Walking on Water

Walking on Water
and Other Stories

Edited and with an Introduction by
Allen Wier

The University of Alabama Press

Tuscaloosa and London

Copyright © 1996
The University of Alabama Press
Tuscaloosa, Alabama 35487-0380

PS
558
.A5
W35
1996

All rights reserved

Manufactured in the United States of America

The paper on which this book is printed meets the minimum requirements of American National Standard for Information Science-Permanence of Paper for Printed Library Materials, ANSI Z39.48-1984.

Cover art, original watercolor, *Walking on Water*, by Donnie Wier. Reproduced by permission.

Library of Congress Cataloging-in-Publication Data

Walking on water, and other stories / edited and with an introduction by Allen Wier.
   p. cm.
  ISBN 0-8173-0785-0 (alk. paper)
  1. Short stories, American—Alabama. I. Wier, Allen
PS558.A5W35 1996
813'.01089761—dc20   95-12753
                                                CIP

British Library Cataloging-in-Publication Data available

For Don F. Hendrie Jr
1942–1995

At the time this book was going into production, fiction writer and teacher Don Hendrie Jr died of a heart attack in Exeter, New Hampshire. "Hendrie" was one of my closest friends. For ten of the fourteen years that I taught at the University of Alabama he was my colleague, and daily contact with him was one of the pleasures of my life in those days. He was an essential ingredient in the success of Alabama's Master of Fine Arts program. Most of the writers who have stories here were his students and friends. I count Hendrie's friendship among my blessings and dedicate *Walking on Water* to his memory.

—Allen Wier

Contents

Acknowledgments — ix

Introduction — 1
Allen Wier

Fighting — 5
Michael Alley

Duck Hunting — 15
Yesim Atil

Epilogue — 17
David Borofka

The Taming Power of the Small — 28
Will Blythe

Héma, My Héma — 40
Mathew Chacko

Foley's Escape Story — 49
Tom Chiarella

Mississinewa — 57
Cathy Day

Prance Williams Swims Again — 64
Matt Devens

Charlotte — 71
Tony Earley

Forced Landing — 83
Jennifer Fremlin

Wau-Ban-See — 95
Ashley L. Gibson

Crawford and Luster's Story — 109
Richard Giles

Howard in the Roses — 121
Dev Hathaway

What Comes Next *Laura Hendrie*	124
The Twin *J. R. Jones*	138
Won't Nobody Ever Love You Like Your Daddy Does *Nanci Kincaid*	150
Stairsteps *Celia Malone Kingsbury*	164
Hardware Man *Tim Parrish*	176
The Wunderkind *Johnny Payne*	189
In the MacAdams' Swimming Pool *Nicola Schmidt*	196
Sipsey's Woods *Ronald Sielinski*	201
Walking on Water *Kim Trevathan*	209
Carl's Outside *Brad Watson*	218
Stoner's Room *Hubert Whitlow*	227
Contributors	239

Acknowledgments

THE FOLLOWING ARE reprinted by permission of the authors or of the publishers of the works in which the stories first appeared:

"Fighting," by Michael Alley, first appeared in *Quarterly West*, no. 21, Winter 1985;

"Duck Hunting," by Yesim Atil, first appeared in *Passages North*, vol. 6, no. 1, 1985;

"Epilogue," by David Borofka, first appeared in *The Missouri Review*, Spring 1993;

"The Taming Power of the Small," by Will Blythe, first appeared in *Epoch*, vol. 35, no. 2, 1986-87 series, and was reprinted in *The Best American Short Stories 1988* (Houghton Mifflin);

"Héma, my Héma," by Mathew Chacko, first appeared in *The Missouri Review*, vol. 15, no. 1, 1992, and was reprinted in *Stories*, Fall 1992;

"Foley's Escape Story," by Tom Chiarella, first appeared in *Foley's Luck* Copyright © 1992 by Tom Chiarella; reprinted by permission of Alfred A. Knopf Inc.; reprinted in the United Kingdom by permission of Brandt & Brandt Literary Agents, Inc.

"Prance Williams Swims Again," by Matt Devens, first appeared in *Story*, vol. 37, no. 1, Autumn 1989;

"Charlotte," by Tony Earley, first appeared in *Harper's* and was reprinted in *Here We Are In Paradise*. Copyright © 1994 by Tony Earley. By permission Little, Brown and Company;

"Crawford and Luster's Story," by Richard Giles, first appeared in *Ploughshares*, vol. 18, no. 4, Winter 1992-93;

"Howard in the Roses," by Dev Hathaway, first appeared in *Black Warrior Review*, vol. 10, no. 2, 1984, and was reprinted in *The Widow's Boy* (Lynx House Press, 1992);

"The Twin," by J. R. Jones, first appeared in *The Kenyon Review*, vol. 11, no. 4, Fall 1989;

"Won't Nobody Ever Love You Like Your Daddy Does," by Nanci Kincaid, first appeared in *Southern Humanities Review*, 1995;

"Hardware Man," by Tim Parrish, is reprinted from *Shenandoah*: The Washington and Lee University Review, vol. 44, no. 1, 1994, with the permission of the Editor;

"The Wunderkind," by Johnny Payne, first appeared in the *Chicago Tribune Sunday Magazine*, October 6, 1991;

"In the MacAdams' Swimming Pool," by Nicola Schmidt, first appeared in *Alaska Quarterly Review*, vol. 9, nos. 3 and 4, Spring and Summer 1991;

"Carl's Outside," by Brad Watson, first appeared in *The Greensboro Review*, vol. 50, Summer 1991;

"Stoner's Room," by Hubert Whitlow, first appeared in the *Beloit Fiction Journal*, vol. 1, no. 2, 1986.

Walking on Water

Introduction
by Allen Wier

WHEN MALCOLM MACDONALD asked if I would edit for the University of Alabama Press a collection of stories from Alabama's graduate program in creative writing, I had no idea how difficult it would be to select stories from the many submitted by former students, good writers and friends every one. I hesitate to call them students; each came to Alabama with demonstrated talent and determination. For every story here, there is another that deserves to be here, and I've no doubt that we will be reading them in magazines and books to come.

The Master of Fine Arts Program in Creative Writing has completed twenty years. I wanted every fiction writer who'd been in the program to know about this anthology; I hope I tracked down each one. The first few classes were small, and few stories were submitted by writers who graduated before 1980. The two dozen stories I selected span a dozen years, almost as long as I've been teaching in the program.

Long before my time, writers had been spending their time in west-central Alabama. In an earlier generation, the biographer, historian, and travel writer Hudson Strode had drawn writers from all over to his creative writing classes at the university and gained for Alabama the reputation as one of the two or three best places in the United States to study creative writing. Strode had hundreds of successful students and helped foster the careers of such writers as Harriet Hassell, Borden Deal, Elise Sanguinetti, and Helen Norris. Strode retired in 1963, and during the next several years creative writing at the university lost momentum.

Tom Rabbitt, a poet from Boston, was brought to Alabama in 1972 to design the curricula for a Master of Fine Arts program (the MFA having become accepted as the terminal degree, equivalent to the Ph.D., for writers in academia), and Alabama graduated its first small class of MFAs in the spring of 1974. MFA students founded *The Black Warrior Review* that fall.

The university offered me a job in 1976 and, after circumstances made me decline, surprised me by maintaining friendly contact. When the offer came again four years later, I accepted and drove an old two-lane highway through red-clay and pine-thick Alabama hills to Tuscaloosa, remembering something Wright Morris, one of my literary heroes, had said: *Where there is little to see, there one sees the most.*

A miserably hot August afternoon in 1980, Tom Rabbitt welcomed me to campus. The next year we hired the novelist Don Hendrie Jr, who left San Miguel de Allende, Mexico, to join us in Tuscaloosa. Rabbitt and Hendrie are writers I admire and enjoy, and they are teachers of skill and integrity. I have come to count on them in ways large and small, and I take this opportunity to thank them for years of unusually good comradeship.

Over the years the "permanent" faculty has included poets Dara Wier, Chase Twichell, and Robin Behn, and fiction writers Barry Hannah, Sandy Huss, and Lex Williford. Poet Elizabeth Libbey and fiction writers Valerie Martin, Chuck Kinder, and Deirdre McNamer have filled in semesters for writers on sabbaticals and grants. The MFA program's Visiting Writers' Series—begun on a shoestring, then supported for years with university-matched grants from the National Endowment for the Arts, and now in the process of being generously endowed—brought a dozen or more writers a year to Tuscaloosa for readings and short residencies. The university awarded the program a Coal Royalty Endowed Chair in Creative Writing, held first by Wright Morris, who set a precedent of literary stature and excellence. Here's a list of chairholders, writers who followed Morris and spent a semester at the university: Margaret Atwood, James Tate, Andre Dubus, Michael Harper, Desmond Hogan, Cornelius Eady, Russell Banks, Gerald Stern, Marilyn Robinson, Jack Gilbert, Mark Costello, Heather McHugh, John Keeble, Brendan Galvin, Ted Solotaroff, Greg Pape, and George Garrett. Following their residencies, two chairholders—George Starbuck and the late Richard Yates—moved permanently to Tuscaloosa.

Many of the writers who visited became my friends. But, of course, the students are the ones who make a writing program succeed. Students came, of all ages, from all over the country and from other countries, with amazingly different backgrounds, to spend two, three, four, or even five years at this university beside the Black Warrior River. They came with the same burning intention—to write well. As a writer who teaches, I couldn't have asked for better.

Writers need the support of a community that takes seriously the toil to make poems, stories, novels. There's a smokestack in a mining town in eastern Kentucky (Harlan, I think) which has painted down its long brick face EAT, DRINK, SLEEP, THINK COAL. I've asked members of my fiction writing workshop to imagine that, here, at Alabama, the slogan is EAT, DRINK, SLEEP, THINK FICTION AND POEMS. And I tell them not to lament where *here* is, either; and not to lament what's not here. The best writing programs tend to be in out-of-the-mainstream places—places where a writer isn't as likely to be caught up in culture or glitter or social good times; places where a computer screen may be the only late-night show in town. A writer who's never before been to Alabama, never been in a Deep-South, steam-press August, never eaten fried okra or red-hair eye gravy, never looked up at the nightmare shapes of kudzu gone berserk, should consider all this exotic. If you're a writer, anything alien should be pretty wonderful—at least until you've exhausted all its possibilities. A writer may never again have the luxury of such a place—a place where so many people turn out to hear a fiction reading, then go drink and rehash the story till the wee hours of the morning, and then go home, tired and hung over, to work on other stories, novels, poems.

The MFA program's goal has been to maintain an atmosphere in which writers are able to write well and are helped to discover the values and develop the resources that will sustain them once they have left such a community and must rely on themselves alone, to write and to write again. We've kept literature classes close at hand. Nowadays, writing workshops are some of the few classes in which literature is still taught as literature—to remind us of the traditions out of which we write. We've tried to recognize the difference between wanting to be a writer and wanting to write. That you cannot teach creativity is well known; creativity, talent, is a given, but does not guarantee good writing. If you can't teach creative writing, you can teach someone to read as a writer reads—not as a literature professor, not as a literary critic—and you can help that writer become his or her best reader, best critic.

We've tried not to pay too much attention to grants, prizes, and publication, any of which may be corrupted—at worst by greed or politics, at best by someone's poor judgment. Recognition is not necessarily the measure of a work's quality.

Even down in Alabama, we hear about the latest literary fashions. But there may be less pressure in places such as Tuscaloosa, far from the center of publishing, to keep up with the trends. Prevailing trends, like prevailing winds, are subject to sudden shifts, they come and they go. I'm suspicious of any writer who seems more committed to aesthetic theories than to the demands of an individual story or novel. We've asked members of our workshops to keep their own counsel and be patient—to try not to let what's merely fashionable influence their goals, their aesthetics, or their integrity. What's popular, even in as small a venue as workshop "publication," what's fashionable and apparently marketable, is as reassuring as good manners, but not nearly as lasting nor as important.

Ezra Pound says, "Gloom and solemnity have no place in the study of literature intended to make glad the hearts of men." We've tried to be serious without taking ourselves too seriously. We've allowed room for whimsy, but kept holy our undertaking—not the institution, not the program, not the classes, but the aspiration to write good fiction, good poems.

With the exception of a few times when I was on leave (three semesters as a visiting writer at other universities, a semester on sabbatical, and a semester enjoying a writing fellowship) I've taught fiction writing at Alabama for the past fourteen years. My time at Alabama, the good fortune of making my living doing mostly things I enjoy, reminds me of a couple of lines Waylon Jennings used to sing about being a country music star: "I got my name painted on my shirt / I ain't no ordinary dude—I don't have to work." At the time that Malcolm MacDonald asked me to edit this book, I had no idea that I would be leaving the university. But, as things have turned out, I'll be at the University of Tennessee in Knoxville by the time *Walking on Water* appears. Hendrie, as Don Hendrie Jr is affectionately known, retired two years ago; Tom Rabbitt will take early retirement in three more years. If I indulge myself, I can think of this anthology as signaling the end of a small era. The making of stories, novels, and poems will continue in Tuscaloosa, but many of the names and faces—faculty and student—will be new.

I take genuine delight in marking my departure with the book you hold in your hand. The stories I've chosen are spoken in a variety of fictional voices and represent widely different sensibilities and visions. Some of these writers' literary careers are well begun, while others (it pleases me to note) appear here in print for the first time. I use *Walking on Water*, from the story by Kim Trevathan—his first published fiction—as the book's title, because walking on water is an apt figure for what the fiction writer attempts with each new story's beginning. One reader may see such an effort as a stunt, a slick bit of sleight-of-hand, while, for another, such a struggle may succeed in ways sufficient to approach the genuinely spiritual. As different from one another as they are, these stories all remind us that good fiction doesn't just imitate life but, rather, reinvents life. I hope, and trust, that after you've read this book, fiction will have merged with real life—that you will have found at least one story so convincing, so moving that it will have become part of your experience, as alive in your memory as all of these stories are in mine.

Fighting

by Michael Alley

First, the telephone rang. Twice. Kerry had not been asleep. He had been lying on his back, his right arm crooked under her pillow. He was waiting for her to fall asleep so he could leave.

When she answered the phone, she did not turn on the lamp. She sat up on her pillow, her back to him, the receiver cupped under the fall of her short blonde hair. As the hotel drapes swayed in the rush of the air conditioner, streaks of ocean-green light fell across her neck and shoulder. Her skin—ocean green, then shadow, then ocean green. He touched her shoulder, but she was not wet. Not even damp. She was as dry as his days—his mornings of sleeping late, then eating breakfast, then sleeping again until he had to drive the half mile to the Pizza Hut where he worked.

"No," she said into the phone. "No. Wayne. You have no right to call me this late. No. No, I won't." In the stillness of the hotel room, her voice was shrill. Her name was Sharon. Kerry figured her thirty-five, maybe thirty-six. She had about ten years on him. In the Camelot Lounge she had told him about her ten-year-old daughter Elizabeth back in Lubbock and her ex-husband Wayne who worked for Iowa Beef here in Amarillo. Sharon lived in Lubbock, in a brick duplex east of the university. She was up this weekend for a training session so she could become a realtor.

From the pack on the near end table, Kerry slipped out one of her menthols and held it between his lips. Just held it, not lighting it. He didn't smoke. In the dark mirror above the dresser, he watched himself lying in bed, his pillow propped against the headboard, the cigarette in his mouth. Gray sheets were twisted across his chest. The streaks of light from the window painted the sheets mint white. Kerry traced the streaks of light across his chest, then across the narrow space between his side and her back, then over the curve of her shoulder. When he touched her, she did not move.

"Piss on you, Wayne," she said. "No, I won't. I'm not coming." She ran her hand through her hair. "Don't even think about it. I'm asleep."

In the mirror she was not tall. She was curled on her side, her left arm folded over her breasts. Earlier tonight she had seemed tall. Maybe it was her high heels or the way she had danced—her back slightly arched. She was not beautiful, but she was pretty, girlish pretty. She was smooth and slender, her face narrow, her blonde hair cut Dutch-boy style. What gave away her age though were her eyes—thin and hard and ice-blue. The half-circles beneath were shadowed gray. "No," she kept saying into the phone. "Just piss on you, Wayne."

It was almost one-thirty. The Camelot would close in another half hour. Above the hum of the air conditioner Kerry thought he could hear the band, the muffled beat of drums. He held the cigarette over the edge of the bed and flicked imaginary ashes. For the past three months he had come here regularly—at least once a week. Buddy Webb, his manager at the Pizza Hut, said it was an easy place to meet women. He said it held an older crowd. You don't have to be much of a talker at the Camelot, Buddy always said. Buddy had gotten married last December.

Most nights when he came here, Kerry just drank. The Camelot never had a cover, not even when there was a band. Draw beer was fifty cents, and on Wednesdays you could do tequila shots for a quarter. When there were single women, Kerry sometimes asked them to dance. Two-step mostly. Kerry wore calfskin boots, Levis, a tapered cotton shirt. He was a good dancer.

"Good-bye Wayne," she said. "You don't want me to go. Good-bye. No, you don't. Take Karen." She hung up the phone and disconnected it from the wall.

He waited for her to roll back over, but she just sat there, half-sitting on her elbow and staring away from him toward the drapes. He rested a hand on the curve of her hip. She made no move. The sheets were cool with sweat—his sweat. When he had made love to her earlier, she had just laid there. She turned her face into the pillow and did not kiss him.

He rolled out of bed now and walked to the window to turn down the air conditioner. His jeans hung on a chair by the drapes. He turned the air conditioner to low and opened the drapes halfway. At the window he could hear the band—the drums, the electric guitar and organ, the husky voice of the woman vocalist. In the bar, when he first asked Sharon to dance, she had said nothing. She did not even look at him. She sipped from her drink, then took a drag from her cigarette. He was about to walk back to his seat when she stood and said, "All right."

Now, outside, I-40 was bathed in purplish-white circles from mercury vapor lamps. Pockets of darkness lay beneath the lamps that were burned out. Semis disappeared into the pockets, then reappeared in the light, their gears grinding down on the Ross-Osage overpass. Kerry touched the window. It was warm. "I'm going to go ahead and leave," he said. Not looking at her, he slipped on his jeans.

She didn't say anything. In the reflection of the window he could see that she wasn't looking at him. He shouldn't even have told her, he thought. He should have found his clothes and walked out the door. He looked for his socks. One was behind the drapes. The balcony outside her window was a half-circle, the white stucco railing shaped like the top of a castle wall. He knew all the second-floor rooms had that kind of balcony. Still, the design looked odd from up here. The two times he had spent the night in this hotel, he had stayed in the ground floor rooms on the back side that faced the pool.

Sharon stood and pulled a folded nightgown from her suitcase and slipped it on. The gown was sheer. It hung just below her waist. She sat on the bed and lit a cigarette. "I'm sorry about the phone call," she said.

"Don't be." He couldn't find his other sock. He swept his hand under the table and drapes. Nothing.

"I don't know why he keeps bothering me."

Maybe the sock was under the bed. "How did he know you were here?"

"I don't know."

"You didn't call him?"

"No. I don't want to talk to him. Maybe one of his friends saw me. He's got a lot of friends." She lit a cigarette and flicked the match in the tray. "He says he's got this special deal for a vacation down to Cancun. He says he wants me to go."

"Do it," Kerry said. "Do you see my other sock?"

She took a long drag from her cigarette and stared at him. "What do you do?"

"What do you mean?"

"You know, what do you do—besides hang around hotel bars and ask older women to dance?" Her eyes were thin and hard behind the orange circle of cigarette ash.

"What if I told you this was it?"

"I'd say you'd starve in a month."

He sat up and tried to laugh, but his laugh fell flat in the silence of the room.

"You live anywhere?" she asked.

"I got an apartment on Bell."

"You got a job?"

"I got a job," he said.

"What is it?"

He thought about saying his old line—that he drove a bulldozer for the caliché pits west of town. But he decided no. What did it matter what she thought. "I'm a cook at a Pizza Hut."

"Why are you embarrassed about it?"

"I'm not embarrassed. It's just a temporary job."

She took another long drag and tapped ashes in the tray. "You wear one of those floppy red hats and stand in the window?" She smiled at him.

"Yes," he said.

"You throw dough up in the air and catch it with your fist?" She started laughing, a soft easy laugh.

"Sometimes." He stood and walked over to the bed and sat next to her. He ran his hand over the sheet along the outside of her thigh. "It's not like you think. All night, red neon flashes in my face. It's always the same—dark and red in there. A couple of years ago, a waitress was killed in the Hut on Western. You hear about it?"

"No," she said.

"You should have. My manager tells me it was on all the news."

"I don't watch the news," she said.

"It happened before I came here. This guy held it up and locked everyone in the freezer, all the customers and the two cooks and the manger, everyone except that one waitress. They say he raped her on the breadboard table and forced her head in the dough mixer. It crushed her skull. Afternoons sometimes, lots of times, when I make dough and the spindle's scraping around the bucket, I think about her. I think about her when I'm in the freezer and the cooler motors are running and it's like I can hear her outside screaming. It's strange I should think about her like that, you know? I mean I never knew her. I've never even seen her picture. How can you care about someone you've never even seen?"

"I don't know." She ground her cigarette in the tray. Smoke spiraled in two gray ribbons above the ashes.

"You got to care about something," he said.

She was staring at him. The green light from the window danced smooth on her face. He kissed her. It was the first time tonight he had really kissed her. When he broke the kiss, she placed a hand on his shoulder, and he kissed her again. Her lips were smooth and soft. In the light they had a silver gloss.

Someone knocked on the door. Four sharp knocks, then silence. Then four sharp knocks again. "Sharon, I want to talk to you." It was a man's voice—low and dull and slurred. "Open up, hon. I just want to talk."

Sharon pulled away.

"Is that Wayne?"

"Shh," she said.

Four more knocks. "Sharon, I know you're in there. I just want to talk."

"Is that Wayne?" Kerry whispered.

She nodded.

"Damn," Kerry said. He walked back to his chair and started putting on his boots. He wasn't sure what he was supposed to do. Maybe he should sit quiet and wait for Wayne to leave, or maybe he should try to get out. The drop from the balcony to the parking lot was a good twenty-five feet. No shrubs or cedars directly below to land on. Just the black hood of a Trans-Am sloping to hard sidewalk.

"Sharon, I'm not leaving till you talk to me."

"I'm asleep. Go away."

Wayne knocked again. The knocks had a sharp metal echo. Kerry imagined a brass ring on Wayne's knuckle. The ring was large and cold and hard.

"Hon, I only want to talk for a couple of minutes. Now open the door and talk to me."

"Go away. I've got to sleep."
"Sharon, open the door right now."
"No."
"Open it."
"Piss on you, Wayne."

Kerry's right foot without the sock was cold in his boot. He looked for his shirt but couldn't find it. This was a domestic quarrel. He had always heard that domestic quarrels were the worst, that if you're ever near a domestic quarrel the best thing to do is run.

Four more knocks—softer this time. "Come on, Sharon. I only want to talk. You can spend five minutes and talk to me."

"I'm calling the police," she said.

"No, you're not," Wayne said. "I know you. You're not going to call the police. Now just open the door and talk to me."

Kerry slipped over by the bed and connected the phone back into the wall. "Maybe that wouldn't be a bad idea," he whispered. "Does he have a gun?"

Wayne knocked again.

"Damn it," Kerry whispered, "does he have a gun?"

"At home," she said. "He doesn't carry it. Relax, will you? He can't get in here."

There was silence. The drapes barely swayed now. Kerry walked back to his chair and pulled it into the shadows. He hoped she was right about the gun. Still, it was better to be near the window in case something happened. Wayne knocked again.

"Leave me alone."

This could go on all night, Kerry thought. He wondered what Buddy would do. Would he call the police? Or just sit quiet? Or would he open the door and tell Wayne to get lost? Silence again. The wind pressed against the window. Kerry listened for footsteps—Wayne leaving—but there was nothing. Just the wind outside and the rush of the air conditioner against the drapes. From where he sat he couldn't see the door. It was blocked by the closet partition.

Four sharp knocks.

"Goddammit, Wayne. Leave me alone."

"You want me to do something?" Kerry whispered.

"What the hell are you going to do?"

"I'll answer the door."

"Just stay quiet. He can't get in here."

Silence again, then the doorknob jiggled. Kerry was about to ask if she had fastened the chain when he realized the door was going to open. He knew it was going to open just before it did, just before a yellow shaft of light sliced around the closet partition and fell on the oak-stained dresser, the television, the green carpet, the foot of the bed. Centered in the yellow shaft was Wayne's shadow—his shoulders were thick, he wore glasses. For a moment no one moved.

Then Wayne slowly stepped into the room and shut the door. Again it was dark. Silently Wayne walked around the partition. He edged to the foot of the bed and groped for the mattress.

"Get out of here," Sharon said. She pulled the sheets up around her nightgown. "How did you get in here?"

"I just want to talk," Wayne said. Wayne wasn't tall. His forehead was sloped, his hair receding. He looked out over the bed, not directly at Sharon. He hadn't seen Kerry yet.

Kerry sat silent in the shadows. He had been in only one fight before. In the tenth grade, a boy named Stan Sparkman had clipped his jaw. They had danced around each other a while, both waving their fists, a small crowd cheering, then Stan Sparkman had uppercut him. The punch had chipped the front face of a lower molar. Kerry never had it capped. Now in the darkness of his seat, he ran his tongue over the rough edges. Over the smooth half, then the rough.

"How did you get in here?"

"Hon, I just want to talk." His voice was low, stilted.

"I'm not saying anything till you tell me how you got in here. You broke in, didn't you?"

"I didn't break in."

"Breaking and entering is against the law. I can have you arrested."

"I didn't break in. I got a key from downstairs."

"Goddammit, they gave you a key? How can they give you a key?"

"Listen, just calm down. All I want is to talk. Why won't you talk with me?"

Kerry stared at Wayne's jacket looking for the bulge of a gun. If Wayne pulled a gun, Kerry was going out the window. He was going out the window and jumping off the balcony. So what if he sprained an ankle? He wasn't going to win any fight with a gun.

"Wayne, no. I'm tired and you're drunk."

"I am not."

"Call me tomorrow."

"I'm not drunk."

"Yes, you are."

Wayne rubbed his forehead and sat on the edge of the bed, his back to Kerry. He placed his hand on the curve of Sharon's foot. At work, Buddy sometimes had to throw out drunks. Three things to know about dealing with drunks, Buddy said. First thing is don't talk. Second is if you're sure there's going to be a fight—absolutely sure—then throw the first punch. And third, don't stop winging until the other guy can't get up.

"I'm not drunk," Wayne said. "I'm *not* drunk." Sharon glanced at Kerry. Then Wayne turned and saw him. "Who is this guy?" Wayne stood. "Who are you?"

Kerry stood, too, his back peeling wet off the chair's vinyl. He clenched his fists. He watched Wayne's hands.

"Get out of here, Wayne," Sharon said.

Wayne started toward Kerry, but stopped. "What the hell are you doing here with my wife?"

"Hey," Kerry said.

"Hey nothing, jerk." Wayne rolled his shoulders. His neck was thick. "This guy's just a kid," he said. "What the hell are you doing with this kid?"

"Wayne, it's none of your business," Sharon said.

"The hell it isn't. You're my wife."

"You mean *ex*," Kerry said.

"I mean wife, punk."

One more step and Kerry would swing. He wasn't sure where on Wayne's face he should hit. His jaw? His nose? An emptiness hung in Kerry's gut. Earlier tonight, Sharon had said that she was divorced. Had she lied? Or was Wayne lying now? The air conditioner blew cold on Kerry's back.

Sharon stood and pushed Wayne in the chest. "Get out," she said. "You have no right to comment on what I do, how I sleep, who I sleep with." She slapped him hard across the face.

He stepped back and adjusted his glasses. "I just wanted to talk," he said.

"You come in here when you have no right to. You wake me up, you violate my privacy. I'm up here trying to learn a trade so I can support myself and our daughter, and you come breaking in here wanting to talk about some damn pleasure trip to Cancun. You wouldn't even ask me except that your girlfriend stiffed you."

"That's not true." Wayne smoothed his hand over his cheek. "That's not true."

"On top of that, you try to tell *me* how to live my personal life. Just who the hell do you think you are, Wayne?"

Wayne looked at the door. "Can't you step out in to the hall and talk with me alone for a minute?"

"I'm in my nightgown. I'm not going out there where everyone can see my tits."

Kerry stepped close behind Sharon. She smelled good, a strong musk smell. He wanted to hit Wayne. Wayne's glasses were black circles glinting yellow flecks of light. His forehead was creased with sweat.

"Damn," Wayne said and started for the door.

"Go into the bathroom," she said.

"What do you mean?"

"Just do as I say." She pushed him and he bumped into the bed, his hand catching the mattress for balance.

Kerry started to follow, but didn't. He waited for a sign from her, a couple of words, a nod, something to tell him what to do. But she didn't even look at him. She disappeared with Wayne behind the closet partition. The bathroom door creaked open, a light came on, then the door clicked shut.

It was quiet. Kerry was just standing there. Then he turned on the lamp over the end table. Did she want him to leave or stay? From the bathroom there were muffled voices. Wayne's voice was low and slurred. Sharon's was shrill at first, then soft. Kerry opened the door to the hallway. No one was outside. The ice machine at the end hummed, then crinkled as ice slid down. How could he just leave? What if she needed his help? He turned on the room's overhead light and walked back in. In the covers of the bed he found his shirt, wrinkled. The sheets were cool with sweat. An hour ago, just an hour ago, he had been with her on that bed. Inside her. He had to do something. He was supposed to do something. He turned on the television—just the picture, not the sound. A basketball game was on. The Knicks were playing the Lakers.

There was a slap in the bathroom. He walked round the closet partition and listened for Sharon's voice. Nothing. A black skirt and navy blazer, pressed and covered with plastic, hung in the closet. He started to call out for her, but then she was talking, soft and smooth.

He shut the door to the hallway, then opened it. Better to have it open, he thought. He walked back to the drapes and opened them all the way. The moon high in the north had the same purplish-white glow as the streetlamps. Its light tinged silver the leading edge of some horizon clouds. In the corner of the drapes he found his other sock and put it on. Then he sat down in the chair and waited. He was waiting for Wayne.

There were two more slaps in the bathroom. Sharon's voice turned shrill. Then someone was crying, either crying or laughing. Kerry couldn't tell. Again he walked around the partition and again he waited until Sharon's voice came through soft before walking back.

On the television the players flashed up and down the court, their bodies colliding on rebounds, their sweat glistening in the lights during foul shots. Why had she told him that she was divorced? How did Wayne find out she was here? In this room? A man walked by the door and looked in. The man was fat and had gray sideburns and a dark suit with no tie. Kerry stared hard at him until he moved down the hall.

Kerry slipped off his shirt and studied his own chest in the mirror. It was milk-white with brown freckles. His chest was thin—too thin. Long veins ran across his biceps and forearms, but the muscles were soft. When he had first come to Amarillo, he had gotten on with the caliché pits west of town. He had ridden on the back of a gravel truck with some Mexicans shoveling spillover and coughing in the thick white dust. The work was hard and hot—he was always scrambling to keep up—but the pay was fair and the Mexicans made the days go fast with their stories and their teasing. At first, he had been scared that he wouldn't make it, that he would collapse in the dust and heat. But after a couple of weeks, he proved to himself that he could make it. It was then that he started worrying about something else—whether he could keep doing it, day in, day out, week after week. So one morning, the morning of a day he was sure he could make through, Kerry decided to quit. He finished eating breakfast, took off his work clothes, and went back to bed.

Kerry wrapped his shirt around his hand and imagined his arm extended and connecting with Wayne's forehead, sweat and blood spewing, Wayne falling back off the bed. He turned the chair toward the partition and flexed his arms. This was how Wayne would see him when he came out. Kerry imagined himself hitting Wayne again, this time Wayne falling through the window, out onto the balcony, then over the white stucco railing and into darkness. Tomorrow night he would tell this story to Buddy. He would make a big breakfast tomorrow. Early. If there were any eggs in the refrigerator he would scramble them with salsa. Then he would buy a newspaper and check the want ads for jobs. Next month, Buddy was quitting the Hut. Got an oil field job, Buddy said, a real job where you sweat and you work hard and you can barely lift your arms at the end of the day.

Kerry was quitting too. He didn't know what he was going to do, but he was going to quit.

The bathroom door opened. Kerry stood. Better to be standing, he thought. He clenched the shirt around his fist. He was ready to fight now. In the mirror he saw Wayne come out first. Wayne's face was flushed. Kerry took a small step forward, but then Wayne slipped out the door into the hallway. Was that it? Wasn't Wayne coming back? Kerry started to call out for him, but didn't.

Sharon shut the door, fastened the chain, and turned off the overhead light. Quietly she walked around the partition. Kerry watched her eyes to see if she was surprised that he had stayed. There was no change. She really didn't look at him.

"Where's Wayne?" He was still clenching the shirt.

She didn't say anything. Her cheeks were not red. She had not been slapped. She slid by him to the end table and turned off the lamp. Then she pulled off her nightgown. In the light of the television, her skin was gray.

"Where's Wayne?" he asked again.

"How long are you going to watch that?"

"Is Wayne coming back?"

"No," she said.

"How can you be sure?"

"I'm sure." She slipped into bed and pulled the sheets around her.

"How did he know you were here?"

She didn't say anything. She reached over and checked the alarm on her clock. Then she disconnected the phone from the wall.

"How did he know?" Kerry asked again.

"I told you—maybe one of his friends saw me. I don't know. Turn that off, will you?"

"I told you—maybe one of his friends saw me. I don't know. Turn that off, will you?"

Kerry clicked off the television. At first, the room was black, but then Kerry could see her—her legs, her shoulders—in the curve of sheets. She was lying on her side, facing the window, her back to his side of the bed. He unrolled his shirt and slipped it on. "Are you still married?"

"Kerry, I'm really tired."

"Are you still married?"

"Yes."

"Why did you tell me you were divorced?"

She didn't say anything.

"I want to know why you told me you were divorced."

She sat up in bed, her back against the headboard, the sheets twisted around her thighs. Then she slowly lit a cigarette. She blew out the match and tossed it in the tray. "If I had told you I was married, would you have come up here?"

"You wanted me up here, didn't you? You wanted me up here when he came?"

She didn't say anything for a while. Cigarette smoke hung green and dry in the light from the window. "Is that what you think?"

"I'm leaving," he said.

"Kerry, why are you leaving?"

He tucked in his shirt.

She smiled. "Kerry, why are you leaving?"

"I'm going to find him," he said. "I was ready to fight."

She started laughing, a shrill laugh, and he had to fumble with the chain before getting the door open. He slammed it behind him. The hallway was empty. Ice crinkled in the machine. He started for the stairwell, then decided that Wayne had taken the elevator. Better to retrace Wayne's steps, he thought. The elevator doors opened and closed in a windless rush. Downstairs, the lobby was deserted, just the desk clerk reading a magazine. Kerry checked the lobby's bathroom. The white porcelain on the sinks and urinals was hard and bright. No one was there. When Kerry came back into the lobby, the desk clerk asked if he needed help.

"No," he said. He stopped at the cigarette machine. He did not know where to go. He didn't even know what kind of car that Wayne drove. The carpet was red shag. A black grill gate was closed across the entrance to the Camelot.

"Are you a guest here tonight?" the desk clerk asked.

"No," he said.

"Then I'm going to have to ask you to leave. The lounge is closed."

Kerry stared hard at him. The desk clerk was young. He wore a red blazer and black silk tie. "Go to hell," Kerry said and stepped outside into the dark silent wind.

Duck Hunting

by Yesim Atil

MEHMET SITS IN the back seat of the '68 Corvair. All his mother has to do is hold the steering wheel straight on the crushed seashell road and try to see around Mehmet's father, who is sitting on the hood. They are driving by Dardenelles Channel in Bandirma, and although the village is just below Istanbul, there are no more houses along the channel. They head west and all the car windows are open. Through his mother's sunglasses Mehmet watches the fading maple leaves. The dark glasses turn the gray morning brown and leave the bright yellow leaves in midair, flickering like sunlight through lace curtains.

Occasionally, Mehmet sees mud huts in front of which boys smaller than himself sell fish. Mehmet takes off the glasses to watch. They wave at the car and yell, "Cheap shad!" His mother repeats the phrase. His father waves back with the barrel of his gun and Mehmet watches it blend with the dark sky. It is early morning and the Marmara sea air blows cold in the windows. Just beyond the trees on their right side he can see the water. On their left, the lake is still and reflects nothing on its surface. They are driving, Mehmet hopes, to the point where the sea joins the lake. The fish which breed there could be kept in any aquarium. Mehmet wants to combine his saltwater fish with the freshwater ones and someday have a giant wall of glass full of many fish.

All around them marsh grass leans with dew as if under water. Mehmet sticks his tongue out to taste the salt in the air. His mother leans her head out the window, keeps it there for a long time, trying to see the road. The uncovered parts of her hair fly in the air, the moist sea wind glittering in each strand. Mehmet's mother has cotton in her ears and she doesn't respond to the shots. When they go over bumps, the blue dots on his mother's scarf blend together; the beads of water in her hair break into one another as if the shots are hitting her. Mehmet jumps high in the back seat to signal each blast for his mother. For a long time it is fun and Mehmet makes scared faces to go along with the jumps, then he is bored. He leans back in the seat, sips Coca-Cola through a straw. He counts seven ducks as they fall into the marsh grass. First they spin with the blast as if in some sort of fancy flight, then fall, brown and heavy like stones. There will be too many for dinner tonight. This is easy hunting. They will simply pick up the ducks on the way back, his father tossing them into the trunk by their heads. In the trunk and in the air ducks are brown and colorless. Mehmet knows that in the white porcelain sink in the back yard the ducks will glow bright green and blue. When his father plucks them, some of the feathers will blow out of the water and swirl over his head. That is Mehmet's favorite part and he will clap for the show. Then, his father will dance in circles around the sink, his black hair gleaming with duck feathers.

Mehmet watches the back of his father's jacket. It is pressed into little roads on the glass. When he shoots, it is like an earthquake—the road crumbles, the whole earth shakes. More ducks fall. He counts ten. "The whole neighborhood is going to eat ducks," his mother says. Mehmet thinks about delivering duck. When you bring gifts people are happy. He will give them the ducks and they will pat him on the head.

Tips of a duck's wings flutter in the open window, and, as if a pet intended only for him, the duck falls through the window and into the seat next to Mehmet. Its legs buckle under; it sits too low for his mother to see. Mehmet offers his straw. The duck is bright green with some purple-blue patches. It pulls its head away from Mehmet. Its chest is soaked with blood, which drops on the tan corduroy seat. Mehmet reaches for it. He wants to pick it up so it will not stain the seat. Suddenly, its wings cover the whole back seat, as bright as if the sun has just risen. Mehmet's mother screams a long time before she stops the car. His father hops off the hood, popping out the dent he has made. He reaches in the window, pulls out the duck by its neck.

Mehmet's mother has her hands over her eyes. She is outside, leaning against the car, swearing. Mehmet watches his father raise the duck, a green flash over his head. The bird, still light with life, treads air with its wings. Mehmet watches his father snap his arm and lower it, heavy and tired with the weight.

Epilogue
by David Borofka

WHAT AM I to say about two brothers whose wives have argued, who are thus forced by their immediate loyalties not to speak to one another? Or the surgeon in love with the deftness of his hands, the choreography of his fingers, and who has been forced by illness to set his scalpel aside? Or the woman who refuses to act on her own desires because she is attracted to a married man, one who represents moral integrity and uprightness of heart? What can I say but repeat the usual clichés: that life is indeed a garden of pain, that men and women are born for trouble and heartache? That the world which seems to lie before us like a land so various, so beautiful, so new, et cetera, et cetera, is in reality a smoking landfill?

Let us say instead, that one hot June morning, the dew even at five-thirty already burned away, Len Farrington returns from his daily run sweaty and happy, illuminated by the sunrise and pleased by his own virtue, to find his brother with whom he has not spoken in a year and a half sitting on the bench to his front porch.

"Frog," his brother says, using a nickname he hasn't heard since his childhood, "how you can sweat like that, I'll never know."

His older brother Max, pudgy and uncomfortably Episcopalian in his short-sleeved black shirt and white collar, is the very image and picture of grief. His forehead is creased by anxiety, his eyes are clouded. Ever since he and Max stopped talking out of deference to Sylvia and Patrice, he has intuitively known that Max's life is nothing he would trade for. He knows that he and Sylvia are miserable, their lives circumscribed by her cycle of anti-depressants and sleeping pills. He knows that Max harbors resentment toward his parishioners for their savage and selfish complaints, their dull needs, springing from loneliness and dread. He once envied Max his sense of calling; he does so no longer.

"Sweat's a blessing," he says now, using his brother's language. He chooses to ignore the recent history that hangs between them. Instead he focuses on the bright front of his white house, the gleam of newly painted black shutters. "After a run, I've drained all the poisons out of my soul. No offense."

His brother visibly winces at the word "soul," as if he doesn't possess the qualifications for its utterance. *Fuck him*, Len thinks. Fuck him and his black shirts of depression, his white collar of propriety. Anger radiates through his whole body like heat. He cannot know that Max only winces whenever the language of his trade reminds him of his own shortcomings. He cannot know that even now Max is thinking that Leonard Farrington, independent insurance agent representing all lines of life, homeowner, and auto, the Frog Man of their childhood now thirty years in the past, so named for his refusal to touch their slimy green bodies, his general refusal to dirty himself, would have made the better priest.

"Maybe I shouldn't be here," Max says, looking to the pale, flat sky, his round face gone gray in dawn's twilight. "But I've needed to tell someone."

"Tell who what?"

It is here that Max buries his head, with its few pale threads of sandy-colored hair, into his hands, groaning from a well of despair. "I'm in love." This last syllable of misery still hangs in the rising heat of the morning when Patrice steps outside onto the porch for the morning paper.

"Love," she sniffs, her eyes still smudged by last night's mascara, "the most highly overrated thing on God's green earth." She pulls her flowered house coat more tightly around herself, picks up the paper, and snaps free the rubber band with at whack that echoes along the quiet street like pistol fire. She steps inside the house again, leaving in her wake nothing, not a word, not a greeting, not a single acknowledgment of her brother-in-law.

"Maybe I shouldn't be here," Max says again. "It was a bad idea."

"No, no, you're here. After all this time. And you're in...." Len sighs. "Maxie, you're forty-three years old."

"And in love. Again. Fat and stupid and terminal with love."

"And married. Still."

"Yes."

"And Sylvia."

"I'm not in love with Sylvia."

He says this with such utter seriousness, such Episcopalian gravity, such obvious adolescent misery mingled with joy that Lennie can't help but laugh. If Max knew how pitiful he looked, how pleased with himself, he would be mortified. This is not the first time that Maxie, resonant with rectitude, has listened to the dictates of his hormones rather than the doctrine of his church. He has, after all, known his share of organists and secretaries, the bored and the lonely. But now, this affair of his heart has left him so fragile that this morning he was nearly driven to his knees by the sight of a young woman riding in the bed of a pickup truck. In the glossy heft of her auburn hair he could see, he was sure, all the promises of eternal life. In matters of yearning, he has the emotional stability of a fourteen-year-old.

"So," Len finally asks, "who is it?"

"No one you know. A woman named Virginia."

"You want to come in?" Len asks.

Max shakes his head. A failed counseling partnership has left Patrice and Sylvia—the sisters-in-law, registered marriage-family therapists—embittered, and their anger extends to their respective families. Office furniture now decorates both houses. Three feet from Len and Patrice's front door, a cherry wood rolltop stands accusingly. A couch, upholstered in industrial grade fabric, faces Max's fireplace.

"No," he says, "I better not."

"Come on." Len pulls his brother's arm. "Patrice won't mind. Have some breakfast."

"No." Max's face brightens for a moment. "Let me buy you breakfast." He names the coffee shop on the corner. "A brother can buy his brother breakfast, right?"

Doubtful now, Len checks his black runner's watch. "I've got an eight-thirty meeting." He checks the watch again. "Oh hell, I'll cancel the meeting. But I've got to shower."

"I'll get us a table. Eggs sunny side up, hash browns, rye toast?"

Len shakes his head. His brother has named his breakfast of the past, as if it had come from a time capsule. "Oatmeal. Half a grapefruit."

"That's not a—"

Len raises a hand before Max can go further. "My cholesterol's at 215, my blood pressure's a little high. I'm forty-one years old, and I'm trying not to fall apart. You get to do the funerals, but I have to write the checks."

"Okay, oatmeal. Half a grapefruit. How about some prune juice? Maybe some Geritol? A Maalox and Metamucil shake? A hair shirt to every fifth unhappy customer."

"Get out of here. I'll meet you." He steps through the doorway into darkness.

After the door closes, Max waits for just a minute on the front porch. The sky is cloudless, a dome shaded from black to azure to aquamarine. Bands of pink and red outline the mountains in the east. By noon it will be nearly white, a furnace. This isn't an easy land to live in, he thinks, putting on sunglasses against the dawn.

Patrice stands in front of the bathroom mirror, outlining her lips. She wears one towel like a turban, another as a wrap. The thought strikes Len that the probability of him standing his brother up could be measured in the thickness of terry cloth and gym shorts. When he turns the tap for his shower, Patrice also turns: "Do you mind not doing that while I'm here?" she asks. "It's steamy enough as it is."

So he goes to the shower built into one corner of the garage and curses the cold cement under his feet. The water begins hot then peters out to lukewarm while he is mid-shampoo. Patrice, he thinks, wiping soap from his eyes. Goddammit. Goddammit to hell. Ever since the collapse of their office and her estrangement from Sylvia, Patrice has been a different person. She took a state job, issuing counseling and prenatal care information to teenagers who look at her with bemused and barely tolerant expressions. She hates them. They remind her too clearly of how fine the line is between success and failure. Patrice now speaks of retirement as her career objective; her résumé has become a ticket to old age. As the cold water drains from his legs, Len once again feels a surge of anger that his money must be used to pay loans for a business that no longer exists. He has an urge to chop the rolltop desk into kindling.

She is dressing when, irked and shivering, Len enters their bedroom. From behind he can discern only the barest outline of the woman he married seventeen years ago. He imagines that he hears his son and daughter begin to stir. They are the children that he and Patrice never bothered to conceive except as jokes, images of misfortune they've avoided. When the toilet clogs they blame it on the girl, the second child they never had. Could real children have made life worse than this? he wonders. Or has the joke been on them?

His life could be worse. His work is routine, his material needs are met. His neighbors are decent and, in a pinch, generous. Although abstracted and unsatisfied, his wife says she loves him. But there are those unpredictable moments when a voice breathes the word "Tahiti" into his ear, when he imagines himself as Gauguin. Why, he wonders for the umpteenth time, does his brother the priest seem to understand matters of sex and desire better than he does?

In such a mood he watches as Patrice packs her brassiere.

"Don't watch," she says. "It ain't pretty." She shrugs into a blouse, steps into a jumper, choosing clothes as cover for her multitude of sins.

"So how is Max?" she adds. "And how is the poor bastard's wife?"

By chance Max meets a parishioner in the parking lot of Gaylord's. Dr. Klinefelter has been retired for seven years, ever since he diagnosed himself as suffering from multiple sclerosis. The disease has worked quickly. He walks now with twin canes in a jerking, spasmodic hitch-hop gait. His hands resemble talons, his mouth twitches between words. Dr. Klinefelter has attended St. James's, Max's parish, for thirty years—since long before Max was on the scene—and Max measures his Sundays by Klinefelter's lurchings as if the condition of the older man's debility were a barometer of his own unrest. He counts the doctor's illness as one complaint that is entirely verifiable, distinguishing him in this regard from the dozens of other complaints he so often hears.

"Don't eat the hash," the doctor grunts as he settles himself into the booth by the door. It's an old joke—they first met when Max had food poisoning. "Try the waffle," the doctor advises. "Safer."

"The waffle it is."

The doctor places his hand on Max's arm. "I have a riddle for you, Father. How can Paul consider the Law to be an agent of death, when it is by the Law that sin is made known and the Grace of God is made both necessary and manifest? Is the Law then not an agent of life by virtue of its role as the causation of Grace?"

Max smiles. "You're more argument than I can handle."

He knows that Klinefelter will be unsatisfied without an answer, but Max has no intention of debating Paul's Letter to the Romans. Max gently refuses the doctor's offer to share his booth. Klinefelter is widowed and childless, lonely as well as crippled. Any other morning, Max would be glad to eat breakfast with him. His mind is as sharp as any scalpel, and he is a devoted, albeit untrained, student of theology.

"You be good, Father Farrington," the doctor says, "or I'll open you up." He makes a slicing motion with his shaking right hand.

"Goodness," Max says, fully aware of all the attendant ironies, "is a vocational risk."

Actually, Max's conscience has been buried for months. He has not allowed himself to think about the ramifications for himself or for Sylvia; he is still thinking only of his desire rather than its consequences.

Max goes to the bathroom to wash his hands. In the one stall another man is on his knees. He is throwing up in great shuddering heaves.

"Are you all right?" Max calls. "Is there something I can do?"

"No, no," the other man sings out—cheerfully, Max thinks—before another surge hits him. "I need to get to work anyway."

Leaving this unexplained, the other man rises and throws the bolt on the stall door. He holds the metal frame as if to steady himself. Flecks of vomit dot his shirt, his sport coat looks slept in, and the whites of his eyes have turned muddy as swamp water. He exudes the odor of alcoholic decay.

"You're okay?" Max says. He is more than willing to play the part of the Good Samaritan.

"Tip top," the other man says. "Absolutely."

He aims himself for the sinks, and Max moves out of his way.

"If you're sure," Max says.

"Of course. Absolutely. Sorry you had to witness that." He buries his head in the sink and opens the valve wide. Spray jets everywhere.

"It's quite all right," Max hears himself say.

This courtly graciousness has become a little strange, and he edges out of the bathroom, flagging down a waitress before he sinks into his own booth. He gives his brother's meager order as well as his own, then stops the girl with one hand on her arm. "Do you know that man?" He tilts his head toward the bathroom door from which the other man has just now emerged, his hair sticking up in wet, unruly spikes.

The girl wrinkles her nose. "All this week, he comes in at five. We draw straws." Her face darkens. "He's never a problem though," she says. "He didn't ask you for money, did he?"

"No."

" 'Cause if he asked you for money, we'd ask him to leave, but if he didn't ask you for money, then we generally let them stay. Unless the smell gets too bad or something, or if they start making dirty jokes to old women or kids."

"I just wondered."

He sits down to wait for Len. His brother has surprised him. While he knows there is no love lost between Sylvia and Patrice, he expected greater shock from Lennie, his puritan brother. Moral outrage. Judgment. Castigation.

As if to solve his problem, the sun frees itself fully from the rim of mountains to the east, and its full potency pours through the plate glass windows next to the booths. The harsh light has the force of a fist, and Max turns his head away. So this is the answer, this stark exposure. Max turns back toward the glare and thinks, *Give me your worst, go ahead,* until the waitresses come by, lowering blinds, pivoting louvres.

As it happens, Len is not the first to meet Max. Virginia has beaten him to it. She called his home only to hear Sylvia's sleep-thick, pill-disfigured voice; she disguised her own hoping to sound like an elderly church member, but Sylvia evidently doesn't care. She doesn't know where her husband is, he could be anywhere, she says. It is obvious that she only wants this bothersome caller to go away. She called St. James's and listened to a recorded message announcing the times of worship. Then she called the number just above Max's in the phone book, his brother's, a long shot at best but there it was: Patrice, much more cheerful and accommodating than Sylvia, told her about Gaylord's.

When Len enters the coffee shop, he first sees Max's worried look, and then Max stands, a polite gesture that he doesn't understand until he sees the glossy dark hair in the seat opposite Max's.

"Lennie," Max says, looking at the other tables, glad that there are not too many others besides Klinefelter—an older woman with a grandson, both eating pancakes, two men at the counter, drinking coffee and smoking cigarettes, the drunk from the bathroom, his hands tentatively raising a glass of water to his lips. Max nervously shifts from foot to foot, hands restlessly jingling his change in the pocket of his standard, diocese-issue pants. "I'd like you to meet Virginia. Virginia, my brother Lennie Farrington."

Her eyes are red, and Lennie is struck by these twin facts: first, that this woman is so young and beautiful, and second, that his brother could mean so much to such a woman to cause her to shed tears.

In fact she has just told Max that this will never work. They were fools ever to think it would. In the first place, she has realized that she loves him *because* he's a minister; she's attracted to men—she knows this now—who represent stability and order, the sanctity and meaning of human life.

"Don't you see," she has just said, "if I get any further involved with you, I'll start being the cause of evil in the world?" When she said this, her nostrils quivered as if she were about to cry, and it was all Max could do not to leap across the table, force her down onto the vinyl seat, and tell her in the language of sex that she had it all wrong, he was neither stable nor pure, she couldn't begin to corrupt him. But would saying that undo the attraction all the more certainly? He could feel a headache beginning to bloom behind his eyelids.

"And truthfully," she added, "I think I just may be nutty about the uniform. You know, the vestments, all that brocade. The Eucharist at passiontide." And here she did begin to cry.

Which was when Lennie entered, to shake her warm hand, to marvel at this young woman's presence, to feel the pulse beating steadily at her wrist, to wonder all over again what she could possibly see in this fat, confused older brother of his who once again is the perfect picture of misery caused, Len can see it now, by the pure pain of loss. He feels sorry for Max. He can't help it, even as he is relieved that such a messy situation might be so easily resolved.

They are each given a moment of reprieve when the waitress comes with their orders. Virginia sniffles, says she must go. Max says, No, wait. And to his brother, he says: "We met at the movie theater, did I tell you that? At *The Fisher King?*"

"No," Lennie says, "I hadn't heard that."

"Isn't that right?" Max says to Virginia.

"I have to go."

The waitress has placed Lennie's breakfast in front of Max; Max's plate has landed in front of Lennie—scrambled eggs, sausage links, hash browns, a biscuit and gravy. Intent on the byplay in front of him, he puts a sausage in his mouth without thinking, and is in the act of swallowing when the taste of pork grease hits him. When he tries to spit it out, it happens. This piece of pork makes the roller coaster ride over the top of his dumb, half-asleep glottis and wedges itself into his airway like a cork—*thunk!*—the sound of suction audible in his own ears.

"No, please," Max is saying. "Stay a little longer. We need to talk."

"No." She's crying again, dabbing at her eyes with a paper napkin.

"I'll call you, then."

"Please don't."

"I need you. I haven't talked to my brother for years, but here we are—I had to tell him about you. You're good for me."

His mention of Lennie reminds them that this is a scene with an audience, but when they look at him, everything else is forgotten. His face is red, nearly bursting. Soft squeaking noises come from his wide-open mouth. His hands are at his throat. This has come as such a surprise that Lennie has had no chance to panic or thrash around. His body is rigid with confusion and puzzlement. In front of him are Max and his maybe-maybe-not girlfriend, and their faces begin to twist and run; he cannot get a fix on color or shape.

"Dr. Klinefelter!" Max is screaming from somewhere far off. "My brother! Look!"

The doctor rises slowly to his feet, pushes himself forward on his canes. "Heimlich," the old man says. "Do the Heimlich."

Max dimly remembers descriptions from television and magazines. He pulls his brother to his feet, his fists underneath Lennie's breastbone. His efforts are spasms of anxiety. Lennie squeaks, his face the color of wine. Max feels tears of failure falling onto his brother's shoulders. He has wasted his own life on riddles and tootsies, tootsies and riddles, and by the queerest sense of divine fairness it is his brother who is going to die.

Dr. Klinefelter fumbles in his large pockets, extracts a silver penknife. "Hold him good," he says, pulling the stiff blade free.

It is the one thing Lennie sees, the bright bead of light from the silver blade as it erratically moves toward the hollow of his throat. He does not review his life, nor does he think with fond regret of Patrice. He does not ask forgiveness for his often uncharitable spirit. He only has room in his consciousness for the bright silver blade and the bright pinpoint of light that burns his eyes.

"Hold him now," the doctor says.

"Oh God, oh God," Max says, then yells to Virginia: "Call 9-1-1."

Then Lennie feels his legs go out from him. Has his brother dropped him? If he could just get some air, he would cry for this, he knows it. For his pain, for the unfairness, for the fact that Maxie the minister, his oversexed, irresponsible older brother, is the one who will get to live. And now other arms are around his ribs.

Max has not dropped Lennie. The drunk from the bathroom has shouldered the doctor and his knife aside and pushed Max into Virginia's lap. He takes a large sour breath and jerks so hard that Lennie's ribs crack. The sausage flies across the room in a weightless arc, a lazy pop fly through a clear summer's day.

Lennie comes to in the sour draft of his rescuer. As his eyes clear, he believes that God looks like Christopher Lloyd undersea, that he has died only to be revived into an odor of piss and rotten shellfish. Max is holding one of Lennie's hands in both of his own and crying. "Oh, dear sweet Jesus," he says over and over again, the strangest sort of mantra for this most professional of Episcopalians. "Oh, dear sweet Jesus, it was all my fault."

"Let him have his air," Dr. Klinefelter says, his tone critical of the stranger, who, although ignorant and unwitting, has succeeded where sobriety and knowledge failed.

The man from the bathroom stall stands. The color drains from his face, he looks like he's about to faint, but he edges backward, surrendering himself into the waiting lap of an empty booth, and the critical moment passes.

Others now cluster quietly around their little group. The waitress has come with water. A Vietnamese busboy flaps his apron, working a breeze.

Virginia quietly leaves. She touches Max's shoulder with two fingers, leaving him with her blessing, although at this moment she is forgotten. He will, she knows, think of her later.

For now though, Max cries. Lennie breathes. Breathing, for the moment, is sufficient. The front door opens, admitting a gust of sunlight and a large, startled trucker. All these people on the floor, he must think, what is he walking into here?

"The Frog Man," Lennie croaks, patting his brother's arm, "the Frog Man lives."

Grace caroms around the room with the velocity of hockey pucks.

What am I to say to such things? That this is a small story after all? I suppose it is, I can't call it otherwise, even with its few moments of danger and risk. It would not even make a credible subplot for an hour-long courtroom drama. Two brothers, their wives, the young naive lover who comes to her senses, the aging doctor, the purple, bloated face of the virtuous victim. The improbable savior, a drunken *deus ex machina*. How can we believe it? What *am* I to say?

That on an early June morning I had just sat down at a booth in Gaylord's coffee shop unsteadily holding a water glass to my lips when a man began to choke? That I had most recently knelt down, my head inside a toilet bowl, vomit burning my esophagus? That my week's odyssey had begun when my wife and daughter and son packed our station wagon with the barest essentials, saying enough is too much, before driving west into the harsh central California sun? That I had begun to believe that our birth is but a sleep and a forgetting, and that the dreams of this life are nightmares only?

I could say that, I suppose. But then, I could just as easily claim that I am Lennie or Max, or Dr. Klinefelter, or Virginia, for that matter. That these multiple lives are merely fractions of one life. I could say that in the moment when I fell backwards into the booth at Gaylord's, my vision blurred by strange clarity and the fluttering of some ethereal curtain, I saw in those figures before me my own life revealed, my own apocalypse, an uncovering, a lifting of a veil. I could say that. Absolutely....

Yet why not say what happened? That and merely that.

That in those dark hours before our early dawns, I would wake to hear the sounds of our house: my wife, her back to me, muttering in her sleep, confused even in her slumber over what was to be done with me—with my rages, my silences, my criticisms, my depressions, my sarcasm, my self-loathing; my daughter turning over, restless in the rush of change that was overtaking her; my son crying out against the terrors of the darkness. I would wake to the distress of these sounds, stripped of any capacity for compassion, overwhelmed only by the realization that I could no longer remember the slightly fetid taste of a particular girl's skin. A Gypsy girl with orange hair who made her living by vandalizing parking meters and duping unwary tourists. A girl so exotic to me now that she might as well have been a native of some south Pacific island. One who made me believe at the age of nineteen that the future was indeed limitless, that no wrong choice could not be undone.

Some days before they left, my daughter asked me what it would take, since I was so obviously miserable, for God to forgive me. She is twelve, theologically precocious, with a penchant for Socratic irony. The lines above the bridge of her nose are clear signs of her resentment towards me. Arguing with her is a debate with the Grand Inquisitor; I lost without speaking a word. How could I begin to explain to her what it means to be forty-two years old, to read the next thirty years as if they had already been written, to be choked by the twin pains of longing and regret? That such pains, no matter how clichéd, can drive weak souls into the arms of willing accomplices, and souls weaker still into the passive madness of bitter daydreams? That to forgive oneself, and thereby embrace the forgiveness of God, would require—for the sake of virtue—some forfeiture of dream and desire?

In the room above our garage, the windows face east, and during the summer there is not a morning that is not clear. The sunrise above the Sierra is magnificent, the sky gradually lightening, the red glow of morning throwing the dark mountains into stark relief. These days, since my unconscious heroism and surrender of this past June, I am awake to see the daily miracle of rebirth and admonition; it washes me with its tides of honesty and grace, and I am reminded that long before my family left, I had already orphaned myself with yearning and self-indulgent woe.

In the sunrise, for a small time I become them all. I know their lives intimately, projections of my own failure, my own pain: Max and Lennie, Patrice and Sylvia, Dr. Klinefelter and Virginia, my departed family, the cretin on the bathroom floor whom I no longer claim. They are mine, after all, my responsibility, my children, adopted without their knowledge or consent; I pray for them to understand that in a choice between inevitable evils, the noble embrace the greater hurt.

What am I to say to such things?

That in this land of light and shadow and make believe, the dream may school the dreamer?

Oh, yes.

And that the character that is my own—poor passing fact if ever there was one—may find within that dream the breath that will let him live?

Yes.

Yes.

Absolutely.

Yes.

The Taming Power of the Small
by Will Blythe

Two men and a boy were driving in a battered Mustang toward the Texas border, with the wind and ahead of the rain. Every now and then, heat lightning flared in the night sky, illuminating the landscape like a photograph. Miles behind them were black cumulus clouds and what they believed was their old life. The men sat in the front seat, the balding, curly-haired one driving, cradling a quart of orange juice between his legs, the other one passing him french fries from a paper bag. "Boom," he said, aiming a gnarled french fry at the driver's head. Wedged over his thigh was a worn copy of the *I-Ching*. The boy was hidden in the trunk, wrapped in rope like a kite spool.

Baron handled the wheel with one hand, ignoring Napperstick. "What does that chink book say about a motel?" Baron said.

Napperstick just smiled, ketchup flecking his pale, wispy moustache. He shook his head like a man who was tired of the same old joke.

They meandered down the moonlit highway, the center line phosphorescent, floating above the asphalt in the car's weak headlights. At last they came to a green sign with a longhorn steer and a moon rocket. Texas. For most of their hurried trip, Napperstick got excited whenever they crossed into a new state. He hadn't been many places. But this border let him down; his disappointment hung in the car like the odor of fried food and rotting upholstery. "Idaho was better than this," he said, looking up from his book.

He'd never been to Texas, but the name had already betrayed him, had promised him more than this land, which was as bleached as bone, luminescent only in its blankness. Baron looked straight ahead and said, "We're in the middle of the desert. What did you expect?"

"Something else, I guess," Napperstick said. He was ignoring the state of Texas, studying his *I-Ching* by the green glowing numerals of the radio dial. He'd picked up the book from a waitress he'd slept with in Las Vegas. She was a headstrong woman who used to dance at the Sands. She made everything she did seem appealing. She'd shown him how to toss the coins, the basics. She taught him to respect the book, to treat it with a dignity he granted nothing else in his life. "There are Chinese sages," she said, "who study this book for forty years and still get surprised." But he told Baron that he'd already mastered the *I-Ching*. He liked the system, the way it applied to everything. He liked having something help him figure out what things meant, what was supposed to be.

In Baron's eyes, he acted like the book was something alive, something that sat faithfully with him on the hot car seat.

"You'll get over it," Baron said. He rolled his eyes. Napperstick was such a boy. They were both in their late twenties, but Baron looked at himself as the leader, as the voice of experience.

They drove on across the Texas flatlands, hewing to the speed limit like an old couple, pulling into drive-ins for food, buying gas at lonely self-service pumps, and stopping occasionally to empty their bladders on the shoulders of long stretches of road. As they pissed, they watched oncoming headlights looming faintly in the distance, drifting toward them across the desert night in slow motion.

"What if he needs to piss?" Napperstick asked.

"Then he'll piss," Baron said. "We're not taking the chance."

"He doesn't cry much, does he?" Napperstick said.

"It's tough with a gag."

By afternoon of the next day, they crossed into Louisiana and entered the terrible green woods of the South, where the midday roar of locusts ricocheted in the greenery with a sepulchral buzz, like voices in a pipe. They passed by kudzu-covered fields and trees.

"What the hell is that?" Napperstick asked. "Looks like something from outer space."

"Some kind of plant," Baron said. "That's obvious."

"That's one mean plant," Napperstick said. "I wouldn't take a nap around it."

They drove on, crossing from light into darkness in quick-blinding succession. Tree shadows dimmed the road and cooled the air like night. Ahead in a gloat of sunlight stood an abandoned Sinclair station, the cheerful green brontosaurus pockmarked with bullet holes. This seemed like the kind of country a man could hide in, but Baron knew better than that. People in this kind of country knew when outsiders in strange cars came through; they noticed the cars even more than they did the flat twangy western accents. The dark green safety of hackberry and water oak and hickory was an illusion.

"I used to collect dinosaurs," Napperstick said. "I had a lot. My mother threw them down the toilet when I broke a two-by-four on my sister's head. I never forgave her for that."

"Jesus Christ, man."

"Yeah, I know. It's strange the things you get attached to."

"No, I mean your sister. What happened to her?"

"I don't know. Brain damage maybe. It could be why she married that black guy."

"Man, you almost give *me* the creeps."

"*I* do? How about that?" Napperstick grinned like a shy man given a compliment.

The light was vanishing slowly from the afternoon. Every now and then, they passed a Cadillac or a Lincoln coming from the Gulf Coast. The cars all had gauzy screens stretched across their grilles to keep the insect world from their fiery pistons. "When I'm rich, I'm going to get me one of those cars." Napperstick said.

It was midevening, summertime dusk, when they came to a brick motel with a lustrous sign, the color of moon, that pleaded VACANCY. If the motel had a name, Baron didn't notice it. They had been traveling for three days straight. It was a motel. That was enough.

A year before, Baron's wife had left him for nothing in particular—"anything is better than this," she'd said—and he began blowing back and forth across the country in his Mustang, a man tumbling in crosswinds of rage and numbness. Baron was a terrible husband but he had loved his wife with a passion that made him tattoo her face with the blue and black marks of his fists. "I'll never stop loving you," he cried, pounding her around the bedroom that night she left, thinking *she's history, she's history,* pounding her until he was sobbing and she was spitting at him like a cat from the corner of the room. "Thank God I didn't have your baby," his wife spat. "Thank God for small favors like that."

So he had gone driving. He felt like a guest in his own life, someone wearing the wrong clothes, not knowing whether to kiss or shake hands. In the summer, he had been speeding through Nevada, lost in a fragile glory of amphetamines and desert light, able, as long as both persisted, to maintain an acceptable vision of what lay ahead. Of course, he had narrowed his vision to where the future was a matter of days, and next month loomed as blank as outer space, an emptiness he did not even want to imagine.

For a man whose future extends about as far as a windshield, automotive difficulties can mark a sea change as profound as divorce or death in the family or winning the lottery. Somewhere in the desert, between Reno and Carson City, Baron's Mustang threw a rod. A piston heated up as orange as an ingot and the motor locked. The radio was playing so loudly that Baron did not hear the engine's clattering, the sound of a steam radiator banging away in the dead of winter. He noticed the acrid smell of burning oil, though for a moment the odor was unattributable in the swelter of sagebrush and baked sand.

Then the car just quit.

Baron let the Mustang roll onto the shoulder and finished listening to a song, "Dead Flowers," by the Rolling Stones. The speed was still pumping through him, a river of energy. He kept beat with the song, tapping on the dashboard, his arms as brown as a Mexican's.

The desert spread out around him, yellow and white, the monotony broken only by a few shriveled yucca plants, sagebrush, rocks. It felt like home.

When the song was over and a commercial for an airline roared onto the air, he switched off the radio, grabbed his sunglasses and his pills, and began walking. "Fuck you," he yelled in a voice that was his and that came from nowhere. He had a rage that he was born with. A mountain range as black as coal cut an austere and parallel track miles to the north. He plunged on down the highway, walking with an antic speed that did not wilt in the sun. It was Napperstick who finally stopped, placid and smiling, a young man, baby-faced, with an incongruous scar slicing down his cheek.

"How about an ice-cold beer?" Napperstick said, dangling a Budweiser out the window.

"All right, buddy," Baron said. As he reached for the beer, the man jerked the can inside the car. "Jesus H. Christ," Baron said. "Is that supposed to be funny?"

"I'm just fooling with you," Napperstick said, grinning. "Here you go, man." He handed Baron the beer and opened the passenger door. "That your Mustang back there?"

"I'm walking—cross country," Baron said.

"That's a good one. Serves me right."

They drove together, first to a mechanic Napperstick knew in Monroe, then to the grocery store for another six-pack, after which Napperstick decided to quit his most recent job as a day laborer on a new hospital. Baron sat drinking with the man, remembering the joy of exchanging words, stories. He didn't know a soul in the world. They spent the rest of the afternoon finishing a bottle of tequila in the mechanic's backyard, listening to the ring of a hammer and the clang of engine parts on the cement floor of the aluminum shed, watching stars nestle in the darkening blue space between the sharp peaks in the distance.

They remained at ease in their silence for a while. Then Napperstick said, "I figure you're my 'approaching emperor.'"

"What in hell are you talking about?" Baron said.

"The Ching said I had to 'advance over the plains with an approaching emperor.' I take that to mean you; you can't take these things too literally. We don't have emperors anymore. Anyway, I've got to get my butt in gear, change my life. I've been stuck here too long."

"What the fuck's the Ching?"

"The Chinese book of prophecy."

"You believe that stuff?"

"Sure. Why not? I mean, I might as well."

Toward one o'clock in the morning, the mechanic hoisted the motor back onto the block, took what was left of Baron's money—Napperstick had already made him a loan—and went to bed. "You can sit around all night if you want," the mechanic said. Through the bright haze of the tequila, Baron felt a camaraderie for the baby-faced man with the scar and the lank, blond hair. He wanted them to move, to do something before the pale, dissipating edge of daylight sapped him of his sudden ambition, his sense of infinite possibility.

"Let's go somewhere," Baron said.

"I've got something else to do," Napperstick said.

They got into the Mustang and barreled out of town, going north, through the desert, toward the range of mountains. Baron rolled down his window with a pair of pliers and inhaled the aroma of sage growing out in the desert. The wind was blowing away the hair he had carefully arranged over his bald spot, but he was drunk, and it was cool and dark, so he didn't mind. He admired his own insouciance.

"This is what it's all about," Baron said.

They kept on driving for months, hemmed in only by the Spanish language to the south, tundras to the north, and oceans on either side. There was still enough space to roam, and both of them had all the time in the world.

At the motel, Napperstick was reclining on one of the beds, leafing through the *I-Ching* and watching a porno movie. He kept clicking the toes of his cowboy boots together and trailing his fingers down the knife scar that ran like a gulch down his cheek. His touch was as light and dreamy as a lover's.

"You really love that scar, don't you?" Baron said, chewing a vitamin C tablet that was as bitter as a child's aspirin. He'd read that vitamin C prevented hair loss, and he kept touching his scalp to check on his hairline.

"Love what?" Napperstick said, gazing at the screen's wan light.

"You know what," Baron said. His voice had the sharp edge of rebuke to it.

Napperstick smiled and scratched his cheek. A warm breeze blew in the window from the parking lot, heavy with the scent of gasoline. "It's Channel Blue," he grinned. "Twenty-four hours of uninterrupted sensuality."

"They don't do much for your self-image, do they?" Baron meant anatomically.

Napperstick just smiled, as enigmatic as a woman in an advertisement.

"We have to pay for those movies," Baron added. "They're not free."

"That's all right. We're going to be rich," Napperstick said, still smiling.

"You little pissant. Turn that shit off."

Napperstick just lay there, studying his book. Baron snapped the TV off.

There hadn't been any news since the weekend, three days ago, no news, no word, no deals, no ransom. They'd taken the boy from a backyard pool in the resort of Sun Valley, high in the mountains of Idaho. It had been as simple as circling the brown-eyed boy with curly dark hair in *People* magazine. "The Wealthy at Play." The boy was going to be a heartbreaker when he grew up. Most rich people were, Baron thought. "He's ours," Baron said. "He's ours if you're up to it. I think we're entitled, and I'm emperor." Napperstick went along because he always went along, succumbing to the prophecy and the profane eloquence of Baron's flat voice.

The boy had been sitting at the edge of his parent's pool, lazily kicking his feet back and forth in the cool blue water. He was reading a picture book, green elephants and pink giraffes, his chin perched on his hand, his eyelashes long and feminine. Baron came up behind him, his tennis shoes squeaking on the smooth cement. The boy didn't even turn around. Baron cupped the boy's mouth and whispered in his ear, "You're a sweet little gumdrop," wondering where that came from. He kept cooing sweetness into the boy's ear, carrying him as light as balsa back to the car where Napperstick was gunning the motor. They raced down into the flatlands on their way south. When the news came on the radio, they panicked, tying the boy up and shutting him in the trunk. Then they continued on down the highway, laughing in their daring and relief like college boys on a prank.

But that had been the last of it. There'd been no ransom delivered, and no explanation, no news. No one had shown up in Reno, no one had shown in Vegas. They'd had enough time to get it straight.

"What are we going to do?" Napperstick said, his voice as toneless as he could make it.

"I've been thinking about it," Baron said.

"Well?" Napperstick said.

"I'm still thinking."

"If it would make it easier on you, I'll shoot him."

"It's not that simple," Baron had said. But maybe it was.

That night the boy screamed out in his sleep. Baron heaved himself out of unrecallable dreams, unsure of whether the scream had been nightmare or worse, and listened intently to the room's buzzing silence. The boy cried out again, full-throated fear, and Baron went to him, kneeling against the cold porcelain of the tub where they had bound him, shaking him gently by the shoulders, rubbing his hair, whispering *Hey man, hey man* into his ears.

The boy's eyes opened wide for a moment, then closed, and he mumbled something unintelligible. "What was that?" Baron said. "What did you just say?" As if the boy were telling him important news, prophecies from beyond his waking knowledge. But the boy's body relaxed again into more comfortable sleep; he licked his lips in somnambulistic contentment and was silent. Baron pulled the blanket smooth over the boy and left him sleeping in the bathtub.

"This is getting on my nerves," Napperstick said. He was rolling a joint, using a telephone book to collect the seeds.

Baron said nothing. The smoke swirled across the room, as sweet in his memory as the scent of rain on a parking lot. He drifted off to sleep, dreaming of traveling to a new place, fresh and unencumbered.

Despite the emphatic light of midmorning, the room remained as gray and grainy as a newspaper photograph. Baron, half asleep, his face burrowed into the pillow, was listening to the maids wheeling their carts down the sidewalk. The maids' voices were husky, full of confidential laughter; to Baron, the women were speaking a foreign language with inflections of menace. One cart clattered to a stop and a maid began rapping on the door.

"Get the fuck out of here," Baron yelled. The cart rolled on down the sidewalk, to the accompaniment of a sudden, aggrieved silence.

Baron went into the bathroom, shadowy and cool, and pissed with relief. The boy was watching him, as wary as an animal. His cheeks were red, imprinted with tiny circles from the shower mat he'd slept on.

Baron closed the lid and sat down on the toilet.

"How'd you sleep last night?" he asked.

"Fine," the boy said, his voice timorous, faint.

"What'd you dream about?"

"I don't remember," the boy said, looking down at the drain.

"You were having a nightmare," Baron said.

The boy said nothing.

"Don't you remember?"

"I had a bad dream," the boy said. He looked shy and embarrassed. Baron marveled at how adaptable the boy was, how all children were as pliant as water, taking the shape of the lives they were leading, warm when it was warm, icy when it was cold.

Baron knew a little something about a boyhood in motels. "Watch TV for a couple of minutes," his father had said, twenty-two years ago, leaving their room for a beer and a pack of cigarettes and going all the way to Flagstaff, Arizona, to get them. Baron had watched TV for the next three days, drinking warm Cokes and listening to coyotes out in the Mojave and to the blue laughter from the room next door. He'd kept the curtains shut against the desert and just sat there, watching his shows until his mother showed up, all the way from Norfolk, Virginia. *I had to leave a good time for this mess*, she said, gesturing at the boy, the cartoons, the rumpled bed. *Oh be nice to him*, his mother's boyfriend had said, settling down on the bed to watch cartoons.

That kind of thing ran in the family. Baron knew that much by now. His heart had been chipped by hard weather into a muscle as clean and as sharp as obsidian. He was proud of that; he could stand almost anything.

And yet he felt a flash of love and pity for the boy, as sudden as a bolt of electricity striking him just beneath his ribs. It wasn't the boy's fault that he'd had such an easy time of it, that he had floated through his life like it was a warm pool. That was the way his world had been. Now he knew that there was more to it than that.

"You hungry?" Baron asked the boy.

The boy nodded.

"Speak up," Baron said. "You have to speak up for what you want."

"Yes."

"Yes what?"

"Yes, I'm hungry."

"That's a good boy," Baron said. "We'll go get something to eat real soon. Get out of this place. It's getting kind of old here."

"Yes."

"Yes what?"

"It's getting kind of old here."

"There you go," Baron said. "That's my little man."

When he crossed back into the bedroom, he saw Napperstick, shirtless, wearing only blue jeans, hunched over the edge of the bed, throwing the *I-Ching*. He rattled the pennies together and let them fall to the carpet, as intent as a man in a casino. He was sweating. Another porno movie flickered on the screen, spattering him with a tropical light, green and orange. The sound was turned down, but Baron could still hear saxophone music and occasional moaning.

"I've got a better idea," Baron said. "We'll let the boy decide what his future's going to be."

Napperstick turned and stared. "I'm telling you, it's no joke."

"Okay," Baron said. "Let's be fair about it. It's his fate."

"It's all of ours." Napperstick sounded like a minister; the *I-Ching* was one of the few things he took seriously.

"Yeah, yeah. Go get the kid."

"You're serious. Great, man. That's fantastic. You'll see. It'll tell you the right thing. It always does. You just have to approach it seriously." He held up his tattered green copy as if it were a Bible. "I mean it, I don't know where I'd be without it."

Napperstick unbound the boy and brought him into the bedroom. The boy's gaze landed for a moment on the movie. "Look at him watching that movie." Napperstick laughed. "You ain't never seen any tits like that, have you?" he asked the boy. The boy shook his head.

"Can you believe that?" Napperstick said. "He said no, he'd never seen any tits like that."

Baron shook his head, bemused. He lay down on the bed, crossing his legs, looking up at the paneled ceiling.

"Okay," Napperstick said, giving the boy the three pennies. "Shake these up and throw them down. Just like you were playing Monopoly or something.

Six times. Ask the *I-Ching* what we should do with you. Concentrate real hard. Okay? Let's do it."

The boy closed his eyes, as if in prayer, and shook the pennies in both hands, rattling them together for a long time before he let them fall to the carpet.

"All right," Napperstick exclaimed. "That's a good one." The boy smiled, pleased with himself. Napperstick recorded the tosses on a sheet of motel stationery, a series of lines, some full, some broken. His brow was wrinkled, a child concentrating on a drawing, Baron thought. He was whistling, too, a slight hissing sound as he sucked the air inward between his teeth.

Baron kept watch from the bed, drumming his fingers on the night table, smirking as he always did when confronted by someone else's idea of the inevitable.

The boy finished throwing the pennies and knelt on the floor, staring at the television. Napperstick was glancing back and forth between the stationery and the book. He let his pencil drop to the floor. "The Taming Power of the Small," he announced.

"What's the word?" Baron said.

"Dense clouds, no rain from our western region," Napperstick intoned.

"Is that the weather report?" Baron asked.

"That's the Judgement, man. Listen to this Hexagram: 'Wind Blowing Over the Heaven.' You don't fuck with the wind, I know that much. 'By it the Model Man renders his virtuous excellence worthy of admiration.'"

"So what's the verdict?" Baron asked. He was rubbing the small whorl of hairs, baby-fine, that were left at his crown.

"Hold on, listen to this one, in the fourth place. 'Owing to Confidence, bloody and terrible deeds are avoided.' That says it all. We've got to let the kid go. The Chinese didn't fuck with the winds. No way. You can't do it."

"We're not chinks," Baron said. "We're white people."

Napperstick wasn't listening. "You lucked out, little fella," he told the boy, thrusting the stationery with its pencil lines of yin and yang in the boy's face. The boy looked at the lines as if they were hieroglyphics, math problems.

"Take it," Napperstick said. "You'll want to keep this. This is your passport home."

The boy took the prophecy, holding it in front of him with both hands like a choirboy with sheet music. It was Napperstick who watched the movie now.

"What does that book say about our fucking money?" Baron asked. The whole charade had gone too far, had sickened him with scorn. He'd never seen successful people, rich people, peering into sheep guts, consulting palm readers, staking their lives on a coin toss. The only people who tried to figure out the future were people who needed more luck that they were ever going to get.

Napperstick looked up from the movie, startled, wild-eyed. "Hey, I thought we were going to score some big bucks. I really did. I never lost hope, no matter what it seemed like. I thought we had a pretty sharp deal going."

"Don't we?" Baron asked.

"We shouldn't be thinking about money," Napperstick was beseeching him, his voice as soothing and intense as a preacher on TV. For him, the matter was settled. "Virtue. I know it sounds weird but we've got to get us some virtue. Virtue is its own reward. That's not just my opinion; that's the universe talking."

"How do I know you understand what that book says? How do I know you can make any more sense out of those squiggles than that boy there?"

"Read it, read it yourself." Baron said. "I can just look outside and see what the weather's like." He gestured at the curtained windows.

"The I-Ching cannot be wrong," Napperstick said.

"We'll see," Baron said. He wasn't sure what he would do.

That evening, they left the motel and drove into the countryside, the wind gusting from all directions, buffeting the car, bending the pines like limbo dancers, sweet with the scent of approaching rain. The whole green world seemed in motion, flooded with eddies of air. "The winds of heaven," Baron smirked.

"Still hungry?" he asked the boy.

"Yes, I'm hungry," the boy said.

Baron smiled. They pulled into a Dairy Queen where the red umbrellas over the picnic tables had been blown inside out, a row of red canvas tulips.

"You can have anything you want," Baron told the boy.

"I'm getting some french fries," Napperstick said.

The boy ordered a hamburger and a milkshake, and sat between the two men, like a child between his parents. He ate the hamburger with slow precision, wheeling it around, taking tiny, evenly spaced bites. He was still wearing his bathing suit and terry cloth sweater.

They left the Dairy Queen and drove east, the woods swaying and creaking around them like a green ship. The boy sucked on his milkshake, holding the cup to his chest. Fifty miles down the highway, Baron swerved into the parking lot of a Holiday Inn.

"Are we stopping already?" Napperstick asked.

"We're getting a room for the boy," Baron said.

"We'll be rewarded for this, I guarantee you."

"Aren't you going to come say goodbye?" Baron said.

They paid the clerk for a room and took the boy there, Baron leading him by the hand. He unlocked and pushed the door open. The boy stood hesitantly in the doorway, cradling his milkshake. The wind had brought out goosebumps on his legs.

"Go on in," Baron said to him. "Make yourself at home." Napperstick and Baron followed, Baron tapping the door shut behind them with his foot. Baron flipped on the TV, spinning through the channels until he came to a nature documentary. The scene was Africa, at the edge of the forest. A gold moon hung over the trees, while down on the floor of the savannah, photographed by stealth, were two chimpanzees pounding on a log. The narrator said that they were looking for insects, but why then, Baron wondered, out there on the grasslands, all by themselves, while the other chimps were sleeping in the trees?

Baron thought of himself and Napperstick, their epic voyages of futility, crisscrossing the country, bickering like old maids, killing nothing but time.

The boy had scooted up on one of the beds, and was watching the chimps. Napperstick remained standing by the door, waiting for something to happen.

Baron went into the bathroom, slipped his Smith and Wesson from under his jacket, and clicked open its chambers. He turned the gun upside down and shook the bullets into his palm, where they gleamed golden in the room's fluorescence. He pocketed the bullets and emerged into the bedroom spinning the Smith and Wesson's cylinder.

"Here," he said to Napperstick, handing him the pistol by the barrel. "Russian roulette. Let's see how smart those chinks are." The boy was watching them in the mirror that ran behind the TV. He just sat there, as still as stone.

"Go ahead," Baron gestured toward the boy.

"This is too cruel, man."

"You already said you'd shoot him."

"I would have, you know me."

"If this is his lucky day, you won't stop him from enjoying it. Go ahead. I'm emperor, man. Like you said. Let's see how seriously you take that I-Ching shit."

Napperstick shook his head slowly, mournfully, twirling the cylinder himself and placing the barrel at the base of the boy's skull, just below the V of his haircut. The barrel was blue and cool, about the circumference of a flute. He held the gun there, as lightly as a finger. "Damn," he said. "Damn."

The boy flinched at the touch of the gun, and Baron held him by the shoulder, the way a man would steady a subject for a photograph. Napperstick closed his eyes and pulled the trigger.

Nothing.

"I told you," Napperstick burst out laughing. "I told you." The boy was crying, silently, still facing the TV. "This is your lucky day, little fella," Napperstick said, tousling the boy's hair.

Baron opened up the pistol and said, "Look Mom, no bullets."

"Oh my God," Napperstick howled. "I'm such a fool, I'm such a fool."

They left the boy in the motel room, sitting on the edge of the bed, watching the strange habits of animals in the wild. Baron swung the Mustang westward, back toward the clouds, the country they'd been fleeing. The wind was rattling the car, still holding out the promise of a sweet rain. The trees were still dancing.

"It really was his lucky day, after all," Napperstick said. "The I-Ching doesn't lie." The book was sitting in his lap.

"You're full of shit," Baron said, satisfied again with his knowledge of the world, his vision, his command. "That book is full of shit. I rigged the whole deal, you know that. You think *this* was his lucky day?"

"I do," Napperstick said. "I really do. He was saved by the I-Ching, no matter what you say. We're virtuous men. Our reward will come. I hope it's money."

They drove on into the night, retracing their path, whirling past hamlets they'd never remembered, past fields and dark green woods.

"Well," Baron finally said, the fire rising within him. "I'd just hate to see him have an unlucky day, if you know what I mean."

But Napperstick did not respond. He was slumped back on the seat, mouth open, his head against the window, sleeping the easy sleep of the virtuous, of the true believer.

Héma, My Héma

by Mathew Chacko

Héma, my beautiful Héma, is determined tonight. I knew it the minute I crawled into our home. I don't mean crawled in a figurative sense. It accurately describes what I did. Our house, you see, is a little on the cozy side; six by six feet to be exact. A perfect little cube it is, made of tin cans that my Héma's late hubbie took apart and flattened into sheets. The result has been quite colorful—white Amul milk powder sheets next to yellow Dalda tin sheets, next to rose-red and aquamarine Asian Paints sheets. Of course, rust, like a leprosy of tin, has eaten away most of the color, and the *Jai Sena* have scrawled their fascist slogans in black paint all across our walls.

Still, it is our house. And a convenient one it is. Since the tin sheets are fastened only to each other, and since our house has no fancy thing as a foundation, it is possible to move from site to site very easily. When the rains come and the water rises waist high in our house—bringing with it turds and bloated dogs-cats-rats—Héma and I can simply lift up our house and move it to higher ground. That is if higher ground can be had. Our slum lies in a valley between the Dadar and Mahim roads and in the rainy season the upper slopes become coveted property. As the black and stinking water spreads its skirt higher and higher up the slopes, shacks begin to squeeze upward. Even what narrow paths we have close up. Families wake up and discover they've been interred in their homes and can escape suffocation only by tearing open their roofs. Sometimes, they are not able to do this in time. Last season, a shack whose occupants were all children was boxed in. The neighbors later insisted that they did not hear any shouts or poundings on the wall. The claim is suspect.

The rainy season, you see, reveals the true nature of the slums. It shows up all those fond myths about the generosity and selflessness of the poor. It puts rout to stories about starving families cheerfully sharing their last morsel. All through the monsoons, families fight over the smallest inch of dry ground like starving dogs over a scrap of meat. Slum citizens throw boiling water into each other's faces and introduce scorpions among their neighbor's sleeping children. Heads of families end up face down in the slum soup along with the disintegrating dogs-cats-rats. That, in fact, is what happened to Héma's ex-hubbie.

But the rains are at least two months away, and, for now, we have the illusion of a peaceful community and the luxury of a stationary house. Coming home in the evenings, I don't have to risk my weight on the neighbors' flimsy roofs or endure their friendly greetings. I can walk along a two-foot-wide path, right up to our door. Although, when I arrive there, I have to get down on my hands and knees. This because our door—covered by an export quality Basmati rice sack—is only three feet high.

Tonight, the first thing I see when my eyes have adjusted to the dark is Héma, my darling Héma, sprawled on the mat in her Rekha outfit. It is an ominous sign. One that I do not even want to acknowledge. I spent the last ten hours waiting patiently at the Public Hospital to interview the Medical Officer about the recent cholera cases in the city. I was there on behalf of the local *Marathi* newspaper for which I am a free-lance—a euphemism for my unemployed status. Superstitions about cholera must have prevented the regulars from taking the case. The wisdom of which I could see as I stood in line with slum parents and their sick children outside the M.O.'s office. The charming presence of cholera was all around me. The corridor was imbued with its characteristic stench—that of a heavily perfumed corpse—and pervaded by the hush the disease unfailingly inspires. From the convulsing limbs and the yellow blossoms that appeared regularly between the legs of the children, most of them were already lost to the disease.

When I finally got to the doctor, he was in no mood for an interview. Fatigue and frustration had pushed him into a state of extreme irritation. I found him standing by his desk, trying, ineffectually, to reattach his broken telephone receiver with a splint of pencils and rubber bands. I asked him, just for the record, if it was cholera out there in the corridor.

"Oh no," he said. "Upset stomachs from too many sweets . . . too many birthday parties."

A certain tone of mockery, you see, is common among the more honest officials of our city.

As I was typing up my story of a cholera epidemic in the Matunga slum, the editor came and stood behind my chair.

"What is this alarmist nonsense you are writing?" he asked me.

"Cholera, sir," I told him, looking up into his hairy nostrils.

"What do you think we are? Some kind of rumor-mongering magazine? Putting out unsubstantiated nonsense?"

His newspaper, you see, has close ties with the present city administration and my report contradicted their boast that cholera had been eradicated in the city of Bombay. Although my frank impulse was to crack the editor's skull with the typewriter, or at least to fling a few curses in his face, I offered to redo the story. According to his requirements. My unemployed status and my limited means do not allow the luxury of high-minded gestures. These days, whatever vomit is provoked by people such as the editor, I swallow. All I want is to pocket my princely fee, so that I can return home to my tin box and curl up with the nice headache the adventures of the day have given me.

But crawling in our door, I see that Héma, my Héma, has other things in mind. She is in full form today. Sprawled over the floor in all her seductive charm. Her forty-two-inch breasts-of-a-Hindi-movie-vamp are crammed-to-the-bursting into a bright red *choli*. White underskirt is hitched up to expose heavy thighs. Oil that could have been used to fry a hundred *chappatis* has been rubbed into black hair, spread like a fan over the pillow. There's *kohl* around the eyes, so much of it that for a while I think Héma has been in another fight with Laxmi-the-neighbor. Lipstick the color of passion itself is smeared over Héma's lips, and pink powder is caked over the rest of her face and the twice-broken-by-mother-and-once-by-late-hubbie nose. Héma has named the entire get-up after Rekha, that blouse-bursting, sex-terror of the screen, whose ten-foot-diameter breasts and twenty-foot-wide hips have invaded the fantasy life of every male in the country. Héma, needless to say, is a poor version of the original.

Pretending there is nothing out of the ordinary, I step over Héma and stand facing the wall. Slowly, I start taking off my shirt. Héma is undeterred and enters the second phase of her seduction. She starts crooning her *engleesh* type love ditty.

"I love you, kiss, kiss, kiss; I love you, kiss, kiss, kiss," she sings, trying to inject ardor and a *filmi* tune into the six words.

I hang my shirt on a nail in the wall and start taking off my pants. I try to convey my disinterest by the rigidity of my back. But Héma, with a popping of knees, gets up from the mat and squeezes herself between me and the wall. She locks me in an embrace any wrestler would have been proud of. My nose is buried in oil-drenched hair.

"Hé, hé," I shout. "What are you doing? Nuisance! I can't even take off my pants in peace."

I reach up and try to unlock Héma's arms from around my neck.

"Don't be like that, *baba*," she pleads in my ear. "Please *na*, for my sake only, give some I love you, kiss, kiss, kiss."

Héma's arms release my neck and start doing something else. I realize it was a tactical mistake to take off my pants, because, now, Héma, she of the butterfly fingers, is rooting around in my knee-length, ration-cloth underwear.

"My skull is splitting open with a headache," I shout. "I spent the whole day standing in line with defecating cholera victims, and when I come home for some rest, there you are, waiting to eat me alive."

"Oh *baba*, I didn't know you had headache. I'll make you tea right now. I'll massage your forehead nicely. Oh *baba*, I didn't know."

Héma stands on tiptoe and starts kissing my forehead.

There's a certain desperation in Héma today that makes me suspect something is wrong.

"What happened?" I ask her.

Héma continues her kissing. Blindly. I have even less patience with her than usual. I shake her.

"Aré, I asked you what happened."

Reluctantly, Héma's eyes open. Jaundice-yellow, *kohl*-edged eyes are swimming in tears. Two drops overflow the edge and clear a path through pink powder.

"Our leper died in the afternoon," Héma sobs.

So that's the reason. The leper who lived in the shack opposite ours is dead. Finally. The eating away that began at birth with tips-of-tiny-toes and end-of-baby-nose has been completed.

More streaks in the powder. Black streaks now, because the *kohl* has begun to run.

"Aré, what's the bad news here?" I shout. "You think it's fun being a leper? You think it's fun to wake up every morning and tie a piece of rubber to your rotting rump and go scraping on it all across the city, asking for ten *paise*? You think it's fun to have flies laying eggs in your sores? What's the matter with you? Are you mad?"

"But still, *baba*," Héma weeps, "who to talk to now? Who to joke with?"

I am defeated. I know that tonight, although it feels like rats are gnawing at my brain, I'll have to submit to Héma. The alternative would be to lie awake all night listening to her weeping.

Héma is covering my neck and chest with tear-wet kisses. I look down and see a trail of red butterflies descending toward my navel as she sinks to her knees. No, it's not sex that Héma wants. Not that thing she is so ardently kissing. What Héma wants is a story. Not just any story either, but a particular kind of story, with a certain kind of ending. Without which Héma can't go to sleep, and for which she is willing to do anything.

You see, every now and then, Héma sinks into a swamp. A sentimental bog, if you will. When this happens, it is my job to go in and pull her out. At first, I had tried to attack the bog itself. When Héma came home from blockbuster tragedies—the kind where Prakash Khanna is dying of cancer and devotes his last days to bringing happiness to his fellow patients—and cried for weeks, nonstop, I tried to din it into her head that the actor was alive and well in his Juhu Beach mansion, surrounded by a harem of eighteen-year-olds. I showed her pictures of the star in his lotus-filled, olympic-size swimming pool. I read her gossip about gold-plated faucets and dinner parties that degenerated into orgies of food throwing. To no avail. The swamp was too vast.

When the weeping continued into a second week and our tin box began filling up with a foul miasma, I began to consider drastic remedies.

Héma's weeping was often accompanied by questions to God. "Why no last-minute miracle, Lord?" she would ask. "Why no last-reel discovery that X-rays had been switched by accident and it was someone else who had the cancer? Why no twelve-hour operation with big, big doctors and ten bottles of blood?"

Héma could conceive of happy endings only in *filmi* terms.

"But there *were* ten bottles of blood," I told her on the eighth day of wailing.

Héma lifted her swollen face from the soggy pillow and looked at me in puzzlement.

"There were ten bottles of blood," I repeated. "There was a big, big operation, with London-returned doctors and made-in-U.S.A. machines..."

"But which film are you talking about now?"

"... while outside the operating room people prayed. Street vendors with cracked feet and baskets of mangoes sat next to gold-chain-and-perfume-wearing college *wallahs*. Hindus with holy thread and *tilak* mark on forehead sat next to bearded mullahs and turbaned Sikhs. All in brother-brother, Indians-first-religions-next attitude. On the altar before which they prayed was a Koran, a garlanded picture of Guru Nanak, and a statue of Sree Krishna. Blue-skinned, playful Sree Krishna. With peacock feathers in his hair and a flute held to his lips.

"'Bhagavan, Sree Bhagavan,' they prayed, 'Ocean of Mercy, Sea of Love. Save your servant's life.'

"Tears escaped from shut eyes and rolled down devout faces. Prayerful voices rose in unison, singing *kirtans* and *bhajans*. Bells were rung and coconuts broken, divisions forgotten and hearts united. The crippled girl of ten, Prakash Khanna's favorite, sat at the foot of the idol and sang the songs of Mira Behn. Songs of adoration, songs of love. While inside, doctors struggled with a tumor whose tentacles were wrapped around kidney and intestine. So many tentacles that the doctors were ready to give up."

"*Nahi! Nahi!*" Héma screamed.

She sank to her knees and joined the other devotees. "Sree Bhagavan, Sree Krishna," she prayed, "Sea of Love, I kiss your feet."

Prayers were heard. The rapt adoration of the crippled girl bore fruit. Gradually, while needles on American-made machines flickered and swayed, while ten bottles of blood dripped into barely alive body, blue-skinned fingers guided doctors' hands. So that at the end of half a day, an octopus lay fingerless in a metal pan.

To tell you the truth, it made me quite nauseous to lie there beside Héma, ladling this sentimental syrup into her mouth. This sweet lyric that is the stock-in-trade of our film industry and the staple food of the masses.

When I got to the end of my story, Héma burst into a fresh bout of tears. Tears of happiness, mind you. Which did mitigate my disgust, somewhat, and encourage me to persist with the cure. The cessation of Héma's wailing was more important than anything else.

The story needed repeated and detailed telling, of course, but by the end of a week it had begun to stick. Brick by brick, and as adeptly as any Hindi film maker, I constructed a house of illusion for Héma to occupy. Sobs and snuffles gradually ceased. Héma's face lost puffiness. The fog grew wispy and blew away. Her faith restored by lies, God's love and *dharma* rescued by fiction, Héma washed her face and returned to life. No, she bounced back to life in true *filmi* fashion. Soggy-with-sweat-of-labor rupee notes were extracted from her waist pouch and spent on colored paper. The inside of our house was transformed into a dizzy kaleidoscope. There were yellow sunbursts of happiness and red triangles of harmony, pea-green hexagons and purple dots, perfect pink squares and orange cones. An explosion of kindergarten cheerfulness on the walls. While on the floor, in barely available space, Héma drew a white circle of love. In it she put multi-colored chalk-powder representations of the flora and fauna of the universe. Sticks-and-circle dogs and cats, flowers and coconut trees, other squiggles and commas of creation. Tadpoles all, Héma wanted to say, swimming in a sea of love.

For Héma everything comes in threes. So before I had recovered from the wild geometry and the primal soup, Héma made me shut my eyes and lie on the mat. When I opened my eyes! *Bapré bap!* Hémaji! Eighth wonder of the world! Across the ceiling, on a dark blue background, a silver moon and a constellation of tinsel stars!

Alas! The enthusiasm of rebirth did not last forever. Not even the mighty fortress that I had built could withstand the daily onslaught of the slum. The stench of excreta rose above the ramparts. The day-and-night wailing of Laxmi's son, as gangrene crept up-and-up his leg, fell like a steady pickaxe on the walls. Whole sections collapsed when Héma accidentally witnessed the scraping off the road of a ten-year-old, run over by a bus. Slowly but surely, the fortress sank back into the bog. And I was forced to run out with blueprint and fresh cement.

This has become a pattern. I construct solid walls of untruth and the slum destroys them with cannon balls of truth. It has become a game between us—a game into which I am pushed, each time, by Héma's merciless weeping. However, to boast a little, I'm getting better at the game, more and more adept at masonry. I'm learning to bake harder bricks and lay deeper foundations. More importantly, in recent months, I've made a certain discovery. I've realized that 70 mm tragedies and neighborhood happenings are merely an external stimuli. The real cause for Héma's distress lies elsewhere. Yes, the true invaders of Héma's fortress come disguised. It's not the harshness of the slum that pulls Héma down. What brings her down is her own past. Her own memories—bearing spears and dragging cannons.

You see, Héma had a bad childhood. One that has left behind stubborn remembrances; against which there is no permanent defense. Nevertheless, it's more effective to engage the real enemy. So tonight, when Héma and I are spooned up on our mat and I put my lips to an oily ear, I avoid the shallowness of "once upon a time, there was a leper who died and went to heaven." Instead, I begin:

"Once there was a cruel mother of the slums..."

Héma flinches.

"Once upon a time," I repeat, "there was a cruel mother who gave birth to a baby girl. When the baby was placed beside her, she put a hand between the new born's still slick legs and searched for something. 'Haré Ram, Haré Krishna, let it be there,' she prayed. But between the legs—a shocking absence. Not even the slightest sign of a divine blessing. Despite a nine-month bribery of God, no wrinkly little sack with two marbles in it. No tiny trunk of elephant-God. No prospect of a dowry. No old age insurance. Only a bitter wound, like a knife slit.

"The mother screamed and beat her breasts. Her blouse became soaked with milk. '*Aré, aré,*' Mumbai, the midwife, tried to placate her, 'what is wrong with you? Instead of thanking God....'

"The cruel mother picked up the framed picture of the blue-skinned God sitting next to her mat, and spat on his smiling face. Then she leaned over the baby girl, over her newborn face, and repeated the act.

"Mumbai had to attend to another birthing and left the baby girl in the grasp of her mother. When she returned ten hours later, she found the mother fast asleep on her mat. The baby lay on the bare floor, in a pool of urine and shit, surrounded by flies. Her hands were clenched into little fists of helplessness, her sparrow chest heaved with sobs.

"Mumbai took the baby away and circulated her among the recent mothers of the slum. After their own babies were fed and if any milk was left, they would suckle the baby girl for a while. But, by and by, they became reluctant to do this. They looked at the baby girl lying patiently on their floor and saw a parasite. A beggar whose silent, beseeching eyes pestered them for the milk they needed for their own children. Sometimes, they gave her a wet rag to suck. At other times, irritated by the imploring eyes, they put the baby girl outside, on the slum path. Mumbai had no choice but to return her to the cruel mother's house."

Héma is curled up tight as a shrimp now. The pillow is getting soggy.

"But then," I continue, "something happened. The white car of a childless couple, the white car of a rich couple, stopped. A woman in a blue silk saree and a man in fresh white clothes got out. They asked the urchins who crowded around them where the shack of the midwife was. Clean feet descended into the slum soup. Waded through rubbish, stepped over rotting things whose guts had spilled out, and over stinking, yellow blossoms, crawling with flies. The edge of a blue silk saree became dirty and the white clothes of a man were splashed. But still they went, deeper and deeper into the slum, led by a midwife. Until they came to the shack of a cruel mother and her baby daughter. A sack curtain was pulled aside, two visitors entered a tin box. A baby was seen lying on the bare floor. The woman in the saree saw the fists of helplessness and could not stop the tears from springing to her eyes. The man in white clothes saw a sparrow chest and pulled bundles of rupee notes from his pocket and offered them to the cruel mother. A baby was wrapped in the end of a blue silk saree and carried out of the slum. Into a white car. Which stopped outside a white house on the beach. A big house with broad windows, lace curtains and breeze. Whose best room had already been readied. Hung with silk drapes and wind chimes. Under whose canopy of music, a baby girl was settled. By a couple who had, till then, ached with childlessness."

At the end of an hour, after spoonfeedings by a kind mother while a father watched; after the blowing out of candles on birthday cakes while pictures were taken; after nights of fever when every light in the big house blazed and a mother and father kept anxious vigil beside a bed; after red balloons and a bicycle with a shiny bell; after the pigtails and yellow bag of school days; the combing of a daughter's silky hair by a mother while a proud father watched; after all this and more, Héma was pacified. Sobs died down. Forty-two-inch-breasts-of-a-hindi-movie-vamp began heaving peacefully in sleep.

Tomorrow the story will be repeated in greater detail. It will take time and careful telling on my part, but in a week or so the fortress will be rebuilt. For a while at least, the fallacy of a white car that came will take hold. Denying the reality of a baby who remained on the bare floor and a cruel mother who looked at her with a sudden excitement. Because there, right under her nose, was a means for taking revenge on the blue-skinned God, for all the miseries He had heaped on her. Because there, in the corner, was something over which the scalding waters of hatred could be poured.

The truth is that Héma's mother became an expert in torture, even by the high standards of our slum. There were beatings and hair-pullings and finger-smashings-with-rocks, of course. But there was also the forced eating of excrement, brandings with iron rods and unnecessary poking around in festering sores. Until Héma was five, the cruel mother would tie her to a stake in the shack floor by a rope attached to her ankle. Thus, offering Héma, for the ten hours she was away at work, as a cure for other people's miseries as well. Hollow-eyed, rib-showing urchins showed up for visits. With sharpened bamboo sticks and pet scorpions on strings. Once, two starving dogs got smart ideas. Héma-the-four-year-old's struggle to escape caused rope to rasp on white bone and a scar like a pink anklet to appear.

I have also been told of a deal struck between mother and gold-toothed pimp. As a result of which urchins and senior citizens, men with paunches and rotten teeth, heaved themselves atop a thirteen-year-old and pushed something like knives into a knife slit.

Héma will not talk about any of this. It was Mumbai who told me. When I heard the story for the first time, I was still new to the slum. Unused, as of yet, to its daily realities. I had been aware, of course, of the physical condition of the slum. From my third-story window on the opposite side of Dadar road, I had

had a bird's-eye view of it. I had seen the excreta-paved paths and the pitted, eroded tin boxes. Because I shared my ten-by-ten abode with two others, and the toilet at the end of the veranda with thirty more, I had even thought that I had some experience of the excessive neighborliness of the slum. So, when I was abruptly relieved of my duties as a reporter and in four months had exhausted my savings and the charity of friends, without finding a new job; when, in other words, the slum became the only option, I thought the change would be manageable. At least for a few months. I even attempted to provoke in myself a certain thrill at my descent into the valley. The thrill of a challenge. I had secretly admired the slum dweller's ability to exist in the conditions that he did. I had envied his capacity to endure harsher realities than I had ever been exposed to. I had always wondered if I, the loyal fan-of-truth-and-reality-no-matter-how-harsh, could equal him.

Alas! I must acknowledge failure in this regard. I was quite ignorant of the sheer magnificence, the sheer brilliance of the realities one is privy to in the slum. Elsewhere, the fan of truth may be asked to forgo a story or even a job. Here, he is asked to remain in the constant presence of a far-too-dazzling vision of his idol. The consequence of which is a gradual blinding of the eyes.

The option of taking refuge in a fortress is, of course, not available to the fan of truth. The night I first learned of Héma's past, I had to take recourse to a full bottle of *arrack*. By the time Héma got home, I was quite an emotional swamp. A sentimental bog, if you will. I wept all over her. I showered her with promises of eternal devotion. Héma, being more experienced than I in these respects, cautioned against such extravagance.

"*Aré, aré, baba,* little will do," she warned. "Don't be making all these marriage vows."

Even a little, of course, is proving a lot these days. The day-and-night glare of slum visions gives me a perpetual headache, and makes everything an irritation. The slum offers no middle ground, nothing between the fortress and the desert, between swampy emotionalism and complete dehydration. I am not certain anymore which is the better choice. There are times, I confess, when I envy Héma, envy the peaceful heaving of her forty-two-inch breasts, and the violent weeping that precedes it. At other times, I am driven to fury by her addiction to lurid melodramas and her steadfast faith in illusions. I try to remind myself then of the midwife's tale. But even that charming story is becoming commonplace against the backdrop of the slum. Slowly losing its capacity to move. Just as I am losing the capacity to be moved by it. These days, when Héma approaches me with her "I love you, kiss, kiss, kiss," it's all I can do to keep from screaming at her. These days, when Laxmi-the-neighbor's son starts his nightly wailing, I am quick to rap on the wall, so that Laxmi can beat or threaten the boy into silence.

Foley's Escape Story
by Tom Chiarella

DAN'S FATHER DROVE the hearse straight by the main house and the barn. As they passed the house, a yellow light went on behind the curtains. It was then that Dan caught a glimpse of Marrissa Tamsley, who was in the sixth grade with him, standing in the window watching them like a silent, bony cat.

"She knows what we're here for," he thought to himself and that was his first real thought of the morning. Less than an hour before, when his father shook him, Dan had said "Hunting?" That was only a word, an instinct really, brought on by his father waking him so early, so abruptly. The half-hour ride since then, slicing the drizzle and mist that blanketed the Sauquoit Valley, had been a blank. Even so, he knew what they were here for. His mother had whispered it to him when she handed him his uncut slice of toast before they left. They were here for one of the Tamsley brothers. They were on removal.

He felt himself waking up a little and guessed that they were headed to one of the Tamsleys' other houses, a new one it seemed, since the road they were on was nothing more than two parallel ruts in the field. "Why didn't they bring him down themselves?" he asked. But his father concentrated on the road, which was slow going, and did not answer. They rocked along in the hearse for two or three hundred yards before his father brought it to a stop. "Now we walk," his father said. The road ahead was deep mud that the low-riding hearse could not handle without getting stuck. At the back of the hearse, they pulled out the shovels, the toolbox, and a large piece of canvas his father had stored under the gurney, and then began walking up the road. His father, carrying the canvas under his arm, a shovel over his shoulder, was quiet. Dan trailed, head down, carrying the tools and the other shovel, watching for dry places.

This was Dan's first removal. His father had always used Hank, Dan's older brother. Although he had no real idea why Hank wasn't there, Dan knew that his father was fed up with Hank. Hank was a tense subject in the family. There was a catalogue of things he did wrong. He drank. He disappeared for days on end. He ran his car off the road. He backed out of work at the funeral home.

While it was possible that his father had chosen to break Dan in on this particular morning, it didn't seem right that Hank wasn't there too. Their father was not much of a teacher, and Dan had counted on his brother helping with the first few removals, offering pointers, providing warnings. But here Dan was, alone, trudging along behind his father, hoping he didn't make some incredible mistake. He tried to remember Hank's stories then, to call up his words.

"Nothing to it," Hank had once told him about removals. "There's nothing you don't already know." Dan hung on that now.

After half a mile, the road swung through a patch of young pines. Just beyond, the land rose up meanly in a large swath of wet earth stretching at least a quarter mile, from the forest on their left, down the slope, across what was once pasture, to a distant line of trees. The road ended abruptly at the wall of dirt in front of them. It was five feet high.

"Mudslide," Dan said softly.

His father looked up at the sky. "If it keeps raining," he said, "there'll be more of these."

"Have you ever seen a mudslide?" Dan said. "I mean while it's happening."

"Wouldn't want to," his father said, walking down the slope. "Look what it did to the house." He extended his arm straight out, pointing his shovel at the tree line. Dan couldn't see over the mud. He had the sensation that everything had been swallowed up, that he was looking at nothing, at a point where the sky simply butted up against the earth. Yet when he jumped he could see the peak of the house poking out of the mud in the distance. He father walked on ahead, picking up speed.

Dan started after him. The rain, which had fallen for weeks, hung like a sickness in the air. Now he could see the beginnings of a path where the grass had been trampled down by the Tamsleys on their trips out to this disaster.

Dan caught up. "Is it buried all the way?"

His father shook his head. "No, but it's pushed up against the trees pretty good."

They walked. Soon Dan felt the dampness seep into his boots. The world seemed out of scale. Next to him was a ridge of earth born only this morning. A mass of earth as long and high as the ridge that ran behind his father's funeral home, a ridge that Dan assumed had been there for centuries. But this mass was new to the world, fresh and wet. He wondered if it might still be moving, at a pace too slow to detect. "This is just like the glaciers," he said out loud. "Or like a river when you look at it from underground."

His father stopped. "What?"

"From underground," Dan said.

His father turned and looked at the mudslide, then back at Dan. "What is it you're saying?"

"This looks like a river from underground," Dan said, putting a hand out and twisting it over. "If you were standing underground. I mean completely upside down."

"What river? Where's the water?"

"If you were under it, Dad. Say the world were upside down."

His father shook his head and put the shovel back over his shoulder. "This is mud here, Dan," he said, looking straight at him as if to make sure that Dan understood.

They walked a little farther and soon Dan could see the house clearly. It was flipped up on its side, and the wedge he had seen was not the peak of the house at all, but one of the corners tilted and pushed against the trees. The front porch lay splintered and crushed against a stand of young birches. Dan felt almost as if he were looking at a normal house from above. He decided not to mention this to his father.

His father leaned in a window. "In here."

Dan moved alongside his father and looked in. The room was hip-deep in mud that had poured in the window from the top corner of the room. The bed stuck up at an awkward angle. A lamp was pinned against the wall by the dresser. Dan saw no body.

"Where is he?"

His father pointed to a patch of red in the mud just to the side of the bed. Dan squinted and began to see the slope of a human back. The red was a flannel shirt. "Why didn't they dig him out?" Dan said.

His father clumped the bag of tools up and into the window. "Why should they? That's what we do."

"How do they know who it is?" Dan said.

"This is Jimmy," his father said, lifting a leg up into the room. "It happened three days ago. They hadn't seen him in a couple of days, so they came out here and saw what happened. Even then, they didn't notice him at first." He pulled himself into the room and turned to help Dan. "Hand me my shovel," he said. "I wouldn't want them to dig him out. It's hard enough on people. That's what a removal is, Dan. It's my job."

Dan passed the shovel to his father and then climbed in behind him. His father placed one foot on the wall and one foot on the floor and began to gently dig away the mud, which had hardened around the body since the mudslide. Dan started in. "Dig a trench around him," his father said, "and we'll pull him out with the rope."

They dug for an hour. Periodically his father would sigh, raise a hand and stop to smoke a cigarette. He didn't say much to Dan, who watched the rigid shape of Jimmy Tamsley grow out of the hole they dug. As they broke the mud from his face, they found that his mouth was open, his eyes closed. His arms were frozen in front of him, bent inwards as if he were holding on to something big, like a tree. They broke as much of the mud away from his hair as they could. What was left formed a corona of blond hair and dark earth around his contorted face.

Dan had seen corpses all his life, so he didn't mind looking at Jimmy for long stretches of time. Jimmy never bothered him while he was alive, either. He had never really struck Dan as much more than an unlucky farmer in a valley of lucky ones; a lanky, dirty man, who paced the floors of Dan's mother's diner with a curious nervous energy, moving from booth to booth, seat to seat, in a clumsy attempt to pick up gossip and tips from the other farmers. Now, in this posture of death, trapped in the motion of escape, he seemed peaceful, and Dan found himself staring.

When they dug down past the waist they found that he was naked below the red flannel shirt. Dan's father ran a rope down under the legs, but the mud at this lower level was still wet and wouldn't give. They pulled—his father heaving, the rope tied over his back like an ox—but the body would not come free.

So they dug. More slowly now, as they were tired and the space got tighter when they dug deeper. Soon they found that his calf was pinned underneath the bed, snapped in half, and it took them another hour to dig down under the bed to free it. Then the body came loose, and they lifted it with the ropes and rolled it to the window, where Dan pushed it out to his father.

They laid the body in the wet grass. It was late morning by then, the gray skies spread above them, the clouds higher than before. The mist had pulled up and away. His father reached down, stuck a finger in the mouth and pulled out a plug of dirt lodged in it. "Tamsleys might want to see him before we leave," he explained, wiping his hands on the canvas as he bent to wrap the corpse.

Dan threw the last flap over Jimmy Tamsley's broken, crouching body. One leg curled beneath the body, one leg—the broken one—was splayed out, so that Jimmy looked something like a dancer, arms frozen in embrace, hands clenching the hardened mud like a knife behind an unseen partner's back.

Dan's father pulled the flap back immediately. Dan knew the tenor of the motion. His father had seen something he didn't like. "For the love of Christ," he said, throwing his cigarette to one side. "Will you look at this?" But he wasn't speaking to anyone in particular, Dan knew, only out loud. He reached down and pulled something like a belt that was wrapped around Jimmy Tamsley's waist. He pulled and yanked until the flaps of mud and grass that covered the groin and belly began to fall away. Dan reached in to pull at the dirt, but his father pushed his hands away. Soon Dan, standing at some distance now, could see that Jimmy Tamsley was wearing a leather harness, one that clamped his penis into a muddy hard-on. As his father cleared the last of the mud away, Dan stepped back a little. His father pulled a knife from the tool bag.

"What are you going to do?" Dan said softly.

"Jesus," his father said to himself as he knelt down next to the body. "Jesus,

Jesus, Jesus." He slid the knife beneath the harness and began to cut it away. When the harness came free he carried it around the house and lobbed it up on top of the mudslide. Dan sat down on a birch tree bent under by the house, while his father resumed working, wrapping the corpse again. As he tied a rope around the bundle he said, with his eyes down, hands busy, as if talking to no one in particular, "No one should have to see that kind of thing." Then he signaled Dan to come around and lift with him. "No one should even have to know about it. Not me. Not you. No one."

He gave Dan a look then, a look that asked for a mutual understanding, a contract between father and son. "No one should know."

"I won't tell anyone," Dan said. "Don't worry."

His father walked back to the house and looked in the window at the ruined bedroom. Dan sat in the wet grass. "You could dig and dig," his father said, shaking his head.

Suddenly Dan knew. His father was looking for someone else, another body buried in the mud. It was as if a voice were whispering in his ear, telling him things, showing him the things he had never seen before. *A woman. They were doing it. They were holding each other. Grabbing each other.*

Dan came up alongside his father. He scanned the room from side to side. "I don't see anything," he said.

His father nodded. "Maybe there's nothing to see."

It took them more than fifteen minutes to drag the corpse back to the hearse. By then it was past noon and his father was anxious to get the embalmment under way. He pushed the gurney to one side in the back and laid the body, wrapped in canvas, on the floor. Then he backed the hearse out and turned at the barn. He drove past the house without stopping. "They can see him after I get done with him," he said, before Dan even wondered if that was the usual practice.

Dan could guess what the embalmment would consist of. He had seen bits and pieces of these, and Hank had told him the rest. They would hose the body off in the second bay of the garage, which doubled as the spare embalming room, then lift it onto the table in the real embalming room and "blood" him. Embalming fluid would be pumped into the carotid artery until it came out the jugular. Then the joints would have to be broken, the limbs pushed into place. The eyelids and mouth sewn shut, cotton balls pushed into the ears. Makeup applied, a suit chosen, a casket.

Dan wondered about the hard-on, though. Hank told him they sometimes had to cut them off. "Depends if it's an open casket or not," Hank said. Dan felt sure that Hank was teasing, although, as with everything about his father's business, he could never be sure.

Now they drove back across the valley and once again they did not speak, though Dan, clearheaded now from the work and the long morning, knew there were things to talk about. He wanted Hank now. He had things to tell him. There were questions, real questions, to be answered.

His mother's diner sat in front of the lot on which their house stood. On the other side of the house was the funeral home and a small parking lot for the services. Beyond all this the valley fell away, pastures sloping into roads and lines of trees and then pastures again. As they pulled in, Dan saw his mother behind the counter, talking across the passthrough with Pete, the day cook. Hank's car was parked along the side of the diner. This made Dan happy, as he wouldn't have to do the embalming. The rest of the day would be his.

Once inside the garage, with the body on the table, Dan's father lit a cigarette and leaned on the edge of his equipment tray. "You must be hungry," he said, breathing out the smoke, which immediately filled the room with its smell.

"A little," Dan said. He was starving, but he didn't want to let on.

"Go get something to eat," his father said. "He can help me from here on out." Switching his cigarette from one hand to the other, he pointed an index finger straight up. His father meant Hank, and Dan could see that he had avoided using his name, but it seemed a good sign to Dan that this father wanted Hank to work at all.

"You did well, Dan," his father said, coughing a little as he exhaled. "You're a real Foley. A Foley can look anything straight in the face." He dropped his cigarette and stepped on it. "That's a hard thing to look at and you never flinched. That's good." Nodding to himself, Dan left.

He tried to think about what he had seen, but nothing registered. Jimmy Tamsley in a harness. The wall of mud. The chaos of the tilted bedroom. The other body, there and not there at the same time. He wondered briefly if there were mudslides in the Bible and made a note to check with his mother.

There were other questions too, but he wasn't sure now about what was secret and what wasn't. He couldn't tell his mother what he had seen. He needed Hank there to press him into the act of telling. Now he wanted to be sure of what he *shouldn't* know. Finding Hank was important.

"Took a long time," Dan's mother said when he came in the back door of the diner. She looked him up and down and Dan realized for the first time that his clothes were caked with mud. "Pretty rough?"

He sat down in a cane chair by the door. "There was a lot of mud," he said, picking at a clod stuck in the folds of his pants. "The whole house was on its side."

"You dug him out?" she asked. "Jimmy, right?"

Dan nodded, closing his eyes. He could smell tomato soup cooking on the stove. "You're hungry," his mother said as if he had held out his hands for food.

Dan nodded again and she slipped a bowl off the top of the stack and ladled it full of soup.

"Where's Hank?" Dan said as she set the bowl down in front of him.

"He left," she said. "I'm not sure." She crumbled a stack of saltines and dropped them in the soup.

"You don't know where he is?"

"He left about an hour ago. He came in here drunk. He went out the back door of the diner," she said, brushing the crumbs on her apron. "He went I don't know where."

"What do you mean you don't know where?" Dan set down his spoon.

"Just what I said. I don't know where he went."

"What if he really left this time?" Dan said, standing.

His mother turned to the counter and began chopping vegetables. "I don't know," she said, looking out the window above the sink. "His car's still out there." Dan stared at the back of her dress. Finally she turned to him. "I don't know if he'll *ever* leave."

More puzzles. Dan couldn't figure what his mother meant by that. He left the kitchen without a word and hurried up to his bedroom to change. He wanted to go find Hank, who—he felt sure—was stumbling away from them out the flooded pastures that lay below the house. He might be leaving them for good, as he sometimes threatened to do. This might be his escape. But Dan would stop him. He could lead Hank back.

But when Dan walked into his bedroom, he immediately smelled Hank, who was lying in the bed, and felt his panic drop away. It was a stale smell, like dirty clothes, which he knew to be the alcohol on Hank's breath. On the chair next to Dan's desk was one of his father's legal pads on which Hank had started a letter. "Dear Dan, I got sick," it read, the sentence unfinished. Dan thought about shaking him awake, telling him to get downstairs, that he was needed.

He found himself speaking. "You should see what I saw," he said, barely aware of his own hope that Hank might roll over and open his eyes. "Hank," he said softly and then once again, louder this time, "Hank." But Hank was too drunk to wake up and give anything to Dan and Dan knew that. He wanted something simple—an explanation, a nudge, a joke. Anything that made things clearer and smaller.

He kneeled down on Hank's scattered clothes and leaned against the bed. Bending close to Hank, he listened to his breathing and became aware of the way Hank had fallen onto the bed—his head perfectly centered on the pillow, his hands joined, the stiff posture of his legs, the parting of his lips. Hank was unshaven. If Hank were a corpse, they would shave him, adjust him, fold him and unfold him until he looked just right, until he looked ready. That much Dan knew.

This man was his brother. This brother was a drunk, unable to take the burden of the morning from him, unable to laugh off the big things with Dan so that the small things might fall into place. Dan reached out and ran a hand along his brother's whiskers. Hank didn't stir. Soon, over Hank's soft, even breathing, he heard the rain begin again.

Then Dan could see himself, kneeling against the edge of the bed in his own dim room. He could hear his own words from a distance, telling the story of a morning. This is something ancient, he thought, something learned long ago.

Mississinewa

by Cathy Day

Two miles outside Peru, the Mississinewa Reservoir sits, a big, brown puddle of river water, backed up and stagnant. I've seen it in spring, all that Mississinewa lapping against docks and half-submerged trees. The trapped water still smells of river, and I cannot help but think of the Flood of 1913. It's the same water probably. Surely in all this time, the water has run its course and found its way back here to our dam, the way old elephants return to their own boneyard to die.

The Mississinewa River almost broke its banks every year, which was maybe why we weren't expecting it in 1913, the year the rains came so fast there wasn't time to sandbag. We were living out by the winter quarters then, me and my husband Charles, and Margaret, who was just a week or two old. Charles was doing work for old Wallace Porter, building his circus wagons and animal cages, sometimes cutting curlicue designs on the staircases of Porter's mansion.

Old Porter was friends with my folks, so I knew about his wife, his great love, dying on him, and that he'd said he'd never marry again. He was small and bone thin, the kind of thin people turn into when they stay up all night worrying and forget to eat for days at a time. He had tiger eyes, tan and gold and green, but they were rimmed by dark circles, so the eyes sunk in and you caught yourself sometimes leaning forward to look into the hollows. His eyes were the only sad thing about him, though, because he carried himself like a gentleman, all poise and polish, right down to his voice, which was the same for respectable folks like my parents as for the gypsies and strange rabble who ran his circus, which he bought with the money after he sold the biggest livery stable business in northern Indiana.

Understand, I lived through the Flood of 1913, but also I was living near the winter quarters where I could hear the animals screaming, where, after the waters went away, all the carcasses rotted in the fields where they'd settled, like the grey, open-eyed fish you'd find in a dry creek bed.

In 1913, Porter practically owned the town. He bought about a hundred acres along the Mississinewa River, built a bunch of barns for all those animals, and built himself a mansion on the top of a hill with white columns and stained glass windows. Since his wife was gone, Porter lived up there all by himself, except for the maids and butlers, of course. Some folks say that at night, he'd go down the hill to the winter quarters and play poker and drink with the roustabouts, or sometimes they'd find him in the barns, watching the animals mate. He said to Charles once that he was just making sure that the mating was getting done, that things would keep on going. Charles even heard that sometimes Porter would get all hot and bothered watching those animals and he'd pay calls on the star acrobat Jennie Dixianna, who had a bunkhouse all to herself. Maybe he did and maybe he didn't. It was never any of my business, but I believe what Porter told me once:

Ruth, what I always wanted was to have many children, to scatter my name like those proverbial seeds in the wind, but God didn't make that possible for me, so I'm just going to make something on this earth really big and put my name all over it.

Most people simply buy a company or make a doo-dad and go about making a name for themselves that way, but Porter was different. Around here, people use that word, different, like a slur, but he was the better side of different.

Our two-story rented house was awful plain, so Porter loaned us some old furniture from the bunkhouses, a ratty davenport and a stained mattress. Charles stayed up late into the nights, making us chairs and a headboard by the light of the kerosene lamp. A few weeks later when I found out Margaret was coming, he carved a cradle, and, after she was born, he painted it sunflower yellow. The rains started while I was still weak and shaky, inching my way through the house in my nightdress.

The rain never let up, not for a whole week. At first, the water covered the back yard, creeping up the back steps, one by one, and then spilled its way through the door and into the kitchen, where I was standing at the sink. The water rushed in like the tide, but instead of soothing me, the cold Mississinewa grabbed my ankles with frozen hands, sending icicles shooting up my legs. Charles found me there, shrieking, holding my nightdress up out of the water. He carried me upstairs, sloshing in his big boots through the living room while I cried for him to save the only nice things we had, my mother's books and my photographs, which were floating around the feet of the kitchen table. Charles piled sandbags around the doors, but it didn't do any good, so he brought up all the food and blankets and the soaked things. I placed the books and photographs on the bed and watched them swell and curl while Charles rocked Margaret in her yellow crib.

After the second day, when the water was a quarter way up the wall on the first floor, Charles and I saw a dinghy across the widening river set out from Ballard's farm. Charles waved a shirt out the window, and the two men inside the boat waved their hats. But the river was churning brown rapids and an uprooted tree tossing in the water capsized their boat. They grabbed the tree and went floating on by us. Charles and I watched them from the bedroom window and neither of us said anything.

That night, the animals screamed. Lions and tigers were roaring to be let out of their cages in a horrible refrain. The elephants blew their high-pitched cry through their trunks. Over the pounding of the rain, I heard water lapping against the house, as if we were on a boat going down the Congo River, and in the jungle on either side of us were animals clawing each other's backs in the darkness. We heard men yelling, and although we could not make out the words, the tone of their fear and their frantic trying to get the animals free echoed in the night. I got out of bed and opened the window to pitch black and saw jewels in the trees, the yellows and greens of squirrel eyes and possum eyes and snakes, too, blinking into the river that wouldn't stop coming.

I slept in fits and starts, and when I opened my eyes at sunup, I saw what looked like a snake climbing over the window sill. I screamed and woke Charles, who walked to the window with a shoe, but then he laughed and told me to come see. A big bull elephant from the winter quarters had stuck his trunk in the window, and when he leaned against the house, his shivers sent vibrations running through our feet. The water covered his legs and was starting to come up his body and his eyes, brown like a horse's and fringed with long lashes, kept looking at us, like we were at fault. Until then, I realized, his life had been one of show and strain in return for human kindness and some hay. I couldn't stand to see him look at me, pleading. I sat back down on the bed and took Margaret up in my arms.

Charles, I said, give him some food. Bread. Do something.

What do you want me to do, Ruth? We need all our food.

Make him go away then.

So Charles threw my hairbrush hard against his back, but the brush just glanced off and floated away.

I can't make him leave. Maybe he'll go by himself.

But he didn't. The baby wailed in my ear, and the elephant bellowed all day long and shivered the house and I couldn't look out the window at his eyes all afraid of the cold and death. The elephant's trunk poked around the window sill, like a tongue licking the corners of a mouth. Toward noon, Charles remembered a straw tick mattress in another room, slit it open and fed the straw to the elephant out the window, but there wasn't much and the elephant just wailed louder when the straw was gone. By five, bitter cold water almost covered his back. Both the elephant and the baby stopped crying, and then there was only the silence of waiting and the steady thumping of current against the house.

Charles stood at the window. *He's just standing there with his head down. He knows it won't be long.*

And about the time the sun went down, the trunk slipped out of the window sill and I got up, too, and watched the elephant sink down into the brown water. There wasn't a splash, just a swallowing up and a big spray of his last breath of air.

I kept Margaret away from the window all that time. There are some things children shouldn't see, even as babies. Folks think they can carry on in front of their babies as if they aren't even there, like they won't remember. But they do, because it's like planting a kernel in their heads that one day explodes and the memory comes rushing back and fills their head with revelations of things long forgotten. See, we don't live just once. We live the first time when things happen and every time we remember that first time, we live it again.

I thought the elephant had floated away in the current, and I imagined his grey bulk bumping off underwater trees, a rollicking tumble head over tail in the brown water. But the darkness outside and the thick, brown water shrouded the elephant completely. He sank below our window and never moved, and when the water finally receded he would still be there, stiff and cold, and so big that even lying on his side, he was almost as tall as Charles. With our team of horses, we had to drag the elephant far enough away from the house so that we could burn him.

But right then, I didn't know that the elephant's body was under my window because the sky was dark all the time, grey and brown, the same as the water that was all around us. Everything flowed, sky and water and time itself, so you couldn't tell the difference between each day, or even where the water ended and the sky started.

The second or third day, a log floated in the front door and started banging away at the piano. Charles laughed at first and said the old piano had never been in tune anyway, but after a couple of hours of the bang-bang-bang, he stopped making jokes. The piano was only partly covered by water, and the log, pushed in a steady, thunderous rhythm by the current, struck the keyboard in random chords. Every hour or so, the current shifted the log to a different set of keys and a new song banged out to the beat of the river.

I'm going to float the piano out the front door. I can't stand the racket.

But I cried and said, Don't. I'm too weak to help if you get into trouble. We'll put little pieces of cloth in our ears and it won't be so bad.

The earplugs worked for Charles and me, but not for the baby. She kept pulling them out and wouldn't stop crying long enough for me to feed her and give her something to take the place of the tears. The water continued to rise, lapping against the pictures hung on the downstairs walls and coming slowly up the stairs. Then the bangs and chords changed and the sound came from underwater, so it sounded like you were swimming in a pond, listening to someone playing piano on the bank while you were underwater. Charles and I took out our earplugs, and even though the plunking was muffled, Margaret still cried, wailing, gulping air and tears.

That night, the sound of the underwater music drifted into my sleep and I dreamed I was playing the piano in our sunken house, moving my arms and fingers through the sluggish Mississinewa. Charles stood beside me, clapping the beat of the current on top of the piano while Margaret squirmed out of his arms and floated up and up, her white baby gown trailing like wings behind her.

I sat straight up in bed then, awakened by Margaret's screams. Grabbing the baby and her crib, I shook Charles awake. I whispered to him, Will the cradle float? Charles sat up quickly and took the crib out of my hands.

Maybe we're going crazy. From the din.

I said, We can't stop the noise and we can't make her sleep.

Well, Charles said, *there's the brandy.*

He got a bottle of apple brandy down from the closet and soaked his handkerchief in it and stuck it in Margaret's mouth, rewetting the cloth every few minutes, and she sucked enough of it to finally fall asleep.

Some days later, we were awakened by calls of *Hello in there* coming from outside our window. The rain had stopped, and Wallace Porter had sent some of his roustabouts on a raft made out of the side of a circus wagon. Charles rigged a rope with the sheets and lowered Margaret in her cradle, then me, then climbed down himself. And wouldn't you know that as we rounded the front corner of the house, we heard the piano shatter blessedly apart and watched it float in pieces out the front door. Charles and I cried and hugged each other, pointing to the piano shards and laughing like crazy people, which I suppose we were, from no food for two days. We sat there on the raft, listening to no rain hammering the roof, no baby crying, no piano plunking, no elephant bellowing, just the miraculous quiet of the current.

The men who saved us were strong from raising tents and sweeping barns, but they had dark circles under their eyes, dead eyes in sad faces that hardly nodded to us before they started heading towards the winter quarters. Charles asked, *What's happened to everything?* But they didn't reply, so Charles grabbed a plank of wood and started rowing, trying to keep us on course while I sat at the front of the raft and stared into the muddy water where faces of the dead floated up to say *Help me please*. But it was too late, I knew, and their faces sank back down into the mud. Some of the faces were folks from town, but some were strangers and I wondered how far they had come down the Mississinewa and how far they would go before they would finally stop and how anyone would know who to send them back to.

Animals from the menagerie floated around us or were snagged in branches, and dogs and cats and cows, too. A horse tried to swim to us, eyes wild and blowing water out its nose. Charles threw a rope around its neck and tried to carry it along, but later the rope was pulling straight down, like we'd caught a big fish, and he cut the line off with his pocket knife.

Something big and grey moved below the surface, so I leaned over, when a big burst of air and water in front of me wet my face and I was looking right into the eyes Wallace Porter's prize hippopotamus, Helen. She circled us once and sank back underneath the raft. One of the roustabouts stopped rowing and said *Maybe she will live* and that's all any of them ever said the whole time we were on the raft.

We rowed into the winter quarters and saw Porter's house sitting grandly on an island in the middle of swirling water and most of the animal barns half-drowned. The roustabouts set us down on the island and the maids ran down the hill, wrapped the three of us in blankets, and helped us towards the house. One woman gave sandwiches to the men, who ate them without speaking and set off again to look for more faces and drag them back to Porter's house.

We found Wallace Porter in his study, which smelled of cigar smoke and whiskey. He was drunk and delirious, mumbling about judgment. *Why didn't God tell me to make the circus float,* he yelled and shook my shoulders, *I would have done it.* Then he stepped back and wiped his hands down the length of his face and said in a solemn voice that there was food in the kitchen and plenty of rooms to sleep in. I couldn't stand to see him like that, with so much gone, so Charles and I turned and left his study. We ate some soup in the kitchen and gave Margaret some milk and slept and slept. When Charles woke up, he said *I dreamed last week and lived it all over again* and I told him I'd done the same, every moment.

Finally, the sun came out, and at first, I thought there was no way in heaven that the earth could soak up that much water. I never did think all that water came from the sky, anyway, because it seemed like most of it sprang up from holes in the earth, from a China flood many years ago, a slow tide always moving through the earth. I think nothing ever happens and then stops happening when it's over. Maybe the Mississinewa Reservoir is nothing more than that same flood from 1913, come back to see us again.

When the water was gone, Wallace Porter opened the front door and Charles and I walked with him down the drive and across the field toward the winter quarters. There were no sounds at all, not even birds, and for a moment, I felt as if the only people alive on the earth were those who'd made it to Porter's house. We could barely take a step without moving branches out of our way, walking around uprooted trees, wagons, roofs, barrels. Everything looked as if it had been boiled and burned and tossed in a tornado, settling down like silt wherever it was.

This must be why the animals were scattered over the fields in the strangest poses, their eyes open and looking up at the flat sky. An elephant lay on its side, big chunks of its hide gouged out, but the blood had all flowed away somewhere. A Bengal tiger hung by its hind legs from a tree down by the river, caught up in the branches. We walked into the gorilla barn and found three dead, trapped in their locked cages.

That day, every time I turned away from death, there was another carcass, another body, and I'd start shaking again. But I don't think I was as sad as Porter was when we walked into Jennie Dixianna's bunkhouse and found her pinned to the wall, trapped by her four-poster bed. Charles and I walked back outside, where we heard Porter crying, moving the bed to set her free.

I whispered to Charles, Why didn't she just swim away? Charles had no answer until Porter let us in and we watched him pick up all the empty whiskey bottles scattered over the floor. When his arms were full, he looked around, as if for a trash barrel, and seeing the state of the room, started crying. Her face is still with me, grey as fire ashes, with leaves and branches twined in her hair like some kind of brownie or fairy.

Charles carried her body up to Porter's house and I asked Porter what we should do about all the carcasses. He sighed like a man letting go of his last breath.

Burn them. Tell the men to cover them in kerosene and burn them.

Maybe if we'd had one of those backhoes, like the ones they used to dig out the reservoir, we could have buried them in one mass gave and erected a cross to mark the place. But we did what we could. We set all the animals on fire, then closed all the doors and windows in Porter's house to keep out the smell, but the stink of roasted, rotten flesh seeped in through the wooden shutters and under the doors, and none of us could eat for those two days.

When we walked outside again all the skeletons were charred black in the sun, not an ounce of flesh left on them. No one knows what Porter did with the skeletons, and most don't care, as long as the bones of the past are sunk somewhere for good. Eventually, though, everything is revealed, floating on the water's surface or tossed on its receding shore. Maybe Porter tossed the bones into a ravine covered now by the reservoir, and one day some shiny ski boat will run smack dab into an elephant's ribcage and crash and wonder how in the world that happened. I'll tell you how. Flesh may burn and rot and wither, but bones stay around for almost forever.

Prance Williams Swims Again
by Matt Devens

I REMEMBER WHEN America was spelled P-A-N-A-C-H-E; when I was six years old and hid from San Francisco's dragontail wind in the folds of Father's greatcoat while he pointed toward the Bay and said, There, son, is nostalgia in the making. We shivered happily on the wharf and watched a hog-tied Jack Fairlane slam through the jagged blue waters off Alcatraz with no fewer than two Cunard liners in tow. Mother's fingers whitened and trembled around her umbrella handle as the bodybuilder parried ink-spitting cuttlefish with gurgling oaths to God and Country and, at least for that day, knocked Great Depression despair on its flaccid ass with a single roundhouse of intrepidity.

Nowadays, Mother and I watch Jack Fairlane's TV show every morning on her old Motorola. I'm sorry, but all the Brilliantine and splendidly monogrammed jumpsuits in the world do not a savior make. This present-day savant of video muscle-moulding simply is not the human tugboat who ferried our hobbled souls out of the Depression. But that fact's lost on Mother, whose daily entrance into the land of the living is cued by Fairlane's five-six-seven-eight. Each morning she sets aside her bowl of farina, shrugs away my token offers of assistance and, with the aid of her aluminum walker, rises to her feet as deftly as any arthritic seventy-five-year-old might. And I invariably flick the set off, free her from her walker, and waltz her through the canyons of bundled old newspapers which wind haphazardly through her small living room. Da-dammit to hell! she sputters as I spin wheatish shocks of her rump-length hair around my fingers. The way Father should have done, and often.

As long as her slippered feet ride atop my own, she's Ginger Rogers. We dip and glide and in this small commotion bump from the wall a lacquered memento of a long-ago vacation in the Rockies, upset the tableau of lead toy soldiers that has occupied the dining-room credenza top for the last thirty years, and dislodge from the bottom of her lungs girlish laughter that's an unfamiliar, but very much welcome salve to my ears. The crash of Mother's onyx paperweight from Carlsbad Caverns punctuates our final jeté and she says That's enough, that's enough. We're no dancers. Now set me down.

Giggles space her short, halting breaths as I lower her into her chair, and seem to retract altogether into the old wedding photographs flanking either side of her. You get weirder by the minute, she's wont to say. . . . No, more *peculiar* by the minute are the words she'll use because I *am* her son.

But it's good to dance, I counter. Did you ever dance with Father?

A surge of memory clouds her eyes and the years that had spun off of her with our every pirouette reassemble themselves in the lines and crags of her face. Your father and I exercised to Jack Fairlane, she says. Now turn my program back on.

Fairlane's a pathetic old charlatan, I grumble.

To which she offers the resolute pronouncement: Jack Fairlane taught us to survive.

She always hangs me out to dry with that one. I used to think day-to-day survival in itself was just cause for celebration. What more could have been asked of people in a time when one had to count his potatoes and patch the soles of his shoes with cardboard? But then, we've all worn new shoes for the last forty years, so why not dance in them?

One day in 1933, a few months after we moved from San Francisco, I asked Father where he and Mother might go hoofing. It was a torpid summer day in northern Illinois, and the waves of the small lake on which we were fishing slapped the prow of our rowboat in a most indifferent way. Father sighed and pulled a spoon from his tackle box. While his thick, work-cracked fingers affixed the lure to my leader, he said, Oh, if we were to go dancing, I suppose the Aragon Ballroom—or maybe the Trianon. But then, we're no dancers.

Oh, I said.

We cast our lines into a rippling image of sun, and not long afterward, Father got the first bite. We got us dinner, boy, we got us dinner! he said, his voice arcing and jerking like his fishing pole. The brim of his dumpy fedora bled dark with perspiration as he reeled the fish in closer to the boat. His fierce, squinting stare wound itself around the line, reinforced it, made it hum.

Sure ain't seaweed, I said.

At the moment, though, all of Father's concentrative powers were engaged in breaking that two-foot walleye pike as if it were an unruly colt; understandably, he neither heard what I'd said, nor felt his fillet knife leave the sheath dangling at his hip. In the same liquid motion, I sliced the taut line with the knife and leapt over the side of the boat. I truly believe I would have caught the fish with my teeth had Father not grabbed my ankle as I was going over. Our capsized boat buoyed us until we were rescued, and unfortunately allowed Father a free hand with which to clench my nape. I didn't wince or cry or try to bite his hand; the bubbly trails of our sinking gear did that for me. He spun the handle on his vice-like grip until I thought my neck pores would spout blood, but he let go when the two-foot walleye surfaced belly-up between us. The fish's body was a putrefying mosaic of scabs and gashes, and the accumulation of old hooks in its gills and snout held the afternoon sun like a gypsy's earrings. Looks as if the old mule simply swallowed its last hook, Father said lamely while the dents his fingertips had left in my neck filled themselves in.

One night about ten years later, Father finally asked me why I did it. By then I had come to perceive him simply as the orange glow of a cigarette bobbing in the dark, the jangle of a belt buckle, the sweet funk of gin vapors. By then he had yet to take Mother dancing, and two weeks later would be stretched out on the mortician's slab, envenomed by his own liver, the thought of cutting the rug with Mother never having seriously entered his mind. For certain, he and Mother had swallowed Jack Fairlane's radio wave vitamins with smiles as healthy as horses', and survived. Father was surviving, if only in the word's most elemental sense, as his *Why?* lolled pitifully in the darkness of my room. I told him if he really wanted to know, it was his fault.

I never would have jumped in after the gypsy walleye had Father not taken me to the Chicago World's Fair a few days prior, where I first saw Prance Williams. At the fair, Father gave me a quarter and the run of the place before he joined the legions of hot-blooded young men struggling for an ample peek at Sally Rand and ultimately resenting her ostrich plumes. I rode the rocket cars until I was nauseated, and let a phrenologist divine the secrets life would soon reveal to me just before two women whose breasts he had felt earlier arrived with a policeman to shut down his booth. On my way back to meet Father, I passed a large, unmarked circus tent which I saw no one enter save two men whose felt berets and handlebar moustaches lent them a certain air of aesthetic sophistication. The men gibbered in Spanish while they pulled a hand truck loaded with movie cameras and banks of lights into the tent. I strolled over to get a better look and saw by signs discreetly posted at the entrance that whatever was going on inside was closed to the public. I wormed into the tent via the shallow rain trench running beneath its canvas walls, and was instantly mesmerized by the talced assembly of muscle and brooding grace that was Prance Williams. While Jack Fairlane was in some sunny part of the country squat-thrusting to visions of candybars and weight machines bearing his name, Prance was, at that moment, emulating the splayed shape of elms with little more than two sewer caps attached to the ends of an iron bar.

After a few minutes of military presses, Prance left his homemade barbells and kicked through the sawdust floor of the tent toward an olympic-size pool of blancmange. The dozen-odd spectators on hand shadowed his every step. The two moustachioed Spaniards had already set up their camera equipment at one end of the pool and, as Prance arrived at the other end, offered him upturned thumbs and a *Ready-when-you-are*. Prance then speared through the surface of underlit gel and quickly pulled himself into a fetal ball which tumbled gently toward pool bottom. As he drifted downward he extended his arms and legs one at a time until he came to rest at bottom—an anthropomorphic starfish sealed in amber. Many minutes later—I had stopped counting them—he emerged at the camera end of the pool, glistening and belching like a newborn baby.

The onlookers gathered around Prance, vying for handfuls of his slick biceps and asking questions.

Prance, when is your next stunt? a fawning member of the press asked.

Stunt? Prance responded, insulted.

The reporter blanched and said, Er, uh . . . sorry. Well, what, in fact, do you call what you do?

The end of it is art; the process, love.

One of the filmmakers had stepped away from the whir of his cameras and draped a towel across the expanse of Prance's shoulders. But Prance, he said, the two are often indistinguishable, no?

Prance's simple reply: That, my friend, is a confusion we might all live happily with.

I saw Prance Williams in person once more after the blancmange event of the 1933 Chicago World's Fair. This second and last encounter took place just after the War at a transvestite show on Bourbon Street. During the intervening years I had, of course, kept track of his exhibitions of love and art, albeit by way of piecemeal reportage. For instance, wire service snippets described with woeful inadequacy Prance's hang-glide through a hellish forest fire in southern California; the glancing morning newspaper reader could not possibly have imagined this quiet Icarus whose wings would not melt. Also, film critics laureled the documentary account of his blancmange swim, which rode the art theatre circuit for a few years before disappearing altogether.

And there were interviews which found Prance in sublime laconic form:

Q: Prance, the big event?

A: An ocean.

Q: Huh?

A: I'd like to swim one.

Q: Which one?

A: The coldest one that isn't all ice.

Plans of a transoceanic swim had yet to see fruition that night I walked down Bourbon Street; and I felt for a few horrid moments that the voice of the barker outside the cabaret I entered sang the death knell of those plans. Come on in, folks! the barker spat from around his fat cigar, Nothing but the finest in live transvestite entertainment!

As if a TV show patron would settle for anything less, I thought as I hurried on past, only to be knocked back by a sight which bored my heart like a musket ball—"Prance Williams: The Human Pedestal" dashed in livid red across the lobby kiosk. The many sordid implications of the phrase washed through my bowels like ice water, though my worst fears were assuaged once I saw what was actually occurring on stage. There was Prance, not in drag, but trussed in an austere black singlet. He was a dozen years older, but one certainly couldn't tell by his stern muscle tone and suede-smooth face. Even if the bright footlights did not obscure the crowd, whose lewd caterwauling and sex stinks glutted the air, Prance nonetheless would have willed it from his vision. All he saw was water. An ocean. And two land masses on either side of it waiting to be inspanned by the wake of one human swimmer. The garish she-he's whom he balanced on his dimpled chin were just so much dead weight—props of the process of love whose end is art.

When I left Bourbon Street that evening, I'd come to love Prance Williams like Jesus. Say what one will of the tawdry forum to which his art had been relegated, his art was still alive. That evening, I'd once again seen mankind's aureate potential realized in the form of Prance Williams, and the strained breaths he had emitted under the weight of a one-hundred-and-seventy-pound transvestite ignited within me an acute philoprogenitive longing that had lain dormant since I first saw him in Chicago.

I was of marrying age when I left Bourbon Street, and soon afterward took a wife. In the early days of our marriage, my wife and I often made love in open fields, beneath heaven-colored bunting tacked across the sky by angels. And we had several children, all of whose faces I saw hours before their conceptions in my wife's ecstatic tears. *Children . . . Children . . . Children* became my locomotive love chant. Our entangled bodies would rock to and fro upon a grassy hillside and I would grunt *Children . . . Children . . . Children* because children are the potential of perfection and perfection is never redundant. After awhile, though, my wife became displeased with our romantic life and said making love to me had become a mystic science. Is that necessarily a bad thing? I asked her. Oh, she said, When we make love, we shouldn't think of children. We should just . . . you know. Anyway, I'm tired of having children.

Seeing that my wife had borne seven children in as many years, I couldn't very well take the last word on the matter. As the bunting of our love arena began to droop with moth holes and dry-rot, I did pray for some god-like capacity to bear children. I prayed for some fissure—vestigial since the heyday of Zeus— to yawn across my forehead or chest. A fissure from which golden-curled homunculi might bound forth into the world to make love and art, with my blessing of a swat to the bare behind. This hope for Olympian fertility was all I had when my wife and seven young children left for Indianapolis with a man my wife considered "sounder" than I.

I nearly lost all hope of ever bearing children one autumn day in 1962 while I sat in a barber shop waiting to get my hair cut like President Kennedy's. I was leafing through a copy of *Argosy* and, amongst the judo school and pistol ads toward the back, came across a picture of a smiling, middle-aged Prance Williams. He was modeling what was advertised as Dr. Pulvermacher's Electrogalvanic Life Belt. "I can still climb the highest mountain, swim any river, do 1000 push-ups—with Dr. Pulvermacher's E-G Life Belt," said the photograph's caption. How desperate was his smile; I didn't think he ever smiled. Could this have been rationalized as a necessary step in the process? I held the page up to the light and searched the photograph for the tell-tale white outlines of a paste-up. It was really Prance, his body the same mechanism of spring-loaded compaction it was thirty years earlier—that's what was so lacerating. Perhaps he felt he'd hung enough flesh on the barbed interface of loving and mere living, and was going to let someone else take the chances for us. Maybe he decided to seal his wounds by hiding in the backs of magazines selling mail-order health gimmicks. I did so by moving in with Mother.

Mother will tell me that if there was ever a charleston, it was that Prance Williams. Was always pulling weird maneuvers and never had an exercise show. Now Jack Fairlane taught us survival, she says. Then I'll tell her that if one really loves life, one's life should be more than a study in survival. If one loves life, all that isn't best is lamentable. The accumulation of an individual's steps should leave him on the top of the world.

Mother will then ask me where are my life's crowning achievements, where are the fruits of my risks, where are the risks? And I'll reply that if one can't change one's world for the best today, one should hope to do so soon afterward, even though such hope can devour a day, a month, a year, as if in a heartbeat. Well, she'll say, if I had Jack Fairlane's philosophy I wouldn't be whiling away my middle years with my old mother. I'd like to tell her that if we collared Prance and Fairlane in their heyday, stood each behind a lectern on either side of Edward R. Murrow, and ran their respective philosophies up the flagpole, we'd see which one we'd salute.

Murrow would open the debate with the following question: Mr. Fairlane, what is love?

Blisters of sweat erupt through the kinescope grain of Fairlane's forehead: Er, uh . . . Love? . . . . He steps from behind the lectern and entertains the audience with a blinding succession of four-point toe-touches.

We're impressed with your athletic prowess, Mr. Fairlane. But again, what is love?

Try my candybar, kids. It's a high-energy, nutritious snack that will tide. . . .

Mr. Fairlane??

And beneath the hot studio lights, Jack's pancake makeup and hair bluing ooze like lava into the open collar of his jumpsuit.

Would you like to take this question, Mr. Williams?

Prance nods politely, steps forward in his black formal singlet, and hands a revolver to his lamé-wrapped lady assistant who's just stepped from the wings. She moves ten paces away, levels the gun at Prance's face and, upon his unwavering cue of "My dear," fires. As the audience recovers from collective fibrillations, Prance removes the spent bullet from the clench of his teeth, holds it to the light like a diamond for all to see, and utters in a voice as sure as his backstroke, "Love."

But that's a fantasy I've kept stoked in my heart for over twenty years. This morning, as usual, I apologize to Mother for having forced her to dance, and join her in front of Jack Fairlane's wrinkly blue image for some deep-breathing exercises. Mother folds her arms into facsimiles of chicken wings, flaps them like a chicken and says, I'm getting old.

I start into some moderately-paced deep knee bends. Mother is now wheezing a bit and says, *You're* getting old. She strains a glance at me through a milky welling of tears while still keeping time with Fairlane. Your seed is getting old, she continues, and dammit, that is life.

Mother's words lock me in the bottom of one of my knee bends; I try to rock myself upward, but end up falling back on my ass with a thud that rattles the pictures on the wall and sends the old Motorola on the fritz.

Dammit, look at this now, Mother growls. Monkey with the rabbit ears till you get the picture back.

I remain on my ass and rest backward on the palms of my hands. Wait a minute, Mother. I lean forward and squint into the flickering tube. Can't you see it? Can't you hear it?

Mother aims a cock-eyed glance at me. She puzzles at the glee my voice undoubtedly registers. What? All I see is a bunch of goddamn snow!

I walk over to the TV on my knees and, as I turn up the volume, rue the infirmities of age which prevent her from seeing and hearing what I do. The *report*, I say. *Watch. Listen.*

The angels seem to have gotten out their tack hammers and are fine-tuning their halleluia chorus. A greased and goggled speck of man and a pace boat were spotted two hundred miles off of the British Isles. He has to be eighty years old! Mother says, and I tell her no eighty-year-old suit of skin and muscle ever hugged bones so tightly. Prance Williams evidently has proceeded quite well through the years, thank you; and I'll be among the jubilarians welcoming him as he steps upon the chalky shores of England and rattles seawater from his body with a heron's aplomb. And I will have never seen Art so wet, so lissome, so anciently young.

Charlotte

by Tony Earley

THE PROFESSIONAL WRESTLERS are gone. The professional wrestlers do not live here anymore. Frannie Belk sold the Southeastern Wrestling Alliance to Ted Turner for more money than you would think, and the professional wrestlers sold their big houses on Lake Norman and drove in their BMWs down I-85 to bigger houses in Atlanta.

Gone are the Thundercats, Bill and Steve, and the Hidden Pagans with their shiny red masks and secret signs; gone is Paolo the Peruvian, who didn't speak English very well but could momentarily hold off as many as five angry men with his flying bare feet; gone are Comrade Yerkov the Russian Assassin and his bald nephew Boris, and the Sheik of the East and his Harem of Three, and Hank Wilson Senior the Country Star with his beloved guitar Leigh Ann; gone is Naoki Fujita who spit the mysterious Green Fire of the Orient into the eyes of his opponents whenever the referee turned his back; gone are the Superstud, the Mega Destroyer, the Revenger, the Preacher, Ron Rowdy, Tom Tequila, the Gentle Giant, the Littlest Cowboy, Genghis Gandhi, and Bob the Sailor. Gone is Big Bill Boscoe, the ringside announcer, whose question "Tell me, Paolo, what happened in there?" brought forth the answer that all Charlotteans still know by heart—"Well Beel, Hidden Pagan step on toe and hit head with chair and I no can fight no more"; gone are Rockin' Robbie Frazier, the Dreamer, the Viking, Captain Boogie Woogie, Harry the Hairdresser, and Yee-Hah O'Reilly the Cherokee Indian Chief. And gone is Lord Poetry, and all that he stood for, his archrival Bob Noxious, and Darling Donnis—the Sweetheart of the SWA, the Prize Greater Than Any Belt—the girl who had to choose between the two of them, once and for all, during the Final Battle for Love.

Gone.

Now Charlotte has the NBA, and we tell ourselves we are a big deal. We dress in teal and purple and sit in traffic jams on the Billy Graham Parkway so that we can yell in the new coliseum for the Hornets, who are bad, bad, bad. They are hard to watch, and my seats are good. Whenever any of the Hornets come into the bar, and they do not come often, we stare up at them like they were exotic animals come to drink at our watering hole. They are too tall to talk to for very long, not enough like us, and they make me miss the old days. In the old days in Charlotte we did not take ourselves so seriously. Our heroes had platinum blond hair and twenty-seven-inch biceps, but you knew who was good and who was evil, who was changing over to the other side, and who was changing back. You knew that sooner or later the referee would look away just long enough for Bob Noxious to hit Lord Poetry with a folding chair. You knew that Lord Poetry would stare up from the canvas in stricken wonder, as if he had never once in his life seen a folding chair. (In the bar, we screamed at the television, Turn Around, ref, turn around! Look out, Lord Poetry, look out!) In the old days in Charlotte we did not have to decide if the Hornets should trade Rex Chapman (they should not) or if J. R. Reid was big enough to play center in the NBA (he is, but only sometimes). In the old days our heroes were as superficial as we were—but we knew that—and their struggles were exaggerated versions of our own. Now we have the Hornets. They wear uniforms designed by Alexander Julian, and play hard and lose, and make us look into our souls. Now when we march disappointed out of the new coliseum to sit unmoving on the parkway, in the cars we can't afford, we have to think about the things that are true: Everyone in Charlotte is from somewhere else. Everyone in Charlotte tries to be something they are not. We spend more money than we make, but it doesn't help. We know that the Hornets will never make the playoffs, and that somehow it is our fault. Our lives are small and empty, and we thought they wouldn't be, once we moved to the city.

My girlfriend's name is Starla. She is beautiful and we wrestle about love. She does not like to say she loves me, even though we have been together four and a half years. She will not look at me when I say I love her, and if I wanted to, I could ball up the words and use them like a fist. Starla says she has strong lust for me, which should be enough; she says we have good chemistry, which is all anyone can hope for. Late in the night, after it is over, after we have grappled until the last drop of love is gone from our bodies, I say, "Starla, I can tell that you love me. You wouldn't be able to do it like that if you didn't love me." She sits up in bed, her head tilted forward so that her red hair almost covers her face, and picks the black hair that came from my chest off of her breasts and stomach. The skin across her chest is flushed red, patterned like a satellite photograph; it looks like a place I should know. She says, "I'm a grown woman and my body works. It has nothing to do with love." Like a lot of people in Charlotte, Starla has given up on love. In the old days Lord Poetry said to never give up, to always fight for love, but now he is gone to Atlanta with a big contract and a broken heart, and I have to do the best that I can. I hold on, even though Starla says she will not marry me. I have heard that Darling Donnis lives with Bob Noxious in a big condo in Buckhead. Starla wants to know why I can't be happy with what we have. We have good chemistry and apartments in Fourth Ward and German cars. She says it is enough to live with and more than anyone had where we came from. We can eat out whenever we want.

Starla breaks my heart.

She will say that she loves me only at the end of a great struggle, after she is too tired to fight anymore, and then she spits out the words, like a vomit, and calls me bastard or fucker or worse, and asks if the thing I have just done has made me happy. It does not make me happy, but it is what we do. It is the fight we fight. The next day we have dark circles under our eyes like the makeup only truly evil wrestlers wear, and we circle each other like animals in a cage that is too small, and what we feel then is nothing at all like love.

I manage a fern bar on Independence Boulevard near downtown called P. J. O'Mulligan's Goodtimes Emporium. The regulars call the place PJ's. When you have just moved to Charlotte from McAdenville or Cherryville or Lawndale, and Independence is the only street you know, it makes you feel good to call somebody up and say, Hey, let's meet after work at PJ's. It sounds like real life when you say it, and that is a sad thing. PJ's has fake Tiffany lampshades above the tables, with purple and teal hornets belligerent in the glass. It has fake antique Coca-Cola and Miller High Life and Pierce-Arrow Automobile and Winchester Repeating Rifle signs screwed onto the walls, and imitation brass tiles glued to the ceiling. (The glue occasionally lets go and the tiles swoop down toward the tables, like bats.) The ferns are plastic because smoke and people dumping their drinks into the planters kill the real ones. The beer and mixed drinks are expensive, but the chairs and stools are cloth-upholstered and plush, and the ceiling lights in their smooth, round globes are low and pleasant enough, and the television set is huge and close to the bar and perpetually tuned to ESPN. Except when the Hornets are on Channel 18, or wrestling is on TBS. In the old days in Charlotte a lot of the professional wrestlers hung out at PJ's. Sometimes Lord Poetry stopped by early in the afternoon, after he was through working out, and tried out a new poem he had found in one of his thick books. The last time he came in, days before the Final Battle, I asked him to tell me a poem I could say to Starla. In the old days in Charlotte, you would not think twice about hearing a giant man with long, red hair say a poem in a bar, even in the middle of the afternoon. I turned the TV down, and the two waitresses and the handful of hardcores who had sneaked away from their offices for a drink saw what was happening and eased up close enough to hear. Lord Poetry crossed his arms and stared straight up, as if the poem he was searching for was written on the ceiling, or somewhere on the other side, in a place we couldn't see. His voice is higher and softer than you would expect the voice of a man that size to be, and when he nodded and finally began to speak, it was almost in a whisper, and we all leaned in even closer. He said,

We sat grown quiet at the name of love;
We saw the last embers of daylight die,
And in the trembling blue-green of the sky
A moon, worn as if it had been a shell

*Washed by time's waters as they rose and fell
About the stars and broke in days and years.*

*I had a thought for no one's but your ears:
That you were beautiful and that I strove
To love you in the old high way of love;
That it had all seemed happy, and yet we'd grown
As weary-hearted as that hollow moon.*

P. J. O'Mulligan's was as quiet then as you will ever hear it. All of Charlotte seemed suddenly still and listening around us. Nobody moved until Lord Poetry finally looked down and reached again for his beer and said, "That's Yeats." Then we all moved back, suddenly conscious of his great size, and our closeness to it, and nodded and agreed that it was a real good poem, one of the best we had ever heard him say. Later, I had him repeat it for me, line for line, and I wrote it down on a cocktail napkin. Sometimes, late at night, after Starla and I have fought, and I have made her say I love you like uncle, even as I can see in her eyes how much she hates me for it, I think about reading the poem to her, but some things are just too true to ever say out loud.

In PJ's we watch wrestling still, even though we can no longer claim it as our own. We sit around the big screen without cheering, and stare at the wrestlers like favorite relatives we haven't seen in years. We say things like, Boy, the Viking has really put on weight since he moved down there or, When did Rockin' Robbie Frazier cut his hair like that? We put on brave faces when we talk about Rockin' Robbie, who was probably Charlotte's most popular wrestler, and try not to dwell on the fact that he is gone away from us for good. In the old days he dragged his stunned and half-senseless opponents to the center of the ring and climbed onto the top rope, and after the crowd counted down from five (Four! Three! Two! One!) he would launch himself into the air, his arms and legs spread like wings, his blond hair streaming out behind him like a banner, and fly ten, fifteen feet, easy, and from an unimaginable height drop with a crash like an explosion directly onto his opponent's head. He called it the Rockin' Robbie B-52. ("I'll tell you one thing, Big Bill. Come next Saturday night in the Charlotte Coliseum I'm gonna B-52 the Sheik of the East like he ain't never been B-52ed before.") And after Rockin' Robbie's B-52 had landed, while his opponent flopped around on the canvas like a big fish, waiting only to be mounted and pinned, Rockin' Robbie leaped up and stood over him, his body slick with righteous sweat, his face a picture of joy. He held his hands high in the air, his fingers spread wide, his pelvis thrusting uncontrollably back and forth in the electric joy of the moment, and he tossed his head back and howled like a dog, his red lips aimed at the sky. Those were glorious days. Whenever Rockin' Robbie walked into PJ's, everybody in the place raised their glasses and pointed their noses at the fake brass of the ceiling and bayed at the stars we knew spun, only for us, in the high, moony night above Charlotte. Nothing like that happens here anymore. Frannie Belk gathered up all the good and evil in our city and sold it four hours south. These days the illusions we have left are the small ones of our own making, and they have, in the vacuum the wrestlers left behind, become too easy to see through; we now have to live with ourselves.

About once a week some guy who's just moved to Charlotte from Kings Mountain or Chester or Gaffney comes up to me where I sit at the bar, on my stool by the waitress station, and says, Hey man, are you P. J. O'Mulligan? They are never kidding, and whenever it happens I don't know what to say. I wish I could tell them whatever it is they need in their hearts to hear, but P. J. O'Mulligan is fourteen lawyers from Richmond with investment capital. What do you say? New people come to Charlotte from the small towns every day, searching for lives that are bigger than the ones they have known, but what they must settle for, once they get here, are much smaller hopes: that maybe this year the Hornets might really have a shot at the Celtics, if Rex Chapman has a good game; that maybe there really is somebody named P. J. O'Mulligan, and that maybe that guy at the bar is him. Now that the wrestlers are gone, I wonder about these things. How do you tell somebody how to find what they're looking for when ten years ago you came from the same place, and have yet to find it yourself? How do you tell somebody from Polkville or Aliceville or Cliffside, who just saw downtown after sunset for the first time, not to let the beauty of the skyline fool them? Charlotte is a place where a crooked TV preacher can steal money and grow like a sore until he collapses from the weight of his own evil by simply promising hope. So don't stare at the NCNB Tower against the dark blue of the sky; keep your eyes on the road. Don't think that Independence Boulevard is anything more than a street. Most of my waitresses are college girls from UNCC and CPCC, and I can see the hope shining in their faces even as they fill out applications. They look good in their official P. J. O'Mulligan's khaki shorts and white sneakers and green aprons and starched, preppy blouses, but they are still mill-town girls through and through, come to the city to find the answers to their prayers. How do you tell them Charlotte isn't a good place to look? Charlotte is a place where a crooked TV preacher can pray that his flock will send him money so that he can build a giant water slide—and they will. I prefer to hire waitresses from Davidson or Queens, because when they are through with school they will live lives the rest of us can only imagine, but they are easily disillusioned and hard to keep for very long.

PJ's still draws a wrestling crowd. They are mostly good-looking and wear lots of jewelry. The girls do aerobics like religion and have big, curly hair, stiff with mousse. They wear short, tight dresses—usually black—and dangling earrings and spiked heels and lipstick with little sparkles in it, like stars, that you're not even sure you can see. (You catch yourself staring at their mouths when they talk, waiting for their lips to catch the light.) The guys dye their hair blond and wear it spiked on top, long and permed in back, and shaved over the ears. They lift weights and take steroids. When they have enough money they get coked up. They wear stonewashed jeans and open shirts and gold chains thick as ropes and cowboy boots made from python skin, which is how professional wrestlers dress when they relax. Sometimes you will see a group of guys in a circle, with their jeans pulled up over their calves, arguing about whose boots were made from the biggest snake. The girls have long, red fingernails and work mostly in the tall offices downtown. Most of the guys work outdoors—construction usually, there still is a lot of that, even now—or in the bodybuilding gyms, or the industrial parks along I-85. Both sexes are darkly and artificially tanned, even in the winter, and get drunk on shooters and look vainly in PJ's for love.

Around midnight on Friday and Saturday, before everyone clears out to go dancing at The Connection or Plum Crazy's, where the night's hopes become final choices, PJ's gets packed. The waitresses have to move sideways through the crowd with their trays held over their heads. Everybody shouts to be heard over each other and over the music—P. J. O'Mulligan's official contemporary jazz, piped in from Richmond—and if you close your eyes and listen carefully you can hear in the voices the one story they are trying not to tell: how everyone in Charlotte grew up in a white house in a row of white houses on the side of a hill in Lowell or Kannapolis or Spindale, and how they had to be quiet at home because their daddies worked third shift, how a black oil heater squatted like a gargoyle in the middle of their living room floor, and how the whole time they were growing up the one thing they always wanted to do was leave. I get lonesome sometimes, in the buzzing middle of the weekend, when I listen to the voices and think about the shortness of the distance all of us managed to travel as we tried to get away, and how when we got to Charlotte the only people we found waiting for us were the ones we had left. Our parents go to tractor pulls and watch *Hee-Haw*. My father eats squirrel brains. We tell ourselves that we are different now, because we live in Charlotte, but deep down know that we are only making do.

The last great professional wrestling card Frannie Belk put together—before she signed Ted Turner's big check and with a diamond-studded wave of her hand sent the wrestlers away from Charlotte for good—was Armageddon V, The Last Explosion, which took place in the new coliseum three nights after the Hornets played and lost their first NBA game. ("Ohhhhhh," Big Bill Boscoe said in the promotional TV ad, his big voice quavering with emotion, "Ladies and

Gentlemen and Wrestling Fans of All Ages, See an Unprecedented Galaxy of SWA Wrestling Stars Collide and Explode in the Charlotte Coliseum . . . ") And for a while that night—even though we knew the wrestlers were moving to Atlanta—the world still seemed young and full of hope, and we were young in it, and life in Charlotte seemed close to the way we had always imagined it should be: Paolo the Peruvian jerked his bare foot out from under the big, black boot of Comrade Yerkov, and then kicked the shit out of him in a flying frenzy of South American feet; Rockin' Robbie Frazier squirted a water pistol into Naoki Fujita's mouth, before Fujita could ignite the mysterious Green Fire of the Orient, and then launched a B-52 from such a great height that even the most jaded wrestling fans gasped with wonder (and if that wasn't enough, he later ran from the locker room in his street clothes, his hair still wet from his shower, his shirt tail out and flapping, and in a blond fury B-52ed not one but both of the Hidden Pagans, who had used a folding chair to gain an unfair advantage over the Thundercats, Bill and Steve). And we saw the Littlest Cowboy and Chief Yee-Hah O'Reilly, their wrists bound together with an eight-foot leather thong, battle nobly in an Apache Death Match, until neither man was able to stand and the referee called it a draw and cut them loose with a long and crooked dagger belonging to the Sheik of the East; Hank Wilson Senior the Country Star whacked Captain Boogie Woogie over the head with his beloved guitar Leigh Ann, and earned a thoroughly satisfying disqualification, and a long and heartfelt standing O; one of the Harem of Three slipped the Sheik of the East a handful of Arabian sand, which he threw into the eyes of Bob the Sailor to save himself from the Sailor's Killer Clam hold—from which no bad guy ever escaped, once it was locked—but the referee saw the Sheik do it (the rarest of wrestling miracles) and awarded the match to the Sailor; and in the prelude to the main event, like the thunder before a storm, the Brothers Clean—the Superstud, the Viking, and the Gentle Giant—outlasted the Three Evils—Genghis Gandhi, Ron Rowdy and Tom Tequila—in a six-man Texas Chain-Link Massacre match in which a ten-foot wire fence was lowered around the ring, and bald Boris Yerkov and Harry the Hairdresser patrolled outside, eyeing each other suspiciously, armed with bullwhips and folding chairs, to make sure that no one climbed out and no one climbed in.

Now, looking back, it seems prophetic somehow that Starla and I lined up on opposite sides during the Final Battle for Love. ("Sex is the biggest deal people have," Starla says. "You think about what you really want from me, what really matters, the next time you ask for a piece.") In the Final Battle, Starla wanted Bob Noxious, with his dark chemistry, to win Darling Donnis away from Lord Poetry once and for all. He had twice come close. I wanted Lord Poetry to strike a lasting blow for love. Starla said it would never happen, and she was right. Late in the night, after it is over, after Starla has pinned my shoulders flat against the bed and held them there, after we are able to talk, I say, "Starla, you have to admit that you were making love to me. I could tell." She runs to the bathroom, her legs stiff and close together, to get rid of part of me. "Cave men made up love," she calls out from behind the door. "After they invented laws, they had to stop killing each other, so they told their women they loved them to keep them from screwing other men. That's what love is."

Bob Noxious was Charlotte's most feared and evil wrestler, and on the night of the Final Battle, we knew that he did not want Darling Donnis because he loved her. Bob Noxious was scary: he had a cobalt-blue, spiked mohawk, and if on his way to the ring a fan spat on him, he always spat back. He had a neck like a bull, and a 56-inch chest, and he could twitch his pectoral muscles so fast that his nipples jerked up and down like pistons. Lord Poetry was almost as big as Bob Noxious, and scary in different ways. His curly, red hair was longer than Starla's, and he wrestled in paisley tights—pinks and magentas and lavenders— he had specially made in England. He read a poem to Darling Donnis before and after every match while the crowd yelled for him to stop. (Charlotte did not know which it hated more: Bob Noxious with his huge and savage evil, or the prancing Lord Poetry with his paisley tights and fat book of poems.) Darling Donnis was the picture of innocence (and danger, if you are a man) and hung on every word Lord Poetry said. She was blond, and wore a low-cut, lacy white dress (but never a slip), and covered her mouth with her hands whenever Lord Poetry was in trouble, her moist, green eyes wide with concern.

Darling Donnis's dilemma was this: She was in love with Lord Poetry, but she was mesmerized by Bob Noxious's animal power. The last two times Bob Noxious and Lord Poetry fought, before the Final Battle, Bob Noxious had beaten Lord Poetry with his fists until Lord Poetry couldn't stand, and then he turned to Darling Donnis and put his hands on his hips and threw his shoulders back, revealing enough muscles to make several lesser men. Darling Donnis's legs visibly wobbled, and she steadied herself against the ring apron, but she did not look away. While the crowd screamed for Bob Noxious to Shake 'em! Shake 'em! Let 'em go! he began to twitch his pectorals up and down, first just one at a time, just once or twice—teasing Darling Donnis—then the other, then in rhythm, faster and faster. It was something you had to look at, even if you didn't want to, a force of nature, and at both matches Darling Donnis was transfixed. She couldn't look away from Bob Noxious's chest, and would have gone to him (even though she held her hands over her mouth and shook her head no, the pull was too strong) had it not been for Rockin' Robbie Frazier. At both matches before the Final Battle, Rockin' Robbie ran out of the locker room in his street clothes and tossed the prostrate Lord Poetry the book of poetry that Darling Donnis had carelessly dropped on the apron of the ring. Then he climbed through the ropes and held off the enraged and bellowing Bob Noxious long enough for Lord Poetry to crawl out of danger and read Darling Donnis one of her favorite sonnets, which calmed her. But the night of the Final Battle, all of Charlotte knew that something had to give. We did not think that even Rockin' Robbie could save Darling Donnis from Bob Noxious three times. Bob Noxious's pull was too strong. This time Lord Poetry had to do it himself.

They cleared away the cage from the Texas Chain-Link Massacre, and the houselights went down slowly until only the ring was lit. The white canvas was so bright that it hurt your eyes to look at it. Blue spotlights blinked open in the high darkness beneath the roof of the coliseum, and quick circles of light skimmed across the surface of the crowd, showing in an instant a hundred, two hundred, expectant faces. The crowd could feel the big thing coming up on them, like animals before an earthquake. Rednecks in the high, cheap seats stomped their feet and hooted like owls. Starla twisted in her seat and stuck two fingers into her mouth and cut loose with a shrill whistle. "Ohhhhh Ladies and Gentlemen and Wrestling Fans," Big Bill Boscoe said from everywhere in the darkness, like the very voice of God, "I Hope You Are Ready to Hold On to Your Seats"—and in their excitement 23,000 people screamed *Yeah!*—"Because the Earth is Going to Shake and the Ground is Going to Split Open"—*YEAH!*, louder now—"and Hellfire Will Shoot Out of the Primordial Darkness in a Holocaust of Pure Wrestling Fury"—They punched at the air with their fists, and roared, like beasts, the blackness they hid in their hearts, *YEAHHHHHH!* "Ohhhhhhh," Big Bill Boscoe said when they quieted down, his voice trailing off into a whisper filled with fear (he was afraid to unleash the thing that waited in the dark for the sound of his words, and they screamed in rage at his weakness, *YEAHHHHHHH!*) "Ohhhhhh, Charlotte, Ohhhhhhh, Wrestling Fans and Ladies and Gentlemen, I Hope, I Pray, That You Have Made Ready"—*YEAHHHHHHH!*—"For . . . The FINAL . . . BATTLE . . . FOR . . . LOOOOOOOOOVE!"

At the end of regulation time (nothing really important ever happens in professional wrestling until the borrowed time after the final bell has rung) Bob Noxious and Lord Poetry stood in the center of the ring, their hands locked around each other's thick throat. Because chokeholds are illegal in SWA professional wrestling, the referee had ordered them to let go and, when they refused, began to count them out for a double disqualification. Bob Noxious and Lord Poetry let go only long enough to grab the referee, each by an arm, and throw him out of the ring, where he lay prostrate on the floor. Lord Poetry and Bob Noxious again locked onto each other's throat. There was no one there to stop them, and we felt our stomachs falling away into darkness, into the chaos. Veins bulged like ropes beneath the skin of their arms. Their faces were contorted with hatred, and turned from pink to red to scarlet. Starla jumped up and down beside me and shouted, "*KILL* Lord Poetry! *KILL* Lord Poetry!"

Darling Donnis ran around and around the ring, begging for someone, anyone, to make them stop. At the announcer's table, Big Bill Boscoe raised his hands in helplessness. Sure he wanted to help, but he was only Big Bill Boscoe, a voice. What could he do? Darling Donnis rushed away. She circled the ring twice more until she found Rockin' Robbie Frazier keeping his vigil from the shadows near the entrance to the locker room. She dragged him into the light near the ring. She pointed wildly at Lord Poetry and Bob Noxious. Both men had started to shake, as if cold. Bob Noxious's eyes rolled back in his head, but he didn't let go. Lord Poetry stumbled, but reached back with a leg and regained his balance. Darling Donnis shouted at Rockin' Robbie. She pointed again. She pulled her hair. She doubled her hands under her chin, pleading. "*CHOKE* him!" Starla screamed. "*CHOKE* him!" She looked sideways at me. "*HURRY!*" Darling Donnis got down on her knees in front of Rockin' Robbie and wrapped her arms around his waist. Rockin' Robbie stroked her hair but stared into the distance and shook his head no. Not this time. This was what it had come to. This was a fair fight between men, and none of his business. He walked back into the darkness.

Darling Donnis was on her own now. She ran to the ring and stood at the apron and screamed for Bob Noxious and Lord Poetry to stop it. The sound of her words was lost in the roar that came from up out of our hearts, but we could feel them. She pounded on the canvas, but they didn't listen. They kept choking each other, their fingers a deathly white. Darling Donnis crawled beneath the bottom rope and into the ring. "*NO!*" Starla yelled, striking the air with her fists. "Let him *DIE*. Let him *DIE!*" Darling Donnis took a step toward the two men and reached out with her hands, but stopped, unsure of what to do. She wrapped her arms around herself and rocked back and forth. She grabbed her hair and started to scream. She screamed as if the earth really had opened up, and hellfire had shot up all around her—and that it had been her fault. She screamed until her eyelids fluttered closed, and she dropped into a blond and white heap on the mat, and lay there without moving.

When Darling Donnis stopped screaming, it was as if the spell that had held Bob Noxious and Lord Poetry at each other's throat was suddenly broken. They let go at the same time. Lord Poetry dropped heavily to his elbows and knees, facing away from Darling Donnis. Bob Noxious staggered backward into the corner, where he leaned against the turnbuckles. He held onto the top rope with one hand, and with the other rubbed his throat. "Go *GET* her!" Starla screamed at Bob Noxious, "Go *GET* her!" For a long time nobody in the ring moved, and in the vast, enclosed darkness surrounding the ring, starting up high and then spreading throughout the building, 23,000 people began to stomp their feet. Tiny points of fire, hundreds of them, sparked in the darkness. But still Bob Noxious and Lord Poetry and Darling Donnis did not move. The crowd stomped louder and louder (BOOM! BOOM! BOOM! BOOM!) until finally Darling Donnis weakly raised her head, and pushed her hair back from her eyes. We caught our breath and looked to see where she looked. It was at Bob Noxious. Bob Noxious glanced suddenly up, his dark power returning. He took his hand off of his throat and put it on the top rope and pushed himself up higher. Darling Donnis raised herself onto her hands and knees and peeked quickly at Lord Poetry, who still hadn't moved, and then looked back to Bob Noxious. "DO it, Darling Donnis!" Starla screamed. "Just DO it!" Bob Noxious pushed off against the ropes and took an unsteady step forward. He inhaled deeply and stood up straight. Darling Donnis's eyes never left him. Bob Noxious put his hands on his hips, and with a monumental effort threw his great shoulders all the way back. *No*, we saw Darling Donnis whisper. *No*. High up in the seats beside me, Starla screamed, "*YES!*"

Bob Noxious's left nipple twitched once. Twitch. Then again. Then the right. The beginning of the end. Darling Donnis slid a hand almost imperceptibly toward him across the canvas. But then, just when it all seemed lost, Rockin' Robbie Frazier ran from out of the shadows to the edge of the ring. He carried a thick book in one hand and a cordless microphone in the other. He leaned under the bottom rope and began to shout at Lord Poetry, their faces almost touching. (*Lord Poetry! Lord Poetry!*) Lord Poetry finally looked up at Rockin' Robbie, and then slowly turned to look at Bob Noxious, whose pectoral muscles had begun to twitch regularly, left-right, left-right, like heartbeats. Darling Donnis raised a knee from the canvas and began to stalk Bob Noxious. Rockin' Robbie reached in through the ropes and helped Lord Poetry to his knees. He gave the book and the microphone to Lord Poetry. Lord Poetry turned around, still kneeling, until he faced Darling Donnis. She didn't even look at him. Five feet to Lord Poetry's right, Bob Noxious's huge chest was alive, pumping. A train picking up speed. Lord Poetry opened the book and turned to a page and shook his head. No, that one's not right. He turned farther back into the book and shook his head again. What is the one thing you can say to save the world you live in? How do you find the words? Darling Donnis licked her red lips. Rockin' Robbie began shouting and flashing his fingers in numbers at Lord Poetry. Ten-Eight. Ten-Eight. Lord Poetry looked over his shoulder at Rockin' Robbie, and his eyebrows moved up in a question: Eighteen? *Yes*, screamed Rockin' Robbie. *Eighteen*. Ten-eight. "Ladies and Gentlemen," Big Bill Boscoe's huge voice said, filled now with hope, "I think it's going to be Shakespeare's Sonnet Number Eighteen!" and a great shout of *NOOOOO!* rose up in the darkness like a wind.

Lord Poetry flipped through the book, and studied a page, and reached out and touched it, as if it were in Braille. He looked quickly at Darling Donnis, flat on her belly now, slithering across the ring toward Bob Noxious. Lord Poetry said into the microphone, "Shall I compare thee to a summer's day?" Starla kicked the seat in front of her and screamed, "*NO! Don't Do It! Don't Do It!*

He's After Your *Soul!* He's After Your *Soul!*" Lord Poetry glanced up again and said, "Thou art far more lovely and more temperate," and then faster, more urgently, "Rough winds do shake the darling buds of May," but Darling Donnis crawled on, underneath the force of his words, to within a foot of Bob Noxious. Bob Noxious's eyes were closed in concentration and pain, but still his pectorals pumped faster. Lord Poetry opened his mouth to speak again, but then looked one last time at Darling Donnis and buried his face in the book and slumped to the mat. Rockin' Robbie pulled on the ropes like the bars of a cage and yelled in rage, his face pointed upward, but he did not climb into the ring. He could not stop what was happening. *Please,* we saw Darling Donnis say to Bob Noxious. *Please.* The panicked voice of Big Bill Boscoe boomed out like thunder: "Darling Donnis! Darling Donnis! And summer's lease has all too short a date! Sometimes too hot the eye of heaven shines! And often is his gold complexion dimm'd!" But it was too late: Bob Noxious reached down and lifted Darling Donnis up by the shoulders. She looked him straight in the eye and reached out with both hands and touched his broad, electric chest. Her eyes rolled back in her head. Starla dropped heavily down into her seat, and breathed deeply, twice. She looked up at me and smiled. "There," she said, as if it was late in the night, as if it was over. "There."

Forced Landing
by Jennifer Fremlin

MARSHA DRIVES, indifferent now, along Airport Road, her charm bracelet clinking against the steering wheel. She looks neither to the left nor the right, no longer interested in the cows chewing their cud, the sun setting over the fields. In the distance ahead, the lights of the city at dusk are burning for others. Her neck, rigid, isn't craning to catch a glimpse in the rearview mirror of planes taking off, planes filled with the passengers she ticketed and herded aboard. She pushes away thoughts of Bob Gianelli's invitation.

Her lips are not moving; the radio is turned off. For the past three months, the once favorite part of her day has become a limbo time. She has no desire to arrive home, nor any to go back to work. She obeys the speed limit, and as she approaches the first outlying stoplight she slows for the amber. She changed out of her blue and gray airline ticket agent's uniform and into jeans and a sweatshirt after her shift. Her name tag lies beside her on the seat.

At one time, before Berta's departure, she would have been sitting up tall in her outfit, her hair pulled back in a matching scarf decorated with the airline logo, piloting her craft to a safe landing. There was excitement in the risks—speeding because of an ill passenger, racing to land before the air controllers were needed to direct an in-coming flight, an hour ahead of schedule and nearly out of fuel. As she came into town the last night of the old days (as she thinks of them now), she had made such a trip, the car nearly turning itself at the proper corners. She had pulled onto Placid Drive, wide and quiet at the dinner hour. The streetlights blinked on exactly as she rounded the curve, a well-lit landing strip. Across the way the Schmidts were just sitting down to their dining room table, where they always ate at night, making their meal a formal occasion.

But as the car had pulled into her driveway, the lamppost in her yard was dark. The kitchen too, except for an eerie glow. Nobody stood at the sink washing vegetables. No light by the back door cast the usual shadows, and underneath the carport she could barely see to park. Her chest hurt as she turned her key in the back door, pushed it open. She took deep breaths as she kicked off her outside shoes on the landing, and she stepped into her house slippers before pushing into the kitchen.

The little TV she had given her mother for the previous Christmas was turned on, but there was no sound. Built especially for countertops, it had AM/FM radio, and though it was only black and white Henry had spliced the cable. Her mother had thanked her with what had appeared to be genuine gratitude and immediately plugged it in. She said it kept her company in the early mornings; Henry went to work while it was still dark.

But it wasn't Berta watching it now. Henry sat at the round wooden table, a beer in front of him, staring at the silent turning of letters. He didn't swerve his gaze even when she stood right in front of him.

"What is it?" she had demanded. "What's wrong?" She saw her mother laid out on an operating table, or in a casket, and the memory of the smell of gladiolas overwhelmed her.

Henry lifted his eyes then to the level of her name tag. He opened his mouth, but his tongue formed no sound. A bubble frothed on his front teeth.

"Are you sick?" Marsha asked. "Or is it her? Where is she, what have you done to her?"

Henry nodded. "She's gone."

"You stupid—what do you mean?" It was all she could do to keep from shaking the old man. Always talk with respect to your father, Berta had taught her, no matter what. It's the least he deserves.

Henry remained dumb. Marsha shoved past the kitchen chairs and ran down the hall. The lights in the living room and her parents' room were off. Once, she had come home from school and her mother wasn't in the kitchen to greet her. No warm cookies were on a plate, and the damp heat of the dryer wasn't rising through the vents. She had raced through the house then too, until finally she came to the room at the end of the hallway. There, on the bed, her mother lay on her stomach, still as death, her cotton housedress pulled snug across her bottom. But then she had moved, she had rolled over, a wet cloth clinging to her forehead. "Oh, hello dear, you're home already. I've had a bit of a headache, but I'm fine now." And that had been that. Berta had gotten up, cooked supper as always, and when Henry came in from work there was no sign of anything out of the ordinary.

No such form spread out over the covers when Marsha had looked that last night. The room was neat and empty. The closet door was cracked, as it usually was so Buttons the cat could creep in and sleep on the shoes. Marsha slid it all the way open. Her father's work shirts, neatly pressed, lined up alongside the matching deep green work pants. Several of Berta's dresses, the good ones she wore for bridge night or at Christmas time, hung on her side of the closet, a pair of pumps beneath each one on the shoe rack. But her cotton prints were missing. Berta had washed only the day before, so they couldn't be in the dirty clothes basket. Marsha pulled open the chest of drawers, something she hadn't done since she was a little girl. Small sachet pouches wafted the odor of her mother up to her, the smell that clung to her underwear, closest to her skin, brushing off as she moved through the house. The drawers were nearly empty—only a girdle and a couple of worn bras, some old pantyhose and summer socks were left behind.

One night a few weeks later, almost two months ago now, Henry was out God only knows where when Marsha came home from work. Marsha, angry with lavender and roses, had scrubbed out her mother's drawers with PineSol. At the back of the top drawer she found a blue box, and inside it was a silver charm bracelet her parents had given her the Christmas she was eight. The charms crowded the interlocking links: a girl's head, with her name and birthday engraved on it; a horse; a pair of skates, and one of skis; a treble clef and a bell that really tinkled; a snowflake; a Santa Claus; a cat with turquoise eyes; and a dimpled orange, "The Sunshine State" in tiny letters underneath. Marsha took it out of the box and put it on, the bracelet fitting snugger than what she remembered. She'd always been big-boned, and her feet were a size nine by the third grade. She stood inches taller than Berta, who seemed petite and fragile at just over five feet.

It was about the time she found the bracelet that Henry took to sleeping on the couch instead of in the large double bed with brass frame that he had shared with Berta. He pulled an afghan knitted by Berta over him, his feet sticking out the end. In the mornings when Marsha came upstairs from her apartment, the blanket would be twisted in a corner of the rose-colored chesterfield Marsha had purchased for Berta a couple of years back. The living room began to take on the smell of Henry, beer and pipe tobacco and the faint hint of sulphur from the steel plant, the smell of his lap when she was little.

Henry still watched "Wheel of Fortune" every evening, but in the kitchen instead of on the big color set in the living room. He grunted in a specific way when he had figured out the puzzle. Marsha and Berta used to sit with him, after dinner, playing along, keeping quiet if they solved it first so as not to spoil it for him. Marsha could tell by the way Berta's fingers popped open on her lap when she had solved the riddle, and avoided her eyes. During the commercials, the women discussed the prizes, the merits of the fridge with an ice dispenser outside the door. Henry complained when they kept their refrigerator open too long, and he could hear the warning beep all over the house. He would tell them to hush, that any fool in his right mind would know enough to take the money, especially when it would be tax-free in Canada.

The car in front of her slows down for the first light at the edge of the city, and Marsha debates turning into Tim Horton Donuts to pick up breakfast for the morning. Henry is likely sitting in the kitchen, no lights on, watching the sports. He will be drinking a beer, not thinking of supper until the moment his stomach growls. There are potato chips in the cupboard, he doesn't even have to leave the room. And then he'll watch while she opens up cans of soup, puts out bread cut in fours already buttered for him. He likes it when she puts cheese on a plate too, but not tonight, she doesn't feel like making another stop. Besides, somebody has to watch his cholesterol. *The Sound of Music* is on at seven, the same time as his game show. She could watch it downstairs, since she moved the big set to her own apartment. By her count, she has seen this movie eleven times, once every other year since she can remember. The first time was at the theater, just her and Berta. They ate popcorn, and Berta cried when Maria came back to the convent, leaving the Captain to his Countess. Every time Berta saw it she cried at the same part. Marsha herself gets teary-eyed when the Captain sings "Edelweiss" with his family. The hospital she was born in is named for Christopher Plummer's grandfather.

Marsha accelerates past the left turn towards home. Instead, she goes straight on down the hill. A weird time to go downtown, just past six-thirty, when all the stores are closed and the early shows haven't yet started. Most of the traffic passes her in the opposite direction. Until a few months ago, she never came down here in the evening, unless it was to the mall with Berta on a Friday night, when it stays open until nine. They would have coffee at the restaurant across from Dominion, where Berta would have shopped for specials on meat and produce. It was kind of like being on a date, and once in a while they saw a movie. *The Turning Point* is one Marsha remembers, and a James Bond film that they both liked.

After she turns onto Queen Street, downtown proper, the street is more crowded, mostly with teenagers in their parents' family-type cars. Which hers looks like, if she had to admit it. She paid for it with her own money. She had bought the chocolate brown New Yorker new off the lot: pricey, but roomy enough to take nice drives on Sundays to see the fall leaves, or out for an ice cream cone after supper in the summer. Just last winter they put the car to the test: 2,500 km to Florida, and the same again coming back. They had left right after the new year, when Marsha had her three weeks coming to her. She had just finished the most grueling part of the season: getting people home to their families for Christmas, helping out students flying standby, taking extra care with the Christmas presents that were checked through to southern Ontario. Some people might think it strange for a ticket agent at an airport not to fly on her own vacation, especially when she could travel just about anywhere in continental North America except Alaska and Hawaii for twenty dollars. She even knew the route: Air Canada all the way, nonstop from Toronto to Miami, only three hours in the air, complimentary cocktails and light lunch included.

But she lets people think what they want, they will anyway; and besides, it isn't anyone's business if she doesn't like the takeoffs and landings, when her stomach lurches and she feels her face drain of color. How can she explain this to Bob, who wants to fly her up north in his little plane this coming Sunday? He says he'll pack a picnic, he knows a lake where the fall leaves have already started to turn. Marsha likes the silver tubes coasting in outside the airport windows, and the people she meets who are traveling to and fro. Some are making connecting flights to Greece, or Africa, and for those people she has to stamp their documents before they can pass out of the country. The thought that she is the anchor, the one constant in all the bustle and importance of business people and world travelers, the one who gets them where they need to be, thrills her.

But when it came to her own parents, an even better way to ensure they arrived safely was to navigate and pilot them herself. Carefully she plotted their route, and watched the gas gauge, and drove with as much confidence as any son. Henry had grumbled at the whole idea, of course, but in the end he went along with it, he always did. He didn't much like his daughter doing the driving, but the truth is Henry's reflexes aren't what they used to be, and his impatience at any car doing the speed limit scared the women to death. So they put him in the back seat where he could spread the maps out and calculate mileages and the price of American gas compared to Canadian. All in all, gas was costing them almost half what it would at home. Marsha couldn't remember the particulars or the equations, but for the most part it had kept Henry content. After each stop he would reach forward and lock both the front doors, and Marsha would relax back in her seat, the cruise control set to the speed limit.

And Berta had been happy then too, or so it seems, even now, in retrospect. In the evenings, the women bathed in the motels they stopped at along the way. They would all rise early, about seven, and Henry would shower. Then they would drive an hour or so before stopping for breakfast at highway restaurants serving berry-flavored syrups instead of maple and whipped cream on the waffles. The waitresses would bring them big glasses of ice water without being asked to, and say "Have a nice day now" as if they meant it, their accents getting softer and prettier the further south they got. Berta, delighted, took to saying it back to them, and to the service attendants at gas stations, and if they stopped to buy pop at a 7-11. She said it made her feel like a nicer person just for thinking it, and maybe it made you live longer. Now, she says it still, to bank tellers and grocery clerks, and to her customers over clean piles of laundry.

After breakfast, Henry usually fell asleep. Not bothering to convert from Fahrenheit to Celsius, the women would note how the temperatures warmed up with each passing mile. Berta would comment on the snow that must be piling up in the driveway back home, and how nice it was to wear only a cardigan instead of a heavy winter coat. She was glad Henry had a break from clearing the driveway; even with the snowblower Marsha had bought him, Berta worried about his heart. Marsha said how nice it was to drive, you really could see the country that way. They played the radio, and Berta liked it when Marsha sang along. Going through Kentucky and Tennessee they started hearing more country music, and pretty soon Marsha knew all the words to songs by Patsy Cline and Dolly Parton and the Judds.

After three days they got to Orlando, and Henry had to admit that the car rode really well. Just think, he would blurt out, turning on the air conditioning in January! Back home, old Werner Schmidt across the street would be plugging in his BMW at night just to make sure it started in the mornings. The three of them sat in the sun by the pool every day, and Marsha thought it was just about the best vacation they'd ever had. Henry loved Disney World and the Epcot Center. Coming back to live at home after her college course in travel agency was the right decision: her parents needed her, relied on her now, it was her turn to take care of them. Before they left Florida they bought a big box of oranges and grapefruits, the kind you shipped home that wouldn't get confiscated at the border, and for two weeks in the middle of winter Henry had fresh-squeezed juice every morning, and every morning he smacked his lips and said he wouldn't ever eat oranges from California again. On Marsha's birthday Berta surprised her with a little silver orange, a charm she picked up secretly on one of their shopping jaunts to Sak's.

The cars cruise up the one-way street, and when she joins the flow of traffic she wonders if they think she is cruising too. It's not a part of town she knows well at night; she didn't even hang out much down here during high school.

And now her mother works here. Marsha pulls slowly past the laundromat/coffee-shop, where a dry cleaner used to be: "Wash 'n Nosh." Bright, the sign lights up the sidewalk out front where several kids are hanging around. Next door an arcade, dark and noisy from the music and video games, pulses out neon onto the sidewalk. All the dollar coins, the millions of "loonies" in these two buildings at once, there must be hundreds of dollars worth between them. At the airport, most people use credit cards.

Marsha looks inside, driving as slowly as she can, which is pretty slow since all the other cars are inching forward too, their passengers straining to get a view of who's out tonight. The laundromat splits in two: along the left-hand side is a counter top, with donuts under glass and bar stools set up; across the aisle washing machines and dryers go all the way to the back. Berta works in the laundry side, giving out change and doing the drop-off loads, thirty-five cents a pound. Marsha had never heard of such a thing before Berta started working here. How much does a towel weigh, or a pair of jeans, she asked Berta. Oh, honey, I guess maybe a pound, maybe not quite. It's a good deal, would cost you a dollar a load to wash them yourself, and fifty cents at least to get them all the way dry.

Marsha turns around the corner, circles the block to pass by again, unable to decide whether or not to go in. She has only done this twice before. The first time was that night, after Berta called to say where she was.

The phone had rung in the dark kitchen. She was lying on her parents' bed, only semi-conscious, her face buried in her mother's pillow. The ringing roused her from stupor: at first she thought it was morning. The light glowing 7:31 from the clock wasn't the same as her own downstairs. It must be Berta, calling as soon as Henry's television show was over. Henry didn't pick up the receiver. He never did, so if Marsha ever called home from work and Berta didn't answer, that meant that Henry was likely sitting in the house somewhere, tuning out the sound. Once she had let it ring and ring, insisting that her call be recognized, it must have been thirty times. But her own multiple lines were lighting up, flashing a few times, then going dead again, and at last she could neglect her work no longer. The rings, ringing, her mother waiting for her to pick it up, calling from who knew where—Marsha couldn't see her at the other end, having no location in which to place her.

She had run down the hallway then, grabbing the receiver in the kitchen. Henry, blank in front of the TV, didn't turn.

"Mother," Marsha called into the phone. "Mother, is that you?"

Berta spoke calmly, as if calling from a great distance on a windless day. She instructed Marsha to pick up the pink pen hanging by the phone, so she could give her the new number. I have an apartment, she said, and in a few days, when I've got myself collected, I would like you to come and see it. Here is the address, write it down so when you hang up you'll know where I am. Marsha, nodding, did what she was told. And I've got a job, Berta added just when Marsha thought she was going to hang up, so you won't have to worry about that, you can spend your money on yourself for once. But there's plenty of time to talk about things. I just wanted to let you know everything's all right.

Berta had hung up the phone without asking after Henry, without even asking Marsha how she was, giving her no chance to say everything most certainly was not all right, not in its place. Not as if Berta didn't care, exactly; more like she was distracted, had other things on her mind.

Then her father had at last spoken. "She's downtown, she got a job, working at that laundry place by the old Dairy Queen. Near the bus terminal." He had turned to Marsha then, looked her full in the face for all the world with the eyes of a sore dog. Marsha wondered if he'd eaten.

Without a coat, she had gotten back in her car that night and driven down to the place, a storefront she'd barely even noticed before, at the end of downtown proper. The good stores—Friedman's and Virene's department stores, Savoy's Jewelry, the fancy Italian restaurant—run out about here and only a few places—a used-paperback store, a coffee shop open 24 hours—trickle on until the bus station, which marks clearly the end of the city's center and the beginning of the West End. The hulk of the steel plant hangs on by the edge of the river, its trademark flame rising over the neighborhood. The houses down here have always seemed grungier and the bars too terrible to know about. She thinks that Bob lives down here, in a neighborhood where people paint their front porches pink and green, and plant gardens in the small square front yards with uncontrollable daisies and geraniums. This is the immigrants' section of the city, where they settled after arriving in the new country to populate the plant. There are even a few corner stores with chairs set up outside, men drinking coffee and speaking Italian. Henry at least had the good sense to buy a house on top of the hill. Berta's workplace was right on the border between a respectable section of town where ladies shopped and the disintegration of the city into the water. Marsha shuddered, pulled up in front, and marched in.

The smells immediately had reminded her of the airport snack bar: coffee and ammonia. A small color television perched on the corner of the donut counter, the sounds of a game show mingling with the whirring of the machines and people's chatter. Another older woman, about her mother's age, stood behind the cash register rearranging carrot muffins. She wished her mother at least worked in that part.

But Marsha saw Berta towards the back on the right-hand side. She was folding someone's towels, big red and white ones, not like the kind they had at home. When Berta saw her, she smiled as if she were expecting this. It was also a public smile, the smile she must offer to the strangers bringing washing.

"Your father told you where I was," she said. Marsha could feel the warmth of the laundry rising up.

"I want you to come home," Marsha said. Her mother's smile did not change. And aware of the petulance in her voice, the unforgiving and unrelenting accusation, she turned as suddenly and walked back out, afraid of knocking muffins off the counters with her hips. She was out of line, and out of place, asking for something she couldn't name, but without which she was afraid she would cease to exist.

"Mother refuses to budge," she told Henry. "And I don't want to hear her name again." Henry, not challenging her, shuffled directionless about the house.

"There's a mystery movie on TV tonight," she had called out to his back.

"Won't you come downstairs and watch it on the big set?" She resisted adding "please." And he had turned and followed her down the steps, careful not to spill his beer.

And so the two of them forged a new routine, rising early for work, eating porridge or corn flakes. Henry would head off in his work clothes as always, a meal packed by Marsha in his aluminum lunch box. After a week or so he took to making the coffee himself, so it was ready when she came upstairs, and he made enough to fill his thermos. Marsha could not remember her father ever making coffee before, or standing at the stove except to make wieners and beans on Berta's bridge night. He learned that she drank hers black, and she noticed he cut down from three spoonfuls of sugar to just one.

"Your mother drank milk in hers," he said one morning, a month or so after Berta's leaving. "But I like this half and half cream." And Henry served her up poached eggs on toast, a little runny the way she liked them.

It was that evening that Marsha had visited Berta for the second time. Even before leaving for work she must have been devising the plan, throwing a pile of Henry's dirty socks and work clothes, and an egg-stained T-shirt, into the trunk. When she got to the laundromat, she bunched up the clothes in her arms. Pushing open the door was easy: it was made to be entered by people with their hands full. She dropped the load on the counter in front of Berta.

"Here you go," she said. "I'll pay you to wash these."

Berta took the pile and began sorting through it, separating out the woolen socks from the cotton pants and shirts. The odor of Henry passed between them.

"I wish you would come over to my apartment some time," Berta said, dropping the laundry into a plastic basket. She weighed it. "A dollar seventy-five," she said. "Henry would like that—it must cost more just to heat up the water at home."

"But there you could reuse it with the water-saver," Marsha said. The washing machine was one of the first things she had bought for the home when she started working. "If you come back, we'll pay you, Henry and I. Forty cents a pound?" She tried to crack her mouth into a smile, turn the sarcasm into a joke. She didn't really believe that domestic discontent explained her mother's departure, but she wanted to compel her to return. Berta shook her head.

"No, dear, this is between Henry and me. It's not about you at all. You're thirty-two years old, you have a right to your own life. Sometimes I'm just sorry that we let you, well, use so much up on us." Berta smiled at her daughter, as if asking forgiveness. "Henry and me—well, we let it go, we just let it run out. That's all. It's better this way. You know, I think he might even be happier—he tells me he goes out sometimes, he's meeting new people."

Marsha cringed, the thought of Henry picking up a strange woman at her house, putting her coat around her shoulders for her, the two of them having a drink someplace—it made her dizzy. She imagined this is how it would be if Bob came to take her out; suddenly even putting on a jacket would become unbearable. She knew it had been a long time since looks had passed between her parents in the mornings, a glance that shut her out, speaking of parts of their lives separated off from hers, making her nervous. She hadn't really missed those exchanges; in fact, she enjoyed breakfast with the two of them more when they held themselves apart from one another. She wondered if Bob's airplane had seat belts.

"Maybe I'll come over sometime. We're doing okay, in case you're interested." Marsha couldn't help sounding angry. She wished she could keep her voice as calm as her mother's.

Henry had picked up his own clean laundry the next day, and since then has washed all his own clothes, twice a week, on Sundays and Wednesdays. He had even gone so far as to say that she should do hers separately, that Berta told him his clothes were too dirty to mix in with finer washables. Marsha tried not to laugh when she heard her father use this phrase he must have borrowed from a Woolite commercial, and it came out like a smirk on her face. Henry read it as a smile, and opened his own mouth back in response.

A honking car prods Marsha around the block again. Circling and circling, until she feels the car is bound to be tied up in a knot, she wants to break out, to spin out fast and speed along a straight stretch right into the middle of the West End. She could control the flight path, swerving to avoid unapproved craft zoning in, meeting head-on the one-way traffic. The car feels anxious to test its power. She turns into the parking lot behind the laundromat.

The alleyway is dark, and a large dog sniffs her as she scurries back out toward the lighted street. Inside, it is warm and Berta is there, folding sheets into four straight corners, folding herself in with each tug and shake. "Hello there," she says to Marsha. Berta's hair is longer, and it curls from the dampness.

"There's mildew in the shower," Marsha says. "I used the Tilex in the front cupboard. I think that I got it all." She cannot imagine washing other people's dirty clothes, even for money. She imagines Bob Gianelli's bush shirts, sweaty and rough, in a pile on a floor. Maybe he even drops off his laundry here, on his way out to the airport. In the machines underwear spins in the rinse cycle, faded jeans beat against the dryer windows.

"It smells like snow today," Berta says. She talks while she works, and smiles when a man in a camel-colored overcoat approaches her, calls her by name. He is taller than Henry, but not as big as Bob.

"Got your things right here, Mr. Bell," Berta says, picking up a basket from behind her. "I didn't bleach those good white shirts—it'd turn them yellow." The man smiles, says he'll see her next week. His hair is gray, neatly trimmed.

"You have a nice evening," Berta adds as he leaves, and he bobs his head at her. Marsha wonders if perhaps her mother means something to this stranger, returning regularly with soiled clothes, allowing Berta to clean them with intimacy.

"I just wanted to tell you," Marsha says, "that *The Sound of Music* is on tonight."

Berta nods. "I saw that in the *TV Guide*. I'm off in fifteen minutes. Would you like to come to my place and watch it?" She pours fabric softener in a washer whose rinse cycle light shines on.

"You have a TV?" Marsha asks, surprised. She thinks of the VCR she had picked out for this Christmas, with up to three weeks' advance programming and freeze-frame precision fast-forwarding.

"Oh, I'm all set up. You should see the place. It's not much, just an apartment over a shoe store. It's only about a mile from here, and I take the bus when it rains or snows. I can see the river from my bathroom window, and I've bought some area rugs, and a nice secondhand rocking chair. I painted it red. The cable is included in my rent. I have a radio too." Berta's skin is smooth and shiny under the fluorescent lighting. "I feel like my heart isn't so tacked down, Marsha," she says softly. Then: "Will you come?"

"A man has asked me out," Marsha replies. "Bob. He's tall, and has an airplane of his own. He takes people up into the bush, Americans who go fishing and hunting." As one fear recedes, another moves in to take its place. When she was little, whenever it ached liked this Berta would rub butter on her belly, letting the cat lick it off her to tickle her. Is it the thought of Bob's large dark forearms, the hair tufting out of his open shirt collar, that shrinks her stomach up inside?

Berta glances down at Marsha's wrist, and nods. "There are a couple of things left at the house that I'd like. I already spoke to Henry, and he said it was all right with him if it was all right with you." She folds creases into a couple of pairs of denim jeans. "The water tastes different at my apartment," she says. "Maybe living so close to the river. I'm not sure. But I'm growing used to it." The lights flick off, then on again, signaling the approach of closing time. Berta wipes soap powder off of the counter.

Marsha wonders about bringing Bob here to meet her mother. She has barely formulated even to herself a story to put forward to this stranger, the story of her life, which keeps shifting. She thinks about her mother's heart, about what Berta meant. And wonders if she could learn how to dance, shuffling her feet in an unfettered soft shoe of her own.

Berta steps out from behind her counter, coat in hand. Marsha knows there is no need to say she'll come, that that much at least is understood. Her mother hums as they walk out the door, "I am sixteen, going on seventeen." Berta turns toward the parking lot; she must have seen Marsha driving, crazy, by the store. "Your father never could understand why we liked this movie," she says.

Marsha nods. It's better that they see it without him.

Wau-Ban-See

by Ashley L. Gibson

The Comanches named this place Wau-Ban-See. Mirrored waters. In the flat under the limestone ridge that cuts across the ranch, pecan trees grow thick and hang low over the shallow San Saba. Evenings, the water comes alive, the green-black leaves reflected on its surface blowing in a wind the trees above do not feel. The Texas Rangers built this place. Each rock of each building pulled out of the hard earth with the end of a pickax and calloused hands. More than twelve miles of five-foot-high dry-stacked rock fences wind around this land, sectioning it off, claiming it. This place and its stories came to me whole and I have changed nothing, named no streams, invented no characters, added no buildings that will bear out my presence after I am gone.

Today is the first day of summer, marked in large block letters under the Thursday column on the Hargrove Feed and Seed calendar that hangs next to the kitchen sink. I am alone. The picture above the calendar grid is a grainy watercolor of three bare-chested boys standing on a boulder some ten feet above the Llano River. They all look out over the water. Two of their faces are in profile and a bit out of focus, but the expression on the third boy's face, eyes wide and unfocused, mouth slightly open, speaks for all of them. They are not thinking about what's under the dark summer water but about the few seconds' plunge through the air. There will be no boys playing in my creek, jumping in my pool, today. The visits by family hunters and holiday guests have stopped. No one wants to brave the heat of the unairconditioned Ranger's house or the bone-aching cold of the spring-fed pool, its waters spilling over the dam and running down into the San Saba. They have houses where they can wear sweatshirts at noon and curl up under down comforters at night. They have temperature-controlled pools in their own backyards with water so clear they can count the grains of sand that stray to the level bottom. They leave me with the place to myself. Five hundred acres, twenty head of cattle not including calves, seven peacocks, countless barn cats, no human contact for a mile and a half.

I have gotten used to drinking my coffee standing up in the early morning light, the kitchen floor boards creaking underneath me. I don't feel so alone that way, almost like I expect someone to come in at any minute or like I am about to rush out to go somewhere. But I don't. I don't drive the two hours to Austin anymore, don't visit friends or have a nice meal or buy a new skirt. I am tired of what they have to say about me, about my husband, about his accident. I am tired of repeating my own story. I want to throw my wine glass or my hymnal at them and scream in the bar or the church foyer that of course nobody expects to die that way. Nobody expects the dive platform they're standing on to collapse; nobody expects to lose their grip on the rope swing handle; nobody expects to fall forward as a result of all that and snap their neck on the black slate ledge of the pool. A man expects to die of old age, in bed, asleep, with his hand wrapped around his wife's waist, his nose in her hair. He does not expect to widow her ten days before her thirtieth birthday.

I wanted to bury my husband on the ridge next to the Methodist circuit rider who has no name above his head, only a rough cedar cross with 1934 carved on it. No one knows where he came from, but he worked the Hill Country preaching for food, a place to stay. He went through Art and Mason, Menard and Junction, worked his way back by Eden and Brady, died on this ranch from a bee sting. My husband, Wil Giddry, always felt close to the stranger buried on his land, felt they did the same work in some small way. Fresh out of med school, Wil passed up an offer from a major Dallas hospital and accepted a residency at the thirty-bed county hospital in Mason. I quit my job as a staff photographer with the *Dallas Times Herald*. He wanted to be a rancher. I wanted to be a mother. I would like to say herds of cattle roam our fields. I would like to say Wil left me with a life down deep inside that grew to kick my womb with long, narrow feet that now look like his, but wildflowers spring up uneaten and untrampled in most of the fields and the rooms of the Ranger's house stand empty. As a result of laws and red tape, Wil lies in the small cemetery outside the ranch gate, thirty minutes walking distance from the traveling minister, twelve feet from the bounds of the property the Giddrys have called theirs for three generations. I visit neither man, let nature take their graves.

The grids on the calendar after the one marked FIRST DAY OF SUMMER are blank. Maybe I should fill them with measures of rainfall or hours of sun like the old-timers do. Maybe I should fill them with what I do: repaired gap to south field, picked bushel peaches, drove to Brady—new brakes on truck, lost two peacock chicks to fox.

The phone rings and I ignore it until I realize it is ringing for me. One long ring followed by a short one. We are still on a party line.

"¡Diga!" I answer. I like to see how people react when I answer in foreign languages. They usually do well with the French *Alo?* and speak a few decibels louder, but the Spanish command makes most people sound confused.

"La Señora Giddry está allí?" an older-sounding woman asks, her Spanish slow and accented with a thick drawl.

"This is she."

"Oh . . . well . . . this is Harriet Mauch." She pauses and when I don't respond she adds, "With the Austin Historical Guild?"

"Yes?"

"I was just calling to confirm our visit this coming Wednesday. You know we so enjoyed coming out to Wau-Ban-See five years ago. Your husband told such wonderful stories about the place and that quail salad you served was just lovely. The ladies still talk about it, you know, and are looking forward to doing it again."

I start pacing the kitchen, walking as far as the phone cord lets me. I'd completely forgotten. They'd written over Thanksgiving and my sister, Virginia, read the letter lying unanswered on the kitchen table and encouraged me to accept. She said if I insisted on staying out here I should at least have people over besides family.

"I'm sorry, Mrs. Mauch, you caught me a bit off guard. Of course I'm looking forward to seeing you and the ladies on Wednesday. You say you'll be in around eleven?" I have no idea when they were coming, but it seems a pretty good guess.

"Oh, no, dear. We'd thought more around nine-thirty so we'll have plenty of time for the tour and then have an early picnic down by that wonderful pool. Then we're off to Fredricksburg and do some antiquing while we're out that way."

"That sounds fine. I'll be expecting you."

That's the end of the conversation as far as I'm concerned, but she chimes in as the phone is halfway to its base, "Oh, your husband won't be able to join us then?"

It is silly of me to expect she knows. How could she? I can probably take the easy route, tell her he was busy at the hospital, but I know I'll let something slip when they get here. "My husband passed away two summers ago, Mrs. Mauch."

She doesn't pause in shock, doesn't miss a beat. "Oh, dear, I'm so sorry. Would it be better if we didn't come? I know how hard it must be on you still. Probably Fredricksburg will be enough to wear us all out anyway."

"No, no. I'd like to have you. I'm sure Mr. Giddry would like knowing someone else was enjoying his place." My answer almost makes me laugh. I am not used to talking about Wil like he is a benign ghost who watches over this place and over me. He loved this land, but he hated its history, its ghosts, felt all the stories I learned from his grandfather were products of an old man's mind. What Wil told the ladies on that visit were not stories of this ranch, but factual accounts of the region, population sizes, county boundaries, crops planted. He saw too many people die to think of Wau-Ban-See's ghosts as anything but insignificant tales better outgrown with childhood and forgotten. His death is the only one I've witnessed, and all the spectacular ones that came before help to justify it.

"Well, if you're sure."

"I'm sure. I'll see you Wednesday morning," I tell her, wanting to get off the phone and start the day. "Goodbye, Mrs. Mauch."

I like to be outside by eight-thirty. That's late compared to the schedules other inhabiters of this house have kept, but it gets me out of bed every morning. I do not take the time to write the ladies' visit on the calendar.

Outside, the temperature has already started climbing. I like this place in the summer the best. I like the heat, like to feel my skin warm and sweat at noon. I like the high hum of cicadas. I like to sit on the porch and watch the darkening hills swallow the bright ball of the sun as the cows settle in around the salt lick and small stock tank if I've moved them to the front pasture. The salt lick sits in a galvanized tub outside the fence to the main house compound and slightly behind five perfectly symmetrical cones of deep red and brown rock with loops of thick metal chain between them. The Rangers used to tie their horses there, sometimes as many as twenty, when they came in for a meeting or a meal or one of the barn dances they had on Fourth of Julys. This was never a major post and I doubt the chains ever saw much use, but they hang just as they did when the Rangers left over one hundred years ago and my nieces and nephews like to sit on them and try to swing themselves while their parents shake hands and hug between heavy foreign cars parked in the packed dirt road and try to convince me I'd be much happier back in Dallas, if they are from Wil's family, or in Austin, if they are from mine. They tell me that it's not good to be surrounded by so many bad memories, tell me that a woman as young as I am shouldn't be stuck out by herself, tell me that they have a banker friend or a lawyer friend who just bought a place not nearly as nice as this for half a million, tell me they'll be happy to put me in touch with someone who can move it quick.

I do not tell them I know nothing of hard work or bad memories. I do not tell them of the young Comanche boy who stopped around the bend up from the house to cool himself in the dark creek waters he thought would hide him and was shot twice in the chest while he floated with his eyes closed and was left to drift downstream until his body caught on a mass of tree roots where the bank had cut away in the last flood. I do not tell them of young Joe Donnely, come to join the Rangers and fight Indians and sent to gather rocks and raise fences, who died of heat exhaustion digging the holes that hold the gateposts I drive through on my way to the hay fields. I do not tell them because, like Wil, they have heard those stories before and have chosen not to remember them. Chosen not to remember them because they can't be proven, documented, because they're merely tales passed on by old men who have nothing better to do or to remember.

I spend this morning like most others, tending other women's flowers, weeding and working their sprawling, terraced beds and lawns. I separate the bearded irises Lizzie Turner, the last commander's wife for whom the six room rock house was built in 1860, brought with her from England when she came over as a girl of fifteen. I prune and mulch the twelve antique rose bushes Grandma Alba Giddry, the first and last of the Giddrys to actually spend the majority of her life on this land before dying on it, brought from her family's farm in Maryland.

A narrow slate-lined stream runs across the front of the house and down the two terraces where it fills an irregularly shaped concrete and rock pool built late in life by Old Man Appleton who bought the place from the U.S. Government after the Rangers moved westward. The water filling the channel is knee-deep and full of water lilies ordered from a fancy East Coast catalogue by Fannie Appleton, the old man's fourth wife who was a "frivolous girl" according to Grandma Alba's brief written history of the ranch. The water filling the pool stands ten feet deep and is full of thick, billowing clouds of algae. I have not drained or cleaned the pool since Wil and I did it two years ago. It wasn't so bad last year and I didn't think much about it, but with the warm winter and spring, the algae has more than doubled.

All the water originates crystal clear from a spring enclosed in a small rock building to the north of the front porch. In the summer the water feels cold and in the winter it feels warm, but it is a constant sixty-four degrees. San Augustine grass, undoubtedly planted by another ranch wife, spreads out from the channel and the pool and has crept through the compound's rock wall to the fields. After working in the beds, I trim the grass inside the walls with a red push mower so that it is thick and low. Canna lilies, planted by Wil's mother in the sixties when they used this place for entertaining, grow in clumps around the pool. I have let them multiply and am careful not to get the mower blades too close to the new broad leaves. This year, for the first time, their tall yellow and red heads peek up through the holes in the collapsed platform under the pecan tree where the rope swing still hangs.

After I finish mowing, I kick off my stained tennis shoes, peel off my clothes, and jump in the pool. I don't mind this water and its darkness. Underneath the algae and the layers of rich silt on the bottom I know there is only dirt-stained concrete and smooth-washed rocks. I swim with slow, sloppy strokes up and down the pool which measures three feet shy of Olympic length from the dam to the slate stream. I swim until my body adjusts to the cold. I float on my back with my eyes closed, letting the reflections of pecan and live oak leaves slide over my wet skin, letting the water drift over my body until I have the desire to curl myself into a ball, drop to the bottom, and sleep forever, then I get out. I put only my T-shirt back on, slip my feet into my shoes bending down the heels, gather up my grass stained socks, plain cotton underwear, and khaki shorts, and pull the mower behind me up to the barn where I store it in one of the horse stalls with other lawn tools, rakes, hoes, three hand-fashioned pickax heads from the Ranger days.

I deposit my clothes in a white five-gallon bucket in the breezeway connecting the mainhouse to the bunkhouse and peel off my T-shirt. The bucket is overflowing since it's the end of the week, and the T-shirt threatens to topple the whole mess over until I rearrange it.

I am turning into a vegetarian, not necessarily out of choice or out of lack of meat. I have two deer, one shot by Wil's oldest brother, one by mine, cleaned and packaged in neat white bundles, lying in the deep freeze out in the old tack room. I have ziplock bags of dove and quail shot by me. The freezer also contains pounds of deer sausage, hamburger meat, a side of beef ribs, and one snow goose, an annual gift from a south Texas banker Wil operated on for appendicitis. I like all of these things, have cooked them fried or broiled or barbecued, but I see no sense in thawing and marinating and cooking any of them just for me. I have squash and okra and pole beans aplenty in the garden behind the bunkhouse and I have had decent luck keeping the pillbugs and leafy mildew off my lettuce. Unlike preparing meat, preparing vegetables requires no thinking. You eat them raw with a sprinkle of lemon for dressing or boiled, and that's that.

In the kitchen, I put a pan of water on to boil and skin and cut two 10–15 onions into chunks. I slice three strips off a piece of salt pork, and only when the water is boiling do I remove a bag of snapped green beans from the freezer and add them to the pot with the onion and bacon. They are last season's, but were frozen right after picking and snapping, so will taste vine-fresh as long as they don't have a chance to thaw out. While they cook, I go to my room at the back of the house and put on jeans, thick socks, a white button-down worn so thin and smooth I can feel through the fabric the warm midday air stirred by the ceiling fan.

I eat the beans with a glass of chilled water from the fridge and leave the dishes in the sink for later. I am trying to break the habit of washing after every meal so that I will not be continually using the same plate, bowl, spoon, fork that sit in the dishdrainer.

I put on a pair of hiking boots that sit outside the kitchen door and walk to the barn where I retrieve a camouflaged swivel bucket out of another empty horse stall and Wil's .30-06 from the gun locker. I have replaced the bucket's short handle with a piece of long, soft nylon rope, and have lined the inside with thick black foam so its contents make no noise. It holds no turkey calls, no boxes of bird shot, no cleaning knives, but one Nikon 35 mm camera, a telephoto lens, half a box of 165-grain Federal bullets, a heavy pair of ear protectors like old stereo headphones, and one brown oat bag from Hargroves.

I walk out the compound's back gate and down the narrow dirt road washboarded from erosion and disuse. I pass two creek beds that run only with the spring rains. I pass the granite outcropping where Wil shot a five-foot rattler and the crumbling chimney of the first Ranger outpost whose plank walls cut from the Lost Pines near Bastrop burned to the ground within six months of being put up. I climb through the barbed wire links of the gap gate leading to the Klein grass field.

Midway down the field and back towards the ridge, I set the bucket down on a flat, gray rock near a stand of Spanish oaks and remove the feed bag, which I attach with clothespins to a cedar bush fifty yards away near the edge of a small half-dry stock tank. I have used the bush before. There are several mangled limbs jutting out from it and small pieces of other bags scattered among the twigs and limestone shards and thin grama grass. But this is not what I'm here for. I like to sit out in the fields, the gun across my knees, camera in my hands, and wait for something. Sometimes it is the way the sun hits the Mexican hats and black-eyed Susans. Sometimes it is a wall of blue-black clouds rolling in over the ridge. Sometimes it is a heron flying low from the San Saba and lighting in the tank. And sometimes, like today, I am not in the mood to wait and I take practice shots at the bag.

I wear the ear protectors and even with them the first two shots are loud and echo through me. A large red and white Purina checkerboard marks the center of the bag and I usually try to take it out a few squares at a time if I'm using a gun like this one or a .22 that makes a small entry hole. Unlike a .22 bullet, though, these explode on contact leaving an exit hole the size of a roadside diner saucer. Looking through the telephoto lens, I can see the splintered cedar branches through dime-sized holes in the bag. The shots hit four squares to the right of where the scope's cross-hairs were and a little high. I adjust the scope with a small screwdriver, turning the knob on the side four clicks to the left, and take two more shots which are still high, but more or less on target.

When I'm not in the mood to sit still, I also resort to taking photos of the shot-up bag to finish off a roll. I have at last fifty or sixty good bag shots and Virginia wants me to sell them at the Armadillo Bazaar in Austin this fall. She says people will buy them for thirty or forty dollars if I mount them, but they're still sitting untouched, scattered over the long oak table in the attic. Bags against cedars, live oaks, Spanish oaks. Bags against prickly pears, spiky yuccas, soft caliche rises. Bags all stages of shot-up. In the photos, it doesn't matter if the scope or my aim is off, nobody knows the difference.

When we moved here a little over five years ago, Wil helped me turn the attic of the bunkhouse into a darkroom so I could do freelance work. The high, peaked, tin-roofed attic is an addition from recent history. Before, it was no bigger than a crawl space and was the domain of the women. The ceiling had two trap doors in it and when the Indians caught the roof on fire, the women poured buckets of water out the trap doors to put out the flames. In 1856, Susannah Whidbee, fresh-arrived from South Carolina, took two arrows in the chest but would not come out of the opening, just demanded more buckets until the fire was out. She died on the solid attic floor that still shows the deep burn marks.

I shoot the last two bullets in the clip, reload, and set the gun over my knees again, taking off the ear protectors. The world always seems incredibly quiet right after I shoot, but today I hear the cattle in the field next to this one and the soft rumble of cars on the Ranch Road on the other side of the cattle. I take several photos of the bag and of the shadows the thick, isolated clouds leave on the tank's surface. I add a few more holes to the bag and in the silence that follows, I hear a noise in the brush behind me and turn on the bucket's seat. A man in a summer straw hat, a short-sleeved khaki shirt, jeans, and boots walks my way down the trail. I look through the telephoto lens at him, not so much to take his picture, but to read what the dark official-looking patch on his breast pocket says, to see who he is, what he's made of.

"May I help you?" I call out for lack of anything better to say.

He stops and the way the shadow from his hat falls halfway across his face, I can't tell what he's looking at. "Hope so," he answers. "I'm Cotton Ledbetter, the game warden."

I can't think of what a game warden would be doing out here in the middle of the summer, then realize he's staring at the camouflaged bucket and the gun in my lap. I eject the clip and set it down beside me.

"I promise not to shoot, Mr. Ledbetter," I joke as he comes closer, "but would you mind telling me how you got in here?"

He smiles slightly from a few feet away and I can see his face is as deeply tanned as mine, despite the protection of the hat, and shows the same fine lines around his mouth and eyes as mine does, lines from approaching age, from too many days in the sun.

"You mind telling me what you're shooting at?"

I point behind me to the bag.

"Mighty big gun for target practice." There's no accusation in his voice, but his eyes dart from me to the cedar bush to the field around the pond looking for game.

"I'm adjusting the scope."

"Isn't it a little early to be gearing up for deer season?"

I toss him the screwdriver, then the clip, and he looks startled as I stand up and pitch him the gun. "It's shooting high and to the right."

I toss him an emergency pair of ear plugs out of the bucket, the soft kind that don't do much good with larger guns but are better than nothing, and put on my own. He takes two shots, aiming at the center of the bag, adjusts the top knob, takes two more, adjusts, and finishes the clip, handing the gun back to me.

I put the box of shells back in the bucket and case up the camera and lens.

"Aren't you going to check it?" he asks.

"No. You're the game warden."

"Look," he calls after me as I get the bag, with its four new holes almost perfectly centered, off the cedar bush, "I don't mean to intrude on whatever you're doing here, it's just that I heard those shots from the road, and I can't quite ignore something so loud, now can I?"

"I guess not." My voice hasn't quite thawed. I bunch up the bag around the camera to keep it secure and start for the house. "You still haven't answered my question. How'd you get in?"

"Walked."

"From where? The road?"

"The main gate. Would you like me to carry that?" He points to the bucket and the rifle.

"No. I'm balanced this way. How'd you get in the gate?"

"I have every legal right to be here . . . "

I cut him off. "I'm aware of that."

We walk for a bit in heat, our bootsteps crackling on the rocks.

"I climbed over the gate," he tells me as we get in sight of the house. "We have codes and combinations for most of the places around here, but yours isn't on file anywhere."

"That's because there hasn't been a game warden on this property," I tell him in a repetition of something I've told a thousand times before, "since 1973 when two convicts escaped from the McCulloch County Jail and the wardens helped in the search. They found the men half-dead from dehydration in Tom Green County three days later."

He opens the gate and follows me into the barn where he puts the gun in the locker while I take the camera and lens out of the bucket.

"Man down the road told me this is the Appleton place. Guess you must be one of them," he tells me in the side yard where the slate stream makes a two-foot fall to the first terrace. "Sure is a pretty place."

I nod my thanks, then add, "No Appleton's lived here since 1907."

"Well, Ms. I'm-no-Appleton, I'm all out of small talk then."

I look at him to see if he's joking, but there is no smile in the lines around his eyes. "I'm Kitt Giddry."

He offers his hand and I shake it, matching the strength of my grip to his.

I offer him a glass of tea, and while it's brewing we sit on the porch and watch the early evening set in. He tells me he's thirty-four, never been married, recently returned from ten years as a forest ranger and fire fighter in Wyoming.

He tells me he got the name Cotton when he was a kid and it stuck, even when his hair turned from a shocking white to a darker blond in the eighth grade. I don't laugh when he tells me his real name is Sidney, and he doesn't ask for any details when I tell him I'm a widow. I serve the glasses of tea with mint sprigs courtesy of Fannie Appleton's predecessor, Molly. Apparently, Old Man Appleton had a propensity for frivolous women. I offer to drive Cotton to the gate but he says he can make it just fine. I give him the gate code, but ask he not enter it in whatever files they keep.

"Just remember 1934 backwards," I tell him.

"What happened then?" he asks, stepping down off the porch.

"Not much."

Swimming over the top of the algae is one thing, diving through ten feet of it to unscrew the drain plugs is another. Not a way I like to spend my Saturday mornings, which are usually reserved for an extra pot of coffee and several loads of laundry. I can only drain the pool six inches, a foot at the most, before diving down to plug it again. The algae has to be soft and wet for the water shooting out the high pressure sprayer nozzle to do any good.

I fall into a rhythm of shoot and drain, shoot and drain, and when the green plastic watch on my wrist reads noon, I have four feet done and the water is down to ankle deep at the shallow end closest to the house. I don't stop for lunch. By one o'clock I have cramps in my hands from holding the nozzle trigger down and tie it with my shoelace. By two, the six-inch drains clog with old tree branches, oak leaves, pecans. I stand in the mud on the other side of the dam and jam a broom handle repeatedly into the holes until they clear, only to have them clog again before three when the pool holds only knee-deep water black with sludge and silt. I have given up on the power sprayer and have moved from picking branches out of the sludge and throwing them over the dam to throwing entire cement shovels of sludge over when Cotton Ledbetter calls a hello from the other side of the rock fence.

I can barely see his head in the battered straw hat from my poor vantage point down in the muck, and I'm sure he might be having a hard time seeing me through the speckled layers of mud that cover my bathing suit, my skin, my high-topped tennis shoes. I stop my rhythm of scoop, lift, toss long enough to ask him why he's come in from the direction of the field and not the main house. I know if I stop for long, my muscles will freeze and the next inhabitants of the ranch will find my bones preserved in the rich mud when they decide to clear the green waters for themselves, so I keep working while he yells down an answer.

"Von Dohlen's had one of their Angus go down, thought I'd take a look at yours." He climbs over the fence, careful not to pull on the top rocks, but to press his hands flat on them and push himself up and over. "Don't know why they called me, not a vet. Cow wasn't shot."

"Piss poor excuse," I tell him between shovels. "Vet's out of town. Cow died of old age, snake bite, something like that. You were over for lunch anyway being as you and Jay Von Dohlen go back to grade school. Right?"

"Close enough." He laughs. "Did walk though. Your hay's looking good, getting enough rain."

"Glad you think so."

"Can I help?"

"Should be done with this soon and then I can start spraying what's left right out the drains."

"You sure?"

"Sure." I toss the shovel up on the grass and pull down the faded green garden hose, minus the pressure nozzle.

"Can I at least offer to take you for some dinner when you're through?" he asks, sitting on the slate ledge, jeans and boots dangling down against the clean, white poolside. "Nothing fancy. Cheeseburger at the world's worst Dairy Queen?"

"I'm afraid I won't even be fit company for that once I'm done with this."

"Are you fit company now?"

"Try me."

He asks short, safe, neutral questions about the pool, the fences, the Appletons. I give him the long answers. I don't start with the Comanches. I do not really know them, only what they did to people here. I start with the bunkhouse, the first real building here, with its rows of two-foot-high by four-inch-wide slits not designed for light but for the easy aim of a gun and the protection from most ammunition. There are bullet marks on the outside walls. Inside, there is blood on the floorboards, some of it belonging to Lizzie Turner's oldest, Miles, who took two bullets in the head. Over the door, a historical marker proves this is true. I end with Grandma Alba dying in her sleep in 1961 and Wil's mother, June, planting the canna lilies and covering the hardwood floors with green shag carpet.

I tell him the stories that are as familiar to me as if they are my own. They are the only history I know, the only history I can repeat with the authority of an adult telling a bedtime story a child's heard a hundred times and knows by heart but still asks for. The sky turns a faded yellow-green as I talk, and the spring water in the little channel that runs through the bottom of the pool turns clear.

"Why end it there?" Cotton asks when I finish talking and sit down finally in the middle of the small stream of water.

"Because. I can begin and end it anywhere I want." I don't plug the drains, but will let the sides bake in the sun tomorrow to kill off any algae I missed. As I rinse and scrub the mud from my face, arms, legs, Cotton rises to leave.

"What about *your* story, Kitt Giddry?"

"I don't have a story." I can tell by the way he squints down at me that he doesn't believe a word. I add in explanation, "At least not like theirs. I'm just a caretaker."

"What'd you do with the green carpet?"

I don't see what he's getting at, but answer him anyway. "I burned it. In the burn pit behind the barn."

"See."

"See what? I was just returning the house to what it used to be."

Cotton just shrugs and climbs easily back over the fence. "Can I ask you one thing?" he calls.

"Not if it's going to make me mad." I stand up so I can get a good look at him.

"Hope not. Were you planning to go to the Fourth of July fireworks next weekend?"

After the fireworks, they close down the square and have a street dance, the kind of dance where little girls waltz on their tiptoes standing on their father's shoes and old women sit in folding chairs on the courthouse lawn talking about the young folks.

"Isn't there a dance afterwards?" I tease him.

"Well . . . yes . . . but we don't have to stay if you don't feel like it."

"Are you asking me on a date?"

He laughs and gives me a half smile from under his hat. "Sounds like it, doesn't it."

"A real date where the man drives up and rings the doorbell, that kind of date?"

"Depends."

"On what?"

"You have a doorbell?"

"No."

"Then I don't guess it's a real date."

"Okay. But, but just because it's not doesn't mean you can show up from out of nowhere and make me walk. Right?"

The pool begins slowly filling on Monday, and I sit on the lawn under a new moon sky Tuesday night and watch the final foot creep in. I don't mind that I'm not in bed by eleven. The cooking for the ladies, the cleaning for the ladies, the arranging flowers and picnic baskets for the ladies, has knocked me off the schedule I've kept five days a week, forty weeks a year, March 'til November, two years running, and it's liberating in a way. I watch the water until way past midnight when I finally begin hearing the faint trickle fall over the dam.

The visit goes well the next day, and as I run through each story in my repertoire Mrs. Mauch exclaims, "Oh, how wonderful. I don't think we heard that one last time, did we?"

I think she actually does enjoy them, is not just being polite, and so do the others. After the second question about how long one could actually live after being shot in the neck with a bullet or in the chest with an arrow, I give up my attempts to tone down any violence and blood.

Sitting on an assortment of patchwork quilts by the pool, we have a proper ladies' picnic of potato salad, marinated and chilled green beans, grilled quail, and homemade biscuits. The ladies drift over in twos and threes to admire the pool, remarking on how perfectly they can see their own faces, almost better than in their mirrors at home. I don't join them. I know what my face will look like, and I know I will be able to see more than my own reflection there now that the algae and the silt's been cleaned away and everything's visible from the surface.

They ask to stop by the cemetery on their way out and Mrs. Mauch gives me a ride in the front seat of her blue Lincoln. I hold open the main gate for them and let six large cars pass through before I shut it and join the ladies who are already picking their way through the graves. I point out where the historical marker is back in a half-circle of live oaks and tell them the families are in no particular spot but mixed in with one another. They seem to know their way around, need no directions. Some walk gingerly around the graves respectful of boundaries, others walk right up to the headstones and bend down to read the inscriptions. I don't come here often and can't help noticing some of the inscriptions myself. Ezra Benjamin Turney, a cattleman, a good man. Faith Marie Appleton, a love constant and true. Trevor Mason Whidbee, the world took his mother and then it took him. And, by the ranch fence, surrounded by patchy grass and a single clump of Indian firewheels, and set at the head of a slightly darker colored mound where the hard earth has yet to settle and bleach out, the plain, gray slab. Wilburn Allen Giddry, a mender of people.

They are all here, Turneys and Whidbees, Appletons and Giddrys. The women tromp through them as they did five years before and nothing has changed. Five years from now the lines around my eyes will be deeper, the skin on my hands thicker, but the stories will be the same. Perhaps I will have children, a son or a daughter I will teach to prune roses back to make them grow fuller, to separate clumps of irises so their bulbs will divide, a son or a daughter I will teach to recognize the smooth flight of dove, to replace the rocks in the winding fences with the same precision they were built. When I am gone, a variation of these women will walk here and someone will tell them the story of Wil Giddry with the same note of romance and loss that my voice holds when I talk of Joe Donnely or Susannah Whidbee, when I repeat the names of this place over and over so that they wind around and reflect off each other. And me? What will the speaker say of me? They'll say, she told me these words, these words I tell you. She kept things going.

Crawford and Luster's Story

by Richard Giles

Down the dusty road, and down the river, down below the Bull Cafe. The sun is up and Luster rises. A long hair divides the dog's water dish into the yin-yang. Luster leans to her toothbrush. The roots of her hair throb in her scalp, her heavy hair. She is naked, and sweating already. Uncle Bud and Aunt Judy. Why did she think of them now? They had matching tattoos of lips on the cheeks of their butts. Kiss, kiss.

Now Crawford comes in behind her; he's been watching her from the bed, trying to make sense of her skinny ass. This is a long way out in the country, a long goddamn way out. From the window you can see farther than you can imagine, away off into nothing and then some. Out there are the cows with their long, gaunt faces.

Already the horizon is dusty. Away off and hidden in the huge country, an automobile moves along the roads—a Buick wide as a barn, gravel pecking its dusty chrome. Joe, the driver, believes in the power of the land to redeem him. He leans forward into the oncoming country as if to wish it true.

Luster makes a pass through the kitchen for a glass of water. It's the middle of the morning, and Crawford shouldn't be here, he ought to be out shuffling dirt or throwing hay, doing farmer things. Crawford's got no sense anymore. But here she goes—she stops herself; no need yelling down that well. This is a rickety place, soon to be gone out of their hands. They have surrounded themselves with this land, she and Crawford. Now it lies like a bed gone hard, a thing to be endured.

The air coming through the kitchen window takes a little of the heat off with it. She drinks her water, feeling a push at her gut—some feeling trying to talk to her. The message seems to ride along on the heat, and pretty soon she can't tell the message from the heat.

Crawford goes out the front, slowly. The day stands before him. More than a whole world, a universe. From this moment it spreads in both directions forever, like the ocean. Bigger. Too big. He brings it down, brings his footsteps down the sandy beach he has imagined. Ahead of him a couple romps and laughs. She, in a green swimsuit cut in plunging angles as if to lift parts of her higher; he with a beard. Crawford passes on, to the barn and beyond. He must catch the horses, shuffle dirt, toss hay. Farmer things.

Heat rises. Already he feels the day has beaten him. Ahead, the immense brown hills roll one into the other, dividing the wind in winter, rising now into the heat. From time to time sparrows flush from among the clods and beat off into the white morning.

Luster watches Crawford from the kitchen window, staggering angrily among the cows, pitching toward the big brindle. He stops and slants against the tractor tire, propped like a hoe handle for a long time. Luster is provoked. Why doesn't something kill the idiot? She breathes hard and then looks back out to the catch-pen on the slope below the barn. She has no explanation for her feelings.

The cow comes over the hill fast. Crawford whacks her once with the stick, and then she hooks at him and snorts but misses. She shakes her old head and falls backward. But she's right back up and coming at him again, which surprises him. He raises the bat to whack her again. Again and again, until she falls, bloody snout first, into the dirt, groveling there with her ass still raised up, her long tail thrashing, like she might kick up and lunge at him and kill him this time. So he keeps the bat cocked over his head. Then her legs tangle in her big bag of an udder and she falls, her eyes roll to white, and she sighs like a shot horse.

Tonk Myrkle shows up; he has walked up the road, and behind him is his daughter. Early mornings Myrkle's daughter sings a clear song that comes down across the hills like air; then when she comes to work she's all quiet. Today is Friday. Crawford and Tonk will drag the cow away into the boneyard gully. Turkey vultures roost in the trees along the rim of the ravine and occasionally one of them spreads its wings to air. When a breeze moves, the salty stink of the dead cattle comes up to the house.

Luster goes away from the window and begins her work, but when Myrkle's daughter comes in, Luster goes to the bedroom and stretches out on top of the plowed sheets. The swish of the broom comes and goes—down the hall, out to the porch; the door latch clicks back into its pocket; blackbirds call their rusty songs across the pasture; the fan buzzes Luster to sleep.

When has she slept like this in the daylight, and dreaming, dreamed herself into that long, falling night of silver-streaked music: she and Crawford fucking on the front porch, time and again and throwing the rubbers off into the flower bed; and the earth slipping from beneath them, down into the dark pond where turtles have eaten all of the fish from the dangling hooks of the trotline, except for the fishes' lips left drifting there like the rolled rims of the rubbers, kisses left behind in some years-ago abandoned barroom?

Crawford comes in to lunch in a ripped shirt. "Who's home?" he yells like an idiot from the moon. He waits for Luster to dish up their food from the stove. She's a good cook by habit, almost accidentally. She moves around the stove with the two plates held in one hand and a big spoon in the other. When she sets the plates on the table, Crawford starts in, but she goes back to the stove and dishes up plates for Tonk Myrkle and his daughter, and then she calls the girl to come and take their food out to the porch where Tonk is waiting.

Luster calls the dog to the back, to the screened porch, and pours crumbled food in his dish. Now the feeding is done. She has done this one thing.

Crawford looks up when Luster sits to her plate. "It's good," he says, and then he's back at it.

Luster watches him a minute and then she starts to eat, too. He's the best friend she has.

"Mercy," he says when he finishes. It's like a request.

"So, tell me about your life," Crawford says.

"I don't really have much to say."

He watches her, it must be forever. He says, "No need gnawing ourselves to the bone." Then his smile comes back. They have begun to look like each other, he and Luster. What joy they have comes to their faces and lingers there, a little uneasily, like curiosity. All their lives together they have bludgeoned each other with this happiness.

He gets up to go, but Luster takes him from the kitchen to the bed and they lie still in the wind from the fan. The dog comes in and wants to be petted, his snout propped on the edge of the bed, his face gaunt like the cows' faces. Tonk Myrkle and his daughter wait somewhere outside. The whole countryside lies as if waiting, and scalding blankets of heat rise everywhere off the land.

Tonight, for the first time, Luster goes out across the pasture to look in the neighbor's window. She is drunk but she isn't crazy. Her feet make a trail of black prints on the silver-dewy grass and her legs rise into the light of the high moon and then fall again into the darkness of her own shadow. She walks naked; this is her indulgence.

The kitchen light is on and she watches the woman making dinner. Thin radio music coming out through the thwopping blades of a window fan, the smell of onions. The woman moves from the sink to the stove to the cupboards like a person who believes she is alone. Now and then she speaks, neither to herself nor to the cat who sits on the table—"Don't forget the butter," she says, "and the plate." The cat watches in that predictable way that cats watch, twitching its tail, indifferent, detached.

Her name is Marla, she is a widow, and this is all Luster knows. Almost all. Sometimes late at night she calls on the phone. Neither Luster nor Crawford knows how the widow got their number, their names. How does anybody know anybody else in this country? It's old country, but people come and go. Luster has heard that the widow's house was in her father's family. She came here with her husband to retire, and then he died, and now the woman stays, alone and unknown, because the house is hers.

She calls them late at night, like a drunk. One of them throws off the sheet and goes in to catch the phone. Usually it's Luster. And she listens to endless monologues, about the rabbits the woman had as a child, the unusual color of the walls in a motel room where she stayed once with her husband. Trying to name those memories.

Now as Luster watches, Marla empties a pan onto the plate and sits down to eat with her back to the window; Luster sees only the back of her head, gray hair tangled at the crown, a small, rigid head balanced like an egg above shoulders as knotty as gate posts. Luster is seduced by the quiet order of this life. This awful life.

When Marla offers spoonfuls from her plate, the cat refuses by closing its eyes. She gets up and goes to bring another glass of water to the table, and the cat suddenly stops twitching its tail, perks its ears even more stiffly upward, opens its eyes, and looks directly out the window at Luster.

When she is done, Marla puts her dishes in the sink and turns off the kitchen overhead light. For a moment, the tip of a cigarette moves, as if alone. Luster feels that she might lose her balance, though her feet are on the ground.

Then the screen door opens—the cricket sound of the hinges and crying spring—and she steps onto the back porch. In her hand is an oily glass of water, the only hint of coolness in this moment of her watched life. And Luster drifts, she sees the moment play itself out slowly like a slow song, like a season, like a story she is trying to imagine:

In a few minutes the woman will go back into the house, back in to whatever is or isn't there. In the meantime, her feet will remain planted here on the years-ago painted planks of the porch. The back porch where everything should be quiet and cool, but where the leak water has dripped a hole in the planks and now all is dry, and the scars where the men dragged the washing machine across into the kitchen are deep in the wood. And the chinaberry tree that gives no shade, not even a moon shadow—when it put on berries its leaves gave all their strength, and now they hang weakly among the wrinkled berries, things about to evaporate; and beneath the tree is dust, the roots scratched bare by the dog, and now the dog lies among the feathery rootlets imagining that he is cooling himself, but he pants, and he is as hot and dry as the galvanized chain that attaches him to the tree. The woman, Marla, is craving a dragging down; even as she drags on her cigarette, she wants to be dragged into the dust, where she can imagine like the dog that she is cool and in love again, where there is no stopping for caution or for cleanliness, where there is no stopping to brush your teeth.

But she remains, foot planted on the porch. And Luster crouches around the corner beneath the window, wondering and unafraid. In the moonlit yard is a corn cob, forever attacked and scratched by hens.

The oily glass of water, tossed at the heat-drunken dog beneath the chinaberry tree, is no substitute for tears. And the boards of the porch creak as Marla steps back through the already-slamming screen door and disappears into the bleak shelter of the house.

And somewhere inside, the life goes on; in or out, on it goes. The crickets take up their fiddles and bows, and the night is deadly full of their racket. The moon comes out again through the low horizon clouds and then plunges again into the clouds, again and again racing down, poking its blue face again and again at the earth. Luster watches this dance, leaning against the house now, waiting for nothing—the old back and forth, front and back, head and tail, face and ass. But there are no equal opposites, there are only continuous surfaces and continuous dreams, each becoming the other, and the next. And the dashed glass of water is no more and no less kind than the flicked cigarette that lands in the dog's fur. And the dog, who smolders beneath the chinaberry tree, and then flames briefly and gloriously into the night, is no more and no less bright than the sun and the moon and the woman waiting alone through the shabby night.

Luster comes back across the pasture in the night, slowly, like a small swimmer, back as if from sleep, into their moonlit bedroom. She watches Crawford sleep, his hair black, his skin pale in this soft light, bedclothes thrown off because of the late summer heat. She moves carefully into the bed.

"Are you breathing?" she says.

"What's wrong?" he says.

"Nothing," she tells him. She wonders. The bed sinks beneath her.

"Where've you been?" he says.

"Walking in the pasture with no clothes on."

"Really?"

"Yeah," she says, looking over at him. His eyes are closed and Luster can see a smile.

"That's lovely."

She waits for a time in the dark.

"I've been over to the widow's," she says.

His eyes are still closed. He waits, silent, the darkness lying between them. "I watched her burn her dog," Luster begins.

The bed moves; he shifts to listen. "What?" he says. She tells him the whole senseless story. And then he wants to hear it again. He always wants to hear her stories again.

"Do you think she's crazy?" Luster says.

"What was she wearing?"

"Nothing."

"You're lying," Crawford says finally. "She didn't burn the dog."

"She was wearing a blanket," Luster says.

Later he dreams about his childhood friend, a boy they called Fish because he convinced Crawford and his younger brother that swimming was a matter of sucking in huge gulps of water. "Like a fish," he told them. "That's all a fish does."

In the dream, Fish rides across Crawford's pasture on a burning horse. The other Fish, the real one, bottom-upped a Thunderbird and drowned in Runningwater Creek.

Here they lie, Crawford and Luster, sleeping, sucking life from the night around them. Their bodies rise and fall, gently, sheltered beneath the moon-reflecting roof, anchored to the earth.

Joe drives his Buick relentlessly through the country. The swaying needles of the dashboard gauges follow the curves of the road, confirming the motion of the landscape, warning of nothing. The day rushes toward him: hill and woodland, creek and curve and dirty weeds, the smell of heat—shadow patches flash and fade. Behind the speeding car all dissolves into a boiling fog of dust; ahead, wide country begins to open. He is lured forward by each new swell, each new curve, lured by simple lust to see the next and the next, his thoughts galloping ahead of the Buick, his dusty past yapping at the tires like a mongrel dog. And from time to time he leans his big face out the window to get the smells of the land. The air informs him. He knows he is close to the promised land.

From her kitchen window, Luster can see all the way over into the black woods across the river, far beyond the puny trail of dust that rises now and again from the road—so far over that the trees become not trees but a continuous rough and nappy mat covering some secret or abandoned part of the earth—and beyond the corner of the lowest field, where the river makes its hard bend to the north, she sees the bright water. Back on this side of the lowland, the hills come up in careful stages, rolling toward her easily in long folds, one into the other, like muscles, or bedsheets in the morning. The land is in motion beneath her, slipping ever so gently. A small, shiny lake is caught between two of these folds of the earth, and nearer the house several thickets of cedar stand on outcroppings of chalk from which the dark earth was allowed to wash away in the times of cheap land.

Behind her, she hears Myrkle's daughter slopping the string mop in and out of the steel bucket and then swishing it across the brick floor of the kitchen. The noise is buoyant, tireless, like the sound of the ocean—collapsing, collapsing, and ever lifting its huge weight to collapse again. Luster wishes for the ocean, that child's place. Used to be, when she was a girl, Bud and Judy took her down to Biloxi every summer. Late on those Friday nights they took off south in the Plymouth, through the heat and crickets—Macon, Shuqualak, Wahalak, Scooba, and Meridian, and down into the pine woods. It all seems one long trip now: years compressed into a child's night in a broad back seat: exhaustion and exhaust fumes, Bud stopping somewhere south of Laurel and the hissing sound of his piss leaking onto the road bank, and when the Plymouth moved off again Luster watching the moonlight walk through the palmetto swamp, and ahead dawn and the car pulled down on the hard sand, hot sleep and flesh and ribbons of paint peeling from the flank of the Plymouth where hot exhaust leaked against the metal. Bud and Judy's sweaty tattoo lips kissing on the front seat.

Now Luster is dribbling Three Roses whiskey into a coffee cup. She moves and the earth moves. Earlier this afternoon Crawford and Tonk drove the yearling cattle over into the ravine. She watched the stupidly awkward animals stretch their long necks and hurtle toward the lake, and then turn, at what seemed the moment before they would plunge into the water, and sweep out of sight beyond the thicket.

And now, away off, Luster sees the horses, running wildly, their riders bent like boys against their necks. Up and up the hills they come, disappearing into the shadowy cleavage where one hill lies against another, and then reappearing larger, nearer, until she can see the horses heaving against the earth and against the heat, running with their ears pinned, running with their hearts. And then nearer, the riders, Crawford and Tonk, lanky, one white and one black but both dark now against the white horizon, girthed to their animals and stretching forward, grinning like mischief and death, thrusting themselves into the last few yards of the race to the corner of the house.

Then they are past and out of sight. Luster backs away from the window, breathing out a long, held breath, the clap of the hoofs and the throaty grunts of the winded animals coming to her like afterthoughts, like recent memories. They'll ruin the horses. What will be lost? Everything.

Myrkle's daughter bends double, wringing her dirty mop into the metal bucket. The girl has left a dry island where Luster is standing—the rest of the kitchen shines like fresh perspiration—the cool odor of brick. Luster leans and kisses the girl, and she speaks to her: "Odelia."

In the past, evil seemed a sinister and invisible disease—the sound of a single coughing calf coming across the hills at night, the unplanted crop, the interest on their bank notes mounting darkly against them. Again Luster feels the seductive motion of the earth beneath her, and she reaches for the table. She is ashamed, and she finds no relief. Meanwhile Odelia moves forward, bluntly and smoothly like a fish.

Then Crawford comes in at the back door. Here he is. And behind him she sees Tonk Myrkle, a stick of a man, sucking a cigarette, his black face disappearing into his jaw socket with each drag. And the smoke comes out, and there is his face again. And Odelia, standing like that over her mop. Something important is happening. Crawford knows this, too; he stands grinning, his hair wild. What can she expect of him? What does she expect? But the silence, the stillness must run its course. And they wait.

Tonk Myrkle and his daughter are here like witnesses, not to a crime, but to their lives. "Here they are," the witnesses might testify at any moment. "Here they are; their lives are happening." And after they are gone, after the farm has been sold, the tales Tonk and Odelia will tell of their lives—tales told over long hours, told with beer breath, told to women and men who have already heard again and again—the stories becoming part of the landscape, evidence of passing, like the automobile down there among the cedars, rusted and shot full of bullet holes, fading with days and weather. They will be a long time gone from this place; they will be forgotten soon enough.

Luster is wearing only a shirt. She could lift it over her head and lie down naked on the cool bricks, and they could take their pleasure like punishment, she and Crawford, take their false penance here in front of the witnesses. The story would be over. She is astonished at their life together.

She goes to the bedroom and pulls her pants on. She tries to imagine the moments Tonk and Odelia will remember, the moments they will tell again and again. The men and women at the Bull Cafe will remember them carelessly. But Luster buttons her pants, as if this is the only thing happening.

Now she grabs a side of the bedclothes and pumps them once, so that they buoy with air and come back down to the bed slowly; she smooths the thick spread toward the pillows with her forearms.

Myrkle's daughter stands in the bedroom doorway, Luster's dark shadow. "Mister Crawford say . . ."

"What is it, Odelia?"

"He say him and Daddy out to the truck."

Luster finishes her work. "It doesn't make much sense, does it—making up the bed?"

"People got to do," Odelia says, her typical wisdom.

Luster kisses her again. "We'll be good tonight."

And then they are in the pickup, Luster between Crawford and Odelia, and Tonk next to the door, the little dash-mounted fan blasting breathy air into her face, the bite of the Three Roses gone now, but resting somewhere. Tonk smells of salt and of sour oats. The hot outside air comes toward them like the road and divides before them—from the corner of her eye, Luster sees the fringes of the hot, stirred air fluffing the dust-powdered bushes along the sides of the road—but she looks ahead now, as if for some new road sign pointing toward occurrence, her confidence in the moment slipping.

The evening will begin and end with beer sucked from long bottles. Pleasure has become habit.

Some ways ahead, Joe's Buick rockets down the dusty road. On and on he passes, past thicket and gully and abandoned silo. Past thin Leota, walking fast. Past the Bull Cafe where three men turn quickly into the parking lot, throwing beer cans to the heat, throwing bits of dry gravel from beneath the rolling wheels of their car to ping against the tin wall of the cafe-shack.

And inside, the band is warming up for the long Saturday evening; two men playing guitars, another with a horn, playing without style, as if this were part of their punishment. Inside, long-faced men and women tell stories and lies. But Joe passes on, heading directly for the land he intends to buy, looking for the place where he will begin his glorious new life. The cloud of dust behind the Buick rises, like a message, hundreds of feet into the white sky. Beneath this fading cloud, Crawford and Luster and Tonk and Odelia make their evening journey to the Bull Cafe.

On the long rise before the abandoned church, the pickup coughs and digs into the road like a tired mule. From the crest of the hill, scraps of music come to them; they roll easily on down.

The saxophone player blows into his dented horn, his song like something learned in the metal-walled classroom of a vocational school, a song to be dismantled like an automobile engine. Voices call to them from the dark edges of the room—the crack of pool balls, smells of dirt and cement and metal. Later Crawford holds beer bottles to his ears and invents the music: noise, landscape, motion, and human touch. Tonk and Odelia dance, incestuous and chicken-necked, like interpreters of the song.

Night has come wholly on when Joe walks in, the Buick left idling in the parking lot, headlights on high beam and thrown directly into the doorway behind him—a shadow just a step ahead of his own dust—all darkness with a silver skin. He stumbles in, he hesitates. To the bar then, and back with arms full of beer, straight to the table where Luster and Crawford are squandering their lives, he moves without steps. "Hello, lovers," he says and sits and spreads the beers around, and some cash falls and lies heavily on the table like the damp heat.

Luster looks at Crawford and says, "It's Jesus."

Crawford says, "He's the savior all right, returned at last."

They both look across at Joe. His face says ha ha, but his mouth is saying something else. Money. An obscene offer.

"He wants the farm," Crawford says as if the music might have deafened Luster.

"I heard him," she says. "What about the cattle?"

And Crawford turns back to Joe. "What about the cattle?"

"All of it," Joe says, this time speaking directly to Luster.

"We don't own it," she says. "We owe it all to the bank, and then some." Suddenly she wishes it weren't gone. She sees the farm again through these new eyes—raw with possibility, raw like it was when she and Crawford moved in here eight, nine years ago, anchored their lives to this piece of earth.

"I know," Joe says, "I've been to the courthouse. And the bank." He nods to Crawford.

She looks at Crawford. His face is long and eroded, like every inch of Mississippi.

Next week is banging at the door, and the saxophone keeps up its battered tune.

"That's not enough," Crawford says. "You pay off the bank and we're still busted." Tonk and Odelia dance lazily around them like evidence of desire—the game of need and want.

Joe reaches into his jacket and pulls out a wad of money the size of a small cabbage. Crawford thinks of a nightmare he has almost every night but has never told anyone: thousands of hungry hogs line up at an endless trough and Crawford pours an endless stream of slop from a bucket. For a moment he is frightened. Here is the money, like evidence.

"We need a ride," Luster says. Something has gone wrong here. She repeats the word "need" to herself, silently. She straightens up and looks pretty. She notices her skin against her clothes. The heat is her friend, something she can touch privately. Crawford is her friend, too. This man across the table has happened to them like a tattoo happens: in an hour their lives have changed.

Crawford follows Joe out the door and into the parking lot, and from where she sits Luster watches their stretched and drunken shadows play in and out of the headlight beam projected through the doorway and against the far wall of the Bull. Tonk and Odelia move their smaller shadows among these, gently like the shadows of small trees.

Joe pulls one suitcase from the trunk. He unfolds a quitclaim deed onto the hood of the car. "Here it is," he says.

When they come back in, Crawford says, "Even the dipstick's broken on that car." He bends forward like a shy dog.

Luster says, "Let's go, baby," and she gathers up the cabbage wad of money. She has counted, something over eleven hundred dollars. She doesn't look at Joe. Soon she won't look back at all; she tells herself this story. A kiss for Odelia. In this moment she wishes it was cabbage leaves she was folding into her pocket.

Tonk inherits the pickup truck. One night on the slope of the hill before the Bull, a piston will drop down through its oil pan and the truck will stop, resolute and quiet. Tonk will clutch it and roll down into the borrow pit, and there it will rust to nothing. Tonk, too, will remain here, until he falls asleep and Odelia's song can no longer raise him. Luster feels drunken and crazy.

Outside, the night has swallowed itself. The Buick rumbles south toward the Gulf of Mexico with deceptive speed, like a large cow. Just a short ways across the country, the widow, Marla, comes to her window, her face as disorganized as the face of a young child awakened suddenly in the middle of the night. For the moment, her whole existence is framed in her window, her self distilled into a single beam of light spilling now out into the barnyard, where her chickens chuckle from their roost in the mimosa tree, the barren yard around them and the hot night spinning with insects. The smell of the seared dog is in the air. Spoons that she has suspended by threads hang in front of the window, and these turn slowly in the air, reflecting but not mirroring. She stares at the window, but not through it. No one watches her.

She wears a heavy winter blanket around her shoulders, Indian-style, the way a child might play dress-up with a tablecloth or an old fur coat. The blanket is pinned at the neck with a heavy, jeweled broach. She has her hands over her ears now, her mouth is open, her eyes wide and blank. If she sees anything, she sees only the window's reflection of her kitchen and her startling self. When she turns away the blanket trails behind her across the kitchen floor.

At the far side of the kitchen she reaches up to open the gray circuit box mounted on the wall. She studies the breakers for several minutes, patting the side of her neck, and she reaches up and begins flicking switches until there is no light in the house.

She dials a number on the phone.

She waits in the dark. The silence and the darkness fuse. She has unpinned the blanket from around her neck and now she stands naked in the thick darkness, feeling for the finger holes in the phone dial. Even the silver spoons hanging in the windows are invisible in the darkness.

She dials another long string of numbers.

"Betty," she says in a high, child's voice, "the most awful thing. The power is out. I don't know what to do, sweetheart. All the lights are out."

Luster watches the hills roll and fade past the open window of the Buick—like the humped shadows of large, gentle dogs; like the warm ocean miles ahead, licking toward her as if to wake her, as if to lift her onto its fat, rolling belly. Crawford imagines the ocean, too, imagines unanchoring himself and floating out. He's been to the barrier islands several miles out beyond the beaches—years ago, on a strange fishing trip—and he remembers the brilliant green water that moved into and out of the shell lagoons along the outer coast. He's not afraid of the water in the daylight. Maybe tomorrow they'll spend some of the wad of cash to boat out to the islands. Crawford can see the time ahead of him, clearly and broadly as if it were lying beneath that clear water—the peaceful monotony of the ocean floor. In time he will be better, he thinks.

Miles of the earth run under them. They have crossed the river, and Crawford is thinking about their table in the Bull. Their old friends have begun to lean toward the table where they were sitting drinking their beers a few minutes ago. The small empty space they left will close and heal. Crawford speaks quietly into the song of the Buick, something that sounds to Luster like "Hogs lapping at the trough of sorrow."

No, maybe he said "Hogs laughing . . . " Luster looks across at him; his face points into the night—the smiling face of the man who kills the cows. More of the road runs under them. She watches him. First chance she gets she will put back a hundred, maybe two, for herself.

She wants the feel of the soft, steady earth, but the land passes away, and Luster feels herself adrift again in the dark dream-water. She and Crawford together, surrounded but not yet drowning. Union and motion. The hot, wet wind blasts against them, but they hold to the night like shadows. What day is it? she wonders.

Howard in the Roses
by Dev Hathaway

In the Glow of the Bug Light

An August night, and stars are falling on Alabama, in a song on the high-pitched patio radio, scratchy like an old 45, grating with the deep-fried static of the poolside bug light. Maybe one true shooting star razorcuts the sky over the backyard tree line, then a moon grows round and white—rhyming with bright, and right, all my might. Meanwhile beetles dive-bomb the bug light's ultrablue glow, their resistance no match for voluptuous voltage. One bug then another spirals in, turns brilliant, is nerve-wracking, arc welded, and explodes, dropping to the poolside, bouncing twice.

And there, rising from blue-cast waters, are the two lovers we've imagined. Huffing and spewing. He, then she. Don't they look like a fresh god and goddess, a baby Adam and Eve, like newborns to each other anyway, as lovers briefly do.

Briefly then, as he scratches on the first try, hoists himself pushup style, stubs his hip on the edge of the pool, and falls back with a seal slap. And she, rising, oh clearly paunchy in her blue-black two-piece, grips the shaky aluminum ladder as though it were a walker and stares at her first firm step, at the popcorn corpses of beetles sprinkled on wet concrete.

How exhausted she appears, repulsed, irritated—see the corner of her lip line lengthen—how doggedly refreshed, pulling her short hair back. She pushes away from the ladder, slings herself forward with a heel thump and a crunch, and gives revulsion her full, breaking voice. "Jesus H. Christ, Howard."

Hopping mad, she's safely reached the lawn, and wipes her foot on the shining grass. "Why in God's green earth did your mother buy that contraption?"

No answer. With all his might, our Howard kicks himself up once more, arms locked straight, still unable to swing a haunch over the poolside. He gazes at his love, his eyelids drooping like a man with diabetes, elbows giving way, and slops back into the pool.

She sighs, looking away, hugging herself inconsolably.

The moon has withdrawn a little to the side. The song concludes. The bug light glows seductively on, like an errant runway marker; crackles again, like a drive-in speaker on the fritz.

Howard in the Roses

All the love shit. But Howard's heart is strong as a dumpster. Hear the whining grind of the forklift truck, the slam-bam. He can take it.

He's eaten love's dust. He's been sandblasted by good-byes. It sure stings, he says, but it leaves you clean as hell.

Howard's seen it all. The rosebud rising darker than lipstick from the tube, smooth and round as a candy kiss. He's been bitten before.

He told this woman he loved, everything. Dumped out love's steamer trunk right there in her kitchen. The burgers were crackling. She stepped back, reaching behind her for something on the counter.

He knows about long distance, too, and why the heart grows fonder, on the other side of the fence. When his old lady hit the road, she wrote she loved him with all her heart. Sure that made him smile, it was a first.

His great-aunt, actually, was very first, and smothered him in her rose perfume. She hugged him tight, in her own image. Oh you're my Howard. It's a wonder he has capacities.

He has this dream now. The lovers kiss madly then stand apart flustered as scaredy-cats. They start kidding themselves in baby talk.

In another dream they get good and sore slip-sliding. Strictly last ditch. So they take off their skins like scuba suits, dropping them in the burning sand. Who are you? And who are you?

Then the jeweler squints through his lens, reading inside the ring. This is you, right? Was, says Howard, and how about my forty bucks.

In the last dream they're standing apart in their blank, fluorescent bodies, waving bye-bye. Now she lets him have it with all her heart. Sure it stings, but it leaves him clean as hell.

Saint Howard and the Alligator

Howard, Howard, he's our man. If he can't do it, nobody can. Sooner or later, boys and girls, he'll fall for everybody. Or at very least come to the rescue. Just you wait, oh best beloved.

And ye who travail and are heavily parched by love's departures, here's your boy. He sees you when you're sleeping, he knows when you're awake. That's him at the desert comfort station, his canteen full to the lips with raw honey.

Moreover, this lap cat, this old sympathy card, wrote the book on country and western warning signs. He's seen the writing on the wall himself: saintliness is next to antsiness, dear husband, dear ex.

And isn't it so. Five times now he's thrown himself, spread-eagle, on the live grenade of relationship. Five times saved an entire company, and lived to tell. You could say our boy has a calling.

And he can find an alligator, oh cheating heart, in almost any septic system, one with grenade-like skin, a familiar and friend-like grin. He's been there, he says, he can tell a story or two. You know how the elephant child got his nose, and Pinocchio his.

Is your house on fire, ladybug? Quick, more honey. Poor alligator—here's molasses for you. And a baby blanket for your sugar shock, dear hearts.

What Comes Next
by Laura Hendrie

Sarah is waiting in her car at the drive-up bank, and when she looks up she sees an Indian in her side view mirror. He is crossing the parking lot in a slack-armed, sideways sort of way, as if he has traveled a long way on foot, or as if he has been sleeping on the ground and woken up not knowing where he is, or as if he's expecting something to jump out of her trunk. He is coming, she realizes quite suddenly, towards her. As she puts down the checkbook, he slides between the drive-up machine and her car and turns to face her, resting his hands on the bottom of her window. "My truck ran out of gas," he says. "I need to borrow a gas can."

It does not sound like a question. She has an impression of gray hair, braided, froggy lips, and a ruined face. He is wearing an oversized blue denim jacket that looks new and a brown plaid shirt buttoned wrong. "Let me see if I brought mine," she says. "I don't think I did." She does not want to appear unfriendly. She looks over her shoulder into the back. She does not own a gas can. "Shoot," she says in an easy way. "I guess I don't have it with me." There is a pause while the Indian looks at her and she at him and then he turns, the ends of his braids catching on his jacket, and looks out in the direction her car is pointed. He does not let go of her door. It occurs to her that he has no intention of letting go. Her heart speeds a little. She has never been robbed. From a certain angle, she can find it interesting. She can almost find it funny. There is a sound like a vacuum cleaner and a "thank you" over the loudspeaker behind the Indian, and the canister containing her money thunks home in its socket.

But instead of turning and helping himself, he remains where he is, staring out at the drive-up lane where she will turn left and then left again at the stop sign back onto the main street when this is over. She looks in the same direction. She has gotten used to Indians since she moved to Taos, standing behind her in the checkout lines or beside her at the laundromat, or sitting in the Arby's where she sometimes stops for breakfast, ordering refills, flipping their braids back to read the paper. But she has never spoken to one. Like actors on break from a Hollywood western, she used to think when she first came. As she sits waiting for him to make the next move, she feels something like guilt creep into the car. Maybe he's not going to rob her. Maybe he's not even planning to panhandle.

In the stiff new jacket, he isn't dressed for it. Plus, he's old. He's just an Indian, she thinks. He's probably late for work. Maybe he'll lose his job. Maybe he's already lost it. Maybe his wife is stranded somewhere, wondering why he isn't back yet to pick her up. Whatever it is, she can see he is not planning to tell her. His fingers are hooked over the edge of her window as if they have grown there like roots. He looks as if he is thinking of everything he does not know how to do next.

"There's a gas station across the street," she says. "Over there. Maybe they have a gas can." He looks at her sitting in her car. Despite what her life has become this last year, she is aware that her face has denied it. Beneath the tightness at the corners, a tightness that makes her mouth look at times almost as if it has been re-sewn with thread pulled too tight, she still has a ridiculously open face. She holds up her hands, palms up. "I'm sorry, but I don't have a gas can. Excuse me." She reaches past him, removes the cash and places the canister back in the machine. "I wish I could help you out," she says. "But this isn't my mine to give away. I'm picking it up for my mother." This is not a lie, not exactly, but she knows what it must sound like, what she must look like, reaching past him to stuff a wad of twenties into her bag. She closes her bag and looks up, smiling. He is not smiling back. She feels as if he has climbed into the car with her and shut all the windows and vents. He has placed his hands on her window again. "Look," she says. "You've picked the wrong person. That's all I'm saying." She stares out at the street and then looks up again. "I can offer you a ride if you want. You want a ride to the gas station or something?"

For a moment, she thinks he's going to go on holding on to the door of her car, but then his hands slide off and he backs up. She waits until he turns to start around the back and she jams her purse under the boxes of samples piled on the seat behind her. Her right hand turns the key and falls to the gear shift. Her left hand goes back to the steering wheel. She looks in the side view mirror. Over at the passenger door. Maybe he's rethinking his decision. Maybe he's offering her the chance to rethink hers. She looks out over the hood, seeing nothing. The idea that something is wrong with him that has nothing to do with gas cans or money has just occurred to her. My God, she thinks.

But when the door on the passenger side opens, it's not the Indian she talked to. It's another one, a big teenage girl, big, maybe two hundred pounds in gray sweat pants and a maroon sweat shirt and a wide swath of hair that drapes to her hips. She is talking rapidly in a language that sounds like bird imitations as she opens the door, and then, gathering her hair and throwing it like the pelt of a large black animal over one shoulder, she pulls herself inside and wedges herself on the emergency brake between the seats. The back of her head is pressed against the roof, and her shoulder is inches from Sarah's cheek, a shoulder that is about the same size as Sarah's thigh. Before the blanket of hair slides forward, Sarah gets a glimpse of her face: flat, fierce, and bruised with pimples, unhappy looking. She calls out sharply and another Indian, a boy about the same age but half the weight, with quick, deer-like eyes, climbs in and slams the door. In the rearview, Sarah sees no sign of the old man.

The big girl rotates her head toward Sarah, staring out black-eyed at her through a crack in the drape of hair.

"What are you doing?" she snaps. "Go."

Sarah puts it into first, apologizing when her hand knocks the big girl's leg. She pulls out of the drive-up lane, turns left and left again. At the corner she stops and leans forward to see past the girl's hair for traffic. It is starting to rain. The boy presses back in his seat on the other side as if he does not want to be seen, and this fact, that he appears to be unhappy about being in the car, that he looks almost as if he's the one who has been bullied into it, is reassuring to Sarah. She decides to ignore the feeling that something odd is going on between the two teenagers and that they are wrapped up in it and giving every indication of not wanting to deal with her. It is, after all, her car.

"Sorry about the boxes in the back," she says. "I just started this job last month and until I know all my samples, I have to carry them with me. It's not a bad job, though," she says. She wants to talk. "All I have to do is take samples of sandstone around to the galleries to see if they want to order it for their displays and table tops, that kind of thing. It's pretty easy, I guess. At least I don't have to dress up."

The big girl leans forward, trying to make room, her hand gripping a Kleenex in a fist pressed to her knee. Sarah waits while a faded red Ford truck crosses the intersection. There are children in the back, peering between the wooden sideboards, sucking on popsicles and holding a blue plastic tarp over their heads to keep off the rain.

It occurs to Sarah that the big girl has been crying and is close to tears again.

"So. You guys run out of gas?"

The big girl lifts so that Sarah can shift into first. As they turn onto the main street, it begins to really come down. Sarah turns on the wipers. She hears the boy on the other side rolling up his window and reluctantly she rolls up her own. The air in the car is very close. Mixed in with the smell of the big girl's hair, a musky, animal smell so thick it's almost a touch, she can smell the bag of her mother's soiled bed sheets in the far back. She has been meaning to take them to the laundry, let the people there deal with them, but she wishes now she had just thrown them out. "Sorry about the smell," she says, as she slows down in front of the gas station and puts on the blinker. "My mother's been sick."

"What are you doing?" The big girl has braced herself on the dash.

"I'm going to the gas station." Sarah looks at her and leans forward, trying to see around her to the boy. "Don't you guys need to buy a gas can?"

"A gas can?" The big girl hits her forehead on the mirror, knocking it askew. The boy reaches for the dashboard and pulls himself forward.

"Our baby boy died last night." When Sarah looks past the black curtain of hair, she sees a face as white as the moon. "We need to go back to St. Mary's Hospital for the release papers," he says. "We forgot to sign them. We were bringing my dad back to the hospital and we ran out of gas."

Sarah turns off her blinker and drives past the gas station. Without knowing it, she has her right hand on the girl's arm, her fingers curled into the blanket of hair draped over it, lost in the black. She has nothing she knows how to say. She wants to tell them she is sorry, but she is always saying she is sorry lately. Sorry to everyone, for everything. Sorry, sorry. Even when she doesn't care one way or the other. And though she does care this time—certainly she cares, my God, she can feel it pinching and swelling in her throat—what difference would it make to say it aloud? Sorry for the mess, sorry for the bother. She's always apologizing. Why? Because she has to. Why? Because. She drives several blocks without really knowing she is driving, before she realizes she does not know what hospital they're talking about. She's never heard of St. Mary's. The only hospital she knows is Holy Cross, where she takes her mother, who has Alzheimer's, for tests. She wants to tell them this. She wants to tell them she knows what hospitals are like. She looks at the big girl and sees that her eyes and mouth are pressed shut, her whole face shining. The boy is leaning against the door, holding the handle. They are half her age, but they are depending on her to shut up and get them there now, they are trusting the fact that they have said enough, that despite being a white person, she must be competent enough to at least get them there without making them explain that, too. They probably know where it is by heart. They probably know it better at this moment than they know who they are anymore or what they are doing in a car that smells like stone sealer and soiled sheets. "I don't know where the hospital is." It comes out in a burst, like a confession, almost a wail.

But here is something they can fix, something they have the answer for. She keeps asking "Which left? The next one? You mean here? At this light?" and they say yes or no and point out the streets. The rain has stopped and they have opened their windows to let in air. They are all three craning forward, leaning into each other, the girl's forehead nearly touching the mirror, the boy holding onto the dash. They are looking younger by the minute, too young to know enough to cry, too young to believe something this bad could happen to them. There's an urgency, as if what has happened hasn't yet, as if it is there still ahead before them, waiting for them to change it. When the entrance sign to the hospital comes into view, they point and half shout it out. Sarah puts on her blinker.

"Shit! They're not there!"

"Where? Who?" cries Sarah. "Is this the wrong place?" But the big girl is talking in Indian and the boy is staring up at the building, his liquid black eyes blank, the muscles around his mouth working. Sarah drives through the parking lot and pulls up to the emergency entrance door beneath an overhang.

"I'm not sure what's going on," she says, but the big girl and the boy have already left. They are running up the ramp to the door.

Sarah leans over and pulls their door closed. The hospital is flat-topped three-story, small for a hospital, and covered with some kind of dark vine that has managed to crack through the cement skirt surrounding the building. On the second and third floors, air conditioning units poke their backsides out the windows, and where the vines have parted below the casements, Sarah can see yellow stains. Inside the glass doors are a gurney and wheelchairs folded in a corner and beyond that a metal handrail and a black rubber mat leading up a ramp into a pale blue hallway. She can imagine what it's like inside. She realizes the wipers are still going and turns them off. She pulls out into the parking lot, turns the car around so that she will be facing the exit and returns to the same place but on the far side of the emergency lane. After a moment, she turns off the ignition.

She leans back to breathe in the smell of the rain-washed pavement, and catches the smell from the back seat again. There's probably a dumpster behind the building, but if they come back while she's gone, they may think she's left them. Besides, doesn't she have a right to carry dirty sheets in her car if she wants? She can't afford buying new ones for her mother every week. What they need is a washing machine. She has one in her apartment in California, but her mother has always done laundry kneeling on a pillow beside the tub in her attic, drying the wash on clothesline strung from the low rafters. "Don't tell me I'm getting too old for work," she would mutter, her rump jiggling against the tub, her voice striking the porcelain. "Besides, if I bought one of those things, you'd go to school every morning smelling like a damn piece of machinery. You and your little sisters don't want that, do you?" No, Sarah had thought at sixteen, slouched against a steamer trunk, flipping angrily through a *Vogue*. *We* want to smell like moldy insulation. Now, of course, the debate over modernizing is moot. Her mother wouldn't know what a washer and dryer looked like now, let alone how to turn them on. Sarah's mother is in bad shape. When Sarah first came home, thinking that her sisters were exaggerating, that her visit would be only temporary, she found every inch of the attic strung with clothesline, the place like walking into a ruined game of cat's cradle. The laundry turned out to be down in the garage, several weeks' worth hidden in the back seat of her mother's old station wagon, the smell like something dead when Sarah opened the door. And that was only the start of what she's found since. She leans her head back and closes her eyes, then pulls her list of clients' names out from under the boxes in the back. She is hoping for a sale today. When she first took the stone job, she saw herself pulling down contract after contract. She saw herself coming home from the galleries to make phone calls and write up orders, too busy to even think. But although hiring Mrs. Andrews to look after her mother has been a godsend, her job, it turns out, is a mistake. She's no good at selling. She talks too much, for one thing. She keeps bringing up personal problems, they keep spilling out of her at the wrong time—a weakness she doesn't remember having before she moved back home with her mother—and people forget why she's standing in their gallery holding a thirty-pound box of samples. Sarah does not want to talk about her problems, especially with her clients, but she forgets. At one gallery, a place full of Mexican ironwork and Guatemalan textiles and dried flower arrangements, she ended up sitting at the owner's insistence on a $10,500 bed in the display room, trying not to get the Navajo blanket wet while the woman ran in the back office to get Kleenex. She looks at her watch—10:00, plenty of time—then raises her head to look over at the emergency entrance. It is not much of a hospital. It looks worn down, almost grimy. It is probably the one all the local Indians use.

Sarah stares at the dashboard and then back at her list. She has recently begun to have nightmares about driving her mother to the cemetery, of circling a cul-de-sac in a wealthy suburb, looking for a pair of iron gates that have vanished. Sarah doesn't need a shrink to analyze it. On bad days, she knows she's going to be relieved when it's over. In her mother's lucid moments, which occur only rarely, mostly when Sarah is unprepared for them, even her mother has admitted it. Sarah sometimes suspects that even Mrs. Andrews will be relieved, despite her heavily starched speeches about God's will and the personal rewards of helping people. Although Sarah usually comes home to a fairly tranquil scene nowadays, when she drives off to work she often imagines Mrs. Andrews luring her mother into the basement and then jamming the door with a kitchen chair. Mrs. Andrews in front of the TV set at the far side of the house, her orthopedic shoes off, her ears plugged with cotton, the volume on high.

This is not true, of course; Mrs. Andrews has come from the day-care agency with the highest recommendations. When things get crazy, she is quick to remind Sarah that she has handled people like Sarah's mother for over thirty-two years. Besides, if Mrs. Andrews did not want the job, she could say so and leave. She could take her money and go. Still, there are times when Sarah watches Mrs. Andrews folding herself stiffly into the taxi at the end of a day and can't imagine the poor old woman doing anything else but rolling her eyes all the way home, panting with the relief of being freed. Sometimes Sarah can see herself at the funeral doing the same thing. Other times she can see herself bawling her eyes out. She has imagined her mother's funeral so often and in so many different ways lately that she knows when it finally happens, whether she cries or not, she will probably not be able to feel it for a while.

Sarah raises her head, wondering what she is feeling now. She squeezes her eyes shut and then opens them wide. What in the world is she doing? As if she thinks that for everyone all deaths are equal? An infant or a mother, one no less than another, all of them ending the same way, in a kind of numb relief, a rough-and-tumble circus of the emotions that suddenly stops, with nothing? She can feel the blood rush to her face. She crushes the list and throws it under the seat. "Wake up," she hisses through her teeth. And when she looks over at the hospital, as if on cue, she sees the big girl coming down the emergency hallway towards the entrance at a near run, blasting the doors apart with both hands.

The big girl stops short, her mouth drops open and her husband blunders into her from behind. He is holding an enormous vinyl pocketbook and he steps back to brace the door for a rigid-looking old woman in a brown sweater coming behind him. Sarah guesses it must be a relative, his mother, perhaps, or an aunt, and she leans over to the passenger window, waving. "Here I am." The big girl takes the old woman by one elbow and the boy takes her by the other and, nearly lifting her off her feet, they hurry across the emergency lane towards the car. Sarah glances at the back seat. She'll have to re-pile the sample boxes to make room or dump them in the parking lot and come back for them later, but before she can get out, the big girl climbs in and then the boy, handing the pocketbook to the old woman and then pulling her in onto his lap. Sarah's too surprised to suggest anything. Everyone leans towards Sarah, sucking in, and the boy manages to get the door shut. It is a very tight fit.

"They've taken him," says the big girl. She is out of breath. "She signed the release paper and they took him."

"I had to sign it," says the old woman in a shrill voice. "You weren't there. How was I to know you'd run out of gas?" She is clutching the dash with one hand and her huge pocketbook with the other, looking in the direction they will go next, her face inches from the windshield. When she turns, Sarah is shocked. She is withered in the face. The eyes remind Sarah of her own mother's eyes, black as raisins pushed deep into cookie dough. With difficulty Sarah gets past the big girl's knee to the key.

"Where do you need to go?"

"She thinks they took him to the funeral home," says the big girl.

"They did take him to the funeral home," snaps the old woman. "Swan's Funeral Home. I remember. That's what they told me."

"Okay," says the boy. "Let's go there. Oh, God," he cries, his voice leaping. "I forgot to ask. I don't know where Swan's is."

"You what?" The big girl rotates her head, aiming the "what" like an arrow.

"I know where it is," says Sarah quickly. "I think it's just up the block." She pulls out to the street and asks if it's clear. The boy tells her it is, but he is so crushed by his wife and the old woman that he probably can't turn his head to look. She leans forward over the wheel. All she can see is the side of the big girl's face, a flat boulder outcropping veiled in black, and beyond that, the old woman on the boy's lap, holding her huge pocketbook with both hands. Hoping for the best, Sarah creeps forwards, easing onto the main street.

"I'll take you there and wait outside," she says. "In case you need me."

Nobody answers.

The funeral home has a yellow stucco front and a low, red tile roof. There is a gate in the shape of a gothic arch and a brick walkway lined with white petunias. The old woman struggles with the door and the three of them tumble out. "I'll be here," calls Sarah, but no one looks back.

She looks at her watch—10:20—and waits five minutes. She can see it in her mind, now that she is awake, clutching the baby and their clothes in the dark and shaking the old woman awake, they must have run out to their car, yelling at each other, searching for the keys. They must have had no idea what they were supposed to do once they got to the hospital. They must have sat on the orange plastic benches in the hallways like things without souls. No one had bothered to tell them this might happen, they had never suspected it, never imagined it, not the way Sarah has with her mother. At some point, it must have occurred to them that getting back into their car and driving home made sense, that they could understand everything from the start if their father was there to tell them what comes next. Their father, she thinks, and sees him again gripping the door of her car at the bank, his big, froggy mouth clamped shut and that denim jacket, probably a birthday present, his shirt buttoned wrong. Asking her for a gas can. Five minutes pass and she begins to wonder if she is doing the right thing. She might be able to help. She knows nothing about what it's like to lose a baby, but she knows about making funeral arrangements. Three times she has come home to find xeroxed *Reader's Digest* articles Mrs. Andrews has left for her to read, articles about how to avoid being taken. The first time her mother met her at the door with it, saying it was a note from "that woman who keeps coming here." Sarah was fairly certain her mother had not bothered trying to read it, but as soon as she got her undressed and put to bed, she called up Mrs. Andrews. There was a row over the phone in which Sarah nearly fired Mrs. Andrews and Mrs. Andrews nearly quit. Back then, Sarah could still afford to doubt that she needed Mrs. Andrews's help. But she has since read the articles, and although she has not told Mrs. Andrews, she has followed much of the advice. She has discussed the future with Mr. Pry, the attorney, with Mr. Sims, the minister at her mother's church, with Mrs. Stumps, the woman who plays the organ, and with various funeral directors, including the one who owns this place, though she cannot remember now one thing about him. She has even picked out the coffin. The pages of the catalogue felt like white satin under her fingers, the coffins floating on a glossy white background like baby bassinets. The prices were printed in Old English text. She does not remember which one she chose or what it felt like to make her decision, only that after the funeral director left her in his heavily carpeted library, a phone began to ring, unanswered, out in the front office. Later, when she called her younger sisters to tell them, they told her it was probably a good idea, but she could hear in their voices what they thought. But now it's done, and she's glad of it. Mrs. Andrews was right. It will be one less thing to think about.

On the other hand, maybe these Indians don't need any help. Maybe they just want to be left alone. Chances are, they've already forgotten her. She is the last thing they need to think about right now. She is just another white person with no idea, no idea in the world. The truth is, Sarah feels a little crazy just sitting there, not knowing what's going on. She gets out of her car and goes through the gate.

Inside the front door is a rectangular anteroom with a pair of glass doors to her left leading into the main building. The walls are yellow and the floor is yellow linoleum with an astro-turf doormat trimmed in black. Against the far wall is a plastic raincoat hanging on a wooden coat rack and a single pair of galoshes, the old-fashioned black kind with buckles. When the heavy door sighs shut behind her, the light coming through a diamond-shaped stained glass sky light in the ceiling turns the narrow room a thick, dusty gold. It is like stepping into an underwater air lock. Sarah tucks her T-shirt in and steps in front of the glass doors, pulling one open.

She expects the heavy, perfumed smell, the dark wainscot paneling, the venetian blinds on the front window throwing weak bars of light across the blood-red carpeting, carpeting that seems to be standard in all the funeral homes she visited; but she is unprepared for the confusion. The room is filled with Indians. The walls, the deep couches and chairs, and the bench behind the organ by the window are lined with Indians, shoulder to shoulder, young and old, holding coats and hats and purses like a tribe waiting for a bus. Everyone is talking, some with their arms folded or hands in their back pockets, some leaning against the fireplace or sitting on the edge of the Spanish-style coffee table in the center of the room, some restraining small children, babies between their knees. Everybody looks disheveled, as if they have slept in their clothes. She sees no sign of the funeral director. She waits for someone to notice her and to stop their neighbors from talking, for everyone to stop, go silent and turn and look at her, *her*, walking in on them like this. As if she owns the place. As if she has a right to watch. She holds still, feeling the blood pump into her face.

"Hold on a sec. Everybody?" At the far side of the room, holding up his hand, a young Indian stands at a door marked OFFICE that he has just closed behind him. He is about twenty or so, a rosy brown color and very fat, his hair pulled back and braided into a thick rope down his back. He is wearing thongs, a rumpled T-shirt, and green plaid shorts that stop at the knees. When he crosses the room to speak to someone, Sarah recognizes the big girl, her head thrown back as if pulled by the fierce weight of her hair, and her hand, still holding the Kleenex, jammed angrily into her side. They may be related because they look somewhat alike, though she is not soft and rosy with fat like the boy. Just big, her massive weight hard on one foot.

"It's not that they doubt our family," the fat boy announces. "The law says when there's a crib death, they have to do an autopsy. It's the law."

"They don't have to do anything," cries the big girl. "I'm the mother, aren't I? They can't take him away from me without my permission. Did I tell them they could take him to Albuquerque?" She turns to the silent room, flinging one arm. "I'm the mother," she cries.

The room falls silent, everyone watching the fat boy. He puts his fingers to his forehead as if to think, a gesture older than he looks. "But that's what we're trying to tell you. They couldn't get hold of you. You'd already left the hospital. She had to sign—"

"The truck ran out of gas," howls the big girl, stamping her foot. "Didn't you tell them that? They can't just take him from me. How am I supposed to know where he is now?"

There is pause, a feeling in the room of looks being exchanged, and two elderly women stand up from the couch and move towards her. The big girl slaps their hands away, her black eyes burning, on the edge of violence. She reaches into her back pocket, takes out a handful of bills, and goes to the corner, hauling someone away from the wall. It takes Sarah a moment to realize it is her husband. Against the dark wood paneling, his young face looks almost skeletal, his eyes huge. He looks ready to bolt. She pushes the money in his hand and pulls him towards the front door by the wrist like a bad child. The women follow her with their mouths open. Sarah opens her mouth, too, but the big girl cuts her off.

"I want you and him to go get a gas can and go get his father and bring him back here." She seems ready to hand over her husband's wrist to Sarah, but then drops it as if she does not even know what it's doing there and turns away, the women parting as she shoves past them.

Sarah and the boy go outside. As they are getting in the car, his mother comes out, shielding her eyes against the light and calling them to wait. The boy, who looks too young to have ever been a father, holds the door for her and they get in. Sarah drives one block down to the Wal-Mart. Unreal, she thinks, as a fat, boiled-faced man in a cowboy hat and a cigar crosses in front of the car pushing a shopping cart of dog food. The boy gets out before they've stopped, leaving the door open.

"Wait a sec," calls Sarah. "Have you got money?"

The boy freezes, slaps his breast pocket and his face clears. "Yes," he calls.

His mother closes the door and they watch him go into the Wal-Mart. The old woman has her hand cupped over her mouth and she is mumbling something. For a moment, Sarah thinks she is praying, but then it occurs to her that in the confusion and panic of the night before, in the yelling and running out of the house in the dead of night only half dressed, only half awake, being jerked along by her son and daughter-in-law, none of it has been real for the old woman, not until now, until she is sitting here alone with a white person in front of Wal-Mart and aware all at once that her teeth are not in.

"This must be awful for you," she tries gently, looking the other way. "All of this."

But when she turns, she sees she is wrong. The woman has a better set of teeth than Mrs. Andrews. "I couldn't sleep last night," she bursts out. "I don't know why but I kept getting up. I kept asking myself 'Why don't you go to bed, old woman?' but I couldn't. I knew something was wrong. I could feel it. I went to the living room, I went to the kitchen, I had a glass of milk"—the old woman is pointing these things out with the crabbed edge of her hand as if she is naming objects on Sarah's dash—"I even went outside and swept the porch." She stops, turning to Sarah. Looking into her face is like looking through the cracked basement window of an abandoned house and finding someone inside, looking out. "I went everywhere in that house last night, honey. But I didn't go into his room."

"Why would you, though? You didn't know. It was a night like any other night. That sort of thing," Sarah says, "you don't know when it happens. It just happens out of nowhere, doesn't it? And then it's done?"

"But I *did* know," wails the woman, her eyes rolling back. "I *heard*."

"You heard?"

"Yes. Of course. The last time I went to bed. His crib is right on the other side of the wall from where I sleep. I hear everything. My room is next to his. And my God . . . " the woman falters. "I kept thinking I heard a little scratching sound. As if he was reaching through the bars of his crib, trying to call me, his little hand, you see . . . but I was so tired by then—I kept thinking I'd have to get up early to fix everyone's breakfast—" She stops, putting her hand over her mouth.

"Don't. It's never anybody's fault. It could have been just a dream he was having. It could have been anything. You could have been dreaming—"

But the old woman is shaking her head. When Sarah tries to go on, she hisses and grabs her sleeve with sudden force. Sarah turns and sees the boy trotting towards the car with a red plastic gas can. He opens the door, jams the gas can into the narrow space between the boxes of stone samples and the roof, and climbs in beside his mother. "I got it," he says. "Got the gas can."

"Good," says Sarah. The old woman is staring out the windshield. Sarah pulls out of the parking lot, bumps over the median and into the gas station on the other side of the street. The boy gets out, yanks the gas can from the back, and trots over to the pumps.

"I just wish I could help," says Sarah, pushing her comfort at the woman, feeling her eyes well up. "I feel so badly for you. For all of you," she hastens. "It must be awful, what you've been through."

"That's right, honey." But she says it without feeling, turning her head away. "He kept saying stupid things on the way to the hospital. You wouldn't believe how stupid. He kept saying 'Why do we have to do this ourselves, Mom?' "

Sarah stares at the back of her head. "It was shock," she says. "People in shock don't know what they're—"

"Oh yes, he did." Her voice has suddenly gone bitter. "He kept saying 'Why didn't you call an ambulance, Mom? Why didn't you?' Can you believe that? He was holding my grandson and he kept saying that to me. His wife told him to be quiet. She slapped him." The old woman turns to Sarah, her eyes empty. "I know it sounds terrible of her to slap my youngest boy like that, but she was right, don't you think? The baby's face was blue when I saw it. It was blue as a cornflower. I can tell you it was. They couldn't have used an ambulance. I'm sure of it. They have no right to blame me. Besides, I didn't ask them to move in with me. They just came. I know I'm getting old, both my husband and me, but we've done our best to look after the three of them since they moved in, haven't we?"

"Of course you have. Your son wasn't thinking straight. He must just have been so upset when the baby—" She stops, instantly ashamed. Who is she to say it out loud, to speak it so casually? She feels as if she is a tourist taking photographs, as if she has spat in the woman's face.

"I know, honey," says the woman. "Do you want to know the worst part?"

But Sarah does not want to know the worst part, or any of the parts. She is getting mixed up now, and she wants it to be over, this confession and this woman and her son out of her car.

"The worst part is that we can't bury him at the pueblo because his mother is Apache," says the old woman. "We're going to have to put him in the public cemetery, I guess. It's going to cost, too. The one behind the Allsups. Do you know which one that is? I'm not sure if I know where it is or not."

For a moment, Sarah has the idea that the old woman has Alzheimer's. The boy opens the door. "I got the gas," he cries. "Three dollars." His face has a bright rosette of color on each cheek.

They drive down the street, the boy pressed against the door with the gas can against his chest. When they pull into the bank, it occurs to Sarah for the first time that the old man has been waiting here for them, probably standing there in his new jacket, watching the street, no idea what to do next. There is, however, no sign of him. The drive-up bank is busy now, cars moving in and out, all the lanes full.

"Maybe I should stick around?" she asks the boy as he helps his mother out of the car. "I could stay until you find out where your dad is."

The old woman is bent over her purse, searching in it for something. The boy shakes his head. "I got the gas can and the truck is down the street. We'll find him. He's around somewhere."

"Are you sure? Are you alright?"

He shuts the door, in his bottomless black eyes a meaning she cannot understand. "I don't know how—"

The old woman pulls the boy aside by his jacket. "Take this, honey," she says, thrusting a dollar bill at Sarah. "I haven't got much but you're welcome to it. You've been so kind—"

"No." Sarah holds up her hands. "Don't."

"You have to. Please."

"No," cries Sarah, suddenly frightened. "I would do it for anybody. Anybody would."

"Mom," calls the boy. "Come on." He is looking back at her from the edge of the parking lot, the gas can on his shoulder. When the old woman turns, confused, taking her hand with the dollar in it off the door of Sarah's car to shade her eyes, Sarah drives away.

For the rest of the morning, she visits the furniture art galleries in the center of town. She does not stop for lunch. She feels her heart beating in her wrists, feels the familiarity of her own life returning. She feels as if she has just stepped out of one of those terrible made-for-TV movies. By the afternoon she has seen four stores, two more than she expected to have the energy for. No one has ordered anything. The tourists are gone, the buying season over. Her clients, all pale women in southwestern jewelry and geometric haircuts, glide through their display rooms to piped-in music, pausing to fluff a pillow or straighten their skirts, watching the door, waiting. Sarah goes from gallery to gallery. "You wouldn't believe what just happened to me at the bank," she says. Then she puts down the boxes of stone. She doesn't care whether they want to look or not. At one gallery they do, two of them crouching next to the box so that their stockings turn their knees to alabaster, the wings of their hair falling forward. They smooth the samples of stone under their long fingers, clicking burgundy nails on it as if testing the shell of an egg. Sarah crouches next to them while they look. She keeps explaining what it was like from different angles, what it was like to drive away afterward. She knows it's not the way to make a sale, but she doesn't care. She's no good at selling anyway. She feels strange and lightheaded, almost as if she's witnessed a miracle. "What an incredible experience," they say, brushing off their skirts. "With a story like that, you should become a writer." Sarah is vaguely aware that she is being indulged, that if they are fascinated, they are less fascinated by what she is telling them than by Sarah herself. The thought is unpleasant to her, almost offensive. At the next gallery, she keeps reminding them of how quickly it happened, how the whole thing was over so quickly. Forty-five minutes, an hour, max. She didn't even find out the name of the baby or how old he was. She never even learned their names.

All she knows is that they are Indians who lost a baby. Lost a baby, she keeps saying. When a customer wanders in the front door, the younger woman murmurs an apology and moves off to see if she can help, straightening her Navajo turquoise necklace. The other woman, the owner, is still pretending to listen, but Sarah gets the point. She hands her a business card, gathers up the samples and leaves. It is three o'clock by the time she gets to the supermarket. Her feet are singing as she hurries up and down the aisles, picking out food for her mother at random. When the checkout boy, whom Sarah knows from the Alzheimer's support group in town, asks her how her mother is doing lately, it is all Sarah can do not to tell him the story. She piles the groceries beside her in the car, takes a detour to avoid the funeral home—because what would happen if they saw her now, if they saw the look on her face, if she saw them and did not stop?—and she drives home, eager to tell Mrs. Andrews.

The Twin

by J. R. Jones

T HE CROWDED TRAIN rocked from side to side and I held on to the vertical seat rail, concentrating on the paper I'd folded in to the day's races at Arlington. I'd lost forty bucks on Tara's Song in the third and twenty-five on Dear Alba in the seventh. On top of that, I'd bet three hundred on the Black Hawks–Islanders game tonight, and if the Hawks lost I'd have to face my bookie with an empty pocket. A perilous situation—plus, the pawn ticket on my Rolex ran out in two days and I needed the winnings to redeem it. My kid brother Eddie gave me the watch as a graduation present. "Yeah, it's being repaired; stem came out," I'd told him. Christ: if he ever found out, he'd give me a half-hour lecture with one silent shake of his head.

But he wouldn't find out, and tonight I'd bring home Hawks tickets; my boss had given me two tenth-row seats he couldn't use. Hard to have a bad day when you've been in the right place at the right time.

The doors opened at Fullerton and a blast of freezing air fought the Lincoln Park gentry as they piled out. Just as the door was closing an ace of spades pushed it open and boarded the train in a final, mad burst of wind. He wore a knee-length jacket and a knit cap, a twice-folded *Tribune* tucked under his arm.

"I'm Matt the Clown, here's what's goin' down," he announced. "If you're sad or blue, I got money in my shoe."

Across from me, two married professionals stiffened and ignored him. The wife crossed her gorgeous legs and stared at herself in the darkened glass of the train. Her husband was trim, dapper, his hair short, his jaw set tightly like the buckles of his London Fog overcoat. His fingers were smooth and blocky like a package of hot dogs as he tightened them around her shoulder.

First Commandment: Never Make Eye Contact. Love Your Fellow Man, but if he's a hustler or a crackpot, Never Make Eye Contact.

Matt the Clown set the smeared, worn-out rectangle of newspaper in his lap and laid down three whiskey bottle caps, one covering a brown cloth ball like a burnt peanut. He spirited the caps this way and that, braiding them slowly but smoothly, and without a break in the flow of his patter. "You can trust you eye or you can trust you luck, but you eye ain't worth a fuck." Round and round the bottle caps swam. "Watch de ball watch de ball whey is it? watch de ball."

At the other end of the car, Matt's partner made phony small talk with an office girl. Tall dude in a beard and flak jacket; I'd seen him before too. He never got involved, just kept his eyes open. They always worked the back of the car, away from the conductor; always worked the rush hour going north, when the office workers rode; never boarded until Fullerton or Belmont, when the cars emptied somewhat.

"Take a chance, mama, come on," Matt the Clown urged the young wife. The couple looked resolutely away. "I been ridin' this train four years, I know the money's here. I wanna tell you it's true, 'cause I got money in my shoe, watch de ball watch de ball whey is it?"

I stared out the window, swallowing. The first person to play him always won. I'd seen him do it twice. *Shee-it, I picked the wrong train. Did you see what she done to me?* The second player was the one who got sheared. I could double my last twenty bucks, no problem.

A cold sweat hit me: my watch sitting at the pawnbroker's. Learn to say *when*, for God's sake. The line between a good bet and a bad one had grown so thin I could barely find it without my reading glasses. Twenty bucks would never buy the watch out of hock anyway. I needed a really big win to clear all this shit away.

Wrigley Field swept into view. "See the boys in the ballpark hit them home runs, it sure look like fun." No one would touch the bet. The husband blinked and fixed his gaze on his wife's legs. *You coward*, I thought, *you want that bet worse than I do*. At least I could admit it.

The last time Eddie and I went out with Pop was an exhibition game at Wrigley: Cubs versus the Minnesota Twins. Two days later he walked into the boiler room at the Jesuit school where he was maintenance chief and the boiler blew up in his face. *God has a reason for everything*, the priests kept saying, and our neighbors, *It was just a freak accident*; both were trying to console us. When my mother drank her liver into submission I was at U of I, Ed a sophomore in high school. This time it was no accident—Mama believed in the sure thing. At least now we could cut Mass. And I cut loose any of playing baseball, put all my energies into an accounting major. Sure, I know. But it doesn't look half as bad when you're thinking about three squares a day.

"How 'bout you, friend?"

Matt had caught me off guard. "No thanks."

"I bet you twenty you can't find the ball, all's you gotta do's bet on yourse'f and you take home twenty. You got a twenty you can show me?"

"I got all my money on the Black Hawks."

"Shit, *they's* worth bettin' on."

Laughter from the other passengers. The young husband was grinning. Sweat collected on my back. I pulled off my glove, reached into my pocket and brought out the crumpled twenty. "You're on," I said with a hint of a sneer.

Now the eyes of the riders were focused on us, papers lifted in the air unread. They were safe now: I was the attraction. Matt smiled. His hand closed over the bill like a crab. "You gone and done it, pal, you already won it." The cash drove him into a frenzy of congeniality. "Find the ball you win a twenty, findin' it's element'ry. Watch de ball watch de ball whey is it? watch de ball." He was moving the bottle caps two at a time, with the fingers and heel of one hand, but I followed the ball easily. I was the decoy; I was betting on that, not the shell game. The Lawrence stop approached, and I readied myself to bolt. Second Commandment: Take the Money and Run.

The caps stopped moving. "Which is it?" Matt the Clown demanded. There was no rhyme now. I shifted nervously, fingering the good luck coin in my pants pocket. I pointed to the right-hand cap, and Matt turned it over. Nothing.

"Shit!" I pounded at the air with my fist.

"I'm sad to say you got to lose, the only way out's to never choose," said Matt the Clown as he stuffed the twenty deep into the pocket of his long leather jacket. Other times I'd seen him go up to the next car for another game, but he'd found his mark, and at Lawrence he and his partner headed out their respective doors. "G'bye folks!" he yelled. "I'll be comin' back for you, 'cause I got money in my shoe, y'all remember that, now!" For a moment I thought they'd burst into applause.

The last four stops were long ones. I glanced over at the man and woman. The husband tipped his finely barbered head with a faint smirk. "Tough luck," he said to me.

"Yeah, what the hell," I muttered. The doors of the train flew open at my stop and I escaped onto the platform, walked as fast as I could down the line of cars, bumping people in my haste. The train jumped twice and began to move, picking up speed as I fought to think of the hockey game.

A huge gob of spit leapt across my coat. I whirled around, stricken, and roared, "You cocksuckers!" Two kids hung out a conductor's window, laughing at me as the train retreated in the distance.

I lived five blocks from the Granville stop (three safe, two dangerous, each block its own entity). My apartment building seemed secure enough, with buzzers and intercoms and glass and steel. But this was a Disciples neighborhood. Last week a guy—twenty-two, same age as me—got greased up on the north platform. Three dudes hit him up for his wallet and he decided to show them the spirit of Chicago. They gave him the spirit of the city, all right, point-blank in the face.

I'd been on that platform much too late for my own good. The entrance was still closed off and covered with a thick layer of vomit sand. They must have had trouble with the stains. *You'll get it someday*, I told myself (knock on wood).

The odds would play it out on me—but when? That's what drove me crazy, the waiting. "Always know the odds," my bookie Mike says. Well, I know them—we just about *party* together—and one thing is, they always take their time.

Eddie wasn't at the apartment, and a few phone calls failed to turn him up. He'd blown his first semester at Champaign-Urbana and I was lodging him until he started at De Paul in March. He drifted around, killing time, slam dancing at punk clubs. Got the shirt torn clean off his back once, lost his coat, came home on the train naked from the waist up in ten-degree wind. I tagged along to the Metro one night and sat in the balcony. Below me a mob of young, sweaty boys thrashed, kicked, and slammed into each other as Hüsker Dü played at pile driver pace. Eddie climbed onstage, doing the clumsy, kicking, steel-booted step, then dove into the audience, where he vanished in the midst of their hands, bobbed back up onto his feet and started hauling toward the stage again. Punks crawled onstage, hurled themselves, flipped themselves, somersaulted into the pack of colliding bodies to land on their feet and catch some other idiot.

"How can you do that?" I asked him after the show.

"Leap of faith."

"What if they decide to clear a space for you someday?"

"Guess I break my neck."

"You might as well play Russian roulette."

"That wouldn't be as much fun with a band."

After dinner I took a shower and dressed for the game. Still no Eddie. The only other place I could think to look was the Grenada. We'd discovered a hidden fire escape to the roof of the abandoned movie palace this summer. It gave me the creeps, but Eddie still went there.

I would try the Grenada and, failing that, scalp the other ticket at the game. I'd get good money for it, too. But it wouldn't be the same.

The Grenada loomed above me like a Moorish whorehouse, a trashed temple to the gods of vaudeville and Hollywood. Over the marquee a stone facade rose in a soaring, fifty-foot arch that came to a point ten feet above the roof. Its center was a great arched window of stained glass, and flanking the glass on either side were stone columns, a corroding, neglected forest of sculpted foliage and gargoyle heads. A row of three tall windows began at roof level. I found Eddie's silhouette in one of the windows. It disappeared as I moved closer, so I crossed the street to the theater and slipped into the shadow of its north alley.

A minute or two passed. Shit! He must not have recognized me, and since he was trespassing I couldn't yell up from the street. I'd have to go up after him. He'd left the fire escape down, thank God. It wheezed and rattled as I climbed up the steps.

The roofscape was broad, shallow plains of tar separated into rectangles by knee-high walls of brick and mortar. An explosion of white paint announced

"DISCIPLES" to all visitors, and other artists had elaborated a maze of spray paint, white and yellow and pink and blue, overlapping and intertwining like a sea of wild snakes.

I called Eddie's name.

"Tom?" He moved out from the shadows, translucent in the streaming moonlight, cradling a seven-ounce bottle of Christian Brothers brandy.

I told him about the Hawks tickets. "That's great," he said.

"You know, you must be nuts drinking up here."

"No, it's cool. View's magnificent." I took the bottle from him. "What?"

"Come on, are you crazy? You'll wind up like Mama did."

"Since when are you my nursemaid?"

"Too long ago."

"Ah, fuck off." He walked up to the windows overlooking Sheridan. They were full-length, and I didn't like being too close to them. "Come look. It really is great."

I walked over to his window and hugged the side. Below us a river of passing cars, a river of chrome and light, flowed in opposite directions. "You're lucky the Disciples haven't kicked your ass out this window. I bet you couldn't get enough punks gathered on Sheridan to catch you."

"What is this luck bullshit all the time? There's no such thing. I could do a backflip out this window right now, and if it wasn't meant to be I'd never hit the street. The earth would rotate backwards and the lake would catch me."

"Yeah, well, life doesn't rotate backwards."

"It doesn't *rotate* at all. I mean, shit, what's the point of pushing forward? What's forward? I called De Paul today and told them I was withdrawing."

"You *what*?" His mouth gave a twitch and he looked out the window. I could tell he'd been planning to bring it up more artfully than this. "You really called them and pulled out?"

"What's the point? It'll be the same as Champaign."

"How do you plan on feeding yourself? You can't stay with me forever."

"I'll get a place, get a job. Greenpeace gives you a hundred bucks a week. Maybe I'll be in a hardcore band with some guys. Greg Marelli's got a set of drums. We're gonna write a song called 'Baby Let's Sordid Out.' Get it? S-O-R-D-I-D?"

"Oh, brother."

"The point is, why do I need a safety net? It's a false god. Why follow it into a little white cubicle?"

"It pays the bills," I said icily.

"Yeah, I know. I'm sorry. I'll give you some money."

"Keep it. You're gonna need it now."

He turned from the window and walked to the east edge of the main roof of the building. I followed him. A tower of sorts stood southeast of us, its roof ten-foot-square and walled in by brick. A brick wall extended out at a right angle to connect with our roof, and the blacktop caved in about a dozen feet to form two gulleys, one on each side of the wall. East of us the moonlight cast dancing bangles in the lake.

"Is that all you want, Tom? To pay the bills?"

I thought of the young couple on the train, the husband who had the money and the beautiful companion and didn't have to sweat out his last twenty bucks in a shell game. Contempt or envy? The line was so thin I needed my reading glasses. "I don't know what I want," I said to him. "But I know I don't have it."

"Besides, most of your bills are for Mike Curran."

I punched him in the chest; he laughed, and before I could get a word in edgewise he'd mounted the brick wall and walked quickly, evenly to the tip of the right angle.

"You're a fucking nut case. If you fall I'll never get you out of there. I'll have to call the fire department and we'll both be busted."

"I'm not gonna fall," he sneered. Looking straight ahead, he turned and crossed to the roof of the tower.

"So who's the nursemaid now, scolding me because I make a bet now and again?"

"And again and again."

"Talk about sanctimonious."

"Look, I don't give a shit one way or another, Tom, I'm just pointing out a fact."

"I never bet more than I feel like. I never bet unless I can feel it in my bones."

"Hey, throw me that brandy, will you? Let me feel some of that in my bones."

"Why don't you make me?"

Eddie grinned. He reached into his back pocket, unfolded his wallet and peeled off three bills. "Here's fifty bucks. Enough to settle you up for the week? Walk that bottle of brandy over here and it's yours. You'll make it, luck or not, I'll bet."

I stepped up to the wall and started out. "As if you could spare fifty bucks." I'd win his money and give it back to him, the little shit. The wall was two feet wide, and balancing was simple if you moved slowly and carefully.

"Don't look down!" I raised my head and stared at the moonlit water. "Okay, take the turn slow."

"I've got it," I said irritably. I glanced down for an instant to negotiate the turn, and the vortex pulled me over; Eddie shouted as the angled wall bit into my arms.

Holding on, I saw everything in a queer slow motion; as though he were swimming miles, Eddie shinnied out on the wall. He yanked me up. Somehow I got my leg over the wall and straddled it. We made our way to the main roof, my heart pounding. I lay on the blacktop and breathed hungrily, gratefully. Eddie kept pacing around and saying "shit." He stuffed the fifty bucks in the breast pocket of my coat and wiped his face on his sleeve.

"Swear to God, Eddie." I struggled to catch my breath. "You *are* lucky. Some people are like magnets: it sticks to 'em."

Snow settled on us as we approached the elevated tracks, and above us a train roared past. We paid our fares and went up to the south platform. Eddie walked up the platform, and I took cover inside the glass shelter. What was he thinking? A heatlamp hung from the roof of the shelter and generated a small, rectangular zone of warmth.

The lamp snapped off and I hit the ON button; the heat came in sixty-second doses. I worked my hands for warmth. Eddie was right: my life was utterly out of control. I hadn't seen a movie in two months, hadn't eaten out since Christmas. Every fucking dollar always on the line, always that tremor deep at the core when it hit me I was going to lose *big*. Now I was in hock and betting three hundred bucks I didn't have. The lamp went out.

What was the point? Life is a trap, a marked deck and a gun on the table. Draw: ace of spades. What difference would it make if I were dead instead of counting other people's dough? Eddie thought I was shit. The money was still in my pocket, and I thought of throwing it on the tracks, but I knew I'd never do it and the knowledge made me want to rend myself, pound on the wall of the shelter. Eddie had given me the money in a spasm of guilt, even though he'd never ask for it back. That was his way of reacting to any problem—immediately.

The twin headlights of a train appeared as it rounded the corner heading north from the Loop. It would be going forty when it reached our end of the platform. This summer a bag lady had jumped. "Man, you don't want to look," the cop told me. "There isn't enough to fill a bowling bag." What did it take? Three steps, and—what? Courage? Hopelessness? The kind of curiosity Eddie pulsed with? Every time I saw a train coming nowadays I hungered for the experience, but fear kept me in place. Tonight was different. The Hawks game, the watch—it was all shit when I saw Eddie waving that money around and grinning at me. You'll make it, luck or not, I'll bet. Numb, I took three steps to the edge of the platform. The train screamed toward me, a chilly wind stirring gently at its approach. I could feel the physical effects of terror but wasn't afraid; in fact, a strange pride welled up within me. I braced myself for the pain.

The lamp snapped on, and I turned. Eddie smiled at me as the train roared by. Its wind pushed me back a step.

"Wrong train, you idiot. We're going downtown."

Before long we were descending the stadium steps to our seats overlooking the Islanders' goal. Full house tonight: beer-stoned granddads in plaid shirts, chewing on their dead cigars; square-headed prep school jocks, slamming down beer and pounding on the railings, their bellows collecting among the girders overhead. We sat with the fanatic brigade, crew-cut kids and army reserve parents, amiable dopes with their buttons and flags and stupid hats. A Spanish announcer for Channel 26 sang the national anthem to an all-white crowd.

As a peace offering I went to the concession stand and broke one of the bills Eddie had given me on a couple buckets of beer. Each held 32 ounces of foaming Old Style, and by the end of the second period we were blind drunk. The Islanders led 5–3. I bought myself another bucket of beer when it dawned on me that the Hawks were out of gas and I would probably lose my bet. I'd never welshed before, and my mind was full of back-alley punishments from a thousand gangster movies. In reality, Mike would just shake his bald head, adjust his glasses, give me an extension and make my name shit all over town.

Al Secord drew up to the net on our side, big as life and with a decent opening. He shot and the goalie dove on it. No score. I cursed and kicked the seat in front of me.

"Cool out, Rambo, it's just a hockey game." I stared into Eddie's calm eyes, my face frozen in a confused grimace. I wanted to tell him about the watch but turned back to the game. Being shit all over town is one thing, but not at home.

"How much are you in for?" he asked me.

"What are you talking about?" I shot back. "I made a chintzy little five-dollar bet at work, will you get off my back?"

"I'd love to know what your blood pressure is right now. Look at this vein on your head, look at this." I felt his cool fingers graze my temple and slapped his hand away. He laughed. "You'd think there was a mortgage on your house riding on this game."

"I like hockey."

In those few seconds Denis Savard had made a good drive forward and scored an open-net goal on the Islanders: 5–4. The Hawks crowd erupted, and I shook my fist in the air, cheering. As if the goal somehow vindicated me, Eddie went back to watching the game.

The Hawks scored again in the middle of the last period, and with the score tied my hopes sprang into flower again. Thank God I hadn't told Eddie about the watch. Tomorrow night it would be on my wrist again.

The clock ran down under two minutes. The Islanders were hanging on to this one. One of their linemen drove Doug Wilson into the Plexiglas barrier facing us. With a thunderous slam his face was crushed into the Plexiglas, and his twisted nose and eye against the glass formed a cavity that filled with blood like a rising thermometer.

The crowd shrieked and a fight broke out. Wilson was carried off. After some deliberation the referees threw the Islanders lineman out of the game. The smear of blood hung on the Plexiglas in front of us, and I shuddered as I recalled the wide, unseeing eye that stared at me through the glass in the moment before the blood leapt over it.

The two teams bore down on each other, the crowd a barely controlled scream of fury. Thirty seconds. The Hawks got possession of the puck and lost it again. My hands tightened into white fists. Eddie was saying something.

"What?"

"The jeweler called. Your watch will be ready Friday."

"The jeweler?" I stammered, confused. He was trying to trick me. The Hawks had gained possession and were surging toward us. "Your watch'll be ready on Friday."

Our eyes met. A triumphant grin tugged at one corner of his mouth. "God damn you," I muttered.

Al Secord found Olczyk open and gave him the puck. Olczyk had the opening, a little left of center, and I yelled even as he shot, for I knew he'd score.

The puck slammed into the net—goal!—and bounced out again. The players, still scuffling, sent it flying over the net, over the Plexiglas and straight at me. I dove for the ground, then heard the puck connect and Eddie cry out.

He was arched up over his seat, his hands covering his right eye. Blood ran through his fingers. A couple of college jocks held him by the shoulders and another ran for a medic. The crowd surged up around us like iron filings to a bar magnet. We got him down in his seat and tilted his head back.

"It's okay, Ed, it's okay, we got a doctor coming." His howl crumbled into a stuttering moan, like that of a crabbed baby fighting for breath. He clamped a bloody hand over mine. The players of both teams swarmed up against the Plexiglas for a look. "Where the fuck are they?" The college kid had only been gone a few seconds, but surely word had spread.

"Here!" A round old woman ripped a pad of pocket tissues from its plastic wrapper and applied it to the eye; a spot of blood spread over the pad, soaking it. The woman was festooned with a dozen Black Hawks buttons, and above her head a green plastic fist signaling "thumbs up!" danced at the end of a coiled antenna.

We commandeered a bunch of coats and wrapped Eddie up so he wouldn't go into shock. "I can't feel my eye," he told me.

"He's on his way, man. Just hold on."

"Think I'm gonna be blind?"

"Of course not." But my own words played back at me again and again: *God damn you*. I gritted my teeth and squeezed Eddie's hand, trying to force the words out of my head. *God damn you*.

Finally the Hawks' medics showed up with a stretcher. "There's an ambulance on the way. Let's get it bandaged." They put a cotton pad over Eddie's eye, wrapped up the top of his head, took his pulse, and sedated him with a hypo. "Are you with him?" asked one of the medics.

"I'm his brother."

"Okay, let's move him," said the other.

"Mister! Mister!" the old woman called after me as they hoisted Eddie up the steps. She held the puck before her. It was grimy with blood. "Take it to him, Mister. He deserves it."

"Thanks." A wave of revulsion rolled over me as I picked up the heavy chunk of rubber. Something told me to get rid of it, some weird jinx that made my skin crawl. I sure as hell wouldn't give it to Eddie. If you had a bullet pierce your brain you wouldn't want it handed to you like a Kewpie doll.

They took him to Rush Presbyterian. I wasn't allowed in the emergency room, so I sat out in the waiting room in a molded chair of pebbled orange plastic, pushing hard against the floor with my legs to see if I could snap the back off it. After about an hour a Dr. Desmond approached me, rubbing his pinched, red face. Eddie was in stable condition and they had him under heavy sedation. A specialist, Dr. Mellon, would operate on the eye tomorrow morning. I couldn't get a straight answer whether he would keep the eye or not. Desmond agreed to let me sit up with Eddie, although he would be out cold until after the surgery.

Eddie shared a room with a skeletal old man who had lost a leg to cancer and spent much of the night shifting unevenly in a restless, murmuring delirium. The room was dimly illuminated and smelled of antiseptic. They had bandaged both his eyes, the whole top of his head, in fact. An IV needle trailed down from his forearm, which was taped to a board with thin white tape. I heard a nurse pad by occasionally, and the hostile, heavy step of a doctor. The chair at Eddie's bedside was upholstered, and I curled into it, drifting in and out of sleep.

Dawn was beginning to take shape when I heard his voice. "Tom!"

"Hey, how you doing?" I asked, standing over him.

"Tom, I'm falling. I'm falling."

"No you're not. You're not falling."

"Help me." His hands shot out and touched me, then he sank back into bed. I settled his hands and held onto the taped one. "Am I blind?"

"They're going to operate. A specialist is coming in to work on you. Everything's gonna be fine."

"I can't see you, Tom."

"It's only a bandage."

"I can't see you." His free hand found my arm and climbed up it. He touched my face. The man on the other side of the curtain began to stir.

"When's the surgery?"

"Not for a while. It's about five right now. You should sleep. Do you want another shot?"

"No. No shots. I'm scared. What if this is it? What if I just sink down and don't come back?"

"Just go to sleep. You'll come out on the other side of this. You of all people."

"Oh yeah, Mr. Lucky. You're the guy who won all the money tonight. How much did you rake in?"

"Eddie..."

"How *much*?"

I turned away from him, bracing myself against the IV stand. Across the room the old man thrashed around feebly. "You never kept that promise," he muttered, his voice thin, "You never never never never..."

Light had begun to seep through the venetian blinds. I saw the puck approaching, and a chill swept through me; I wanted to dive out of the way as I had then, and leave it to blow Eddie's eyeball open. I closed my eyes, blacking out the horizontal lines of light. The train was flying toward me, along the same path. No, it was *right* to run, I would run from the train if it jumped off the track after me, I would run for the rest of my life and outrace the odds, but only if I could drag him after me. *Wrong train, you idiot. We're going downtown.*

"Eddie?" I said. But he had fallen asleep.

The surgery was scheduled for 10:30 a.m. Even by a conservative estimate Eddie would be in for an hour and unconscious for quite a while after that, so I took a cab home, showered, changed, and got on the train to go back. Staring out the window, I wondered how so much havoc could be wreaked in twenty-four hours. *I could do a backflip out this window right now, and if it wasn't meant to be, the earth would rotate backwards and the lake would catch me.*

Then I saw him, in the next car. Seated before his eager students like a teacher of old, cheerful in the knowledge of his control, bottle caps moving like the gears of a fine watch as the world sleeps. I walked to the end of the car and climbed out the door onto the coupler, the wind a long metallic shriek as we flew down the subway tunnel at top speed. I wrestled open the door of the car and entered, closing the maelstrom out behind me.

"Watch de ball watch de ball whey is it? Watch de ball. If you don't know what to do, I got money in my shoe. My name is Sylvester, I'm the world's best eye-tester."

"I thought your name was Matt."

He recognized me at a glance, kept the shells moving. "I'm Dr. Sylvester, I'm the world's best eye-tester. You can trust you eye or you can trust you luck, but you eye ain't worth a fuck."

"Here." The puck was still in my pocket. "I'll bet you this." He looked at the puck, studied the NHL seal as I held it up in front of his face. "A hundred bucks. Got it at the Hawks-Islanders game last night. Game-winning puck."

"All right, m'man, a hundred. I know a man who likes a good bet. Find the ball you win a C, lose the ball the puck comes home with me. Watch de ball watch de ball watch de ball whey is it?"

He moved his hands away from the caps. I closed my eyes and let my hand fall on one of them. He turned it over, empty, and stared deep into my eyes, trying to burrow into my soul and claim it.

The signs for my stop began flying past. I tossed him the puck. He caught it and studied its brown crust of dried blood. "Hey, what's this shit, man?"

"Blood. It hit my brother in the eye. Blinded him."

"I don't want none of this evil shit, man."

The doors flew open. "You gone and done it, pal, you already won it." I walked out and headed for the stairs. The doors closed and the train pulled away. As its tail passed I turned to watch it go and found myself before a shelter. I hit the ON button and stood under the meager warmth of the heat lamp. Eddie would be coming around soon. What would I say to him? I stared into a sky as flat and gray as pressed tin. The train plowed around the corner and was gone.

Won't Nobody Ever Love You Like Your Daddy Does

by Nanci Kincaid

I

Tammy's mother, Norma June, was a good-looking woman. Everything she did was like a good-looking woman, smile, laugh, tease with her teeth in a way that can't be explained. Smoke the friendliest cigarettes anybody ever saw, when she wanted to. And fix up. Serious fix up, with a drawer full of Merle Norman creams, lipsticks, eyelash curlers, and powder she patted every place there was.

The women in the neighborhood could not decide what it was about Norma June that nudged her across the line to the good-looking side. Suzanne, her best friend, said it was her hair. She had good hair. Dark brown with shine to it and natural curl and a Falstaff beer rinse once a week. Some of the women said it was her eyes, green like they were, with eyelashes like lips. Eyes that sort of puckered up and kissed out at things. She had good skin too, and talked about Merle Norman like it was a relationship.

"Merle Norman has done wonders for me," Norma June said. "I swear by him, I do. Wouldn't be the woman I am without him." Of course, Norma June thought Merle Norman was a man, since she never heard of any woman named Merle. Besides, as far as Norma June was concerned that's what men were for— to make a woman feel beautiful.

Norma June was married to Barton, who was big. A photo of him in his army suit sat on a table in the living room. It was the way he looked when she married him—big, and soft faced. Now he was just big. Filled up whole doorways being big. And Norma June had sense enough to know some things when she married Barton, like it would take a big man to be married to a good-looking woman like her.

Every Friday and Saturday night Barton took Norma June out someplace. He'd been doing it since before they even got married, taking her out to show her off. Sometimes they got a colored woman to come stay with their kids, Tammy and Tony. But as the kids got older more and more they just let the TV babysit. That and their big yellow dog, Sunset, who Norma June had named.

On Friday and Saturday nights Norma June locked herself in the bathroom and communed with Merle Norman while Barton made Tammy and Tony some mayonnaise and banana sandwiches. Sometimes he made hamburgers, or fish sticks. Got the kids some supper and glasses of milk in greasy tupperware cups and then got himself dressed to go, and sat on the sofa in front of the TV where Tammy and Tony were sprawled out on the floor, and Sunset was too. Sunset with that tail scraping back and forth on the hardwood floor, back and forth, back and forth, like one of those things that hangs down inside a clock and ticks back and forth.

When Norma June was finally ready she unlocked the bathroom door and entered the room like a vision. Norma June liked to wear black. She said it was her best color—black—and had lots of dresses she proved it in on Friday and Saturday nights. She waltzed into the room and made Barton smile as she turned around slowly in her beaded cocktail dress and little black patent slippers. Norma June twirled right up in front of the TV so everybody in the room had to notice. Tony said, "You look pretty, Mama." And Tammy said, "You sure do. Will you save me that dress till I grow up, Mama?"

"I sure will, Sugar Cube," Norma June said. "When you grow up then you and your Mama will share this dress, alright?" And Tammy reached out to hug her Mama, trying hard not to smudge her powder or smash her hair. Norma June blew a little kiss on her fingers and tapped it on Tammy's cheek. "There you go, little Sugar," she said.

Once Norma June was dressed to go it was not unusual for Barton to sit another half hour, him and the kids, while his wife went next door to the neighbor's houses, just two or three of them, to show how good she was looking since people were always interested in that. Her friends were, the ladies in the neighborhood.

Norma June tapped on the back door and tiptoed into the kitchen. "Yahoooo," she sang out, casual, like some woman coming by to borrow a cup of cornmeal. "Yahoooo, Suzanne, you home? It's me, Norma June. Wanted to show you my dress." And Suzanne barrelled out from the back of the house in her pedal pushers and her husband's shirt she was using for a maternity top and her flapping house shoes.

"Norma June Hartell. Let me look at you." And Norma June started twirling again. "Good gracious," Suzanne said, "if Cinderella went around in black dresses she could be you. Come in here, Jack," she yelled to her husband who was already on his way into the kitchen. "Come get a look at Norma June." Jack came in with his glasses on and a newspaper in his hand. He looked at Norma June still twirling around the kitchen, and nodded his head up and down.

"Doesn't she look pretty?" Suzanne said.

Jack just kept nodding. Then one of the babies started crying and Suzanne hurried to the back of the house, leaving Jack to see Norma June out. Norma June tiptoed out the kitchen door, smiling, and tossing her beer-flavored hair in Jack's face as he stood holding the screen door open for her. "Wish me a good time," she said.

"Have a good time."

"Oh, you know I will." Norma June started out across the yard. "Tell Suzanne

I'll call her tomorrow and tell her everything." Jack nodded some more, and watched Norma June make her way to the next house where LuAnn and Blakney Steadman lived.

And when Norma June finally went back home to Barton, heavily dosed with admiration, she smiled and was almost mushy over him. She gave him little kisses and smoothed his hair with her hands, and straightened his tie that didn't need straightening.

When Barton and Norma June said goodnight to Tammy and Tony, Norma June patted Sunset, saying, "Be a good dog, Sunset, and look after the kids." And Barton bent over and whispered something in Tony's ear that made him smile and nod yes, then Barton said to Tammy, "Come here and give your daddy a kiss, little girl." And Tammy put her arms around Barton's neck and gave him a loud kiss you could hear. "That's a good girl." Barton said. "Your daddy loves you, baby." Then Barton and Norma June got in the car and drove off to the American Legion Hall or the Elk's Club or any place that had some music and liquor, and low lights or bright lights—either one. Any place where the people had sense enough to appreciate a good-looking woman.

Sometime after midnight Barton and Norma June came back home just a little bit drunk, or maybe more than just a little bit. Norma June took off her high heels and tried to tiptoe through the living room and back to the bathroom in her stocking feet so as not to wake up little Tammy and Tony who were sprawled out on the floor still in front of a jabbering TV with every light in the house on. The two of them, with the spread off Tammy's bed pulled over them, asleep on the hardwood floor, and Sunset there with them, her back-and-forth tail going. Norma June stepped lightly over the children, careful, in her unsteady, giddy, I-could-have-danced-all-night condition.

And Barton came in, stumbling behind her, with his shoes like those a big man wears. Shoes that sort of shake a floor. He reached down and scooped up the children, one in each arm with the bedspread drapped between them half on and half off. He carried them both back to their beds, flopped them down so gently they never even woke up, and he arranged their arms and legs some way that looked comfortable and pulled a sheet over them, and pulled the hair back out of Tammy's eyes. He did this with his whiskey breath and loud shoes. Aimed to place a wet kiss on each of their small faces, but was off target and kissed their hair, or an ear. Then Barton turned off the lights and went to bed himself, and waited on Norma June to take her makeup off and put her cream on. He always waited as long as he could.

II

When Tammy was almost twelve and Tony was nine, Barton lost his job at the meat-packing plant, but got another one within two weeks, traveling for Golden Flake Potato Chips. Had his own territory. They paid him by the mile, too. But it meant being gone most of the week, just coming home weekends, or sometimes being gone most of a weekend, too. But Barton made up for that. Made good money. Brought presents home from time to time. And in the summer when he could he took Tony with him on the road. A man and his boy doing a job for Golden Flake Potato Chips.

"Tammy," Barton would say when he left, "you take care of your Mama now. Hear me. And me and Tony will bring you something. What you want? A 45 record?"

"Doesn't matter," Tammy said.

"Look after your Mama now. Help her when you can."

When Norma June lost her Friday and Saturday nights to the potato chip company she took it all right. Better than anyone expected. Because, good-looking woman that she was, she had friends. She had Suzanne and Jack next door, her best friends since the day they moved in. Suzanne that she whispered with at the line, hanging clothes, that she loaned a dress to every New Year's Eve until Suzanne gained all those extra pounds and couldn't fit into anything. And when Suzanne miscarried her second baby it was Norma June that lay down in the bed beside her and patted her back until she finally fell off to sleep. Patted her back like a soft little heartbeat—and it helped some.

And Jack was a friend too, a quiet one, that didn't say much, but did not complain when Norma June gave Suzanne ammonia permanents in the kitchen which took four hours altogether and left supper so uncooked that Jack finally took the kids to Tastee Freeze for chili dogs. It was Jack that came up to Norma June's with a flashlight that time she heard funny noises at three o'clock in the morning and Barton was off in Moultrie. And it was Jack that went on and cut the grass for Norma June when her yard got to looking like a neighborhood embarrassment with Barton gone too much to keep it right. Jack would just go on and cut both yards as long as he was cutting.

Sometimes that first summer, when Barton and Tony were out on the road, Norma June got sort of dressed up and took Tammy out to a restaurant for supper. They would go someplace that had good fried fish and served half-price liquor to unescorted ladies. More than once they had got their whole dinner free. Good-looking Norma June and her daughter, Tammy, who wasn't but twelve but already showed signs of promise. Had those kissing eyes like her Mama. Soon as she was old enough to put some mascara on those eyes there wouldn't be no stopping the girl. People said that sometimes.

Once a man at the bar had walked right over to their table and picked up the check out from under a water glass, and when Norma June protested, he said, "Now, honey, don't argue. You and your sister here enjoy your supper. Y'all sure helped me enjoy mine."

And so Friday and Saturday nights kept on for Norma June, with or without Barton. From time to time when Barton came home, pulled up in the driveway like company coming, he'd get out with presents. Something foolish and useless for the kids that they always liked. Maybe nothing but some stalks of sugarcane to rot their teeth and make them sick. Maybe a record for the hi-fi, Purple People Eater or something. Once some coconuts with seashell feet, and crazy faces carved out and painted, and big earrings in each ear. But he brought Norma June presents in wrapped-up boxes, and she never unwrapped them so Tammy and Tony could see. She just took those presents and kissed Barton's face. Him eyeing her like he never saw her before in his life, his own wife, eyeing her while she goes to the back of the house and closes the door to open her presents.

"What you and your mama been up to?" Barton asked.

"Nothing," Tammy always said.

"Well, good," he said, grabbing Tammy up and swinging her around in the air, same as he did when she was six, same as he'd probably do when she was twenty-six. "Your daddy is glad to be home," he said. "Ain't no place like home. Ain't that right, Tony?"

"Naw," Tony said. "There's too many girls in this house when you're gone, Daddy. They run me crazy. I wish I could keep on going with you."

"You got to look after your mama and sister some," Barton said. "Women need a man to look after them, keep 'em out of trouble. That's your job when I'm gone."

"Tammy ain't no woman," Tony said.

"Well, she's gon' be. Soon as me and you blink our eyes a few more times your sister is gon' be a grown woman. Gon' be as pretty as her mama, and worry me to death like your mama did her daddy. 'Cause Tammy is just like your mama. Gets more that way by the minute. You can see that can't you, son?"

"No," Tony said.

Barton smiled at his daughter—the same smile he gave Norma June sometimes—so Tammy recognized it, and knew to go to the refrigerator and get the man a cold beer when he smiled at her like that.

III

When Tammy was almost fourteen she started babysitting Jack and Suzanne's kids after school since Suzanne took a job at the hospital working the three-to-eleven shift. Tammy watched the kids until Jack came home, usually around seven, sometimes later. She got the kids their dinner, and Jack too. Sometimes he came home looking so tired and worn out that Tammy just stayed on and gave the kids their baths, got them into pajamas, and read them off to sleep. She was glad to do it.

Sometimes Jack sat at the kitchen table and smoked cigarettes and listened to Tammy read out loud. Other times he got a beer and went and sat in the living room with the newspaper, or watched TV until Tammy went in and said, "Jack, will you turn that thing down some. Your kids never will get to sleep with that thing blaring." She said that to a grown man and her not fourteen yet. And she liked it how Jack mumbled, "Sorry," and went over and turned the TV down. Sometimes turned it off. And put on the hi-fi, played Johnny Mathis or something nice like that that kids could go to sleep to.

And in her head Tammy started this game. It was about Jack and the kids. She played like it was her house, the kids were her kids, and Jack was her husband. Played it every day after school while she babysat. And when Jack came in from work she had him a place set, and some supper ready. Tomato soup maybe. Or tuna fish. And she kept things picked up, and mothered Jack's children like they were hers, because in the game they were.

When the kids got to sleep she straightened the kitchen and put the dishes away. Jack smoked cigarettes and sometimes took off his glasses. Tammy emptied his ashtray and talked to him as sweet as she could because she was practicing up for how it would be when things came true and she really did have her own house and kids and husband. Maybe a husband sort of like Jack, but probably not. Jack was sort of handsome, had hair so black it was almost blue (Suzanne always said he was part crow—the bird, not the Indian), and with his glasses off he had such nice eyes that Tammy could hardly look at him without being embarrassed. But he always seemed quiet and serious, like he was worried.

Sometimes she felt sorry for his kids. Half the time he forgot to pick up his little girls and swing them around when he came home from work. More than once Tammy had had to remind him to kiss them goodnight—until she had just started bringing them in to him, the girls fresh out of the tub with their curly wet hair and Cinderella shorty pajamas, and Jackie, the baby, in his diaper with a bottle hanging from between his teeth and mismatched socks on his feet. She carried them in to Jack and sat them on his lap—all four of them—every night, so he could love them and wrestle with them a few minutes and throw them up in the air and catch them. But it never happened just that way, mostly he sat quietly while the children swarmed over him, giggling, fussing, like so many pink puppies. Jackie always yanking at Jack's glasses, sometimes pulling them off. And when Jack said, in a too-loud voice, "Bedtime," then Tammy marched the children to their bedrooms and tucked them in, while Jack reached for a Kleenex tissue and began to clean his glasses.

So even though Jack was a good practice husband—fine for the make-believe life she was trying out every afternoon after school—she thought that when the time actually came she would probably marry somebody more like Barton, big like that, and real nice. A man who would lie on his back on the floor, put his big feet on the soft bellies of her children, and fly them up in the air making airplane noises. A husband who brought secret wrapped up presents and called her "Babydoll," like her Daddy did her Mama.

One night when the kids were asleep and the dishes washed and put up,

Tammy was getting ready to walk across the yard home, when Jack said to her, "Tammy, you know how to dance?"

"A little bit," she said. "I can fast dance good. You want me to show you how to fast dance?"

"Naw," Jack said. "Fast dancing is for kids. I just felt like dancing, slow dancing, thought maybe you knew how."

"Sort of," she said.

"Come over here and I'll show you."

And she did. And he did. Taught her to slow dance like Arthur Murray would. Official like that. And as the nights passed they might dance some. Wait till the kids were asleep good and dance and laugh a little bit. Tammy even tried to show Jack the fast dances she knew. He watched her with interest, tried it himself just barely, just enough to amuse Tammy and make her giggle. Tammy thought it got to be the best part of the night.

The first night they danced with the lights off it was because Jack said it was more relaxing that way. They danced at least five slow songs. Jack held her so close she thought it was like they were a couple of candles—like the music lit their heads, and was melting them together. It was the nicest smell. She closed her eyes because there was nothing to look at. And Jack brushed the hair away from her face sometimes, and kissed her neck. And whispered her name with his lips that were a little bit wet against her ear. Tammy thought this meant he loved her.

But Norma June didn't like it. Tammy coming home at ten or eleven o'clock every night, not getting her homework done, not helping around her own house anymore. Norma June said it would not do, and she put an end to it. Wanted Tammy to come home the minute Jack walked into the house. She said Jack was a grown man and could look after himself. Tammy could not protest much because she was too embarrassed to explain about the game.

And Norma June watched to see too, watched for Jack's car in the carport, and as soon as she saw it she would stand on the porch and wait for Tammy. It made Tammy so nervous. Hurrying like that. Jack knowing she's got to hurry because her mama is standing there, waiting, for the world to see, with her hands on her hips. And sometimes Jack gave Tammy a friendly swat on the bottom real easy, as she was hurrying out the door. Swatted her that playful way and called her "Mama's girl."

When school finally let out for that year Tammy quit babysitting because Suzanne hired a colored lady to come and keep the kids and cook supper. And because it was summer again, then Tony went off with Barton every chance he got, going places on business and staying in motels. Barton still saying to Tammy everytime he left, "Look after your Mama, now."

It was mid-July when Suzanne went to visit her people in Louisiana. Took all the kids with her. Jack couldn't get off work to go, said just the peace and quiet of them being gone would be vacation enough for him, and he grinned saying it. His car left the driveway about eight o'clock every morning, came back around seven just like always. A couple of times Tammy saw him go inside carrying a sack from the barbecue place, for his supper, she guessed. Probably gon' sit over in that house and eat his barbecue with the relaxing lights off and the hi-fi going. Tammy could picture it.

Norma June missed Suzanne, but LuAnn and Blakney were good about inviting her to do this and that thing with them, play some cards, drive down to Madison and bet the dogs, fry some fish in the yard. One night they invited her to go see some kind of Rock Hudson–Doris Day double feature at the drive-in and she wanted to go in the worst way. She wanted Tammy to call up a friend and spend the night out, so she would not have to worry about her at home all alone. But Tammy didn't want to call anybody. She liked being alone, having the whole house to herself. She promised to lock the doors. So Norma June finally said okay, and then went in the bathroom and spent one full hour, maybe longer, getting ready, rattling things in her Merle Norman drawer, singing to herself the whole time.

"Sugar Cube, you be good," Norma June said as she left. "Keep the door locked and go to sleep when you want to. I'll let myself in with the key." And she left to walk down to LuAnn's. She looked mighty good to be going off to sit in a dark parked car where nobody would even see her, but that was Norma June's way.

It was hot July when every minute seems like it is leading up to something. When everything you do is wet. It is too hot to sleep. The window fan moans twenty-four hours a day. Tammy watched some TV. Two different boys called her on the phone, but she didn't talk long because it was too hot and she didn't like the boys much anyway. She ate almost a whole bag of Golden Flake Potato Chips, but it didn't help that July feeling.

Around ten o'clock Tammy took a bath. Sat in the tub of water to cool off. Shaved her legs. Got out and put lotion all over and baby powder on top of that. Then just for something to do—she got into Norma June's Merle Norman drawer, got out all the tubes and compacts and polishes and put them on to see who she could turn into. Put on mascara and blue stuff on her eyelids. Did all the magic things to her own face that she had been watching her Mama do for years and years. Was almost good at it, and she liked what she saw when she was done. Liked the way those little tubes of lipstick and pink lotions and powders gave her five more years than she'd really earned, five years she could wash away when she wanted to. Tammy brushed her hair, pinned up one side of it with a hair clip and let the other side hang loose and free. She felt good. As she was admiring her face, talking to herself in the mirror, the phone rang. She blew a kiss at her reflection and went to answer it.

"How's the sweetest girl this side of New Orleans?"

"I'm fine, Daddy."

"You ain't just fine, little girl, you're as fine as fine can be, you know that, don't you? And I'm still your best boy, ain't I?"

Tammy recognized all the energy Barton put into his talking, it was how he did when he was half-drunk. Talk loud, like he was singing.

"You miss me?"

"Yes."

"Where's your mama? Put your mama on the phone."

"She's not here."

"Shit." Barton said. "Where is she?"

"Don't say shit, Daddy. She's gone to the show. Her and LuAnn and Blakney."

"I'll be dog," he said. "Here I am a lonely man calling his wife and she's gone off to the picture show. I'll be dog."

"What are you doing, Daddy?"

"Thinking about your mama's ass."

"Daddy," Tammy said, "don't talk like that. Don't say ass. Me and Mama don't like it when you talk like that. Mama says it isn't you talking, it's Jim Beam."

"Well, she ought to know. Do you miss me, Baby?"

"Yes, Daddy. I already told you yes."

"You always gon' be your daddy's girl, ain't you? Won't nobody ever love you like your daddy does."

"I know. I'll tell Mama you called."

"You do that, little Babydoll."

"I'm not gon' tell her what you said though."

Barton laughed.

Tammy hung up the phone. Her daddy got that way every once in a while. Sort of nasty drunk. Sort of lonely for Norma June and he called late at night, woke up the whole house, saying he just wanted to hear Norma June's voice. Sometimes she acted glad he called. She acted sweet over it. But sometimes she got mad, said she just as soon sleep as talk to Mr. Jim Beam himself. Sometimes she got on the phone and fussed, said why in this world didn't he use the good sense God gave him?

But Tammy didn't think of all that now. She looked at herself in the mirror again. If she ever wanted to she could be one pretty girl, she knew it was the truth. Might be as pretty as her mama. She got bold and went into Norma June's bedroom closet and tried on her best dresses. Some of those black dresses, none of which fit exactly, but some came close. One looked as good as Tammy thought a dress could ever look on her. She zipped it up and pulled the belt as tight as it would go. She twirled. She looked in the mirror from a hundred different angles. Smiling. Tossing her head. She sat in a chair and looked in the mirror. Crossed and uncrossed her legs. Then she lay on the bed and posed like all the glamour women she had ever seen in magazines. She was practically in love with herself over her good looks. Merle Norman magic. It seemed terrible to waste looking this good. Someone needed to see her to make it true.

Jack's car was in the carport, the porch light was on, and maybe one light in the living room. He might still be up. It was only eleven-thirty. Tammy would twirl herself down to Jack's house. Go to the kitchen door and knock. He would open the door with a cigarette in his mouth. He would stare at her in disbelief—he would have to put his glasses on—"Tammy?" he would say. "Is that you?"

But what would she say to him? She needed to think of something to say before she went. She did not want to have to think on her feet, not in Norma June's high-heeled shoes.

"Jack," she would say, "I came to dance one slow dance. Mama is off at the show. So we can dance one slow dance." Tammy decided the lights would probably be off already, the music going already, and she would let Jack kiss her neck again if he wanted to. And when he whispered her name the third time, it would be time for her to leave. She had it planned. Third whisper and she would say, "Well, I better go now," and she would run across the yard, fading into the night like a dream. She would vanish like Cinderella and leave Jack standing there in his sockfeet like a stupefied prince. Then she would wash her face, hang up Norma June's dress, and go straight to bed.

When Tammy got almost to Jack's kitchen door she noticed Sunset behind her in the darkness, slow walking. Doing the old age limp. But it was too late to go back and put her in the house. Tammy's shoes tapped across the driveway in what she thought was a too-loud manner, so she began to tiptoe instead.

She heard music before she even got to the door. That much was good. And the house was almost completely dark, just a pale rim of light around the edge of the window. Seemed like Sunset was making a lot of noise in the flower beds, but Tammy managed to be quiet, and to position herself just right to see inside.

Jack was there. She saw his cigarette burning in an ashtray, and his glasses on the table. It was perfect. Everything was perfect. It was just exactly like she imagined, except for one thing, one detail. Her mama, Norma June.

There was Jack, the pretend husband—his shirt unbuttoned, the hair on his chest as black as a fluttering crow's wing—holding Norma June in his arms like all it was was hugging and there was no music at all. And Norma June's hair—it was a mess. Her good hair all loose and tangled. Jack and her mama blurred together, the two of them so tangled, so blended it made Tammy rub her eyes and smear blue stuff up the sides of her face. "Oh God," she thought, feeling as if she had been dropped from an airplane, fast falling through the night air.

If Jack was whispering her mama's name Tammy could not hear it. Her ears rang so loud she couldn't hear anything. Ringing in her ears like if an ambulance drives up to your very own house with the siren going. She was sure she was not screaming. It was just some siren going off. Sunset's tail flapping away, faster and faster, like a hand slapping an invisible face.

Tammy tried to run home, but her feet wouldn't run, they only stumbled—

right out of both high-heeled shoes, left lying somewhere in the yard. She went in the side door and locked it, unpeeling Norma June's dress as she went. She was hurrying the way a person about to vomit hurries. She ran to the bathroom and began to wash her face, makeup smeared everywhere. Black and blue streaks across her face, red smears from her lips to her nose. "Shit," she said. "Shit. Shit. Shit." She kept rubbing, but it seemed like she was just rearranging the mess—not getting it off.

She put soap on a washcloth and rubbed again, her skin pinkened until it was the same color as the lids on the Merle Norman cosmetics she had left sitting out on the counter by the sink. She swung at them suddenly, her washcloth like a whip, and knocked them across the room where they bounced against the tile, crashed into the tub, and rolled across the floor under her feet, making a noise like Tony's little toy trucks. She scrubbed harder, but those extra five years—they did not wash off.

She threw the towel on the floor and went into her mama's bedroom and began rummaging through the bedside table looking for the telephone book and the mimeographed paper that was kept folded inside it, Barton's travel schedule. It was so Norma June could find him if she needed him, in case of an emergency. Tammy found it in the G pages, G for Golden, and unfolded it. July. She thought she might vomit. July 17. Valdosta. Friendly Motor Lodge. It was almost twelve o'clock. Barton would be asleep. It was a long distance call. Practically midnight. Tammy dialed. An irritated clerk put the call through. Tammy's stomach churned.

"What the hell?" Barton's angry voice said.

"Daddy?"

"Who the hell is this?"

"It's me, Daddy."

"Good Lord, what time is it? What's wrong? What's happened?"

"I just wanted to talk to you, Daddy. That's all."

"What's wrong?"

"Nothing."

"Where's your mama?"

Tammy dug her fingernails into her flesh, gripping hard, to stop the falling. "She's gone to the movie, Daddy. I told you that. She's on her way home right now. She's just a couple minutes late."

"You okay?" Barton asked. "You sure you're okay? I swear to God you scared the hell out of me."

"I just miss you, Daddy. That's all."

"You like to give me a heart attack."

"I love you."

"I love you too, Baby. You know that, don't you?"

"Yes, Daddy."

"You go on and get to bed now. I'll be home in a couple of days, and I'll bring you something nice."

Tammy hung up the phone and scratched through the bedside table for a pen and wrote on the back of Barton's travel schedule, "Mama, your husband called you tonight." She left the note sitting on the pillow on Norma June's bed.

It was after midnight now. Outside she could hear Sunset whining. In her hurry to get home Tammy had locked the old dog out because she was too slow in coming, so now she would have to listen to her whimper, scratch at the door, and whine. All night long she would have to listen.

It was not until she lay in her own bed with the door to her room locked that Tammy began to cry. It was her belly. And it was her face. She rubbed her skin and it burned where she touched it. She put her pillow over her head and the cotton pillowcase felt soothing. She kept it that way for a long time hoping the darkness would help. But no matter how dark it got, Tammy could still see.

She was not asleep when Norma June's key rattled the door, unlocking it. She heard the sound of Sunset's toenails scratching across the hardwood floor, and Norma June whispering to the dog, "Shhhhh," as she tiptoed down the hall to her bedroom. Tammy got out of bed and followed her.

She watched Norma June take off her shoes, slinging them across the room. Norma June picked up the note on the pillow. Her lips moved as she read it. She crushed the note until it was the size of a clenched fist and jammed it into the bedside drawer. Then she walked to the dresser looking at herself closely in the mirror, running her fingers around the edges of her eyes.

"So," Tammy said. "How was the movie?"

Startled, Norma June twirled around and looked at Tammy as if she were reading something written in small letters across the girl. "It was fine." She turned away and began undressing.

Tammy watched as her mother unbuttoned her blouse, took it off, and hung it up in the closet. She unhooked her bra and held her arms out in front of her to let it slide off. She undressed gracefully, as though she were performing before a live audience, as though she were saying to the world, "See, this is the beautiful way to take off a bra and fold it and put it in a drawer." Norma June's immodesty infuriated Tammy, the sight and sway of her mother's breasts as she slid a nightgown over her head, the way she slid out of her panties, left them lying on the top of the dresser, picked up a brush and began brushing her tangled hair. All of this as though Tammy were not watching her—but everyone else in the world was.

"I saw you with Jack tonight," Tammy said, her voice slipping out from under her. "You were letting him. . . . " She stopped and closed her eyes. "I saw what you were doing."

Norma June's half-brushed hair, full of electricity, stood out wildly on the side of her head. She was pale. Tammy pictured Jack kissing away all the make-up her mother had carefully applied. It was as though he had licked her clean, eaten off the outer layer of perfect skin.

"You're too young to understand," Norma June said.

"I'm telling Suzanne."

Norma June looked at Tammy with naked eyes.

"Can't you at least say you're sorry?" Tammy demanded.

"I'm not sorry."

Tammy shook her head to keep the words from settling. "I hate you."

"No you don't," Norma June whispered.

"At least I know right from wrong, which is more than you can say."

Norma June laughed, her voice was a saw slicing the night in two, half for Tammy, half for herself. Her jaggedness frightened Tammy, cutting her off, making her drop like a limb from a tall tree, she fell and fell at the sound of it. "Stop laughing," she ordered.

"Oh, God," Norma June said, throwing her head back, running her fingers through her hair, one side electric, the other side knotted. "Listen to me. Try to understand this." She paused and looked at Tammy as though she was searching for something with no hope of finding it. "Jack and I see this line between us, do-not-cross-or-else, okay? We see it. But the line comes to life, Tammy, and circles us, wraps its tail around us. And before you know it we're all tangled up—and the crazy thing is . . . "

"You're crazy."

"When I was fourteen I had good and bad memorized too, but things change places, Tammy. That's what they don't tell you."

"Poor Daddy."

"Damn it, everything is not about your daddy."

"I'm telling him."

"You want to play God?" Norma June said. "Fine." She went to the bedside table, dug out the travel schedule, picked up the telephone, dialed the number and handed Tammy the receiver. "Play God," she ordered. "Tell your daddy everything. Don't leave anything out."

Tammy put the receiver to her ear. It was ringing. "Jack doesn't love you. If you hadn't been there he would have . . . "

"What?" Norma June said. "Danced with you?"

Tammy pressed the receiver hard against her face with both hands. Tears filled her eyes as if someone had said on your mark, get set. She was going to cry like a stupid little girl.

Norma June stepped close and put her arms around Tammy, a melting, not an embrace. A moment of fear passed from Norma June into Tammy, then gave way to dizziness. Tammy was unsure which of them was the mother and which one the daughter—for a moment they were both the same woman standing in different points in time.

Tammy thought of Norma June in Jack's arms, legs entwined, arms wrapping, wrapping, wrapping, the way Jack was kissing her and kissing her. "I thought Jack liked me," she said.

Norma June rocked Tammy back and forth the way she must have done—although Tammy couldn't remember it—when Tammy was a little girl. "My sweet Sugar Cube," she whispered. "Of course he likes you."

Tammy swayed with Norma June, still holding the telephone receiver in her hand.

"Jack would be crazy not to like you. But, Sugar, he's old enough to be your daddy."

"Friendly Motor Lodge," the telephone voice said. "Hello?"

"And a girl doesn't need but one daddy." Norma June took Tammy's face in her hands, wiping the tears with her thumbs.

Tammy pictured Barton asleep in his underpants, his big, white body sprawled across the motel bed.

"Anybody there?" the voice kept saying. "Hello? Hello?"

Stairsteps

by Celia Malone Kingsbury

A DRIENNE WILSON IS 5′4″, but she has always felt shorter. Her mother Maydean Crockmire is 5′6″. When Adrienne was younger and posed for family portraits with her mother and grandmother, Bertie, both women topped Adrienne. Stairsteps. That is what Maydean calls them. Now age has drawn Bertie up like a wool sweater somebody put in the dryer by mistake. In the photographs, Bertie is 5′8″. The three of them have not posed together since Adrienne's wedding twenty-two years ago.

In Maydean's birch-paneled den, Adrienne sits on a brown tweed Hide-a-Bed and looks at old photographs while her mother irons a dress for church. Adrienne does not go to church. Later she will meet Maydean for lunch, and then they will visit Bertie in the retirement home where she lives. Maydean has sold Bertie's house to the bank, and they plan to tear it down for a parking lot. All that remains of Bertie's possessions litters the den floor. When Adrienne lived in the old house with her mother and Bertie and Granddaddy Albert, she hated it. Now the house routinely visits her dreams. Yesterday they drove by to see if demolition had begun, but it hadn't. Early this morning, Adrienne dreamed about the house. As she looks at photographs, she tries to remember the dream and is frustrated that it won't come back.

In the mildewed teak box on her lap, Adrienne finds the snapshot from her grandparents' fiftieth wedding anniversary. She sees herself there and groans. "I look like I'm fifteen in this dress," she says, lifting the picture for Maydean to see. "Look at my knees."

Maydean holds the picture at arm's length and her eyes become wistful as she studies it. "How old were you?" she asks as if she thinks Adrienne was fifteen.

"Twenty-three," Adrienne says. "I'm standing next to Scott. We got married a year before this party." She is almost as tall as Scott, but the way she looks in the photo, Adrienne does not wonder that he failed to take her seriously. Her naturally wavy hair, flattened each morning on the ironing board, falls to her collarbone in a blonde sheet. Her dress, charcoal gray trimmed with orange at the belt and collar, descends barely to mid-thigh where pale orange tights complete the color scheme. Fresh with the optimism of the seventies, her face beams at the camera even though she hates posing. Her mother smiles too, a stiff expression which wrinkles her oversized nose. The nose matches Adrienne's and Bertie's and marks the three women as relatives.

"You'd never know from looking at Daddy that he'd be dead in three months," Maydean says. She blinks to keep tears from falling on her dress and brings the photo closer. "I always thought you'd be taller. You didn't grow any more after you turned fifteen, did you?"

"Only my butt," Adrienne says.

"Reckon you were anemic?" Maydean stares out the high window toward the street. "You never did like vegetables."

"Dr. Murphy stuck my finger every time I went to see him," Adrienne says. "The ends of my fingers are scarred. I doubt that I have any fingerprints."

Maydean shrugs. "We were perfect stairsteps," she says. "Mama never wore heels because she was so tall. I wouldn't have worn them if Walt hadn't been nearly six feet." She hands the picture back to Adrienne.

"I do look fifteen," Adrienne repeats. "But I promise I didn't marry Scott until I was twenty-two."

"I know that," Maydean says. She slaps the iron into the turquoise dress she presses. "How long have you been divorced?"

"Five years."

"I wish you could find somebody," Maydean says. "I know living by yourself gets old."

Adrienne is silent. Part of her mission this weekend is to tell Maydean that she has found someone, an English teacher named Mark, but she does not want to do it now before Maydean goes to church.

"Are you sure you won't go to church with me?" Maydean asks. "I want you to hear my new minister." She pretends to check a spot on the dress, but she is sneaking a peek, Adrienne knows, to see if Adrienne will give in and go with her this morning. "He's a D.D.," she adds.

"Not today," Adrienne says. "I need to have my car loaded so I can leave from the Hewlett House." She points to a black linen dress which hangs from the top of the den's accordion door. "I have to press this dress, too."

"Did you cut that dress off?" Maydean asks, putting down her iron and turning to stare at the garment, one she has seen Adrienne wear before.

"No," Adrienne says. "Why?"

"I didn't remember it being that short," Maydean says. "They're wearing them shorter this year." Frowning, Maydean pats her frosted hair and turns back to her iron. "I'm just glad I don't live in Saudi Arabia," she says. "You know, they have to wear veils over there."

Adrienne drops the anniversary photo back into the box and stands up. "I'll go pack 'til you get through," she says.

While Maydean irons, Adrienne goes to her room to make the bed and pack her suitcase. After they visit Bertie, Adrienne will drive back to Nashville where she runs a catering business. Today is Mother's Day and Adrienne has a straw purse wrapped up in rose paper for Maydean, who likes purses and pastel lingerie, things she can describe to her friends at the courthouse. Maydean serves her last year as tax collector of Richland County this year. She has told Adrienne she is tired of the courthouse and does not want a political fight with the Democratic party, which would like to see a younger person in office. When Maydean became tax collector sixteen ago, she spent an hour every day delivering cards to patients in the county hospital. Each card, engraved with "Compliments of Maydean Crockmire, Your Tax Collector," contained a dollar's worth of dimes tucked into little cardboard circles. Maydean delivered the dimes because, in her opinion, sitting with someone in the hospital demanded change. Adrienne's daddy had spent months in hospitals and Maydean never had a dime to make a phone call with or to buy a Coke or a candy bar. Discreet when she needed to be, Maydean handed the dimes of dying patients to one of the nurses. "I never give dimes to terminal strangers," Maydean had told Adrienne. "I let Miss Markle, the head nurse, do it. She's real sweet that way." The cards finally stopped when phone calls went from a dime to a quarter.

As Adrienne strips her sheets from the cherry Lillian Russell bed she sleeps on, she thinks of the anniversary portrait. When she accidentally stumbles on her copy of the picture, hidden in a drawer, Adrienne shivers slightly, even though it may be the middle of August. The smiling faces of Maydean and Bertie remind her too much of her adolescence. Maydean's worst horror then had been that Adrienne would become pregnant, and Maydean had done everything she could to prevent it. Only during the days of Adrienne's period did Maydean relax. A small bank calendar on her dressing table predicted the opening date of Adrienne's period and Maydean's too. A neat circle pointed out the date, and beside it, a "me" or an "A" determined whose period it was. This calendar rankled Adrienne to the point of speechlessness. She had prayed daily to grow up and assume possession of herself and her bodily functions.

Adrienne deposits a pile of pastel sheets outside the door and smoothes the bedspread over a bright yellow thermal blanket.

Maydean appears with a comb in her hand. "Would you come and see if there are any holes in the back of my hair?" she asks. "I usually sit in the second row. I don't want all those people behind me to think I need help."

Her things packed and loaded into her red Jetta, Adrienne arrives at the restaurant before Maydean gets there. The routine is for Adrienne to get the table so they can beat the church crowd. This morning, Adrienne sits on the enclosed porch of the restaurant, a remodeled Victorian home. The floral wallpaper behind Adrienne swirls in a burst of green and wine and reminds Adrienne of Bertie's house and her dream last night. She still cannot remember what the dream was about. Maydean has not lived in the old house since 1985 when Deek Stovall proposed marriage to her. For that occasion, Maydean bought a new house, but before the ceremony could take place, Deek died when his single engine Cessna ran out of gas over the rock quarry south of the runway. After the funeral, Maydean made no motions to sell and move back in with Bertie.

Next to Adrienne's table sit the Bartletts, a couple who were in Bertie's Sunday school class, and they ask Adrienne about her grandmother's health. Before Bertie lost her wits, she gossiped about the Bartletts because Vergie Bartlett never wore deodorant. In the seventies, when everybody got into gardening and natural foods, Vergie decided aluminum chlorohydrate was poison. After that, according to Bertie, you had to stay upwind of the woman. Today, Adrienne does not notice anything offensive as Vergie leans her pink flowered bodice over her iced tea and waits for Adrienne to answer.

"Not too good, Mrs. Bartlett," Adrienne says. "I haven't seen her since Thanksgiving, but Mama says she barely knows where she is, let alone who put her there."

"Lord, Lord," Vergie says. "I hope I never get like that."

"You and me both," Buck Bartlett adds. "I'm too old to sit through church now. I don't know what I'll do if it gets any worse."

"We just take it one day at a time," Vergie explains as she buries a spoon in a dish of banana pudding beside her plate.

Adrienne shakes an envelope of Sweet-n-Low into her tea, a thing she would never do in her shop, and stirs. In a way, Vergie reminds Adrienne of her grandmother; she has a wide-eyed innocence about her even though she must be eighty.

In her better days, Bertie had been formidable. Adrienne wonders about her as she waits for Maydean, who is now late. Often late for appointments, Maydean is never late for lunch. Has she received an emergency phone call and been pulled from her mahogany pew to attend Bertie? Or does she stand even now on the church steps talking tax business with the county attorney who is also Methodist? Adrienne brushes a crumb from the rose papered box next to her and sips her tea.

In the shower this morning, Adrienne planned the conversation for this lunch meeting. Maydean will be pleased and surprised to hear about Mark; she will also ask a million questions, which Adrienne dreads. Mark is several years younger than Adrienne, nothing new these days, unless you live in Lancaster. If Maydean has read *People* lately, she will be sympathetic. But then, Adrienne reminds herself, she is forty-four and doesn't need permission to move in with someone.

To Maydean's credit, she has kept her peace since the time she tried to make Adrienne come home from Peabody the beginning of her sophomore year. In those days, Peabody sent midterm grades home. Adrienne's report, which arrived in Lancaster on a Wednesday morning, listed a D in Anatomy and Physiology. By six o'clock that evening, Maydean and Bertie had reached the second floor of Peabody's United Daughters of the Confederacy dorm and knocked on Adrienne's door. Adrienne and her roommate Charmette had just opened a can of Swanson's chicken à la king and were about to eat.

"Knock, knock?" Maydean's head appeared beside Charmette's poster of Mick Jagger. "Can we come in?"

"Sure," Adrienne said. "What brings you to Nashville this late in the day?" Puzzled, she got up from her chair at the study table, then sat back down.

"We came to see you," Bertie piped in. "We thought you might be homesick and want to come back to Lancaster. We think little girls ought to get homesick." She hovered in the open doorway grinning. "Y'all don't have any boys hidden in the closet, do you?" she asked.

"Why would I be homesick? I've been gone for a year and a half," Adrienne said.

"You made a D on your anatomy midterm," Maydean said. She straightened the spread on Adrienne's unmade bed and sat down as if she were afraid she might pick up a parasite.

"You didn't need to drive up here to tell me that," Adrienne said. "I know that."

Charmette sat back on her bed and picked distractedly at an ingrown toenail. Beside her the chicken simmered on the hot plate.

"You must be sick," Maydean said. "You wouldn't make a D if you weren't sick."

"I'm fine," Adrienne said. "If I were in pre-med, I'd learn all the bones in the body. I only need a C." She tucked her pink wool bell-bottoms around her ankles and sat on her feet. "Did I tell you I changed my major?"

"We're majoring in sociology now," Charmette offered.

"I thought you always wanted to write for the paper," Maydean said. Her brown eyes rounded with the threat of tears. "I want you to come home and let me take you to see Dr. Murphy."

"If I do that, I'll make D's in everything," Adrienne said.

"You might have mono or something," Maydean said. "Maybe leukemia. They say listlessness is one of the symptoms." She stroked her chin to stop the quivering that had set in there. "Although nobody in our family has ever had cancer. They say it may be hereditary."

"I promise I do not have leukemia," Adrienne said.

"She might have a brain tumor," Charmette said.

Adrienne picked up her fork and threw it point first at Charmette.

"We've all had hemorrhoids," Bertie offered. "That's the only thing I know of that we've all had. I remember when I had mine removed." She clamped her lips together, smearing her dark red lipstick at the corners. "I think I went in on a Wednesday afternoon, and just in case anything bad happened, I played my album from *The Sound of Music* and had a good cry." She smiled.

"Do you want me to flunk out of school?" Adrienne asked as if Bertie had not spoken. "Look at my tongue." She stretched her tongue out as far as it would go and kept talking. "That's a perfectly healthy tongue."

"I hope we don't get what she's got," Bertie said, and backed tentatively toward the hall.

"I don't have anything!" Adrienne screamed. "Do you want me to come home and flunk out?" She leapt up and ran to the foot of the bed where she kept her biggest red suitcase, a graduation gift from Maydean. "I don't care." Mad and on a roll, she yanked the luggage out and flung it open in the middle of the floor. "I'll need underwear." She pulled open a dresser drawer and dumped its entire contents into the open bag.

"Are we a little short-tempered tonight?" Charmette sat up.

Adrienne shoved the drawer back into place and sat on the floor next to the suitcase.

"Bart Ledbetter just came back from U.T.," Maydean said, as if she had just remembered. "He decided to take some courses at Lancaster Junior College." She did not look at Adrienne when she said this.

Adrienne dated Bart Ledbetter until she left for Peabody. Maydean didn't know it, but Adrienne had written him a get lost letter that had pulled no punches.

"I graduated from Lancaster Junior College," Bertie chirped. "Back then it was a girl's school and boys weren't even allowed to walk on the side of the street where the classrooms were." She raised her straight gray eyebrows and eased back into the room. "Let's see, I took Bible, and Arithmetic, and Sewing. I didn't do too well on the sewing. I never will forget, I made this dress of lavender organdy and I put the sleeves in backwards. Mama fixed it, but I never would wear it." She gripped the handle of her black pocketbook.

Maydean gritted her teeth at Bertie. "If you're not too sick to get out, you could take some courses at Lancaster," she said.

"Mother, I am not sick," Adrienne said. She pulled a pair of black lace panties from the heap and snapped the elastic. "Just because I made a D doesn't mean I am sick."

"Where did you get those?" Maydean asked, looking suspiciously at the bikini underwear.

"Cain Sloan," Adrienne said. "Why?"

"I didn't know they had that sort of thing."

Adrienne stood up. "I hate to rush you," she said. "But it'll be after ten by the time you get back to Lancaster."

"I wish you would go with us," Maydean said. Her lower lip sagged. "What if you get too sick to call home?"

"I'll call you, Mrs. Crockmire," Charmette said, rising to hug Maydean. "Don't worry about our girl. We'll keep an eye on her."

"I'll have straight A's by the end of the term," Adrienne said, regretting her words as soon as they left her mouth.

"I hate to leave," Maydean said, jingling her keys.

"I'll walk you to your car," Adrienne said.

"Oh, you can just walk us to the lobby," Maydean said. "I wouldn't want anything to get you."

For years, Adrienne wondered what Maydean said to herself on the way back to Lancaster that night, if she had considered force, or if she had given up, abdicated what she thought was her responsibility. Out the restaurant window, Adrienne sees Maydean with Mabel Parker, who goes to Maydean's church and has known Adrienne since she was little. Maydean's shoulders, in the crepe dress she is wearing, are small and rounded in a way Adrienne has not noticed before. She rises to greet them as they enter the porch.

"Hey, Mabel," she calls, and hugs Mabel, who has become stouter with the years. Adrienne is glad to see Mabel, but her presence will make it difficult to talk about Mark.

"We had two christenings," Maydean explains. "We left as quick as we could. I hope the buffet is still hot."

She deposits her purse next to Adrienne, and as she does, notices the Mother's Day gift in the chair. "You can open it after lunch," Adrienne says. "I meant to give it to you before you went to church, but we got busy looking at pictures."

Maydean smiles and moves toward the buffet line, which lengthens as they stand talking.

"Your mama told me you were here and I just had to come see you," Mabel says as she ushers Adrienne into the line. "What have they got today?"

"They have chess pie," Maydean offers.

Mabel rolls her eyes.

Adrienne's catering business specializes in continental cuisine and American dishes with a southwestern influence. But when she comes to Lancaster, she forgets what she does for a living. That way she can down helpings of fried okra and squash casserole with no remorse. She searches the buffet now and chooses a predictable slice of roast beef with green beans and okra. Counting calories, she skips the pie.

"Didn't you get a dessert?" Maydean asks, as they return to their table.

"I don't need it," Adrienne says.

"I'll go get you one," Maydean says, and scurries away from the table.

"If she brings it, I'll eat it," Adrienne explains to Mabel. "That's why I didn't get it to begin with."

"It's still warm," Maydean says as she places the pie in front of Adrienne and looks at the package.

"You can open that now if you want to," Adrienne says.

"Ooh," Maydean says. "How pretty." She removes the package, sits, and tears the pink paper quietly. "It's like your purse." Excited, she lifts the bag from its box. "I had told her to get me one like it if she found one," Maydean explains to Mabel. "Thank you." Maydean gives Adrienne a one-arm hug and arranges the paper so she can eat her lunch. "I got Mother some bedroom slippers," she says, testing the temperature of her roast beef. "She won't even know it's Mother's Day." Her voice clouds. "She looks normal, but she doesn't have any mind."

"Does she have Alzheimer's?" Mabel asks.

"I don't think so," Maydean says. "They think it's just hardening of the arteries. Her brain doesn't get enough blood." She waves toward the top of her own head to illustrate. "I'm trying to watch what I eat now so I won't get it."

"I'd just as soon be a vegetarian," Mabel says, picking at the fried chicken breast on her plate. "I'd never miss meat."

"From what they say, you might as well be one," Maydean says, popping a fork full of green beans into her mouth. "I'm eating more oranges, too," she goes on. "They say they help prevent hardening of the arteries. And I quit putting cream cheese on my bagels."

"Get the light kind," Adrienne says.

"I did, but it still has . . . I forget how many grams of fat, but it's a lot." Maydean tastes the beef. "This roast beef is not even warm," she says.

They eat in silence, each wondering, Adrienne suspects, if the next bite will be the one full of bacteria—salmonella, or the dreaded ptomaine, which Maydean contracted once from eating ham pulled directly from the bone at a church supper. The catering business has taught Adrienne to be bacteria conscious, but the impulse to sniff everything she puts in her mouth comes from Maydean.

The silence offers the perfect opportunity to mention Mark, but Adrienne freezes for a moment. Her mother will be happy, probably too happy. She takes a big sip of iced tea and leaps.

"Did I tell you I went out with someone last weekend?" she asks. This statement is true; she and Mark went out to dinner and a movie.

Maydean and Mabel put down their forks in unison and stare at Adrienne.

"He teaches at Peabody," Adrienne says. "English."

"How did you meet?" Mabel asks. She does not attempt to hide her curiosity from Adrienne.

"At a wedding I catered," Adrienne says. "He had never eaten prosciutto before. He followed me to the kitchen for more and that was that." The information omitted—that the wedding was in February—will come out later. Now there is no reason to complicate the issue, to make Maydean ask why she has not been told sooner.

"Well," Maydean says. "Is he nice?"

"What does he look like?" Mabel asks.

Adrienne describes Mark, his blonde beard, his perfect naturally curly hair—Adrienne must perm hers now—his fondness for her cats, his age. They are in fact better matched than Adrienne can believe, yet she is not interested in marriage. She does not say this to Maydean, but it is true. Marriage did not improve her relationship with Scott, so she sees no reason to rely on the institution now.

"He's six feet tall," Adrienne adds.

"You've never dated anybody that tall before," Maydean says.

"When will we meet him?" Mabel asks.

"Sometime soon," Adrienne answers. She feels silly now for holding out. Small things please Maydean and Mabel, and Adrienne is not sure why she thinks she is on trial when she offers news.

"Well," Maydean says again, and reaches for her pie.

In that motion, Adrienne thinks Maydean approves. But when she tells Mark, Adrienne will wonder the same way she wonders about the night Maydean and Bertie drove to Nashville. A boyfriend, even a younger boyfriend, makes Adrienne look normal. Maydean and Mabel know about Cher and Linda Evans. The issue is moot. Disappointment tugs at Adrienne. She is glad to avoid confrontation, but she would have liked to produce a small ripple, if not a wave.

"The Lord," Mabel says, pausing with a forkful of pie at her chin. "I forgot to tell you about Dot Jenkin's daughter, Niki."

"What happened?" Maydean asks.

"She sold all her furniture and disappeared for two weeks. Dot found her in Tacoma, Washington, with this guitar player from some band that went through here." Mabel eats her pie while Maydean considers the news.

"What did Dot do?" Maydean asks.

"Nothing," Mabel says. "The girl is twenty-five or twenty-six."

"Reckon she ought to have her committed?" Maydean says. "I mean she might get on drugs and do something to hurt herself."

Adrienne sighs. Even in moments of abandon, she is always careful. She has never passed out drunk and she thinks too much of her furniture to sell it for a man.

"You're not eating your pie," Maydean notices.

"Maybe just a bite," Adrienne says.

While Maydean pays the check, Adrienne walks Mabel to her car.

"What's your friend's name?" Mabel asks.

"Mark," Adrienne says. "Mark Tyler."

"Well, we're anxious to meet him," she says, and kisses Adrienne on the cheek. "It's time you were happy."

"I know," Adrienne says, but she wonders exactly what Mabel means. After living with Scott, she has been happy just to run her business in peace.

Adrienne waves as Maydean goes to her own car, and they drive separately to the retirement home. She wishes she did not have to visit her grandmother now because she knows what she will see will depress her. Scott never understood the dynamic between Adrienne and her mother and grandmother. For years before Walt died, Maydean smoked behind Bertie's back. At night with the fan on in their upstairs apartment, she drew guiltily on Kents and swore Adrienne to secrecy. Adrienne never told, but she suspected Bertie knew. When the two women bickered at the breakfast table, Adrienne always expected Bertie to accuse triumphantly with a pointed finger, "I know you've been smoking up there all these years." Bertie never did. Scott thought she never knew, that she was too flighty to pay that much attention to anything. Adrienne would have bet her furniture that Scott was wrong. Every day Bertie held her peace about the smoking, she gained a little more power over Maydean. She never used the power, but she kept it just in case, an ace in the hole. This kind of subtlety eluded Scott. When Maydean told Bertie that Adrienne was divorcing Scott, she had smiled. "I never liked him anyway," she said. "Good."

Adrienne turns up the drive of the Hewlett House and watches in her rearview mirror for Maydean's car, a large black Chrysler with a red streak down the side. In her turquoise dress, Maydean is still a large woman behind the wheel of this car. Like Adrienne, she drives too fast. As she pulls into a space and gets out, the engine barely quiet, Adrienne smiles. Without Bertie and Maydean, she isn't sure she would really know how tall she is. The stairsteps have always been her yardstick.

"She won't know who you are," Maydean explains as they enter the brand new wing where Bertie's room is. "She knows who Adrienne is, but she won't know you're Adrienne. Does that make sense?"

"Yeah," Adrienne says. She thinks about turning around and running for her car.

"At least she's happy," Maydean says.

They stop at a door and Maydean pushes it open. Inside, Bertie sits on a blue peacock print sofa. Her head dips to her chin in sleep. Maydean touches her shoulder and wakes her. "Happy Mother's Day," she says, and gives Bertie the gift wrapped in lilac flowered paper.

Bertie looks a little frail, but not much different than she did six months ago. "Is it Mother's Day?" she asks, and looks at the gift, puzzled.

"It is," Maydean explains. "And you're my mother. That's for you."

Bertie's eyebrows dart together as she thinks about what Maydean says. "Am I your mother?" she asks.

"I'm Maydean," Maydean says.

"You are?" Bertie is surprised.

"This is Adrienne," Maydean says as she motions for Adrienne to step forward.

"Adrienne?" Bertie smiles. "What's this?" She looks back at the gift in her hand.

"It's from me," Maydean says. "Open it."

Bertie picks at the Scotch tape at the end of the package, then tears the violet paper. The slippers she pulls from the box are blue brocade, and she slips them on, one at a time. "Thank you," she grins.

"Did they comb your hair this morning?" Maydean asks. She stands over her mother and examines her white curls.

"I reckon they did," Bertie says, looking up sheepishly.

"I don't believe they did," Maydean says, and takes a pink-handled lift from her purse. "It's flat in the back where you've slept on it." With the pick, she lifts Bertie's hair away from her scalp. "I know they didn't comb it," she says to Adrienne. "I came over here last Wednesday and she had her dress on backwards." She raises her hands as if to say she knows she is helpless in the matter. "I guess some days they're shorthanded."

The room smells freshly painted and papered, but is hot even though air conditioning spills from a grill beside the window. Adrienne thinks if she does not get out, she will faint or throw up. She sits for a moment on Bertie's bedspread, which matches the sofa, but the rest does not help her. She moves toward what looks like a bathroom door. "Is this the bathroom?" she asks Maydean.

"Yes," Maydean says. "Are you sick?"

"No," Adrienne says. "I think I ate too much." She closes the door behind her. She feels the way she thinks Maydean might have felt if Bertie had ever accused her of smoking. Maydean wouldn't have known what to do next, except maybe quit, and that wouldn't have been any fun.

The fluorescent light in Bertie's bathroom is so bright Adrienne switches it off. On the toilet, the lid down, she closes her eyes and sees the house, gutted now. Clapboard pulled from beneath the upstairs windows litters the flat porch roof. Windowless holes gape. Layers of stripped wallpaper on a back wall shine through the massive cracks. Last night when they went to see it, the house was only dark. Otherwise, nothing had been touched. This stripped-down version must have been her dream. Maybe in the dream she had been in the house and walked from room to room, pulled off a shred of paper herself, or kicked loose a slate tile from the front hall floor. In the kitchen she sees herself open a cabinet door and find a shot glass, plain except for a band of square etching, like faggoting on the hem of a linen pillowcase. She pockets the glass as she leaves.

Adrienne rises, runs cold water, and splashes some on her face. The water dampens her hair and drips from her chin as she reaches for a paper towel. In a moment, she will go out and tell her mother she has to return to Nashville. She and Mark will visit shortly, she will say. She is not sick at all; she has definitely eaten too much buffet and will be fine as soon as her lunch settles. She will say good-bye to Bertie and in all likelihood not visit her again. Somehow visiting her now is like watching somebody sleep without their permission, when they are defenseless; it just doesn't seem fair. Adrienne drops her paper towel in the wastebasket and opens the door.

Maydean senses Adrienne is ready to leave and gets up from the sofa beside Bertie. "It was good to see you," she says, and hugs Adrienne. "I'm excited about your friend. Maybe he'll come home with you next time."

"We'll see," Adrienne says. She pulls back, surprised at how thin Maydean's shoulders feel.

"Is something the matter?" Maydean asks.

"No," Adrienne says. "Still trying to remember that dream about the house."

"Why don't you drive by there," Maydean says. "Maybe if you see the house, you'll remember. Besides, you may never get to see it again."

"That's true," Adrienne says, but she knows she won't drive by.

"What house are y'all talking about?" Bertie asks.

"Just a house we drove by yesterday." Maydean's eyes redden.

"I gotta go," Adrienne says, backing toward the door.

Maydean follows her and stands there as Adrienne walks down the hall.

"Don't drive too fast," Maydean calls.

"I won't," Adrienne says, and steps into the sunny parking lot. She is wearing high heels with her linen dress and as she strides toward her car, she wishes she did not feel so tall.

Hardware Man

by Tim Parrish

I WAS THE highest-paid hardware man in Baton Rouge. Seven bucks an hour. Doesn't sound like squat, but in the Red Stick hardware war I was big gun. Five years I worked at Leenks. "Leenks—Your Hardware Connection." I started there a month after Allied Chemical fired me, two months after my girlfriend of nine years, kind of my second wife, told me to pack. During those first days I snorted coke on the loading dock just to get through but even then I was good. I only sold people what they needed, and I showed them how to use it. No bullshit. Eight people worked there when I started. On December 24, 1989, when we closed the doors on our mulch and bolts for the last time, only me and the owners, Rodney and Patsy Leenk, were left.

We'd planned to have a close-out party, a slow last morning while we helped an Xmas customer or two, but a record arctic front busted half the pipes in town and flooded us with customers, especially dumbasses that didn't know pipe from their own arms. The store was cold as a refrigerator coil, and my daddy, who came into town for the party, had on a thick, brown coat lined with fake sheep's wool and jeans that hung loose like his legs were dowel sticks. Earlier Rodney had walked up to me and said, "Shoplifting time, Bob," meaning I could have anything I really wanted, and every few minutes Daddy checked out some new feature on the Swiss Army knife I'd salvaged for him. Over in the electrical section, I caught him looking through the magnifying glass at colored light bulbs, then in the garden tools department he had the little scissors out clipping his fingernails. That afternoon Daddy and I'd be traveling to Galveston to see my younger brother, Jeb, my first time to see him since Momma's funeral.

It was almost noon, and I had this brunette holding a piece of PVC pipe while I showed her how to wrap tape on the threads, her slender fingers almost touching mine as she nodded and smiled, flirting back, but Patsy and Rodney walked up with these stricken faces that told me this was our last customer, and I wanted to hurry and finish the sale before a wad clogged my throat. I'd just gathered the pipe and tape when the plate glass window at the storefront shattered into a million pieces and a blast slapped me square in the face. Next thing I was in a tunnel, darkness and flashes and footsteps, and then I was running toward where Daddy had been standing. The freezing wind hit me like a cluster of tiny nails, and right when I saw Daddy stand, a second explosion quaked the store so bad fluorescent tubes, cans of spray paint, and rakes fell into the aisles, clattering and exploding like small arms' fire.

"You all right?" Daddy yelled, coming down the aisle towards where I was crouched. I nodded back, embarrassed.

"Exxon must've blown," he said, meaning the refinery about a quarter mile away. "Guess the cold weather messed up the pressure in their pipes. Well, I'll be. Look at that."

In the parking lot, it was snowing black, chunks of insulation floating down from the sky. I glanced around and saw everybody else standing unhurt. "You okay, Daddy?" I asked.

He put his hands up to the sides of his head. "My ears is ringing. That's all."

The five of us crunched over the glass at the front and looked into the distance where fire roiled on the horizon, splotching the cold blue with black smoke.

"Damn that looks bad," Rodney said. Daddy nodded. While I was in Vietnam, Daddy's plant blew an hour before he was supposed to go to work. The brunette looked at me in a way that told me I was pale green. On a normal day I'd have already had her phone number. I excused myself. On the way to the back I tried lighting a cigarette but I couldn't get the match to be still. I wouldn't be walking these aisles anymore. My mother was gone. I didn't know what I'd be doing.

My brother Jeb and I were in the room when Momma died. Her lupus had given her a heart attack, and for two weeks she'd fought a coma, finally slipping in four days before she went. Jeb dabbed her lips with a wet cloth, the thing he'd done every time he was in the room. Earlier she'd moved her mouth like she was trying to suckle, but now she struggled just to breathe while I rubbed her feet with lotion and tried to shut out Jeb's telling her that Daddy had gone to the cafeteria with their relatives. It sounded like Jeb was talking to a child.

When she went she took one last deep breath like she was ready to rest. Jeb and I each held a hand and yelled, "Good-bye, Momma. I love you. I'll miss you," so loud a nurse came. Neither of us cried because we were tired, too. Then the room filled up with her, and it was like she was hugging me all over at once, and I saw red lights dancing outside the window, Momma saying good-bye back. I walked over and watched the lights lift into the sky, pause above my apartment across the street, spread out and disappear.

When I turned around, Jeb was sitting in a chair next to the bed still holding her hand. I told him what I'd seen, and he just gave me that "Right, sure" look he's so good at. We had the thermostat low to offset Momma's fever, and I shivered, everything metal-and-linoleum cold, knowing Jeb was going to sit there and hold her hand until the last bit of warmth left her, as if her body, that thing that had let her down, still had something to do with her. I waited in the hall. When I heard the squeak of gurney wheels, I told Jeb it was time to go.

In the cafeteria Daddy and the others were paying the bill and laughing at some joke, but when we came through the door, Daddy threw his toothpick on the ground. Jeb and I each put an arm around him and walked him out, and in the elevator Jeb told exactly what had happened using that official college-teacher's voice he uses when he acts like he's Daddy's daddy. I watched the floor numbers tick higher and pictured Momma's lights zooming past the moon, weaving through asteroids, skimming the rings of Saturn, and heading towards burning white Alpha Centauri.

After the explosion, Rodney, Daddy, and I boarded up the broken window. When we finished I hugged Rodney and Patsy, and they told me to keep in touch, but we all knew we wouldn't. The store made us a family. Without it we weren't. Rodney and Patsy took off, then I got a broom from the loading dock and started sweeping insulation on the parking lot into black mounds. Daddy opened his car door and turned the news channel up loud. *Out of Romania come estimates of twelve thousand dead,* the report said as Daddy watched fire swell the oily cloud over Exxon. The air stank like gasoline and for some reason I thought of the black Martian gas in *War of the Worlds,* a book Jeb had sent me in Nam.

"You put in applications anywhere yet?" Daddy asked.

"The store just closed, Daddy."

"You known about it for a month."

"I'll get unemployment. I'm going to take some time off. I want to go see Teddy."

Teddy's my son. He lives with his mother, my real ex-wife, and her family outside Soso, Mississippi.

American soldiers are playing heavy metal music hoping to drive General Noriega out of hiding in the Vatician compound.

"Who would've thought all the stuff that's happened this year would've happened," I said.

"Hard to believe what all I seen," Daddy said. "The Depression, World War II, communist thugs getting back what they gave. The world's finally turning."

Automatic weapons fire crackled from a live report. I imagined Teddy in fatigues, standing with an M-16 at some checkpoint. I was glad he was only fifteen. I said, "Thank God I could do my part to stem the Red threat."

Daddy twisted the corner of his mouth.

"Lots of men had to fight in wars, Bob. I fought mine."

"Yours wasn't total bullshit politics."

"Every war's politics."

"Not like mine."

"You mostly worked in a hospital. You could've had it worse." Daddy walked next door in front of the Radio Shack where a thirty-foot inflatable snowman stood. He tugged one of the guy wires, wobbling the promo balloon. I wished I hadn't mentioned Nam. Like everything else, the wars we'd been in was something we couldn't share. I'd never been able to tell him what had gone on with me, and he'd never been willing to tell me what had gone on with him. He told Jeb about being on Midway when the Japanese fleet passed in 1943 and about being in the first fleet to enter Nagasaki after the Bomb, but all he'd ever said to me was, "I was just a SeaBee, trying not to let my hammer get rusty." When I told Jeb I wished Daddy talked to me like he talked to him, Jeb said, "You blame him for your going to Nam, and he blames you for blaming him. What do you expect?"

I started using a piece of cardboard as a dustpan, and Daddy came back to help. *Record cold temperatures again tonight as the Siberian Express continues to travel through the South.* TV pictures the night before had shown cars sliding on slush in New Orleans and palm trees thrashing in snow.

"Interstate over the Atchafalaya might be froze," Daddy said. "I don't remember it being this cold since right after Winona and me come here."

"Ain't it strange how it's all happening this year?" I said. "The Iron Curtain coming down and the cold front and then that explosion today. I bet Momma's getting a kick out of everything being crazy since she's gone."

Daddy stood and worked his knee like a hinge until it popped, then went off toward the dumpster, carrying the platter of black insulation. I rested my chin on the end of the broom. My hands were numb, the tip of my nose gone. A small explosion rolled like artillery. The sirens seemed like they'd never quit.

This was my war: On the flight to Nam, the pilot came on the intercom and told us if we looked out the window to the right we'd see Apollo 13, the moon shot that got crippled in space, parachuting down. We all crowded over to one side, pressing together and sweating, trying to get our faces close to these little windows, but all we saw was sky and sea. Then the pilot comes on again, real sheepish, and tells us he screwed up, we missed it because he was sitting backwards in the navigator's chair and should have told us to look out the left side.

In Nam I was stationed at Chu Lai. I went out on patrols but mostly I was an orderly and put people and parts in bags. When I had five days left, this fire base not far from us got overrun. They choppered the bodies, about two hundred Americans, back to this air-conditioned warehouse and laid them out until me and three other guys could go over and bag them. Cambodia was on, so we were busy and didn't get to the warehouse until afternoon. It was dark in there after being in the sun, and quiet except for the AC's hum, so we stopped inside the door. When we flicked a switch, banks of fluorescent lights blinked a couple of times before buzzing on. And there they were. All two hundred of those dead fuckers, their muscles contracted, sitting up in neat rows, waiting for us. I turned around and walked back to the CO's office.

"I quit," I said.

The ditches next to the interstate were frozen hard as concrete, but the road had thawed. In the median a tractor-trailer rig had crashed, throwing its load of pipes in heaps except for a couple that had jabbed the ground and angled like turrets. The sky shone deep blue. A pale crescent moon ran away from the sun. A daylight moon spooks me because it's something out of place, like the cold weather, like when Halley's Comet drew all the crazies out of hiding and into the store. Jeb thinks I'm full of shit for watching the sky, but what's happening there fucks with people's heads. If the moon can pull the ocean, it can tilt a brain.

"I hear they're opening a new plant down around St. Gabriel," Daddy said.

"Yeah, and they'll be hiring twenty-two-year-olds to be operators."

"You don't know that. You won't get it unless you try."

"I don't want to work in a plant again, Daddy. All those chemicals at Allied made me sick."

"You should've never lost that job. If you'd learn how to keep your mouth closed."

Coming towards us, headlights shimmered from a convoy of green military vehicles. Following the lead jeep were troop trucks, smaller trucks towing artillery, several armored half-tracks, and a medical truck, regular Army stirred up from Fort Polk by Panama.

"Pastor says all this turmoil's the start of the Last Days. 'Revelation,'" Daddy said, watching the last of the convoy. He wiped his nose with a handkerchief. "Maybe you can get on at another hardware?"

"Could we just drop the job talk?" Daddy looked away and tugged at his ear. "Thank you," I said. Soon we reached the elevated interstate between Baton Rouge and Lafayette. Cypress knees jutted from the water, but the water was frozen white as far as we could see. Around the tree trunks, little ice waves looked like bunched-up visqueen. Bright sun glinted off the ice as if it was chrome.

"You ever seen this frozen, Daddy?"

"Never. I can't recall it ever being froze."

A white egret glided over the road, and I saw Daddy watch it as we left it behind.

"Winona would've loved to seen this," Daddy said. "She always wanted to see a real winter. Look at there."

A bateau with two men in it was slowly sawing a path, the boat rising up onto the surface then breaking through. One of the men had on a droopy toboggan cap the color of a roadside cone—a high-visibility Santa.

"You know how hard your mother worked to make last Christmas like the old ones?" Daddy said. "She told me she wouldn't get to see another Christmas." Daddy kept looking out the side window, the bald spot on the back of his head tanned from working in his yard.

"I think it made her happy," I said.

He nodded. "You know," he said, and tapped a knuckle on the window, "we'll probably never see this again."

I tried to get Momma not to do too much her last Christmas, three months before she died, but she wasn't having any of that. She baked pies and made her green-jello, whipped-cream, pecan dish. On Christmas morning, her smile cut through the swollen cortisone skin, her wit sharp in spite of the drugs that sometimes dulled her. After lunch we ate her special dessert, then Daddy and Conlee, Jeb's wife, went for a walk while we sorted through old Christmas photos.

"Look at this one," Teddy said. He held out a photo of Jeb and me wearing jet pilot helmets, large tin cans strapped to our backs, a big football in Jeb's arms. I was about twelve, Jeb three.

"Steve Canyon," I said.

"Did you always carry that ball?" Teddy asked Jeb.

"Until your dad went to Vietnam. I never would've played basketball if the war hadn't started."

Teddy unhooked my tape measure from my belt. Already he had the start of a moustache, but he also had something I hadn't noticed—Jeb's smirk. I took back the tape.

"You always wear that thing, Dad?" Teddy asked.

"Always," I said. "Protects me from jerks at the store. Whenever somebody gives me a hard time, I stretch this tape out in front of their nose," I stretched it, "and say, 'I got this much patience left for you,' then press the button." The tape snapped back in. Teddy laughed, but Jeb shook his head and picked up another photo.

"What?" I asked.

"Nothing," Jeb said.

"No, I know that expression. What is it?"

Jeb nudged his glasses up his nose. "Do you get in some customer's face every day?"

"What do you think?"

"I think you talk a lot about telling people off."

"So?"

"I'm just saying. You asked."

"Y'all cool it," Teddy said. He drilled me with a look, then put on the headphones I'd given him. I got up to let myself get level again, but when I stood Jeb started tapping his thumb on his thigh, the smirk painted on his face.

"You got something else to say?" I asked.

"You don't want to hear it."

"I'm listening."

He glanced at Teddy who was nodding to a beat. "I don't think it's good for Teddy to always hear you talking like you do about work."

"They're funny stories, Jeb."

"No, they're stories about how bad assed you are."

"Of course you could do better at my job."

"I could be more diplomatic."

"When's the last time you worked in the real world?"

"I deal with students every day. I don't push things in their faces."

"Come sell hardware a week before you start preaching."

"You've got a bad attitude, Bob."

"And you know every damn thing about every damn thing, Jeb."

Momma's rasping snore stopped me. She slumped in her recliner, her chin dropped forward near her chest. My eyes met Jeb's, and he looked down.

"Jeb told me a lady astronaut who lives there's gonna be on the next space shuttle," Daddy said, pointing to a large bayfront house. The houses at that end of Jeb's street, especially the ones on the bay side, were fancy, but the closer we got to Jeb's the smaller they got, the houses on his side looking more like nice weekend getaway camps, the kind people had at False River and Old River near Baton Rouge. "If Jeb would've got his degree in chemical engineering, he'd be living next to the bay," Daddy said. "That's his there."

He nodded at the last house on the right, a place on stilts with redwood shingles on the sides. A fat Christmas tree blinked behind sliding glass doors, a single-pointed red star on its peak. In the front yard, a plywood alligator with a glowing Rudolph nose lifted Santa in a pirogue. The lot next to Jeb's was empty, marsh grass standing like broom bristles around an iced-over pond in the lot's center. Jeb greeted us like we'd been having Christmas at his house forever, exactly like I knew he would. He had these tiny round glasses and a cheesey goatee that made him look like Lenin or some other freak. He hugged Daddy, then me.

"Conlee's gone to the store," he said. "Y'all have to put on the snow chains coming over?" he joked.

"Only the swamp's still iced," I said. Daddy was staring across the street at a seawall being built around a house and at the lot next to it filled with huge chunks of concrete. On the side of Jeb's house, a rusty shovel lay on a pile of sand next to a stack of weathered boards. "Nice place," I said.

"The last hurricane washed away everything on that side, but it didn't touch this house," Jeb said. "I got a great deal." He smiled. "It's freezing. Let's go in." He draped his arms over us. "I saw about Exxon on the news. Were you at the store when it blew?"

"Me and Daddy both. Busted the front glass."

Jeb laughed. "The sensational's always chasing you down, isn't it?" he said.

In the living room, with its fireplace and couches, the house seemed bigger than it had outside. Jeb asked if we wanted a beer, and while he was gone, I ran my fingers over the spines of Conlee's law books and Jeb's Vietnam books. Jeb's a chemistry teacher at a small college, but he's a Vietnam buff. For a while he tried to get me to read some novels about it, but I told him living it had been plenty for me. Next to the books was a photo of Momma and Daddy on their wedding day. Momma wore a long-sleeved, forties dress suit that hugged her middle and showed off her tall slimness. At her throat were cauliflower ruffles next to a white corsage. Her blond, wavy hair was parted to the side and lifted from her shoulders. She smiled her slightly buck-toothed smile and held Daddy's hand as the camera caught him speaking, shy but happy in his double-breasted suit. I wished I hadn't come.

"I better get the suitcases," Daddy said, standing in front of the TV watching CNN. Jeb and I told him to sit down.

A gust of wind came from the direction of the bay just as we opened the trunk. Jeb stomped his feet and bent his shoulders. "I can't believe how cold it is," Jeb said. "Last Christmas we were in short sleeves." His face didn't register that mentioning last Christmas made him feel anything. I handed him Daddy's bag.

"Which room am I in?" I said.

Summer before last, Daddy, Jeb and I got in a big yelling fight. Jeb was in town to do some consulting work, and he and Daddy had ganged up on me saying how I needed to get another job and start thinking how I was going to send Teddy to college. What they were saying didn't piss me off as much as the way they said it, talking to me as if I was a little kid, especially Jeb. I told them both to FUCK OFF and blew out of the house, thinking I was going to leave, but I leaned against my truck to smoke a cigarette and relax. Momma came out after me on her walker.

"You shouldn't be walking this far, Momma," I said, but she kept coming, her face set hard in the blue street light in the front yard.

"What do you think you're doing?" she said. She almost never lost her temper, but I could see her shaking from more than the effort of standing.

"I'm tired of them giving me crap," I said.

"I don't care what you're tired of. This is a family time."

"I'm sorry."

"No you're not. None of you are. I told them, too. All y'all care about are yourselves or else it wouldn't happen. Grown men acting like children. I'm sick of it."

"I'm sick of them."

"Shut up."

She wavered. I grabbed her arms.

"Sit on the swing," I said.

I helped her over. The chains creaked from her weight. She kept her eyes on the ground.

"Momma?"

"I don't understand y'all. We get together once or twice a year, and we can't have peace. How long do y'all think I have?"

My legs went rubbery. I sat beside her. The night sky was dark and moonless. The radio tower on the road behind the house threw flashes like lightning, showing one thin cloud, pointed like a finger, creeping over.

"Why can't you get along?" she asked.

"Why can't Daddy treat me like he does Jeb? He's never thought I was worth a shit."

"That's not true."

"Nothing I do makes him happy. I volunteered for the goddamn Army and all he could say when I came back was 'get a haircut.'"

Momma ran one hand across the back of the other, then looked at the dry skin there. I put my arm around her shoulder, but she pushed it off. I laid my hands in my lap. I was sick of getting hurt and of hurting everybody. Every time one of us looked the other in the eye it was some kind of challenge.

"You have so much anger, Bob. I don't know why. What did we do?"

"You didn't do it, Momma."

Momma wiped her hand across her eyes and then across her skirt. She looked at me. Her face was so swollen her cheeks looked like gobs of putty. "Don't you know your daddy loves you?" she said.

She touched my face with her hand, hot with the fever she constantly had. It was the same way she touched me to wake me after I got back from Nam, even though I might hit her. But I never did hit her. Even asleep, I always knew it was her hand.

After dinner Jeb made us some drinks, and we sank into their living room. Daddy sat in an armchair glancing at the soundless TV, while Conlee and Jeb played curly toes with each other on the couch. Jeb asked Daddy to tell about coming out on the deck of his ship their first morning in Nagasaki Bay. Daddy rubbed his lips with his fingers awhile before he started, then stumbled a bit telling how they got in at night and had to stay below deck. Then he pictured it.

"So when we come out on deck we was surprised by it, you know, the whole city tore up as far as we could see. We hadn't seen nothing like that. We really didn't even understand it. This petty officer points way down on the water and there set this little boat with five Japs in it, pointing this old cannon up at us. They wasn't saying anything, and we didn't know how to talk to them, so we all just kept looking at each other, us with our big boat and them with their little gun. After a while they rowed off to another ship and then another, all day, nobody messing with them, and them never shooting. Finally they went back to shore."

Daddy told it funny, but I remembered the other story Daddy had told Jeb about his truck ride through Nagasaki, about people sitting on piles of rubble staring, about the shadows of people where there weren't any people, about buildings that looked like they'd been sheared by a giant sickle. I saw the bodies still floating there a week after the bomb, and worse I saw the Japs' faces in that boat and Daddy's face looking at them, all of them sharing the most terrible thing that had ever happened, but none of them knowing how to speak.

I wanted to shake the feeling, so I started a story of mine about this kook who came in the hardware store during Halley's Comet wanting to know if we had repellium, a metal he could cover his windows with to keep comet radiation out. I didn't get very far, though, because Jeb busted in and said, "This isn't one of those stories that ends with you saying, 'Then I told the son-of-a-bitch . . . ' is it?" Conlee gave him a kick, but he just smiled. Daddy sat there holding his drink with both hands, looking away at people on TV chipping the Berlin Wall while the fire popped and Bing Crosby sang and the room was way too small.

I saw the black snow falling and Exxon's flames boiling up, and I remembered one day this Chinook chopper passing over, a gigantic net slung under it, filled with dead Vietnamese, their arms and legs sticking out like hair on an insect. The chopper went out over the sea and dumped the net and it splashed and sank into the water. I looked at Daddy sitting there in Jeb's living room, and I wanted to yell, "How do you live with what you saw?" But Daddy just sat there, paper-skinned and bony, his eyes looking through the TV.

"I need to walk," I said.

"It's freezing out there," Daddy said, and I knew he'd say to Conlee and Jeb how fucked up I was. I stepped out into the icy air still buttoning my coat. I lit a cigarette on the go, holding the match in both hands, heard Jeb's voice cracking the cold air, his footsteps hammering to catch me. He grabbed my arm, and I wanted to cock him so hard it'd knock the bullshit out of him, but he grabbed me in a way that told me just to wait.

"Mind if I join you?" he asked.

"Do what you want." I pulled my arm away. We headed away from the houses, the night so still and cold it was like walking inside an ice cube.

"I shouldn't have said that," Jeb said. "It was a joke. I didn't mean to come off like such an asshole."

"Right."

"Everything's just so weird."

"No shit."

He looked me in the eye and smoothed the whiskers on his chin like he was trying to make them grow. I doubted I'd even talk to him if he wasn't my brother.

"Down here," he said. "There's an old pier."

We walked the waterfront road between empty lots and lots with construction under way until Jeb led me over big jagged slabs of concrete toward the water.

"This used to be a restaurant," he said. "People who stayed during the storm say a wall of water knocked the building off its foundation, then dragged it back out."

The boards groaned when we sat. We hung our legs over the black water, and I reached under and broke off an icicle the size of a railroad spike. A sliver of moon sat in the sky. Across the bay refinery fires burned, sending a smoky fog out to hug the water.

"Bad luck moon, isn't it?" Jeb said. "Wasn't less-than-half bad news on guard duty?" I didn't talk. I pulled out a roach, not really enough to get stoned. I lit it, and we each took a couple of hits. "Two hurricanes and a major oil spill here in the last four years," Jeb said. "I figure this place is due something good."

When we finished smoking, Jeb's legs were moving back and forth so fast the wood was shaking. "You're freezing, let's go back," I said.

"No, let's stay. I don't feel like being in yet."

We were quiet again a little while. I wanted to feel about my little brother the way I did when we were close, but what I felt instead were screws tightening in my head.

Jeb ripped up a strip of rotten wood. "I've only seen you once since she died. You didn't come see us last time we visited Dad."

"I was busy."

"No you weren't. You were mad at me. What for?"

"You really asking?" I said.

"Yes."

"Cause you act like you're Daddy's daddy. You act like you can make everything all right."

"So? That's better than you. Here you are, a Vietnam vet, still calling our mother 'Momma.' "

Jeb stood and hugged himself. He spat into the water.

"I try to make it easier for Dad," he said. "All I want is to make the hard times go faster."

I stood. "Let's hit it."

He touched my arm. I faced him.

"Come on, Bob, let's talk. Who knows when we'll see each other again?"

"Who knows? Maybe not even next Christmas."

Jeb inhaled slowly and shot the air out through his nose just like when he was a kid. He raised his hands. "All right," he said. "I'm judgmental. I'll try harder. I worry about Dad, though. You too. You're my big brother."

I walked past him, stepped through the concrete and headed toward the houses. He matched my stride, but we didn't speak. Through the fog on the water, I saw a boat's red running lights, heard its horn.

"Give me a cigarette," Jeb said. I lit two and gave him one. He pulled hard and blew the smoke upward the way I'd taught him when he'd asked me how to look tougher as a teenager. He smiled.

"Asshole," I said.

"You know, I get jealous of you and Dad when y'all tell war stories," he said. "Know what I mean?"

"Yeah, you're fucked up."

"No, really."

"You were lucky. You've gotten great rolls," I said.

"I have, but I still envy you. I know it's perverse. Your life is big. Sometimes I feel like my life's been cut and dried."

"You just got some sense. Don't wish you didn't."

Ahead, I saw a hulking Martian ship on legs. I stopped, a fist in my throat, then realized it was a water tank strung with lights. I blew into my hands.

"I still dream about Mother almost every night," Jeb said. "The worst are when she's alive and young and then I wake up and she's not. You dream about her?" I nodded. "Tell me."

I flicked my cigarette away and started walking again.

"I had one where I was at a table with all these people," I said. "I kept hearing this piano music that nobody else was hearing, real pretty music. So finally I got up like I was going to the john and went to the room where it was coming from. It was Momma playing the piano. She winked at me and said, 'This is our secret, okay?' "

"I never told you about my trip home after the funeral," Jeb said. "It was like she was sending all kinds of omens. Like she was saying, 'Look out, things are going to be different.' "

"What kinds of omens?"

"Nothing earth-shattering, it's just that they all happened that night. First, a gas can wedged under our car. Then a dog about the size of a wolf, maybe it was a wolf, darted in our way so that I had to swerve onto the shoulder. And then, this was the one, a blue meteorite fell across the road."

"Really?"

"Really. I'd never even seen a shooting star while I was driving. It was beautiful."

Jeb stopped in front of his house and looked up at the sky, so filled with stars they seemed to be looking at us from just above the houses. I remembered when I was in basic training, Jeb had sent me a picture he drew. He was only ten and he'd crayoned two astronauts, one big and one small, on the moon. On their space suits he'd written our names.

Jeb ground his cigarette on the sole of his shoe, making a tiny shower of sparks. He put his hands in his pockets. "When all that happened to me," he said, "when I saw that meteorite, I thought of you, Bob. I felt like I was you."

"Sure you did."

At the picture window, Daddy smiled and nodded, listening to Conlee. He pointed over us into the darkness.

"I'm serious," Jeb said. "I felt like you."

I shoved him and laughed. "You never felt that good."

The Wunderkind
by Johnny Payne

At one time, I considered myself a passable example of a type that seems to have found its peak of adulation on American soil, though its name is German—*wunderkind*. Reflecting on it now from the vantage point of my nearly thirty years of age, when I can no longer claim to be a *kind* of any kind, I don't regret that season of conceit, nor do I lament its passing. Feeling our potential well up within us like foolish tears, or like a very German keg of lager begging to be tapped, is a satisfaction that doesn't need to find its objectification in any lasting performance in order to gratify fully. What is *promise*, after all, but exactly what it says?—a pledge that finds its definition in the fact of being deferred. I remember watching with astonishment at a summer starlight concert while a child prodigy played a Bach partita with skill and insight far beyond his meager years, thrilling the audience the more as they tried to imagine how exponentially his talent would have improved ten summers from that date.

I had the good fortune to hear this same prodigy six years later at a symphony hall, on the threshold of his adulthood. He had not, as so often happens with musical prodigies, reached a plateau of achievement by then, and, as his eyebrows attested, he actively searched out more complex interpretations of the pieces even as he played them. Yet, in the pauses between symphonic movements, a tinge of sadness could be heard in the rustling programs as his listeners clearly foresaw the competitions he would win, the recording contracts, the long succession of albums he would generate with the world's best orchestras—in other words, not gold to airy thinness beat, but solid gold. The prodigy had surpassed all predictions, and was about to become yet another productive adult. His aficionados mourned his passage even more than if he had died at a tender age.

We're not, as we pretend, a nation of Benjamin Franklins, resolving to perform what we ought, and performing without fail what we resolve. We do function, without question, often with great efficiency, but I can never forget that *function*—the *f* in the mathematical equation $y = f(x)$—is simply the relation that allows us to plot on a graph the exciting and mysterious trajectory of, for example, a *wunderkind*'s life. The mystique of that plotting is the intangible object of the mathematical equation. It is also the intangible object of our affections.

I recall a conference, at which I was present, that took place between my mother and a guidance counselor at one or another of the elementary schools I attended. Without mentioning specific numbers in my presence, the two of them were discussing my scores on an achievement test with a great deal of excitement. I didn't see those scores, nor did I ever dare to inquire about them (no more than I would have asked my parents to furnish a marriage license to prove the legitimacy of their ostensible marriage date), but I saw the effect they had on my mother.

At that time in her own trajectory, she had trouble enough providing money for our weekly lunch tickets. Only infrequently could she attend parent-teacher conferences, as she was summoned to do in cryptic writing (meant to be deciphered by parents only) on the back of my report cards. Her prospects then were as thin as the hair beneath the brunette fall she'd begun to wear. But she'd taken a half day off work and come, wearing a mauve pantsuit she had bought on layaway at Mr. Lajhre's store but never worn, as if saving it for that occasion.

My mother stared at the blue piece of paper containing my scores like someone who, on the eve of eviction, is handed a contract for an interest-free loan, payable at her leisure. Now and again in the past I had overheard her make remarks about my intelligence which she never intentionally let drop within my earshot and took care to couch in cryptograms similar to those on the report card, perhaps afraid of warping my already severely introverted personality even more. But the test scores seemed to put the matter in an entirely new realm, and my presence at the encounter was tolerated, even necessary. They let me know, by circumspect signs, that I was destined to accomplish some great, though unspecified, mental feat. The prospect gratified me, and I was eager to lay my powers at my mother's service. I somehow took it in my head that she was formulating a plan for putting my aptitude to a practical and immediate task, such as hiring me out to Mr. Lajhre to do accounting without the use of paper, or take inventory at his clothing store by merely glancing around the storeroom, as a kind of idiot savant with a vocational bent. I even imagined I might possess psychic powers like those in the Edgar Cayce books on my mother's nightstand, and spent several weeks telepathically commanding our poodle to go to his water bowl (which sometimes worked) and trying to hold seances with my mother's dead brother Byron—a saintlike figure she was compared to unfavorably by her own mother at every Christmas gathering—to see if he could shed some angelic light on his sister's grand design for me. Mostly, though, these pastimes (along with crossword puzzles) were minor mental exercises to sharpen my mind while I waited for my mother to make her intention clear.

But the conference was never spoken of again, at least not until much later when it had acquired the harmless status of an anecdote. If my mother had plans for me, she never intimated them, not even in an indirect fashion. My parents, if anything, were moderate to a fault about inhibiting their children's free choice. In my later forays into academic study (none of them requited with a degree), they seldom inquired about particulars and seemed to have trouble describing to their friends and relations exactly what I was up to. My knowledge of exotic languages, my monograph on shear geometry and my admittedly failed attempt to prove once and for all Fermat's Last Theorem, both published in (largely unread) scholarly reviews while I was still in high school, are all referred to as "the things Stephen likes to do." When I developed a working model of a pentatonic synthesizer for analyzing urine tests via arrays of musical notes, my invention was met with a knowing smile by my family members, who have such an infinite and vague belief in my capabilities that if I discovered heavenly bodies more distant and luminous than quasars, they'd be as unsurprised as they would be proud.

This attitude used to vex me a great deal, and it's only recently that I've begun to understand that for my mother, a wonder-child was not so much a child who performed wonders as a child she could wonder about. On my eighth birthday, the one that included a swimming party at the Castlewood pool, she set aside one particular gift to be unwrapped last. As I tore away the paper, I was keenly aware of her, cross-legged as a devotee of the Buddha, zinc oxide on her perpetually peeling nose, as she watched me through her sunglasses like a lifeguard trying to keep in sight someone too far out in the deep water. The present turned out to be a hardback, *Brains Benton and the Mystery of the Painted Dragon*. The uncracked spine revealed she'd bought the book without even a peek inside at the details of the mystery. Though it revolved around a painted ceramic dragon inscrutable as the Orientals themselves were reputed to be, and which seventh-grade science whiz Brains analyzed in the secret laboratory of his secret clubhouse, the mystery turned out less mysteriously than my mother might have hoped: fake Chinese art, buried in the earth next to the construction site of the new gymnasium to give the painted dragons a patina so they could be sold on the black market as priceless smuggled goods. Brains and I solved the mystery with a makeshift amateur carbon dating kit and plain common sense, but we wisely kept the method of solution between ourselves and the police. When I finished the final chapter, I intuitively gave my mother an inscrutable Oriental look, one that seemed to content her, and said nothing futher about the matter.

But on other occasions, I tried in vain to resist my prescribed role, which, if it were written as a Brains Benton Mystery might be titled *The Curse of the Hyperactive Mind*, a curse made more grotesque and dragonlike by the randomness with which the investigator's mind (and not the criminal's) grasps for objects to vent itself on. My mother's failure either to voice or relinquish her expectations prohibited me either from giving my intellectual aspirations too directed a form, or from abandoning them altogether. In protest, I once let all my curricular and extracurricular activities languish for months except trading and reading thousands of comic books, and the untidy stacks of them, like the dusty, rutted columns of a mausoleum, made my room begin to look like a probable setting for *Tales from Beyond the Crypt*. A little later in life, I took a twenty-three-day hooky hiatus (or rather a hookah hiatus) from junior high, so my friends and I could spend our mornings smoking Jamaican grass out of a bong, and our afternoons smashing the burned-out neon tubes we found in dumpsters; playing chicken with shopping carts; and shooting bottle rockets into oncoming traffic from behind a stone wall.

When I grew weary of these mindless activities, I tried the opposite tack of ordering out of a magazine the entire set of leatherette-bound Harvard Classics, the first volume for forty-nine cents, the second and third on approval, and the rest shipped en masse. If I couldn't make it as a bona fide bonehead, I resolved to map out a specific and efficient program for becoming a Great Mind, a philosopher maybe, by reading Great Books. I calculated that one book per week would provide me with a solid classical education in less than six months. All I remember of that project is that reading Dante's *Inferno* coincided with a series of bedwetting episodes, and that shortly after I received the en masse shipment, I also got a form letter telling me that the company distributing the Harvard Classics was in some sort of legal difficulty, so I could keep the books without further payment. This form letter should have elated me, but my superstitious mind took it as an ill omen that I should discontinue reading the books, that my presumption in knowing too aggressively would, as a form of *hubris* (a word I'd gleaned from *Oedipus the King*), result in fresh calamities for all us Mileses. After that day I only read those particular books haphazardly and in snatches, as a kind of esoteric encyclopedia, fondling the green leatherette and the gold leaf, and began to think of the experience mainly as having gotten a good deal on a complete matching set of something even more durable than the luggage I'd won the previous year selling greeting cards door-to-door for my school.

Sometimes, in one of the fits of sulky self-indulgence I have yet to outgrow, I would silently wish for my parents to compel me to attend a special summer camp—a place I imagined as a kind of selective Alcatraz for the most recalcitrant child-geniuses, where the children's own tyrannical and flamboyant little personalities would be taken firmly in hand, and they would be forced on little sleep and thin rations to play the violin for eight to ten hours a day, solve quadratic equations rejected from college textbooks on the grounds of their excessive difficulty, and draw up blueprints that would make the summer prison even more escape-proof when we inmates returned the following year. Part of this fantasy always involved my purposeful inclusion of a flaw in the blueprint, a means of escape too subtle to be detected as such by any captor not absolutely attuned to the workings of my mind.

I punished on occasion my own family's inattention to my workings by such means as making incomprehensible remarks at the table. After a supper of fried salmon croquettes and rehydrated au gratin potatoes, when we sat together in a rare moment of satiated silence, I would turn to my mother and, in a French rendered perfect by the brevity of my question, I'd ask *Et alors?* with a look of expectancy, as if we were a Tolstoyan family of princes and princesses accustomed to switching casually back and forth between our native tongue and French as we planned our after-dinner sleigh ride through the *bois*. Remarks like these were sure to nettle my mother, dead on her feet and acutely sensitive to social slights—including in-house ones—and she would then accuse me of acting like a little snob (how much more cutting the diminutive made her reproach!). Her other derogatory term for me first came into use when I was arrested for stealing outdoor Christmas light bulbs off the bushes of houses in an adjacent neighborhood. When I was returned from the police station, long of hair and long of face, sullen and enveloped in my Army surplus jacket, she told me I was a hoodlum. If she never let me know just what a *wunderkind* was supposed to do, she made it perfectly clear that *snob* and *hoodlum* defined the outer limits of his behavior. I walked a line (as fine and as elementary a part of my education as the one dividing numerator from denominator) between indulging in the exotic and making too familiar with it at home, and a similar line between inscrutability and sullenness.

These restrictions on a freedom that appeared otherwise almost without bounds were part of a ruthless devotion to a democracy in which, according to my mother's plan for her offspring (for she did have a comprehensive one), our collective childhood and adolescence would be very, very different from hers—a vow she often repeated without getting too much into specifics. Her credo was that all of us would arrive at adulthood together (with a margin of error for our differences in age) bearing a minimum of trauma-induced scars, or at least with the scars evenly divided among us; no favorites would emerge. Like a scrupulously honest schoolteacher who forbids her students to sign their papers in order to assure them of her fairness to all of them by reading blind, but who nonetheless can't help guiltily recognizing the handwriting of each, my mother forswore preferential treatment and tried to rectify her indulgence in it by approaching our separate talents as so many lovable peculiarities. Mine was smartness, a tic or minor handicap I had to learn to live with as best I could.

Before I went off for the first year at college, my mother threw me a going-away party, a huge lasagna dinner (my favorite dish) to which she invited all the relatives, neighbors and friends she could muster—a sizeable regiment she could infallibly command to social functions on a few hours' notice. Neither of my parents had been much involved in the decision, application, or any other aspect of my preparations to attend college, but once I had figured out how to do so, and was ready to depart, I was honored by this special extravaganza, one my mother could indulge in to the fullest of her peerless culinary capabilities by treating the occasion as she would a significant birthday—for after all, every one of her children was born, and therefore had birthdays, and in that respect I was no different from any of my sisters. I was simply celebrating the birthday of Smartness, and I would go off to college and be a great success at whatever I decided to do, it didn't matter what, and make everybody proud and contribute significantly to the Gross Domestic Product of our collective self-esteem.

Another of her designs revealed itself by evening's end. Birthdays mean presents, and after the party, when we had cleared the lambrusco bottles away and she and I remained alone in the kitchen, she asked me to count up the money in the envelopes I'd been handed in the course of the evening by those invited to the dinner. The checks and bills came to well over a thousand dollars, enough to supplement my scholarships and loans and keep me afloat the first year if I managed it carefully. There had never been any question of my parents being able to contribute to my college costs, pressed as they were by their own overwhelming money worries, and I never considered even opening the subject with them. But hard-times financier that my mother was, she managed to raise a short-term fund, to turn a pretty profit on her dinner party and so contribute to my particular needs, yet in strict accordance with the necessities of her pocketbook and the dictates of her ruthlessly democratic code of child rearing. There was never enough money for any of us, but there always turned out to be just enough for all of us.

Though I didn't ever finish college, lack of money played no part in my decision to drop out. Doing without and making do has bred a certain extravagance in all my mother's children. Elaine will sometimes allow a letter she's written me to lie around unmailed for weeks and then, deciding all at once that it must arrive immediately if not sooner, she'll send it express mail, to the tune of eleven dollars. Judy's weakness, since the advent of call waiting, is to telephone long distance and then put you intermittently on hold while she transacts business with the dry cleaners or cheers one of her aerobics clients out of despond. By a similar impulse, I came to consider college not as training for a career, but as an occasion for lavish expenditures of mind, and even though I came close to receiving a degree more than once, I abandoned each program as easily as I took it up, indulging in a luxury like leaving unfinished an expensive meal in a restaurant. While each of us has become in our own way a workaholic like my mother, there was not, as in the proverbial poor immigrant family, any expectation that we would scrimp and save and apply ourselves in order to enter professions, make good pay, become prominent and productive citizens. It's true that Poor Richard's fifth rule—"*Frugality.* Make no expence but to do good to others or yourself, i.e., waste nothing"—was often forced on us by circumstance. But as an ethos, his Rules for Perfection, in our household, would probably themselves have been put to frugal use, folded up and set underneath a glass of iced tea to soak up the excess condensation.

My decisions to leave school were met with no incriminations except my own occasional ones about squandering talents, and I am free to knock about for as long as I like without chattels or encumbrances, now writing computer software, now helping an oceanographer friend chart wave motions on a well-provisioned icebreaker ship in the Arctic Circle. For myself, I've mostly accepted the fact that my multifarious mental quirks probably won't ever coalesce into a prolific or consistent brilliance. I'm only sometimes bothered by pangs of wishing still to prove myself a Great Mind—the kind that leaves behind works tangible enough to be bound up in green leatherette—and of trying to decide at what point the expectancy of youth irrevocably becomes the procrastination of adulthood. For my mother, no matter how old I get, I'll always be her *wunderkind*, the prodigal son, forever on the verge of yielding up a definitive abundance of something or other, forever offering a deferral of that moment as comforting and predictable in its approach to infinity as a repeating decimal. I don't think she would object to my fondness for using mathematical metaphors to formulate our relation to one another and her aspirations for me. We share an understanding of how numbers are both real and imaginary, finite and infinite, and how the abundance she's always hoped for is as tangible as the balance in the checkbook ledger or the food she put on the table or the son who ate it, yet also is something beyond, which can never come into being completely but only be perpetually imagined. My mother the breadwinner and baker of earthly delights believes, as I do, that it's possible, even if sometimes costly, to have your π and eat it too.

In the MacAdams' Swimming Pool
by Nicola Schmidt

It is cool and bright; the Macs always put too much chlorine into their pool, but Christine opens her eyes anyway; the round light in the shallow-end wall makes the water glow turquoise. The tiles around the sides are sky blue and sea blue and white. She swims underwater to the middle of the pool and surfaces and treads water and breathes. Splashing, she clambers up onto an inner tube, and the dry rubber on top tugs at the skin of her legs. She lies back, her feet and arms and bottom in the water, and as she kicks with her toes, the tube spins. The blank sky above her dips into purple along one edge but is still green and bright on the other side. Ripples slap with faint, tinny plashes against the tube's inside ring.

Little Den-den Welch churns up the water behind Christine; he barks like a seal, splashing and spluttering.

She does not know where Jamey MacAdam has gone.

In front of Christine, her sister Pam sits on the diving board sharing a bottle of beer with Suze MacAdam. They wear one-piece bathing suits with thin straps that cross over and hook in the back, with narrow glossy triangles holding their breasts.

Christine's old tank suit squeezes her armpits and the tops of her legs; her mother told her the new one, purple with a halter top, which like Pam's is all straps and ties but not so shiny or skimpy, is more her age, more sophisticated, but standing this afternoon in front of the bathroom mirror, Christine was unsure; it would be no good for duck dives, for swimming like an otter. Yesterday, in the department store changing room, her mother brushed the bangs away from Christine's eyes and looked at her reflection and said, "How about a proper hair cut soon, Teenie?" and Pam, still grouchy because their mother wouldn't buy her a bikini, said, "You look like a goofy little boy."

Christine says, "Did Dad say you could have that?"

Pam takes a swallow, hands the bottle to Suze, and stares down at Christine. "Teenie, that old swimsuit's way too small for you—you know what I mean?"

Suze wipes her grinning mouth on her knee and hands the bottle back.

"You shouldn't be having beer," says Christine.

"Oh grow up," Pam says, and crosses her legs and looks away and drinks.

Suze touches Pam's shoulder and says, "So go on. What were you saying about—"

And Pam says, "But you can't tell, Suze, this is just between us, no telling, right?"

Suze leans forward hugging her knees. "OK, sure, I swear, so go on." Suze tucks her wet hair behind her ears and nods as Pam talks, but Christine can't hear over Den-den's splashing. Pam is saying something about Carl, his Camaro, quarter of twelve. Then Den-den gasps and splashes once and is quiet, and while he is underwater Pam sighs, and Suze says, "God, what a pain." Suze looks over her shoulder toward the adults, and Christine follows her glance, paddles herself around with her feet until she faces the patio.

The grown-ups—her parents, the Macs, the Welches—are gathered around the picnic table. The grill is still smoking, and the women rewrap buns, screw the caps back on ketchup bottles and relish jars, while the men pass around beers, pour wine from big dark bottles and hand out glasses as if there's a game going on—Musical Drinks. And then, still like an unexplained game, the adults separate, rearrange into pairs around the patio.

Suze whispers, and she and Pam laugh. "It's true," says Suze. Their talk sounds like swishing, like wind and long hair and moving pants legs and skirts.

At the end of the pool, Mrs. Welch grunts and rises from a lawn chair, holding up an empty wine glass. She squats next to a red cooler and some wine bottles, and sets her glass on the concrete. As she fills the glass—she picks two bottles up and puts them down and then pours from a third—she says, almost shouts, to Christine's father, although he is right there in a lawn chair just like hers, "So how're missiles these days?" She rises into a crouch and pulls the chair closer and then without ever standing all the way up flops back into the chair. With one hand she holds the glass to her dark red mouth and with the other points and flutters at Christine's father. "I mean radars, forgive me, it's just radars, isn't it? How're radars treating you, hm?" And she grins, and her upper body sags, and Christine's father grins.

Suze says, "And old Blob Welch—"

"What?" says Pam. "What? Tell me."

"When he kissed me hello this afternoon, he tried to slip me the tongue."

"No way."

"I swear."

Christine frowns and closes her eyes and dips the back of her head into the water. Somewhere down the road, at the turning circle perhaps, firecrackers pop. The inner tube revolves. There are cold soft bands around her calves and arms at the water's surface.

Someone chuckles, and a woman says a long "Oh." Christine raises her head. Mr. Welch and Mrs. Mac lean together against the mesh fence. Mr. Welch touches his green beer bottle to Mrs. Mac's bare shoulder and mumbles something. Mrs. Mac laughs and twists the end of her ponytail with her left hand. She looks up at Mr. Welch over the rim of her glass as she sips and nods, and then they turn together to look over the fence—at the dark back yard, at trees where a purple bug light sparks—and Christine cannot see their faces. Their shoulders touch, level with each other because Mr. Welch bends at the middle, his rear end thrust back.

Small cold hands grip Christine's ankles, and Den-den bobs up between her feet and coughs and spits into the water. Still hanging on, he ducks his head down and wipes the sodden blond-green hair from his face with his arm. He looks up at Christine and blinks. "Wanna play otter?"

"I don't know," she says. "Maybe."

Den-den tugs at her legs, splashes himself with her feet. The inner tube rocks.

And then the sliding screen door scrapes open and bangs shut, and Jamey MacAdam, loose-shouldered and lanky, in his grass-stained white soccer uniform and his blue baseball cap—his red hair curls out through the hole at the back—is looking at the salads left on the table; he peels back the foil over the wooden bowls and pokes, puts carrot disks and cucumber slices and cherry tomatoes in his mouth one after another, chews and chews. His arms and legs are freckled and skinny, and his hands—she has just noticed this lately—seem older than the rest of him, teenaged already, wide and darker.

"Come on, come on, Teenie Otter."

"I guess not. Maybe later."

Den-den lets go, sinks with his arms straight up, and swims away underwater just like a frog.

"Hey," her father shouts. He is standing now and holding up a beer bottle and he steps away from his chair, his back to Mrs. Welch, who frowns beneath her black crescent eyebrows. "Come on, everybody—to Independence! Happy Fourth."

Pam says, "Oh jeeze, Dad," and all the adults raise their glasses and bottles and drink from them, except Mrs. Welch, who takes off her eyeglasses and holds them out in the air, like a stripper with a necklace perhaps, and closes her eyes and rolls her head. Then she puts her glasses back on and sips her wine while her left arm dangles to the ground and her fingers strum the air.

Christine's mother, in her new pink sundress, stands barefoot at the top of the swimming pool steps and balances a wine glass on the handrail. Mr. Mac stands next to her, one hand in the pocket of his tennis shorts. His other hand touches Christine's mother's bare back. She smiles up at him and tilts her glass so that it just nudges his hip. They murmur, and Christine's mother turns away from the pool, and Mr. Mac's hand floats to her shoulder.

Den-den doggy-paddles back towards Christine, and without looking at him she strokes herself away. She says, "I don't feel like playing right now," and then hears him swim back to the shallow end and splash up the steps, leaving her alone in the pool.

The inner tube rocks and spins Christine slowly. The sky is violet-black.

Den-den, squeaking to himself, finds a tennis ball in the grass, throws it up and catches it with splayed fingers, tosses it again and darts stumbling forward, misses, and chases the ball across the patio. Jamey scoops the ball up, bounces it twice, then pitches it across the lawn, and Den-den runs after it. And then Jamey eases himself up onto the table; he reaches for a bag of chips and drinks soda straight from the bottle. He turns toward the pool, and Christine paddles herself around. The adults are dragging lawn chairs onto the grass beside the mesh fence. The screen door scrapes open and shut.

The grown-ups murmur and shift and settle in their chairs. They lean forward to speak low to one another, to touch shoulders and knees. Mr. Mac sits between Mrs. Mac and Christine's mother with an arm along the back of each woman's chair. Mrs. Mac leans away from him with her arms crossed on her knees and her fingers waving and talks with Christine's father. Mrs. Mac's lips move, and her fingers wave and curl and uncurl and brush Christine's father's arm, but Christine cannot tell what Mrs. Mac is saying. Mrs. Welch's head tips back and her mouth is open. Then her head flops to one side and her eyes open and she jerks upright.

"Jesus but it gets dark fast now," Mrs. Welch says.

Bob Welch stretches and puts a hand on the aluminum arm of his wife's chair. "Hey maybe it's time we called it an evening. What do you say?" He stands, rubs his hips, says to Mr. Mac, "Gets toward night and we can't even keep our heads up. We're getting old, Mitch, I tell you, regular ruins."

"And can't do a thing about it, Bob, hey?" says Mr. Mac.

The other men and Mrs. Welch stand, and Bob Welch takes his wife's elbow. Halfway around the pool, he puts his arm around her waist.

At the gate, Mr. Welch turns and says toward the pool, "Hey Denny, come on little guy, let's hustle."

Den-den drops the tennis ball and runs toward his parents, then runs back to fetch his clothes and his sneakers with the socks tucked into them. His wet feet slap the concrete.

The chairs creak as Mr. Mac and Christine's father sit back down.

"Poor kid, I swear," Mrs. Mac says.

Pam and Suze are walking close together, their arms brushing, alongside the pool to the patio. Christine paddles around to watch them. They take a beer from the cooler and sit on the table, their legs crossed, their knees pointing at each other. Suze tugs at the straps over her shoulders. With the bottle opener in her hand, Pam scowls at Christine, and then turns to Suze and says something into her hair.

Christine lets the inner tube spin her around, away. Her hands and feet swing in the water. She closes her eyes. The grown-ups murmur, and she catches fragments but cannot grasp whole sentences or even after a while distinguish the voices:

"—it's beginning"
"must do something—what's"
"and then the next"
"anybody, someone"
"we all know how difficult"
"but if one cares at all, if"
"to do nothing"
"but you know what's true too—"

A buzzing and whispering from farther away joins the sighs and mutters, and she looks up, toward the house; the wavering glow of television shows through the screen door, and Jamey's sneakers rest crossed on the coffee table in the blurred and bright den.

Her mother calls, "Why don't you come in now, Christine? Why don't you go on indoors?"

Christine waves her hands and feet back and forth, and the water ripples between her fingers and toes. She takes a breath, rocks to one side and tips herself over, and for the moment before she surfaces, utter quiet envelops her.

Sipsey's Woods
by Ronald Sielinski

BILLY DROVE SLOW. Six inches of snow was nothing for his Blazer, which had four-wheel drive and a plow, but the window on his side was smashed. Dad put his fist through it back in Sipsey's woods. Now, the faster Billy drove, the harder cold and snow blew in. Even with the heater vents pointed directly at us, we couldn't get warm. Billy had one side of his coat pulled up over his nose and his hands tucked into his sleeves, but he didn't look so cold as me.

My feet hurt. My chest and stomach muscles ached from shivering. The wind had started soon as we left Sipsey's woods, and big gusts blew down the road, tugging at the trees. The sun was nearly gone, the snow was still falling, and the air was too cold to breathe, too cold to do anything but pull our shoulders in and shiver.

I said, "What if Dad dies?"

Billy didn't answer.

"What if he passes out or falls through some ice?"

"Jeff," he said, high-pitched, like I'd said something stupid.

"But what if—"

"Dad's not gonna die." He didn't want me thinking about it. But I already had: Dad lost in the woods, confused by the snow and the coming night, him lying down just to rest, then a drift covering his body.

"He's not dead, and he's not gonna die." Billy said, "We're not that lucky."

But nothing Billy said could change what would happen, what had happened. The glass had cut Dad bad: a hundred razor cuts from knuckles to elbow. He should have been howling Jesus-Mary-and-Joseph, but he was beyond mad. He could walk miles into the woods before he noticed the blood dripping from his hand, the little red icicles at his fingertips. By then he might not have any blood left to bleed.

"Maybe we should go back and check?"

Billy didn't answer.

"We could follow his tracks."

Billy sneered, "I didn't think we had time."

He was blaming me. Billy always blamed me. It wasn't my fault I had a scouts meeting; Mom's the one who said I had to go. She said she wasn't going to pay initiation and dues, buy a uniform and books, just so I could lose interest in three months. I had to eat, get cleaned up, and change into my uniform, all before six. Our next-door neighbor, Mrs. Henslow, was den mother; she'd probably make us decorate styrofoam place settings or memorize directions to the post office. Only once, we made tom-toms out of oatmeal tubes. I said, "I don't even want to go."

Billy said, "Yeah, right." Billy blamed me for everything. Even when the cat got chopped up by his engine fan, and I'd only let the cat outside like she wanted, he blamed me. *What the hell d'you do that for?*

I asked him, "What're we gonna tell Mom?"

"What happened."

"It's not my fault."

Billy took a loud, you're-trying-my-patience breath. We'd left Dad back in Sipsey's woods because Dad wanted to hunt a deer and Billy didn't. Billy wouldn't even let Dad use his rifle. But Dad broke into his Blazer and took the gun anyway.

"If Dad's dead," I said, "you killed him."

"Jeff. Shut up."

"I'm gonna tell Mom it's your fault."

"I *said* shut up."

"I'll tell her you killed him."

"Nobody dies from a cut hand. Now would you just shut up?"

But I knew. I'd already earned my first-aid achievement. Without a tourniquet, you bleed to death. If Dad could just find a sturdy branch and narrow strip of cloth—. But after that they'd have to cut off his arm because gangrene would set in. If the poison spread to his heart, he'd die. Same with frostbite. Scouts had taught me one thing, at least: there's lots of ways to die. "Maybe he'll freeze?"

"Good."

Billy hated Dad. They used to get along okay, before Billy was old enough to drive. But now they couldn't talk without ending up shouting. Lots of times I hated him myself. I even wished him dead. But Dad could be all right. He taught me things. He showed me the right way to use a screwdriver, to let a screw work itself into wood. And when we watched football on TV, Dad knew if a team would run or pass as soon as the ball was snapped. Sometimes he'd take me to the Army Surplus. We'd shoot expensive bows on the practice range and look at pictures of bucks in magazines.

Mom said he liked hunting deer better than he liked her. Really, she didn't like the killing. I was on her side about that. Once, I'd shot a waxwing with my pellet gun, and I felt so bad, I went crying to Mom. I can't imagine what it'd be like to kill a deer.

But Billy hated Dad. Last Friday, Dad caught him with a pack of cigarettes. Dad hates cigarettes. So he taped the pack to the front door, so Billy would remember not to smoke as long as he lived in Dad's house. They got in a big fight, a real one. Billy finally dared Dad to hit him, *C'mon, old man. You know you want to.* So Dad hit him. I didn't see it—I was in the kitchen—but I heard the thwack of flesh. Billy stomped out of the house and didn't come home till two-thirty, drunk. Dad's been real friendly ever since, but Billy stayed mad.

You could see the mad in him as he drove: We slid to stops, spun to starts, and fishtailed around corners. I knew better than to say anything. And he didn't say anything either for a long while. Then the wind got louder. And when the wind got louder, it got colder. I rubbed my arms and legs and jiggled, and that helped a little, but my feet still hurt.

"Stop it," Billy said.

"I'm cold."

"Stop it."

"I'm cold."

"Would you just stop it."

I said, "You *want* me to freeze, don't you?"

Billy bit down on nothing.

"You killed Dad, now you want to kill me."

"All *right!*"

"Then you could say it's all my fault. Then—"

"Shut up!"

"You could kill us both, that'd make you happy—"

My head rang, and I remembered seeing Billy's big brown glove come away from the steering wheel, toward me. I could feel where each knuckle hit. My skin was so cold it felt like whole chunks had been torn from my cheek and nose. My neck hurt in a line from ear to shoulder from twisting so hard. My lip felt warm. I touched it with my mitt and watched the red blood freeze. I looked at Billy.

He looked back. "I said shut up."

I wanted to open the door and jump out and run, but there was nowhere to run. And Billy would stop and catch me, then he'd hit me again because I ran. I hated Billy. "All right," I said, "*Dad.*"

"Listen, you little shit, I *saved* you from Dad."

Maybe I'd thought that, too, when Dad was walking toward us with Billy's thirty-ought-six, but that was just me thinking. "Nuh-uh," I said, "Dad wouldn't shoot us."

"What?"

"Dad wouldn't shoot *me*," I said.

"Are you that stupid? I'm talking about the cold and your stupid scouts meeting."

I didn't say anything.

"I'm talking about having to follow Dad all through the woods, chasing some stupid deer, when you'd rather be anywhere in the world than with him.

Having to put up with his shit because you're not having as much fun as he thinks you should."

Billy was right. When Dad was pissed, he'd holler and gripe so much you felt embarrassed to be yourself. He'd make you feel ashamed because you'd somehow caused all the trouble in his life, because you couldn't do anything to help him. If Dad lived, I was glad we'd be gone when the pain in his hand woke up. Except our leaving would really piss him off. He'd come back to the road, still bleeding, angry about not getting a deer, and find us gone. He'd shoot trees then, and kick snow, and shout our *fucking* names at the sky. And if he ever made it home, he'd be even more pissed because he'd had to walk fifteen miles through the cold and night.

"Maybe we should go back?" I said.

"You got scouts. Remember?"

I told him again that I didn't have to go.

Billy punched the roof, "Goddammit!"

I didn't want him to hit me again.

"You're going!"

"You're not Dad," I said, "You can't tell me what to do."

"Would you just shut up."

"Or what? You'll hit me?"

"Listen, all this started because of you and scouts."

"You're the one who started it, not me. I never would've left Dad."

"Oh, really?" he said. "What are you doing in this truck then? Huh, Jeff? Tell me, why didn't you just stay behind?"

I hated Billy. The whole way home he'd been trying to make me feel bad. I hadn't done anything wrong. I stood as best I could.

"Sit down," he said. I turned and stepped on the seat, then climbed into the back, away from Billy. "Dammit, Jeff." The seat springs were stiff with cold. "Look what you did to my fucking seat."

I lay with my back to the wind, a seat belt in my face. "Jeff," he said, "get back up here."

The vinyl had frost growing in the hollows of its grain.

"I'm warning you, get back up here and clean this mess."

It wasn't my fault that I had a scouts meeting. It wasn't my fault that I'd seen a deer. Billy was the one who pissed Dad off. "It's all your fault," I said, not loud enough for him to hear.

We'd been carrying carrots out to the bait pile. Dad had started the pile about a month ago in the flats where, every spring, old trees pulled themselves up from the ground, and the big rings of roots and dirt made natural blinds. About a quarter-mile shy of Dad's blind, we heard something in the trees, the kush of pine needles. I saw him first, a huge buck, with at least a ten-point rack, only fifty feet away. He struggled to get up, slow and awkward. I pointed, and the buck ran. He jumped through the woods, dodging trees and scrub, still graceful despite the stripe of blood down his thigh.

Dad wanted Billy to run get his gun. Billy said, *He's already gone.* Dad said, *Not with that leg, he's not.* Then Billy said we didn't have time, we had to get back for my scouts meeting. Dad looked playful, *It'll be Jeff's first deer.* Then he looked at me, *What d'you say, Jeff? Eh? Getting too old for that scout shit?*

I didn't much care for scouts, but I was cold, deep-down, painful cold. I wanted to go home, take my boots off and stand on the hot air duct in the kitchen. I didn't want to shoot a deer. I didn't want to kill anything. But I was afraid to tell Dad no.

Dad gave up on me and looked at Billy, *C'mon,* he said. Billy tried again, *Jeff?* But I didn't answer. Billy looked at Dad, said we should get back. I was happy to hear him say that. Dad wasn't. The two of them went back and forth, Dad about the first kill of the season and venison steaks, Billy about the lack of time. You could see their arguing in the air, frozen puffs of breath, bigger and bigger, till they pissed each other off. I thought Billy was going to challenge Dad to another fight, but he didn't. All he said was, *It's my gun,* and Dad lost control. *Don't hand me that shit!* Billy said that he'd drive Dad home and Dad could get his own gun. Dad threw his sack of carrots at Billy's feet, and Billy sidestepped. Dad stomped off down the trail. Billy waited till Dad disappeared around a bend before he said, *Don't forget the keys.*

Billy picked up Dad's sack, and we went on ahead to the bait pile. We met up with him on our way back. He was walking toward us, Billy's gun cradled under one arm, both hands tucked in his pockets. Blood soaked his jacket from his elbow to wrist; he looked ready to kill us both. Billy put an arm down to stop me. He stood in front of me. *That's my gun,* he said. But Dad just kept coming. Billy said, *How'd you get in?* Dad kept coming.

Last summer I shot Dad with my pellet gun. Not once, but a bunch of times. I don't know, I kind of went crazy. I just kept shooting. Back then I really hated Dad, not for any one reason, just for who he was. So when I saw Dad coming down that trail, I knew he was mad enough. I imagined him lifting that gun to shoot, a bullet going through Billy's stomach and hitting me in the chest or shoulder, spinning me in a circle to the ground. I would've looked over at Billy and mouthed the words *This is all your fault!* blood coming up from my throat the instant before I died.

Dad passed us, instead, and Billy started to follow, *Hey,* he said. Dad whirled around, *Don't push it!* They stared at each other, and if Billy so much as opened his mouth, I know Dad would have shot. But Billy didn't say anything. Dad turned and walked away. Billy grabbed my shoulder and said, *Come on.*

Back at the road, I saw nothing but blood; there was a red hole melted into the snow and a red hand-print on the side of the Blazer, like on an Indian's horse. Billy probably only saw the thousand safety glass pebbles scattered across the snow. *Son of a bitch,* he said. And we left.

The Blazer lurched and I looked up. I saw the tall tangle of our oak's black branches. The branches disappeared. The Blazer stopped.

"Open the door," Billy said.

I climbed through the front seat and jumped out. My legs disappeared into the drift of snow. I waded over to the garage and opened the door for Billy. He drove up past the drift, stopped, and dropped his plow. Then he backed up, dragging the white drift with him, all the way to the street, where he turned around, backed into the drive, and started plowing, the snow rolling like a heavy surf in front of his plow, new flakes of snow falling behind him, landing in his tracks, until, finally, the driveway was clear.

He pulled his Blazer into the garage. I shut the big door and closed us in, then I headed for the small side door.

Billy got out. "Come here," he said, "help me with this."

I kept walking. Icy snow crunched under my feet, dry, like the taste of chalk, and it gave me a chill. I wanted to reach the house before Billy and tell Mom what happened, explain how it was all Billy's fault.

"Jeff!" he said.

I turned.

Billy cocked his head and made a fist. "Turn that light on and get over here."

I didn't want Billy to hit me again. He was too far away to hit me. "I'm cold," I said.

He took a warning step.

I turned the overhead on. Billy grabbed the trouble light and held it out for me. He unwound its extension cord and plugged it in. I took my mittens off to warm my hands around the bulb.

"Knock it off," he said.

So I held the light like he wanted, pointing it at his hands while he cut a sheet of cellophane from Dad's paint supplies. He brought the sheet over and folded it to the size of his broken window, then he ran duct tape along the outside molding. The tape didn't stick so well in the cold, and he kept having to redo it. By now, my hands were so numb that I wanted them to hurt just so I'd know they still worked. After Billy taped the sheet from the outside, he taped it from the inside.

Billy put the duct tape away, unplugged the work light, took it from me, and put it away. He said, "Now clean off that seat."

I brushed off the snow in two swipes. "There," I said.

He looked at me.

I gave the seat two more swipes.

"All right," he said and nodded toward the house, like he was doing me a favor, like everything was suddenly good between us.

I hated Billy.

We walked through the little door, back into the cold. I ran ahead and squeezed the handle to the front door between two pain-straight hands. Mom opened the door from the other side, and the warm air hit me, peeling away the cold. My shoulders sagged with relief.

Billy was behind me. I wanted to shut the door on him, let him freeze.

He stepped inside.

Mom plucked my cap off and started unwinding my scarf, as if nothing was wrong. Then she saw the blood on my lip and stopped. I said, "Billy left Dad, Mom. He left him in th—"

She shushed me and looked up at Billy.

Billy took off his coat. "He's hunting."

She flaked blood from my nose, "How'd this happen?"

Billy hung up his coat and walked toward his room.

I whispered, "Mom, Billy—"

"Shush." Mom got me out of my coat and said, "Go wash your face."

I lingered, then followed her down the hall. I walked past Billy's door and peeked in: he lay on his bed, listening to music, and Mom walked toward the stereo. I stood just inside the bathroom door and listened.

She shut the stereo off. "Where's your father?"

"Hunting."

I stepped into the bathroom and turned on water.

Mom said, "I've had a long enough day already."

"We saw a deer," Billy said. "He went after it. Simple as that."

"So you just left him? In the woods. In this storm."

"But he broke into my truck, Mom, and stole my rifle."

I pulled a washcloth from the towel rack. My hair was flat to my head from static.

"Your father wouldn't just *do* that. What happened?"

Billy didn't answer right away. I let the water warm, then filled the basin. When I stuck my hands in, the pain shocked my arms stiff. I took my hands out. Billy said, "Jeff had to get back for his scouts meeting." I knew he'd blame me. I hated him forever.

Mom said something I couldn't hear.

"Well he wouldn't shut up."

Everything was silent for a moment, then Mom walked back to the front door. She put on her coat. She came back down the hall. "So," she said. "Are you going or am I?"

I couldn't help but think how awful Billy must have felt. I imagined him turning to face the wall, lips in a tight frown, pissed at the world.

Mom said, "Well?"

Billy got up and left. He stomped out the door, out to the garage, where he spent half a minute just roaring his engine. Then he left, spinning his tires in the snow.

When I got home from my meeting, the snow had stopped and Billy's Blazer was parked in the drive. The light was on in the garage and I looked in through the side door. Billy stood with Dad. The buck was tied by its front hooves to the rafters, a stick wedged in its empty chest. Dad had his coat unzipped, his cut hand was taped, and the other held a bottle of tequila. He handed the bottle to Billy, who drank. I could hear Dad through the window: "I tracked him down to the lake and around. All the way around. He'd come back for those carrots, and I thought I had him then. God damn, I had him all lined up," he held an imaginary gun and said, "He'd come back for those carrots." Billy handed the bottle back to Dad, who stopped talking to drink. Billy folded his arms, tucked his hands in his pits, and stared at the ground. "So," Dad said. "He'd come back for the carrots...."

I wanted to go into the garage and touch the deer's fur, feel the short, coarse hairs. But I was worn out from Mrs. Henslow's snowflake cutouts and knew, if I went in, Dad would make me listen to his story about a dozen times. Billy looked up and saw me and rolled his eyes. I could have gone in there, and maybe we could have made faces behind Dad's back. That's the only way to put up with Dad when he's drunk. But I went to the house instead.

Mom was watching TV. She asked how scouts was. "All right," I said. She asked if I'd seen the deer, that Billy was out there, why didn't I go have a look? I didn't say anything. She asked if I was mad, and I still didn't say anything. She said I shouldn't be.

"I know."

I wasn't tired, but I went to bed early. I twisted back and forth for hours, the furnace going off and on, off and on, stretching out time. I kept expecting Dad or Billy to come in and apologize. Say something hokey about how we're a family and should try to get along better. Dad sometimes does that. Billy, too, lately. But I never understood how *sorry* changed things. I mean, once a thing is said, how can they take it back? Once a thing is done, how can they pretend it never happened? You can't forget how miserable they made you feel. They only make themselves feel better.

Walking on Water
by Kim Trevathan

Backing out of the truck trailer onto the metal ramp that led to the store's backroom, Eddie Clyde Johnson jerked the handle of the pallet jack and shook loose a case of Log House Maple Syrup from behind where I was pushing. It grazed my shoulder and landed on the ramp with the dull thud of thick broken glass.

"I told you to steady it!" Eddie Clyde shouted. He jerked the jack again, this time so hard that the whole eight foot high load of stacked boxes lurched at me so that I had to slam my body against it to keep from being crushed to death.

Before Eddie Clyde could tell me to, I picked up the dripping case of syrup and walked backwards with it to the produce sink, holding it away from my body and leaving a stringy trail on the floor. Rinsing each of the ten unbroken bottles under the hot water faucet, I stripped them clean of syrup and labels so they'd be ready for Wayne Stone to mark down to half price and put in the discount buggy out on aisle one. With what was left—a box of broken glass and syrup—I headed back to the loading dock and the incinerator. When I opened its metal doors I had to lean away from the heat and hiss of a caseful of loose macaroni and cheese that had been mashed beyond salvage. I reared back to throw in the syrup box, and from behind Eddie Clyde snatched it out of my hand and pitched it off the edge of the loading dock into the pit, the bottom of the downhill concrete ramp that the warehouse truck had just pulled up out of. The box landed in a pool of black water and splattered the gray canvas sneakers of Crawford Keys, the bum, who made his appearance every Tuesday after the truck left. Open pages from a newspaper swirled and crackled between his legs, and the black puddle rippled around the sinking syrup box. Crawford looked up at us—eight stockers standing five feet above him on the lip of the loading dock—and told us the story of how he could walk on the water.

"You boys are young," said Crawford, which we knew, all of us high schoolers except Wayne Stone, who'd worked at the store twenty years. "Even so," said Crawford, "I bet you've heard of the 1915 flood."

Though he'd told us this one before, we all shook our heads no. "Tell us about it, Crawford," said Eddie Clyde, who had a mustache and a red Firebird with a glasspack muffler that grumbled so loud the checkout girls paused at their registers and smirked when he arrived for work each afternoon. He stood closer to the edge of the dock than the rest of us, and in the middle so that Crawford had to look at him while he told his story.

"That river can fool you," said Crawford, glancing over the side wall of the ramp in the direction of Clark's River, a half mile away at the city limits. "It may look harmless—slow and graceful on its way to Paducah and the Ohio— but if it takes a notion it can destroy a town, it can kill you. I know. Back in the summer of 1915 there was no stopping it. It spilled over its banks, over the railroad tracks that run alongside it, halfway up the big tobacco warehouses on First Street, and on up the hill to Third where it covered the courthouse steps and rose above the pedestal of General Robert E. Lee's statue, all the way up past his boottops, six feet off the ground. Gray skies, gray rain, brown water everywhere. I lived upriver from town—y'all know, where I still do—up on a hill above the landfill, up high where I watched the river rise and cover the dump, all your grandparents' garbage and trash and rusty cars and washing machines. The water would never touch me, but over the hill that stood between me and town, I knew it had to be bad."

Crawford rubbed his hand along his silver stubbled jaw. He looked sideways at the sky. Then he snapped his head back around at us and raised his voice. "Did I sit in my shack on the hill while that river swallowed the town and the people I knew?"

"No!" we said, all of us except Wayne.

"That's right," said Crawford. He turned his body sideways and squinted his peacock blue eyes, which he knew made us listen harder. "That's right," he said again. "I walked on the water to help them, all those people sitting on their roofs waiting for the rain to stop. Anybody would help if they could, sure, but not just anybody could make up inventions." He looked down the line at each of us and bowed. "Floating shoes," he said. "Inflatable like those things pretty girls lay on in the water. Except smaller and shaped like slippers so I could wear them on my feet and slide right over the water like I was on ice."

"How'd you think that up?" asked Eddie Clyde.

Crawford smiled and wiped his lips on the sleeve of his flannel shirt. "Didn't have to think them up, Johnson. I already had them. For fishing."

"Didn't really answer my question," said Eddie Clyde to us out the side of his mouth.

"Flood came so sudden," said Crawford, "that everybody's boats washed away down the river to Paducah and into the Ohio. Not one boat left in town, just strong men trying to swim places and drowning. I saw them floating down the river on my way to town. Head down, face up, all of them on their way to Paducah for the last time. No telling where they ended up in that current, maybe on down to New Orleans, where I went one time in my inflatable shoes and played harmonica with Louis Armstrong. Another story."

"Let's hear it, let's hear it," we said, though the only one of us who knew a thing about Louis Armstrong was Wayne, and he was behind us now push brooming the stock room.

"The flood story," said Crawford. "I have to finish it."

"Hell, we've only heard it about fifty times," said Eddie Clyde. "We know you saved the day and screwed all the old ladies." We laughed as we always did when Eddie joked. He dated the prettiest majorette at our high school, and she smiled straight at him where he sat in the stands as she waited for her baton to descend from the moth-littered black sky. Eddie always told us he wasn't stupid enough to play football, though he was strong enough, we knew. Every day he would hit us hard on the shoulders to say hello and if you tried to punch him back, he would dodge and thump you on the side of the head with his finger.

Crawford waited for us to stop laughing and got right up next to the edge of the dock, close enough to reach out and touch the toes of our sneakers, us standing there with our hands in our pockets looking down at him. Eddie Clyde jingled coins in one pocket, a wad of keys in the other. He could lock and unlock every door in the place. They trusted him.

"It kept a-raining," said Crawford, whispering, "like you boys have never seen. No thunder, no lightning, just a hard, cold rain in the summertime, everything as gray as that concrete there. I put on an orange cap so the people on their roofs could see me coming through the rain, and I took along fishing gear and old bread for bait so the folks could feed themselves."

Eddie Clyde made a big show of scratching his head. "How'd they cook them fish," he asked, "in the rain and all?"

Crawford smiled at Eddie and showed his teeth, which made us all stare. His eyes did not smile because he was thinking with them, remembering. A few feet behind us Wayne's broom scratched against the smooth concrete floor.

"Raw fish will not kill you, Johnson," said Crawford. "They ate that fish raw because they were so hungry, because they needed strength against the chill. Ate all kinds of fish, didn't throw nothing back. Not carp, not drum, not even old gar. Ate whatever the Lord sent their way, rich and poor alike. And they were glad to have it, up on their roofs, under their wet blankets and whatnot. And they thanked me for that fishing tackle, they thanked me until the rain stopped and the sun beat down so hard that steam rose from the wet cold roofs and it looked like the whole town was smoldering. And the water went away and people gathered all the ruined stuff to take out to the dump. A procession of them passed below my home to discard their mud-soaked rugs, their broken furniture, their clothes that smelled of death and decay. Then they drove to town and didn't look back. Do you think they remembered old Crawford Keys once the sun come out?"

"No!" we said. And we were right.

"Excuse me," said Wayne, behind us. In front of his broom was a line of trash and dust and broken glass. Crawford stepped back as Wayne pushed the line over the edge into the black puddle. Fine white dust floated in the air between us and Crawford. Wayne went away to put up the broom and came back with a half rotten red cabbage and an overripe cantaloupe, which he handed down to Crawford, who was telling us how he strode down the mighty Mississippi to New Orleans in his inflatable shoes and met Louis Armstrong.

"Who was he?" asked Eddie Clyde. "A boxer or a wrestler or something, and you went down there and kicked his ass?"

"Louis Armstrong," said Crawford, "played a trumpet so loud and clear that the earth trembled and the Mississippi River ran backwards and women shivered and moaned and fainted, and the hardest rich white men smiled and loved Louis."

Eddie Clyde said, "He was a nig—?"

"He was on a riverboat playing lead trumpet for Fate Marabel's band," said Crawford. "He saw me walk up to the side of the boat in my floating shoes and stopped playing to give me a hand up. We become friends right away, and after he got off work, we went to his place to smoke a reefer."

"You mean a joint," said Eddie Clyde. "You went to his place to smoke a joint." From the side of his mouth he said, "That's what happened to him. Too much weed."

Crawford hefted the red cabbage in the palm of one hand like it was Louis Armstrong, and in the other he held the overripe cantaloupe like it was him. The cabbage spoke in a rich, red voice, thick with ripe leaves: "Crawford, where did you find this stuff? It's the best I've ever smoked."

"Kentucky," said the cantaloupe. "Across the river from Missouri in the swamplands of Bullard County."

"I feel so good," said the cabbage, "that I could play a song about this Kentucky reefer."

"Play on," said the cantaloupe.

Crawford got serious. He set the cantaloupe and the cabbage side by side up on the edge of the dock right next to my foot. He folded his arms and bowed his head. "Y'all ever heard the cry of a blue heron in the fog over a smooth lake? When you're not expecting it? Louis's first note hit me like that. And the second. On to the last. You just couldn't get used to it. It was a song about Bullard County hemp, I could tell that, but it made you sad and happy at the same time with something big that filled the room.

"Do you think Louis Armstrong allowed me, Crawford Keys, to accompany him with my lowly harmonica?"

"Nah," said Eddie, the rest of us silent.

"Wrong," said Crawford. "You'd have to know Louis. He never heard his playing like other people did, he didn't know that in his lungs and lips was a power that knocked you in the back of the knees. So I joined in here and there where it felt like there was a gap and Louis needed a break, trying to get across my feelings about the land from which this weed was harvested. When we reached a stopping point on "Kentucky Reefer," we just sat there without talking and Louis filled the silence by humming in that deep growl of his. I went to the crapper, and Louis started playing again, something big and grand and sad, a funeral march for a king, I thought, long shivering notes that made me think of bad times, like that flood I saw, and the Great War overseas, which I couldn't do anything about."

"How come you didn't fight in the war and save the day, Crawford?" asked Eddie. I wanted to say shut up, Eddie, and let the man tell the story, because it was a new one we hadn't heard and Wayne was getting restless at the garage door rope. But I didn't say anything and neither did Crawford. He cleared his throat and went on with the story.

"Louis hit a short high Cee like he'd seen a good-looking woman sashay past the window and the impact of that note made me drop the roll of tissue into the toilet. It was a small roll and in my mind I thought it would cooperate and travel right through the system. No such luck. I had to use Louis's plunger. It made that squish squash splash sound I'm sure you all know, and it got me to thinking as I worked it in a sort of rhythm about how people played music on combs and pots and pans and other things made for something else. I got to wondering what in tarnation could be done with a plunger. I come out of the can with it, having washed it off good, and told Louis to play with the thing over the bell of his trumpet, just to see how it would sound. Well, he laid the horn across his lap and liked to fell out of his chair he laughed so hard. But when he run out of laughter he tried that plunger, his eyes cocked sideways and smiling at me, then rounding out and glassing over as the sound he made surprised him.

"He asked me to go along with him to play in Fate Marabel's band on the riverboat, but I knew my calling was not music. I was just a middling harmonica player and not really suited for the kind of music Louis was inventing. But Louis wouldn't let me say no, he was so grateful for the plunger idea. He insisted we go down to the docks and talk to Fate Marabel that night. I can hear Fate now. 'You want what? This boy who pulled up alongside us in floating shoes, you want him in my band? He plays what? Harmonica? Shit,' he said to Louis, 'you stick to blowing that horn and let me worry about the band.'

" 'Look here what he invented,' said Louis, playing a few notes with the plunger.

"Fate Marabel grabbed the plunger by the handle and threw it out in the middle of the river. 'Have a little more respect for yourself,' he said to Louis and walked away.

" 'At least you can get a ride back to Kentucky with us,' said Louis. 'We're going up that way tomorrow.' But I said no, I wouldn't ride on a man's boat who insulted Louis Armstrong. Not long after, Louis formed his own band and started making history. Y'all know how I got back home?"

"No," we said.

"I tied a rope to the back rail of Fate's boat and in my inflatable shoes did what y'all call water-skiing back to Kentucky. No charge. Yes sir, those were good times, back in 1918," said Crawford, staring at our knees.

"How old are you, Crawford?" asked Eddie Clyde, squatting so that Crawford had to look at his face, then away at the trash heaped around his feet to count the years of his life.

"Because you got to be at least a hundred if you was a grown man in 1918," said Eddie. Crawford's mouth moved as he stared at his reflection in the black puddle where Wayne's dust floated.

"Another thing," said Eddie. "Are you sure they had indoor crappers back then?" Eddie stood, then reared back and looked around at us and back at Crawford. "And if they didn't have toilets, then they wouldn't have plungers either. Now, don't tell me you invented the commode because I know damn well that ain't true. You wouldn't be standing here every Tuesday begging food if you did."

And Eddie hooked his thumbs in his belt loops and stared down at Crawford Keys as if he'd poked a hole in his inflatable shoes. Crawford didn't look insulted or ashamed, he just stared between Eddie Clyde's legs still thinking of New Orleans and Louis Armstrong, I thought. But no, he was watching Wayne walk toward him with some old hamburger wrapped in bloody butcher paper. Crawford took it from him and set it next to the red cabbage and the cantaloupe, and appeared about to start another story.

"You go on home now, Crawford," said Wayne, his voice soft and scratchy. "These boys got to stock the shelves."

Wayne had a silver watch for his twenty years, but he was still only night manager, really just another stocker, and nothing important like dairy or frozen foods. He stocked the smallest, messiest, most back-breaking aisle in the store—sugar and flour. Twenty years of sugar and flour. It was hard on him, but he never complained. He hardly ever changed expression, and we respected that, along with his age, so when he told Crawford to go away, nobody argued. Wayne stood at the edge of the dock a little to the side of Eddie and watched Crawford walk up the loading ramp with the cantaloupe, which was him, and the red cabbage, which was Louis Armstrong, and the hamburger, which would spoil if he didn't hurry up and get home to cook it.

Everybody was real quiet watching Wayne watch Crawford. Until Eddie raised his leg and farted long and loose and loud as the air brakes on a diesel. Wayne had to walk away before Crawford was out of sight. I backed up a couple of steps myself and ran right into the stockcart with the smoothest ride in the store, the one Eddie had written his name on. I had to grab the handle to keep from falling backwards over it. Eddie turned, ran over to me, and hit me on the arm much harder than his hello punch.

"Get away from my cart," he said.

I ended up with the cart that had a wheel missing. Loaded it with two cases of toilet paper, two cases of paper towels, and a case of Kleenex—a high, light load that I had to look around to steer straight. Not like everybody in the store couldn't hear me coming in the crippled cart that bumped and clanged with every revolution. As I turned down the back aisle Wayne was pushing his superheavy load with his old man's body all stretched out. Not watching well enough, I ran up on his heel just as he slowed down to turn onto the sugar aisle.

"Sorry Wayne," I said. He had his shoe off and his sock pulled down and he was rubbing his heel. The back of his leg was blue-white and hairless. He squinted up at me like I was shining a flashlight in his eyes.

"All right," he said and strained to get his big load rolling.

"Wayne," I said. "You know Crawford pretty well?"

He stopped pushing and stood behind his cart. "You reckon he still gets high," I asked, "an old man like that?" I waited a little longer for him to answer this time.

"I know he gets hungry," said Wayne, so quiet I could barely hear him. He took a twenty-pound sack of flour in his arms, squatted, and plopped it onto the bottom shelf. White dust rose and flurried all around him, the biggest particles settling on his bald head, his eyebrows, and the small hairs of his arms. I coughed and moved past him to my aisle.

Wayne quit working at ten o'clock when the store closed. Eddie held the door open for him and said, "Stay out of trouble, Wayne," then he turned the dead bolt with his key and we were locked in the store. We worked a half hour, then Eddie got on the loudspeaker in the office and said, "All stockers to the backroom. Break Time!"

I finished stocking a forty-eight-count box of Tissue Boutiques and could hear Eddie talking through the metal doors that led to the back: " 'Let me drive, Eddie, let me drive,' she kept saying."

I pushed open the doors and there he was, up on a six-foot-high pallet of Blue Lake Green Beans, everybody else lounging here and there listening to him. He forked crab meat from a can and drank from a two-liter bottle of root beer. "And I drove farther and farther out in the county," he said, "lower and lower down toward the big river, the Ohio, just listening to her beg, you know, and thinking. We were sipping pure grain and grape juice and feeling the car cut through the thick swamp, nothing but the headlights in front of us, the sweet purr of my motor trailing behind us. And she kept saying, 'Lemme drive, lemme drive.' So I looked over at her sitting so nice with her knees together and her feet crossed, and I said, 'Take off your underpants,' and she smacked me on the arm with the back of her hand and said, 'Eddie,' the way they do to sound innocent.

" 'Take 'em off,' I told her, 'and you can drive.' Sure enough, she raised her little behind and scooted them out from under her. Then she held them up in front of me on one finger, just a little wisp of fabric, you know, and said, 'Let me drive now?'

"I looked her up and down again, my girlfriend, and she had her legs back together and her hands crossed on her lap. 'Take off your shirt,' I said, 'and you can drive.' Well, she pouted then and said it was cold. I was quiet, just waiting, and sipping from the grain, as I listened to the click of her buttons and the silk shirt coming out of her skirt and off her back and then the sound of her hands rubbing the backs of her arms. 'Stop the car,' she said. 'You're gonna let me drive now,' and she looked so cute just in her little bra and skirt that I almost let her.

" 'No,' I said, 'we got to get just a little further.'

" 'Where to?' she asked.

"And I looked at her and she saw what I meant and turned her head toward the swamp. 'You don't love me,' she said. We were quiet until we were almost to the Ohio and I heard the snap of her bra and the rustling sound of her wiggling out of her skirt. 'There,' she said, so close I could smell the grain on her breath. 'I'm ready to drive now.'

"I didn't even look at her. We started up the hill at the Cairo Bridge, that old narrow thing you don't want to meet anybody on, especially at night. And I took my foot off the gas and coasted, listening to the girders pass above us, slower and slower until we'd stopped smack in the middle of it, right above the wide dark Ohio. I put it in park, turned off the motor and the lights, and waited until the headlights of a diesel showed coming from the Missouri side.

" 'You drive,' I said, dropping the keys between her legs and sliding over into the back seat. She leaned forward and pressed her nose against the windshield and started saying real low, 'Here comes a truck, here comes a truck.' And I said 'Slide over and start the car like you been begging to.' As the truck got closer its headlights turned her hair golden and she started beating on the dash and screaming, 'I can't move! I can't move!' I just laughed and sat there admiring the straightness of her naked back."

We all stood there waiting as Eddie spooned a load of crabmeat into his mouth and chased it with root beer. "Let's get back to work," he said, "I got a date tonight." And in that way he left us in the middle of the Cairo Bridge with a diesel coming right at us, his paralyzed girlfriend in the front seat with the keys.

All the other stockers wadded up their candy wrappers and crushed the aluminum cans they were drinking from on the way back to their aisles. I stood up and said, "Hey . . . " looking right at Eddie, and everybody stopped and turned around. "Did she get you off the bridge or not?"

He walked up to me with an amazed look and stood so close I could smell the crab meat on his breath and see the blackheads on either side of his nose. "Did you ask me if my girlfriend got me off?" His eyes got big with anger. I stiffened myself for the shove I knew would follow and wondered what was behind me. A soft pallet of paper towels, I hoped, and not the iron pallet jack or a piece of jagged glass that Wayne had missed in his sweeping. Out of the corner of my eye I saw the others watching, and figured I had to at least reply to his question. I tried to steady my voice.

"I meant, did she drive the car off the bridge."

"Nah," said Eddie Clyde. "Crawford Keys come along in his floating shoes, did a chin-up to the bridge and stopped the truck with his bare hands." He stepped back and looked around and everybody laughed. "I got me some that night," Eddie added, "but old Crawford didn't. He's like you. He's never had any." The laughter got louder.

After midnight Eddie locked the doors and we walked to our cars. He had moved his Firebird from the side parking lot to the front of the store, right next to the plate glass window between two yellow stripes. In a few years, if he wanted it, he'd be assistant manager, on salary. A few years after that, manager, then who knew what rewards awaited him.

I wondered what Crawford was doing. If he sat on his front porch in the moonlight and listened to the train whistle while he spooned out the soft ripe cantaloupe. Or whether he played his harmonica and thought about his old friend Louis Armstrong. Or whether he smoked a joint and stared out over the landfill thinking hard to make up new inventions to tell us about. I wished he wouldn't come to the store next week. I'd pick out a pound of fresh hamburger, a big can of pork and beans, some potato salad from the deli and fresh buns from the bakery and tell Eddie Clyde I was going home sick. And I'd drive out to Crawford's shack for a cookout. Maybe he'd show me the floating shoes and let me try them out, but I wouldn't insist on it.

Eddie's motor caught and rumbled and I felt the low nose of the Firebird inching toward my back. When I whirled around, Eddie was holding his hand out the window. I stepped forward swinging my open palm toward his, and he squealed his tires and was gone to his girlfriend's house, leaving me there with a handful of nothing.

Carl's Outside

by Brad Watson

I WAS OUT on the front porch when the phone began to ring. A pink sunset was spreading in the sky and I didn't want to leave it. But Lanny was busy with supper so I went inside and answered the phone.

A Mr. Secrist from Carl's school introduced himself.

"Is anything wrong?" I said.

"Well we've been a little worried about Carl," Mr. Secrist said. "He hasn't been himself." He paused. I didn't say anything. "He's been getting into fights, falling asleep in class. Nothing we haven't been able to handle, you know, but it's not like Carl."

There was an awkward pause. Then Mr. Secrist went on.

"Anyway, this morning Carl fought—argued—with his teacher, Miss Fortenberry, and I just thought I'd call and let you know she had to send him to the principal's office."

"I see," I said.

"Carl is normally such a quiet, well-mannered boy," Mr. Secrist said. "I mean, I *know* Carl, everybody at school knows Carl, he's a great kid. I just thought I'd call and tell you, in case it's something you might understand and, ah, know how to deal with better than us." He was choosing his words carefully. "Is there anything we can do to help?"

"No, thank you," I said. "I think I know what's troubling Carl. We can talk to him."

"I don't mean he's been a troublemaker or anything," Mr. Secrist said. "Carl's a good student."

"He's not in any trouble here, Mr. Secrist. Thank you for calling. We appreciate it."

"Well if you'd ever like to come in for a conference or anything, just let me know."

"Sure. Thanks." I hung up. I was nearly out of the room when the phone rang again. I walked back and answered it.

The voice was puzzled.

"Oh I'm sorry," Mr. Secrist said. "I was trying to dial another number and must have redialed yours by mistake." He chuckled. "Busy day."

"That's all right," I said. "I know what you mean." We hung up. I was almost to the kitchen when the phone rang again. I called ahead to Lanny, "I got it," and answered the one on the kitchen wall.

The caller made a surprised sound. It was Mr. Secrist again. "Man, I'm terribly sorry," he said. "I made sure I dialed the right number this time. Something must be wrong with the phones." He paused. "Well, this is embarrassing."

"Don't worry about it," I said. "Maybe you should try another phone, or call the phone company."

"I'll call the phone company from another phone," he said.

"That's probably a good idea," I said. "Thanks again for calling about Carl."

We hung up. Lanny looked at me. She was slicing peeled potatoes into halves on the chopping block. It made a sound that filled the momentary silence between us. *Schock. Schock.*

"What about Carl?" she said. "Who was that?"

"A counselor from school. He said Carl argued with his teacher today and got sent to the principal."

"He called us over that?"

"Well, he said he's been doing it a lot lately."

She looked at me and set the knife down on the block and wiped her hands on a towel.

"I'm not surprised," she said. "Kids know things. They can tell when something's wrong." She picked up the knife again. "It's us he's upset over." She sliced another potato. *Schock.*

The phone rang again.

"Jesus, if that's him again," I said. "He's called three times already."

"Who?"

"The counselor. He said his phone's messed up."

I answered it on the third ring.

"Bob?" the caller said.

"You must have the wrong number," I said and hung up.

"What are we going to do about Carl?" Lanny said.

"We need to sit down and tell him. Explain it to him."

She was quiet. She chopped another potato. *Schock.* Then set the knife down again. "It's not going to be easy," she said. "We've just ignored Carl through all this. We never pay him any attention. And he's going to be the one it's hardest on." She breathed hard and looked down at her hands. They were pink from working in the kitchen and I had a moment of guilt about sitting out on the porch while she started supper by herself. I put it out of my mind. Lanny took a deep breath and seemed on the verge of tears. The phone rang again. I snatched it up.

"Yes?"

"Who is this, please?"

"Who is *this*?"

They paused and hung up. Lanny was looking at me. I hung up the phone.

"We never even taught him to ride his bicycle," Lanny said. "He can't even ride a bike. The kids all rode by here a few minutes ago and they all had their own bikes except Carl. He was riding on the back of Fredrick Nelson's." Our kitchen was in a small separate wing of the house. A window at the sink overlooked the back yard, and our breakfast table sat near a bay window that looked out front. Lanny could see the street out that window. I'd seen the kids ride by too, when I was on the porch, Carl on Fredrick's old splayed banana seat while Fredrick rode the pedals. Carl's legs hanging listless, bare ankles in old sneakers and toes stubbing pavement with Fredrick's desultory lunges.

"Even the little girls ride their own bikes," Lanny said. "We got Carl a bike like that last Christmas."

"I know that," I said.

"Well why isn't he riding it?"

"Look, I know mothers who've taught their kids to ride bikes."

"My father taught *me*." *Schock, schock.* Four large Irish potatoes, halves rocking on the cutting board, crazy beveled edges like fat whittled sweetwood sticks. We seemed to have more than enough for supper. The phone rang again.

"How you been?" a woman's voice said. "I ain't seen you in a long time."

"Who is this?"

"Terry?"

"You have the wrong number," I said and hung up. I felt the urge to turn on Lanny and held it back.

"I'm going outside," I said. The phone rang as I stepped onto the porch but I ignored it. The kids were a couple of blocks down the street on their bicycles. I walked out to the curb, cupped my hands and called out, "Carl!" Down the street a few heads among them turned. The bicycles wobbled to a stop. They talked among themselves, then turned and started my way.

It was seven o'clock on daylight saving time, thin high pink clouds spreading across the sky. They looked like brush strokes in a painting. The lush greens of the trees and grass deepened, the sharp lines and angles of houses and cars and telephone poles and lines softening. The children drew closer, brown-skinned already on their rangy bikes. Poker cards were fastened by clothespins to the bikes' front forks, making stuttering noises they imagined to sound like motorcycles.

They called their group the Roadhog Club. I know how they came up with this. What they loved to do was line their bikes up in the street until a car came along. Then they reared up on their back wheels and stood their ground until the driver got out cussing. Then they scattered and scooted, motocrossing through the yards and whooping like Indians.

They zipped up and skidded to a stop, looking at me and waiting on what I had to tell Carl. They may as well have been reared up, the looks on their faces. The formidable Roadhog Club, defiant. I could hear the phone ringing faintly inside the house. Carl sat loose on the back on Fredrick Nelson's rigged-up banana seat, waiting.

"C'mere," I said to him.

"Aw, I want to ride."

"Just c'mere. I want you to do something with me for a few minutes."

He dismounted in silence, Fredrick slipping forward on the bar to let him off. Carl's a good-looking kid, with his straight sandy blond hair down on his forehead and his tiny wedge build. He doesn't have the wiry or pudgy looks the others have. Carrot-headed Bubba Weeks, Wick's kid, stared at me with a cool gaze I took for insolence.

"Y'all go on. Carl's going to be a little while. Get." I shooed them away with my hand. Carl stood a little behind me with his back to them. The Roadhogs wobbled slowly around and at some silent signal scooted, Bubba Weeks and Fredrick Nelson's sister doing wheelies. They dipped turning right onto Ashland, like birds swerving.

"Come on," I said to Carl. We went around back, phones ringing faintly then clearly as we passed windows thrown open for a breeze.

"What're we doing?" He stayed a few steps behind me, dragging.

"We're going to teach you to ride your own bike. Your mother's ashamed."

He mumbled something, then said, "What's Mama ashamed about?" We turned to the little window above the kitchen sink and saw his mother's head there.

"Nothing," I said. "I was only kidding. We want you to learn to ride your bike." He mumbled something. "Come on now, let's do it."

I got the bike from the shed and rolled it through the back yard, past the cherry tree and out to the alleyway lined and shaded with old wooly oaks and tall, upflung sweetgums. Twice a week garbage trucks rumbled through, stirring dust and a faintly sweet stink. Carl followed like a small prisoner. He stood a couple of steps away, hands in pockets. I heard a breeze and looked up, the thick oaks rustling and the star-pointed sweetgum leaves playing against the sky. I heard something and looked at the little window and her head was still there. Shouting something.

"The phone keeps ringing."

I laid the bike down and went up to the window.

"There have been five calls since you went outside," she said.

"Wrong numbers?"

"Yes. What the hell's going on?"

"I don't know," I said. "Maybe you should call the phone company."

"What are you doing out there?"

"I'm teaching Carl to ride his bicycle," I said. She looked at me and I could tell she was holding back a comment. Behind her in the kitchen the phone was ringing. She looked around at it and then back at me.

I went back out to the alleyway and picked up the bike and grabbed it by the handlebars and the back of the seat.

"Okay," I said to Carl, "get on."

He trudged over, wiped the dust off the seat with his soft grime-edged fingers, wiped his fingers on his shorts. He grabbed the bars and mounted.

"You set?" I said. He put his feet on the pedals and nodded.

"Was the phone for me?" he said, looking up.

"No. You ready?" He nodded. I pushed and got him going a little ways and said, "Okay, *go*." He tried to, but his feet slipped off the pedals and the bike fell over with a crash. The alleyway road's a dirt one, hard-packed sand with a little gravel ridge in the middle and scattered gravel on the edges. Carl got up breathing through his nose and scowling and blinking his eyes. I felt my skin prickle with shame and I ran over to help him pick up the bike.

"Jesus, Carl, I'm sorry," I said almost to myself. "My fault. My bad." I pushed the hair from his forehead and looked at him. He frowned and pulled his head away. "I'll do it right this time," I said. I looked back at the house. Lanny's head still at the window.

Carl wouldn't look at me. He got on the bike again. I grabbed the back of the seat.

"Ready?" I said.

He gave a serious nod.

"Is Mama watching?" he said.

"Yeah."

We took off. I ran beside him, holding on with one hand. He didn't pedal, but kept his feet ready and his eyes straight ahead. He was on the right wheel path, hard-packed, and I ran on the gravel ridge having a tough time of it. Then I let go and ran beside him and yelled *Pedal!* and in a second he did and took off down the alleyway. He was going pretty good. Down where the alleyway runs into the street he slowed and fell over. He jumped up and hopped around, holding his elbow.

I called out, "You all right?"

He stopped hopping and examined his elbow. Then he picked up the bike and walked it back to me.

"Did Mama see that?"

"I don't know." I didn't turn to the window. Carl stared at the house for a minute. A group of kids rode by in the street down where Carl had fallen over. They were younger than the Roadhogs and ringing chrome bells clamped on their handlebars. The ringing faded, *shring-ring*, fainter than their shouting voices, then a faint sound lost in rustling leaves and air.

Carl climbed back onto the bike and I grabbed hold and pushed him going again. He wobbled a little when I let go but didn't fall down when he turned, and got started back to me by himself. He got the hang of it and rode back and forth for a while, up and down the alleyway. I smoked a couple of cigarettes and watched. Carl whizzed past on the bike, kicking up dust.

He was having a time. He started trying to do wheelies, catching on so fast because he'd waited so long, hanging around such good riders. He was being cool, paying me no mind. And he was beautiful, with his hair blowing back away from his forehead. The breeze had died and the air was quiet. The phone lines and power lines dipped and rose from pole to pole along their graceful paths through the trees and in the quiet warmth of the evening I could almost hear them humming. Voices into robotic hums and metallic warps and squawks at near light speed across continents and then cut off with a button. At near light speed once again the gulf between. I sensed a vague feeling of dread creeping in, but then Carl zipped up and skidded to a stop, breathing hard and sweating, his eyes wide open.

"It's almost supper time," I said.

"Can I stay out just a little bit longer?" He leaned forward over the handlebars, pleading.

I remember this moment sometimes, by itself. It stands apart, in balance, like Carl balanced over the handlebars of his bike, wanting another few minutes outside. There are moments like that, and when you remember them they grip you inside. But at the time I only hesitated for a second.

"Go ahead," I said.

It was twilight. Lamps snicked silently on in houses. I walked down the alleyway toward the street, where light bloomed pinkish in streetlamps curved from poles like thin chromed gargoyles brooding over what traffic may wander their way.

I crossed the street and walked on in the relative dark of the alleyways, into a part of the neighborhood whose houses from the back looked unfamiliar. The shadows had deepened. The trees were towering dark shapes. I stood there looking up at them. I felt small and isolated beneath their huge branches. A bit of breeze ran through them like a shiver.

I turned and started back, taking my time. Sounds changed subtly with the light. And in the cooling calm of the settling dusk I became aware, like someone waking up from a dream, of a faint ringing.

Behind one house I stopped in a mimosa's shadow to watch. Under a single lamp, sliding glass door open for a breeze, a fat scarlet man and woman in T-shirts and three near-naked pudgy children sat eating supper. They glistened with sweat. Steam rose from their meal. Their phone was ringing. It stopped for a moment then began again. None of them said anything, glowering, forking food into their mouths with an angry urgency.

I walked on toward my house through the darkening back yards. In every house the phone was ringing. Toot Nelson stood beside his, yelling at his oldest son and pointing outside. The boy ducked his head and came out the back door, his startled, angry face looming suddenly into mine.

"*Yah!*" He jumped back. We stared. He turned wide-eyed and hurried on.

I crossed through a yard and out into the street. Through the screen doors and windows open for breezes I could hear the phones ringing as I walked. A television blared in the Hirlihues' house, blue light filled their empty den. Before I stepped onto our porch I saw the dim figure of a phone company truck parked way down the street.

I cupped my hands and hollered, "*Carl.*" No answer.

Except for the kitchen, the house was dark, and I stood there for a minute in the den, the phone in the hallway jangling dully on, off, on, like a senseless alarm. In the dark the rooms felt vast, everything in the air tingling and electric, jumping needles. I felt I couldn't breathe in enough air. I took a deep breath until I could feel a small tight spot deep in my chest expand like sore muscle. The dread welled up and spread through me. In the kitchen the phone rang, stopped, and began ringing again. Lanny stood at the sink washing tomatoes and ignored it.

"There's a phone truck parked down the street," I said.

"A man came by and said to let it ring while they fixed it." She looked up, her face blank.

"I taught Carl to ride," I said.

She stood at the sink with her hair pulled back tight in a ponytail, wearing an old loose sundress and sandals. She dried a tomato and set it beside two others on the porcelain drainboard beside the sink. Behind her on the stove the potato halves rose and tumbled like the blunt noses of tiny white whales.

"Supper's almost done," she said.

It was dusk outside, the sky a deep dark blue, a thin line of pink above the tree line high in the darkening window. The glaring overhead light in the kitchen cast an odd glow on things. It made her skin look weirdly smooth, like a doll's. I looked at my hands. Skin and veins stretched taut over bone and muscle. The phone rang. It rang again. And then it stopped. We stood waiting for it to start again. She stood at the sink looking down. I went over to her and touched her arm. I felt her stiffen. I put my arm across her shoulders and tried to hug her to me.

"Don't," she said.

I pulled her closer, but she stiffened.

"Don't make a scene," she said. "Carl's outside." I looked but didn't see anyone outside the window. Then I saw someone sitting in the fork of the cherry tree, just a silhouette in the failing light. A bike lay on its side in the grass. I looked back at Lanny, let her go. She stared at the tomatoes on the drainboard. I looked again at the figure in the tree. It was hunkered down on a branch. A shape not sharp but vague in the faint light shading darker in almost clocklike moments. With the kitchen light on, through the screen, you couldn't tell who it was.

"That's not Carl," I said.

"What?"

"Carl's riding," I said. "Must be some other boy, spying. Maybe it's Toot's boy." I leaned toward the window. "Go on, now," I called. It sat still. Too small for Toot's boy.

She looked at it, closed her eyes and rested her palms against the sink.

"Ben," she said.

It didn't move at all.

"What are we going to do about him?" she said.

I looked at the figure in the tree.

"Carl?" I called.

No answer.

"I don't think it's Carl," I said.

Lanny shook her head and turned away. The child in the tree had not moved.

"Carl?" I called out. "Come on in the house."

It sat very still.

"Carl," I said louder.

It was a still, dark statue.

Out front in the street a clamor clapped up. The members of the Roadhog Club, quick shadows in the deepening dark, rode in a furious circle, slapping their mouths with their hands, *woo woo woo woo woo woo woo woo.*

I cut the light to see out through the bay window glass. They broke and curved out of sight. I didn't see Carl. Out back, a soft scrabbling and clatter. When I looked, the tree was empty.

We stood not saying anything, looking out at the tree.

Slowly, sounds came back to our ringing ears. The gurgle of the boiling potatoes in the pot. The quiet hum of the refrigerator motor. The flutter and quiet hiss of the stove eye's blue flame. Lanny reached over and turned it off. The flame snuffed out with a little popping sound. She turned off the oven and I heard the jets chuff once, then the metal crackling and ticking.

She said, "You don't even know your own son," and walked out through the dining room.

I heard the front screen door open and shut. I heard her lift her voice out in the street and call.

Carl? she called. *Cah-arl. Carl.*

I was thinking about the time I stole in on Carl asleep and watched him until he seemed some child I didn't know, some beautiful foundling.

And the nights I lay awake beside Lanny like someone moving through dark space at high speed.

Cah-arl, she called. *Carl?*

Moving away, growing fainter.

Her calling like a bird song you know by heart but never knew which bird sang it. And you always wish you'd found out. I stood very still and listened to it, feeling disconnected, already gone.

Stoner's Room
by Hubert Whitlow

"When I die," said Mrs. Winters, addressing her favorite topic as though nothing were wrong, "I want to go out feet first and with eyes closed." She lay prone on the porch swing and accentuated her last four words by tapping her cardboard fan against the red tiles of the floor. She was a short, stumpy woman whose loose, gray hair fluctuated in a diaphanous halo with each wave of her fan.

"When I die," said her daughter Sue Ann from her rocker, "I just want it to be quick. I don't care which end goes first." Sue Ann was a tall, pale woman with her hair worn in a bun. She looked like she had just been blown up with a tire pump. They both had bathed and powdered and were dressed for bed.

"You're too young to worry about dying," replied Mrs. Winters with a yawn. "You don't have my weight and blood pressure."

"I'm thirty-four years old, Mama, and could go at any time. We never know when we will be called." The two women rocked and swung in the dark and watched the fireflies outside the porch screen signal with their splinters of light.

"Those fireflies look like they are dancing on air, don't they?" said Sue Ann. "Just dancing away. Free as a bird. Just winking and dancing away. I wish I could dance like that."

"You're too heavy to dance," said Mrs. Winters. "You'd fall and break something. Besides, you're freer than anybody I know. I provide you room and board. I even worry for you. I do nearly everything you need to have done except drive a car, and Mr. Mooney does that." Mr. Mooney drove the local cab. Mrs. Winters paused for a minute, then said, "Now if Mr. Stoner should come, Sue Ann..."

"In the night? He was supposed to have been here at three o'clock!" Sue Ann leaned forward and clutched the arms of her chair until her knuckles bulged white.

"If he should come," said Mrs. Winters, "if you see him come up the walk, that is, let me know. I don't want him to see me lying down in my nightgown." The nearby campus clock had tolled ten P.M. and no visitors were likely.

"How will I know him?" said Sue Ann.

"Just tell me if somebody comes up the walk!" Mrs. Winters barked. Large japonicas and boxwood shrouded the porch from sidewalk passersby, and Mrs. Winters could not see the walk from her swing.

"We don't even know what he looks like," whimpered Sue Ann. "Here we are waiting on a strange man in the middle of the night and we don't even know what he looks like." She scratched a knee impulsively.

"Now don't start your fidgeting," said Mrs. Winters. "If he doesn't come for the summer term, we'll wait for the fall term and start off with a regular student. We don't have to start off with Mr. Stoner."

"I think I'll start off and catch the next bus to Jacksonville," said Sue Ann. "Help Ella clean her house for a few days while you get Mr. Stoner settled in."

"Your sister is perfectly capable of cleaning her own house."

"Do you have any idea what Mr. Stoner is like? I don't know a thing about him, you know. You never let me in on deciding anything."

"Mr. Stoner is an art student. Art students are different. They are dedicated and mature. Mr. Stoner will make us a good tenant—the first man in the house since your father's death. He'll not be like Mrs. Clinchfield's rooming house crowd next door."

"It doesn't look to me like he's going to be the first of anything, but if he pays the rent—"

"Oh, he's already paid for the full summer."

"Oh, dear God," said Sue Ann faintly. She slumped deep into her rocker. "Now he'll come for sure."

"Don't have another one of your fits," said Mrs. Winters. "It's just your blood sugar letting go. Remember the doctor said it was all a matter of chemistry, so come on. Let's play the game. Make that chemistry go to work."

Rays from the corner streetlamp slipped through the highest reaches of the closeting shrubs and settled in feathers of light on the floor. Mrs. Winters leaned forward and studied the pattern of shadows intently. "I see a bird with a topknot," she said.

"Don't tell the cat, or that's one dead bird," said Sue Ann.

"Just play the game. Don't worry about the cat."

"Okay, I'll bet that bird's a cardinal," said Sue Ann, shifting her weight and trying to make out any pattern at all on the mottled tiles.

"No," said Mrs. Winters, opposite her daughter. "I see something better than that. I see a plate with a shallow bowl."

Sue Ann leaned forward until her rocker creaked with strain: "Well, I see a funny looking man's hat with a shallow crown."

"That's because you are looking at my plate upside down."

"Your eyes are getting bad, Mama. You are looking at the man upside down. See, the head is right ... under ... the ... hat ... " Sue Ann looked up and peered into the shrubbery. "Oh, Jesus!" she shrieked. She leaped up and bounded into the living room, leaving her rocker in violent, solitary motion. By the time Mrs.

Winters had freed herself from the lurching swing, Sue Ann had slammed and bolted the living room door.

"Sue Ann!" yelled Mrs. Winters. "You've left me behind." She pounded on the door with her fists. "Open up the door and let me in!"

"That lady really moves fast when she wants to pray," came a voice from the other side of the shrubs. The voice was soft, wispy.

"That was no prayer. That was a nervous fit," snapped Mrs Winters. She moved to the deepest shadow on the porch and clutched her nightgown close to her body. "What do you want?"

"I'm Carlyle Stoner. I've come to rent your room." The figure speaking remained hidden behind the shrubs.

"If your name is Carlyle Stoner, why weren't you here at three o'clock?" asked Mrs. Winters, peering out from her shadow. She shielded her eyes from a narrow beam of light that broke through from the streetlamp.

"Because my car broke down and I finally had to leave it in Martinsville."

"But that's only twenty miles away. Why didn't you phone?"

"Because it's long distance, and I didn't have any money," came the voice. "Nobody would cash my check because it was on a Jacksonville bank. So I walked. My feet got sore from walking, and I had to take off my shoes." There was a pause. "That's why I'm still behind this bush. My feet swelled up and I can't get my shoes back on. I didn't want to meet you in the dark with my shoes off."

"Open up the door, Sue Ann," called out Mrs. Winters. "It's just Mr. Stoner."

"How do you know its just Mr. Stoner?" came Sue Ann's muffled voice from within the house.

"Because his car broke down and his feet got sore walking from Martinsville and he's hiding in the bushes with his shoes off," Mrs. Winters said loudly, then quietly to Mr. Stoner: "She's not a quick judge of character."

Mrs. Winters and Mr. Stoner talked quietly in the front yard "so the neighbors wouldn't suspect anything funny."

"There are a few last things to be settled," Mrs. Winters said with her arms crossed over her chest. But essentially her mind was made up. She liked what she saw, even in the speckles of light: his solid, black attire; his Gothic and chalk-like face; his bowler hat now crumpled in his hands; the overlong coat; the baggy trousers. To Mrs. Winters this all bespoke an honest and frugal humbleness. And he was agreeable to her stipulations: thirty-watt bulbs in the ceilings, sixty watts in the one allowed reading lamp, one ten-inch fan, one small radio. No argument. And Mr. Stoner's old Hudson, with one door blue and one door green, would be parked in front of Mrs. Clinchfield's next door when he retrieved it from Martinsville, leaving Mrs. Winters's front curb accessible to more fashionable models.

"Property values must be guarded," said Mrs. Winters the next noon while the two women ate lunch. She had called Mr. Mooney at the cab stand and had him bring over two Big Macs and a large order of fries in his cab. She was still happy with Mr. Stoner. His amber eyes and awkward strides accentuated his tapered build. "He'll help us save pennies," Mrs. Winters said. "And goodness knows we can use the extra money his rent is giving us."

"Maybe Mr. Stoner is a phony," suggested Sue Ann as her Coke fizzled tan around the rim of her tumbler. "Maybe we should call somebody and check him out."

"We don't need to call anybody," said Mrs. Winters. She gulped down the last of her own drink and rattled the ice in her glass. "You just don't know how to judge a man of character," she said with a fierce, porcelain grin. A pellet of ice nestled between her dentures.

"The trouble with you," replied Sue Ann, "is that you don't know the difference between high character and a ten-dollar bill. I just don't think we can count on Mr. Stoner."

"We can count on you, can't we Mr. Hooper?" Mrs. Winters muttered to their thin and yellow cat as she dropped food into its bowl. The one-eyed animal had a neighborhood reputation for wildness.

"Well, Mr. Stoner's been here one night, and I'm tired of making up his bed already," said Sue Ann. "I don't like making up the bed for a strange man. I'm a single woman and it isn't right. He's not one of the family."

"You'll grow to like him, you wait and see," said Mrs. Winters as she cleaned the cat's box. "You just wait and see."

"I'm still waiting," said Sue Ann the next morning at breakfast. "And I'll tell you one thing. He's as dumb as a turkey." She blew steam from her coffee. "I asked him this morning how he liked his room, and he said it didn't sparkle like a K-Mart's. That's being as dumb as a turkey, and anybody who ties a chifforobe door shut with a belt is as dumb as a turkey."

"You just don't understand him," said Mrs. Winters as she dropped bacon fat into the cat's bowl. "Maybe he's just stretching his belt. Probably aims to put on weight. I think we should invite him to supper one night just to get acquainted."

"I hope the two of you have a fine time, Mama," said Sue Ann loudly. "Mr. Mooney can bring over two Big Macs and he and I'll eat out on the grass." Sue Ann marched from the room like she was headed for battle.

That Friday at six, Mrs. Winters, Sue Ann, and Mr. Stoner gathered in the living room for a little refreshment before supper. Sue Ann stretched carefully for a cheese and cracker from the plate on the coffee table. The pink pantsuit purchased that morning at Belk's fit too tightly, and she felt constrained. "How's your belt coming along, Mr. Stoner?" she asked.

"Sue Ann," admonished Mrs. Winters quietly.

Mr. Stoner looked confused. His head turned from Mrs. Winters to her daughter, then back again. "My belt?" he asked and he felt along the top of his trousers to make sure that everything was all right. He was dressed in his usual black. His hair was parted evenly down the middle and combed straight to each side. Strands lapped over each ear.

"Forgive Sue Ann," said Mrs. Winters. "She was taken with that beautiful belt you hang over the doors to your chifforobe." She smiled and offered him a second ginger ale. "Sue Ann's the one who cleans your room so nicely each morning," Mrs. Winters added with a coy smile. "She's a good housekeeper and a good cook, too. A real, unclaimed treasure."

"Oh, that belt," said Mr. Stoner and he suppressed a nervous laugh. Then seriously he said, "Do you want me to remove it?"

"Of course not," said Mrs. Winters. "Whatever gave you that idea? Mr. Stoner can put his belts wherever he likes, can't he, Sue Ann? Is your room all right, Mr. Stoner?" She brushed some cheese crumbs from her own new dress. It was gray and flowered with peach blossoms. Mr. Stoner nodded yes.

"Mr. Stoner?" said Sue Ann. "You make a lot of money? I hear you've already paid the entire summer's rent on that room."

"Sue Ann! Mr. Stoner is a serious art student. You don't ask a serious art student questions like that."

"I'm just trying to keep up my part of the conversation, Mama. Mr. Stoner's mighty quiet."

"You'll have to forgive Sue Ann, Mr. Stoner," said Mrs. Winters. "She may seem rough on the surface but underneath she's pure gold."

"Is that right?" responded Mr. Stoner and he turned to Sue Ann as though he were seeing her for the first time. Sue Ann returned his stare. His upper front teeth, she noticed, hung down like little chisels.

"Yes, sir," said Mrs. Winters. "I want the world to know that Sue Ann is one beauty of an unclaimed treasure." Mr. Stoner squinted his eyes, leaned over, and scrutinized Sue Ann section by section. Sue Ann shifted her weight as though preparing to spring.

Mr. Stoner coughed but finally said, "Beauty is really a matter of shadows and light." He leaned back in his chair and fanned himself with his bowler.

"That's what I've always thought," mumbled Mrs. Winters. She paused and fumbled with the pendant at her throat, then said, "You are a student of art, Mr. Stoner. I can't tell you how good it is to have a student of art in this house, someone to talk to about things . . . cultural. My late husband had a friend who was an artist. Tell me, Mr. Stoner, don't you think that light is actually defined by shadows?"

"Yes," said Mr. Stoner, and his voice dropped and eyes shifted from side to side. "And some say that good is defined by the boundaries of evil." The last of his sentence dropped to a whisper. Sue Ann's rapid breathing could be heard throughout the room.

"Oh, Mr. Stoner," said Mrs. Winters. "That's profound. It's so nice to have a profound man in this house. I wish you could have known my late husband's friend who was a painter. He was so interesting."

"What made you decide to become an art student?" asked Sue Ann.

Mr. Stoner raised his sight from the bowler hat in his lap. His smile vanished into a thin, straight line and his eyes, small and dark, bore into her own. "It's . . . it's something I felt called to do."

"It's what?" asked Sue Ann.

"He said he was called, Sue Ann. Pay attention. She's a good girl, Mr. Stoner, but sometimes she doesn't catch things like the rest of us."

"Well, at least I don't have your high blood pressure," said Sue Ann.

"Mr. Stoner is not interested in my high blood pressure, are you, Mr. Stoner?" Mr. Stoner's pendulum gaze swung from Mrs. Winters to Sue Ann and back and forth again.

At a pause in the conversation, Mr. Stoner took from his coat pocket a pencil sketch of Sue Ann and handed it to her. "Oh," she said with lowered voice. "Where did you get that?"

"I drew it. I drew a little of it each night. Keep it. It's for you."

"That's mighty nice of you," said Mrs. Winters. "Isn't that nice, Sue Ann?"

"And your picture," Mr. Stoner said as he turned to Mrs. Winters, "will be ready at summer's end. It'll be a full-size portrait. I may need you to pose a bit, but you must not see the picture until it is finished. It will be a surprise."

"You mean you are going to paint me?" asked Mrs. Winters and a hand went to her breast in weak protest.

"Yes, you have an interesting essence."

Mrs. Winters touched her hand to her hair and looked to a ceiling corner and said coyly: "But what if I don't like the painting?"

"Mama, don't jump the gun," said Sue Ann. "You've only seen one of Mr. Stoner's pictures. How do you know you won't like it?" Then turning her head to Mr. Stoner, she said: "Don't mind her, Mr. Stoner. She jumps to conclusions too much. Draws too many phony conclusions." The two women glared at each other.

At dinner, Mr. Stoner talked about shadow and light and how a black-and-white portrait could reveal a person's very soul. And he talked about religion. Mrs. Winters shifted uncomfortably, spilling coffee. Sue Ann giggled. Mr. Stoner went on and on about the wisdom in shadow and light. They ate as dusty light sifted through the venetian blinds closed against the day's heat and settled on their lips all slick with lamb. Mrs. Winters sighed heavily.

The next morning at breakfast the two women discussed the evening before. "I thought he would stare a hole in my bosom," said Mrs. Winters.

"It wasn't your bosom he was leering at, Mama, it was that gold K-Mart pendant hanging there," replied Sue Ann through a mouthful of scrambled eggs. "And I thought he would wear out that hat of his just by kneading it."

"And whenever he said anything," added Mrs. Winters, "it was about light and shadows and crosses."

"Mama, have you ever thought that artists may like gold?" Sue Ann licked the jelly spoon clean. "Have you ever actually known an art student before?"

"Not personally."

"Well, I guess we shouldn't jump to conclusions."

"What conclusions?" asked Mrs. Winters with concern.

"Oh, I don't know," said Sue Ann tiredly.

"We'll just leave it at that, then," said Mrs. Winters, whipping up a surge of suds at the sink for the morning dishes. She paused and looked through the little window above the sink. A silver beam of morning light pierced her sight like a dagger. She stared into the relentless glare until her eyes watered and twitched. Finally, she said: "I'll bet my eyeteeth that Mr. Stoner is as honest and reliable as they come."

"I don't know about his honesty," sighed Sue Ann, "but any man who practically locks his chifforobe doors with a belt to keep out two helpless women seems mighty peculiar to me."

The two women often watched through the curtains when Mr. Stoner left the premises. They noted the ever-present umbrella. "He's prepared for the afternoon shower," said Mrs. Winters.

"It's early morning, Mama."

They noted the constant lack of books or artist paraphernalia. "His is a brilliant mind," said Mrs. Winters.

"He's a hoax," said Sue Ann. "Maybe he isn't a student at all." They looked at each other, and there was a touch of fear in the glance. With time, Sue Ann's suspicions grew more serious, but Mrs. Winters, though often touched by temporary doubt, never lost real faith. "He's like a son," she said one day, as much to herself as to Sue Ann.

"Well, he's no brother of mine," Sue Ann shot back. She disliked the man's humming when in his room. But mostly she disliked her mother's waiting to see her completed portrait as though it would be the pinnacle of her life.

Sue Ann's sister, Ella, was married to a Jacksonville policeman, and Sue Ann decided to make inquiries about Mr. Stoner. So the next Thursday evening she boarded the 7:15 Greyhound to Jacksonville to visit Ella and do a little shopping. The trip was a relatively short one, and Sue Ann made the journey about once a month.

"What did you say his name was?" asked Ella at the Jacksonville bus station. She was a large, blond woman, almost albino-like.

"Carlyle Stoner. He drives a 1950 Hudson."

"I don't know anybody who drives a 1950 Hudson," said Ella.

It was dark when they reached Ella's apartment, and traces of moonbeams stretched through outside branches of hawthorn and splayed across the kitchen floor. "Are we going to play the game?" asked Sue Ann. They drew up chairs and studied the patterns of light while Sue Ann described Mr. Stoner. "What do you see?" Sue Ann asked quietly. The only sound was the distant howl of a dog.

"I'm calling Howard," said Ella suddenly, getting up and turning on a light. "Something's not right." Howard, her husband, had access to certain police files during his night duty at headquarters.

"Stoner's not a pervert or anything, is he?" asked Sue Ann. "I'm not going to stay in the same house with a pervert."

Ella made the call and explained the problem. Then they waited in silence for the return call. "I'm awfully glad Mr. Stoner's gone this week," said Sue Ann. "That's when I decided to come over. He's in Ocala painting orange groves."

"How do you know?" asked Ella in a low and husky voice. "He may be down at Disney World stealing hubcaps this very minute."

Sue Ann pondered for a few moments, then said: "Well, that's what the man said. He said, 'I'm going to Ocala,' and he walked out the door carrying a little valise and easel and things."

They both jumped when the telephone rang. Ella said hello and listened in silence for long minutes, then hung up the receiver. "Well, you and Mama really picked out a beauty for your first roomer," she said. Then her solemnity exploded into laughter which came in waves while she told of Mr. Stoner's obsession with painting widows, his penchant for stolen art trinkets, his total lack of education. "He's a non-student," Ella howled with laughter. "I knew a regular student would do better than a 1950 Hudson."

"What'll I do?" asked Sue Ann.

"I wouldn't do anything. The police will catch him in some discount store one of these days loading up that closed umbrella with trinkets, and that'll be the end of your Mr. Stoner. Mama will blush all over. I'll bet that chifforobe's stuffed with junk right now."

"Are you sure that's all on Mr. Stoner?" asked Sue Ann. "That really isn't very much."

"That's all they got on him, sweetheart. Good luck with your next roomer. You and Mama just made a mistake." Ella blew over the mouth of her beer bottle until it went "whooo-whoo-whoo."

"Stop making fun of me," Sue Ann said. She turned her head and peered directly into the whir of the window air conditioner. The cool air blew her loosened hair into waves. "Some days I think Mama wants me and him to be sweethearts."

"You think you want a sweetie?" Ella asked.

"I don't know. I've never really had a sweetie," said Sue Ann.

"Well," said Ella. "If you can't reform him, you could always sell cheap jewelry door to door. I won't tell Howard or anybody."

"If I get me an honest-to-goodness sweetie," said Sue Ann, "I want him to be somebody who can take me away from things. Free me. Show me the world."

Sue Ann's week was up Thursday and she repacked her travel bag. Ella said: "All you bought with all that shopping was that silly rhinestone pendant. Mr. Stoner making you arty?"

"It's all I can afford," said Sue Ann. "But I think it looks good on me. Adds class."

The bus arrived late at Sue Ann's station, and the blue neon sign buzzed angrily over the darkened sidewalk. Mr. Mooney lifted Sue Ann's bag into the trunk of his cab and climbed wearily behind the wheel of the Plymouth.

Sue Ann noticed with mild interest that Mr. Stoner's car was not parked in its usual place. Maybe he's still gone, she thought.

"Wait 'til Mama comes to the door," she said to the silent Mr. Mooney as he set her bag on the sidewalk. "Mama, I'm home," she called as she opened the screen door and crossed the tiles speckled with streetlight. "Mama, I'm here," she called more loudly as she opened the white, wooden door and entered the dark living room. "Mama, why don't you turn on at least one light in the house when you are expecting someone from out of town? Even you can afford that."

She flicked on the overhead chandelier. "Mama, where the hell are you?" She went from room to room, turning on lights and looking behind doors like it might be some sort of a game. The house smelled musty and cat-like. "Mama, have you gone off somewhere?" she asked in a much quieter voice. She moved slowly down the short, dim hall that led to Mr. Stoner's room. "Mr. Stoner," she called in a whisper as she knocked on the door. "Mr. Stoner, you got your shoes on?"

The door swung open, and the cat, wild with hunger and now horribly experienced, fled past like an evil shadow. Sue Ann turned on the ceiling light. Mrs. Winters lay on the floor, scrutinizing the thirty-watt light bulb in the ceiling. An eyelid had gone to the long-starved cat. The chifforobe door stood open, the belt now cut and on the floor, an unfinished portrait within. "Mama, are you all right?" Sue Ann asked. But when she bent over and looked into the vacant eye, she realized that all was over, that the first and final stroke had come.

She turned to the chifforobe. The picture inside was of frozen stars; a heart-shaped moon locked in ice; and light bulbs, streetlights, leaves, and birds all connected by thin wires. From the darkest umbra came Mrs. Winters, naked, clutching a church collection plate. From it spilled trinkets like bits from a shattered rainbow. Sue Ann and her broom hovered over it all like a tornado's threatening funnel. "Mama . . . " whispered Sue Ann. Then she heard Mr. Mooney's horn.

She strode down the hall with long, deliberate steps. She would tell Mr. Mooney what had happened with a voice so calm, so sure, that he would have to believe. But when she waved from the front porch, Mr. Mooney pulled heavily on his cigar and drove off down the street.

"Mr. Mooney!" called Sue Ann. "Mr. Mooney! Come back!" She ran into the street, but he did not hear. The cab disappeared around the corner at the end of the block, and outside the streetlight glow all was dark. But from far down the street came a new, single, yellow light, rumbling and lurching. It was Mr. Stoner's Hudson. "Mr. Mooney!" Sue Ann called. But then she caught herself and said more quietly, "I mean . . . Mr. Stoner. Mr. Stoner?" He came towards her but paused under the streetlight. Her breath was sharp and fast. "You're just what I thought you were," she said in a whispery voice.

"No, I'm not," he answered in his own vapory voice.

"Yes you are. You're a pervert. You painted my mama to death. Only a pervert could do that." Mr. Stoner wouldn't believe until Sue Ann showed him the scene. This time she noticed a collection of trinkets on the chifforobe floor. Mr. Stoner quickly threw his largest suitcase on the bed and frantically started packing. "Where are you going?" asked Sue Ann. "You can't leave me here," she said. "The police might come and ask me things."

"Like what?" asked Mr. Stoner. His eyes were large and restless. The sweat on his face gleamed in the dull light.

"Like . . . why don't I like making your bed. I understand they can get real personal." The room resounded only with their breathing. "If you leave me here all alone," she said, "I'll . . . I'll tell them that you have a police record in Jacksonville." Mr. Stoner held his bowler hat in front of himself as though in supplication.

The Hudson wouldn't start, so Mr. Stoner placed Sue Ann behind the wheel and explained what she must do. Then, from the rear, he pushed. She released the clutch, and the engine fired into action. The car moved forward with a roar. She did not know how to stop or to shift gears, so the machine whined and vibrated in its first gear, gaining speed, leaving Mr. Stoner running behind in smoke.

Where the street ended at the campus, Sue Ann rounded the corner onto University Boulevard. She did not know how to turn on the one working headlight, so she drove by the glow from streetlights and the moon. Her initial terror subsided once she had made the turn, and she felt a sense of pride. "Look, Mama, look here," she said to passing reflections on the dashboard's dark chrome. "I'm doing something you can't do."

At the city limits the streetlights stopped, and there were only the lights from the heavens. She looked up through the windshield to see the stars in their firmament, stilled there like fireflies in ice. She saw them as a halo around the rim of the earth. She extended an arm through the open window and curved it into the night air. For a fleeting moment she felt as though she could soar into the constellation of stars and nestle there in their glowing. She shut her eyes momentarily. It was as though she were dancing with the dark.

Contributors

ALL THE CONTRIBUTORS to this volume have been members of the Master of Fine Arts Program in Creative Writing at the University of Alabama.

MICHAEL ALLEY is from Asheville, North Carolina. He has degrees in engineering physics and electrical engineering. A 1987 graduate of the program, Alley is the author of a textbook, *The Craft of Scientific Writing*, published by Prentice Hall. He teaches at the University of Wisconsin in Madison.

YESIM ATIL was born in Ankara, Turkey, and moved to the United States when she was eleven. She was graduated from the program in 1985. Atil's novel, *On Freedom Street*, won the Outstanding Thesis Award for the University of Alabama and was published by Lynx House Press in 1991. She teaches writing and women's studies at The Behrend College of Penn State University, in Erie, Pennsylvania.

DAVID BOROFKA is from Portland, Oregon. A 1982 graduate of the program, he has published in several literary magazines, including *Southern Review, Beloit Fiction Journal, Witness, South Dakota Review, Manoa, Greensboro Review,* and *Black Warrior Review*. Borofka won *Carolina Quarterly*'s Charles Wood Award for Distinguished Writing and *Missouri Review*'s Editor's Prize for 1992. He teaches at Kings River Community College in Reedley, California.

WILL BLYTHE is from Chapel Hill, North Carolina. A 1986 graduate of the program, he is the literary editor for *Esquire* magazine in which he edits "The Esquire Reader" and writes a regular book column. Blythe's reviews have appeared in the *New York Times Book Review*, and his fiction has been published in several literary magazines. "The Taming Power of the Small" was published in *Epoch* and reprinted in *The Best American Short Stories 1988*.

MATHEW CHACKO, who is from India, has published stories in *India Currents, Chicago Review,* and *Stories*. He won third place in *Playboy* magazine's annual college fiction contest. "Héma, My Héma" first appeared in *Missouri Review* and was reprinted in *Stories*. Chacko's novella, *The Season of Carcasses*, won the University of Alabama's Outstanding Thesis Award for 1992 and was published in *Stories*. He is completing a Ph.D. at the University of Missouri.

TOM CHIARELLA is from Rochester, New York. He has published fiction in *The New Yorker, Florida Review,* and *Story*, among others. Chiarella's collection of stories, *Foley's*

Luck, was published in 1991 by Alfred A. Knopf. A 1987 graduate of the program, he teaches at Depauw University in Greencastle, Indiana.

CATHY DAY is from Peru, Indiana. She was nominated for the 1994 AWP Intro Journals project and she won second place in the *Playboy* magazine college fiction contest. She is a 1995 graduate of the program.

MATT DEVENS, a Chicagoan, lives on the Indiana shore of Lake Michigan. He has published nonfiction in *Novel & Short Story Writer's Market.* "Prance Williams Rides Again" first appeared in *Story.* A 1989 graduate of the program, Devens has taught at Livingston University and several Chicago area schools.

TONY EARLEY is from Rutherfordton, North Carolina. He was graduated from the program in 1992. He has had fiction published in several magazines, including *Texas Review, Witness,* and *Harper's,* where "Charlotte" was first published. Earley's collection of stories, *Here We Are in Paradise,* won the Outstanding Thesis Award for the University of Alabama and was published in 1994 by Little, Brown.

JENNIFER FREMLIN is from Sault Ste. Marie, Ontario, Canada. She was graduated from the program in 1990, having twice won the Alumni Fiction Award. Fremlin's fiction has appeared in *A Room of One's Own.* She is completing her doctorate in English and film studies at Brown University.

ASHLEY L. GIBSON is from Austin, Texas. She has studied writing with R. H. W. Dillard at Hollins College. A 1995 graduate of the program, she held two Graduate Council Research Awards and was fiction editor of *Black Warrior Review.*

RICHARD GILES was graduated from the program in 1988. His fiction has appeared in *Chariton Review, Florida Review, Untitled,* and *Story.* "Crawford and Luster's Story" was first published in *Ploughshares* and is listed as one of the "100 Distinguished Short Stories" in *The Best American Short Stories, 1993.*

DEV HATHAWAY, a 1983 graduate of the program, was born in Norfolk, Virginia, and grew up in Virginia and New Jersey. His fiction has appeared in *Carolina Quarterly, Crazyhorse, Greensboro Review, Missouri Review,* and others. Hathaway's collection of stories, *The Widow's Boy,* was published by Lynx House Press in 1992. He has been director of creative writing at Northeast Louisiana University and director of freshman English at Emporia State University, and currently he teaches fiction writing at Shippensburg University in Pennsylvania.

LAURA HENDRIE left Tuscaloosa for Ojo Sarco, New Mexico, in 1987. Her fiction has appeared in *Missouri Review, Taos Review, Writer's Forum,* and *Best of the West.* Hendrie's novel, *Stygo,* was published in 1994 by MacMurray and Beck and will be reprinted in paperback in 1995 by Scribners.

J. R. JONES grew up in Chicago and was graduated from the program in 1991. A former fiction editor of *Black Warrior Review,* he has returned to Chicago. Jones has published fiction in *New Virginia Review* and *The Kenyon Review*, where "The Twin" first appeared.

NANCI KINCAID grew up in Tallahassee, Florida. A 1991 graduate of the program, she teaches at the University of North Carolina in Charlotte. Her stories have appeared in many magazines, including *Carolina Quarterly, Missouri Review, New Letters, St. Andrew's Review, Southern Exposure, Crescent Review,* and *Ontario Review,* and have been anthologized in, among others, *New Stories from the South.* Kincaid was awarded a National Endowment for the Arts fellowship grant for 1992. Her novel, *Crossing Blood,* was published in 1991 by G. P. Putnam. She is presently a Bunting Fellow at Radcliff College and is completing a second novel.

CELIA MALONE KINGSBURY was born in Pulaski, Tennessee. She was graduated from the program in 1989 and held a lectureship at the University of Alabama from 1989 to 1992. She lives in Tallahassee, Florida, where she is working on a doctorate at Florida State University. "Stairsteps" is her first publication.

TIM PARRISH is from Baton Rouge, Louisiana. His stories have appeared in *Texas Review, Shenandoah, Southern Exposure, Washington Review,* and *Black Warrior Review.* A 1991 graduate of the program, Parrish teaches at Southern Connecticut State University in New Haven.

JOHNNY PAYNE was graduated from the program in 1986. He teaches creative writing at Northwestern University. His novel, *Kentuckiana,* is forthcoming from White Fields Press. Other books include *Conquest of the New Word: Experimental Fiction and Translation in the Americas* (Texas, 1993); a novella, *The Ambassador's Son* (*TriQuarterly*, 1995); *Voice and Style* (Writer's Digest Books, 1995), and *The She-Calf and Other Folk Tales* (New Mexico, 1995). Payne has cowritten a musical, *The Devil in Disputanta,* and has been guest editor of *TriQuarterly* and *Review of Contemporary Fiction.*

NICOLA SCHMIDT was born in England and grew up outside of Boston. Her story, "In the MacAdams' Swimming Pool," originally appeared in *Alaska Quarterly Review.* A 1992 graduate of the program, she now lives in LaSalle, Illinois.

RONALD SIELINSKI was graduated from the program in 1994. He grew up in Michigan, where he now works as an electrical engineer for the General Motors Corporation. "Sipsey's Woods" is his first publication.

KIM TREVATHAN is from Kentucky. Before graduating from the program in 1994, he completed an M.A. in English at the University of Illinois and an M.A. in Journalism at the University of Wyoming. He edited *Foresight,* a quarterly engineering journal, and has published nonfiction in *Transitions Abroad.* While at Alabama, Trevathan won an Alumni Fiction Award and a Hackney Literary Award. "Walking on Water" is his first published fiction.

BRAD WATSON is from Meridian, Mississippi. He was graduated from the program in 1985. He has been a newspaper reporter in the Gulf Shores, Alabama, area for the *Independent* and the *Islander* and for the Montgomery *Advertiser,* where he was also an editor. Watson's fiction has been published in *Intro 10, Story, Black Warrior Review,* and *Dog Stories*. A collection of stories, *The Last Days of the Dog-Men,* is due in 1996 from W. W. Norton, which will also publish Watson's forthcoming novel. "Carl's Outside" originally appeared in *Greensboro Review.*

HUBERT WHITLOW recently retired as librarian at Floyd College in Rome, Georgia. He lives in Athens, Georgia. His fiction has been published in *Louisville Review, Southern Humanities Review,* and other magazines. Whitlow won *Louisville Review*'s Literary Award for Fiction for 1992. "Stoner's Room" first appeared in the *Beloit Fiction Journal.*

ALLEN WIER taught in Alabama's MFA Program from 1980 until 1994 and served as the program's director on several occasions. He is author of three novels, *Blanco, Departing As Air,* and *A Place for Outlaws,* and a collection of stories, *Things About to Disappear.* With Don Hendrie Jr, he coedited *Voicelust: Eight Contemporary Writers on Style.* Wier has had a fellowship grant from the National Endowment for the Arts, a Guggenheim Fellowship in fiction, and the Dobie-Paisano Fellowship from the Texas Institute of Letters. He now teaches writing and literature at the University of Tennessee in Knoxville, where he is completing a new novel.